AMULET BOOKS
NEW YORK

A NOVEL BY
A. G. HOWARD

ENSN

Library of Congress Cataloging-in-Publication Data

Howard, A. G. (Anita G.)
Ensnared : a novel / by A. G. Howard.
pages cm
Sequel to: Unhinged.
Summary: "Alyssa travels to Wonderland once again to free both her mother and Jeb, and to set right all that's gone wrong"— Provided by publisher.
ISBN 978-1-4197-1229-6
[1. Supernatural—Fiction. 2. Characters in literature—Fiction. 3. Rescues—Fiction. 4. Love—Fiction.] I. Title.
PZ7.H83222En 2015
[Fic]—dc23
2014033275

Amulet Books are available at special discounts when purchased in quantity for premiums and promotions as well as fundraising or educational use. Special editions can also be created to specification. For details, contact specialsales@abramsbooks.com or the address below.

THE ART OF BOOKS SINCE 1949
115 West 18th Street
New York, NY 10011
www.abramsbooks.com

To Mom:

I miss you. Thank you for giving me the courage to fly high and catch my dreams, and for being the wind beneath my wings.

MEMORY'S MYSTIC BAND

It's a poor sort of memory that only works backwards.
—Lewis Carroll, *Through the Looking-Glass,*
and What Alice Found There

I once thought memories were something better left behind . . . frozen pockets of time you could revisit for sentimental value, but more of an indulgence than a necessity. That was before I realized memories could be the key to moving forward, to recovering the fate and future of everyone you love and treasure most in the world.

I stand outside the glossy red door of a private chamber on the memory train. *Thomas Gardner* is engraved on the removable nameplate inserted inside the brackets.

"An unnecessary formality, since he's here in the flesh," the conductor—a carpeted beetle close to my size—said when I first requested the nameplate. I shot him an angry glare, then insisted he do as I ask.

Now, as I press my forehead hard against the brass, letting the metal chill my skin, I consider Dad's name, how it means more than I ever imagined . . . how he *himself* is more than I ever could've dreamed.

I almost followed him into the room when we first arrived. He was so shaky, even before we had landed in London.

Who wouldn't be? Shrunk to the size of a bug, flying across the ocean on the back of a monarch. I can still taste the residue of salty air. At dawn, when Dad started to accept we were actually riding on butterflies, we slipped through a hole in the foundation of a giant iron bridge and landed beside a rusted toy train in an underground tunnel. The fact that we were small enough to step into the train made Dad's eyes so wide, I thought they'd pop out of his head.

I want to protect him, but he's not weak. I won't treat him like he is. Not anymore.

He was nine—just two years older than Alice had been—when he wandered into Wonderland and was trapped by a spidery grave keeper, yet somehow he survived. Better he face that memory alone. Otherwise, he might try to protect me. And I don't need protection any more than he does.

It took me losing my mind to gain my perspective. If that's what it takes for my dad, too, so be it.

My fingertip trembles as I trace the letters: *T-h-o-m-a-s*. Dad will find out his real name today, not the one given him by Mom. All the revelations, all the monstrosities he lived as a child, those experiences will lead us to AnyElsewhere—the looking-glass world where Wonderland's exiles are banished. A dome of iron covers it, holding them prisoner and warping their magic somehow, should they use it while inside. Red and White knights keep watch over AnyElsewhere's two gateways.

My own two knights, Jeb and Morpheus, are trapped there. A month has passed since they were swallowed up. I want to believe they're still alive.

I have to.

And then there's Mom, stranded in a crumbling Wonderland, hostage to the same spiteful spider creature who once held Dad in her webby thrall. The rabbit hole, the portal into the nether-realm, has been destroyed at my hand. AnyElsewhere is the only way inside now.

We're on a rescue mission, and Dad's memory is the key to it all.

I drag my muddy feet along the red and black tiled floor, headed toward the passenger car's front. My muscles ache from riding a monarch for twenty-four hours. It would've taken much longer had we not been picked up by a storm and lifted several thousand feet in the air, covering hundreds of miles in mere minutes—a mad ride my Dad and I won't soon forget.

My hair drapes my shoulders in a wild snarl of platinum blond, limp from rain. The tangles are fitting, since that's how I feel inside: chaotic, yet drained. The netherling half of my heart swells to break free of the human emotions ensnared around it. There will be no respite until I've found my loved ones and made things right in Wonderland.

Even then, I know none of us will ever be the same again.

A half dozen queer creatures occupy the white vinyl seats. They aren't waiting to reunite with lost memories. They're here because they're stranded, too. Since the rabbit hole is gone, they have no way back to Wonderland, their home.

One creature is a pale, cone-headed humanoid whose cranium pops open sporadically so she can argue with a smaller version of herself. Next, the smaller version's cranium opens to reveal an even littler likeness. The tiniest one is a male with a large nose. He bonks his female counterparts with a teensy rolling pin before hiding away again. It's like watching a nightmarish nesting-doll version of *Punch and Judy*, a vintage puppet show I studied during drama class at school.

Two other passengers are pixies, and I wonder if they were part of the group I met last year in Wonderland's cemetery. They look different without their miner's caps: bald, scaly heads with tufts of silvery hair. A plastic bag rattles between them as they take turns tossing peanuts at the cone-headed creature, inciting more arguments.

The pixies' long tails twitch and their spider-monkey faces twist to studious expressions as I meet their silver gazes. They have no pupils or irises, and their eyelids blink vertically like theater curtains.

They whisper to one another as I cup a hand over my nose to stifle the rotten meat stench oozing in silvery slime from their hides.

"Alice, sparkly talkeress," one says in a breathy voice as I come within hearing distance. "No ostlay isthay times?"

The dialect is an odd mix of pig latin and nonsense. He wants to know if I'm lost this time.

"Not Alice, stupidess," the other shushes before I can answer. "And only thinkers ostlay here. Thinkers and omentsmays."

I continue down the aisle, too absorbed in my problems to engage.

The beetle conductor scribbles something on a clipboard while chatting with the last three passengers. These are round and fluffy, with eyes affixed to tall, fuzzy stems that look more like rabbit ears than eye sockets. They watch as I pass, their pupils dilating with each rotation of their ears.

The fattest one sneezes in answer to a question the conductor asks, and a cloud of dirt puffs up from its fur.

"Blasted dust bunnies," the beetle bellows, and drags a vacuum cleaner from a holster at his waist, proceeding to suck the dirt from his carpeted hide.

I settle in an unoccupied row up front and hunch down by a window, waiting for the conductor. He was supposed to check on something—lost memories I need to see. They're not mine. I'll be spying on someone else's missing moments.

Mom felt guilty for visiting Dad's lost memories behind his back. Her wisdom makes me cautious. But the one whose mind I'll be violating doesn't deserve my respect. She's vicious and vengeful. She almost stole my body, and has managed to tear apart my life and most of Wonderland's landscapes.

Morpheus always says that everyone has a weakness. If he were here, he would tell me to find hers, so when I face her again I can crush her.

I intend to do just that.

The carpet beetle's vacuum whines, muffling the arguing, sneezing, and shushing going on around me. I lean back and look up at the chandeliers made of fireflies—each half the size of my arm—bound together by brass harnesses and chains. The glowing insects dip and dive, painting brushstrokes of yellow light across the red velvet walls. I tilt my head and stare out the window. More firefly fixtures illuminate the darkness, rolling across the tunnel's ceiling like glittery Ferris wheels.

I suppress a yawn. I'm exhausted, but too keyed up to close my eyes. I can't seem to settle in time and place. Just yesterday, I was at a table in the asylum's sun-filled courtyard, tricking my dad into eating a mushroom that would shrink him. That seems like an eternity ago, but not nearly as long as it's been since I've hugged Mom . . . argued with Morpheus . . . kissed Jeb. I miss Mom's scent, how she smells after working in the garden—like overturned soil and flowers. I miss the way Morpheus's jeweled eye markings flit through a rainbow of emotions when he challenges me, and I miss the arrested expression Jeb always used to wear when he painted.

The littlest things I once took for granted have become priceless treasures.

My stomach growls. Dad and I didn't have breakfast, and my body tells me it's lunchtime. I tuck my hand into the apron tied over my stiff, mud-caked hospital gown and roll the remaining mushrooms between my fingers. I'm hungry enough to consider eating one but won't. The magic within that made us small enough to ride butterflies will make us big once we're done here. I need to preserve them.

My outline reflects back from the windowpane: blue gown, white apron, frazzled blond hair with a streak of crimson down one side.

The first pixie was right. I'm the epitome of Alice.

A nightmare Alice.

An Alice gone mad, who thirsts for blood.

When I find Queen Red, she'll *beg* me to stop at her head.

I snort at the silly rhyme, then sober as the beetle turns off his vacuum attachment. He straightens his black conductor hat and hobbles over on two of his six twiggy legs. The other two sets serve as arms, cradling a clipboard.

"Well?" I ask, looking up at him.

"I found three memories. From long ago, when she was young and unmarried. Before she was"—he looks around and lowers his voice to a whisper—"*queen.*"

"Perfect," I answer. I start to stand but settle in my seat again as he pushes my shoulder with a spiny arm.

"First you ruin the one way back to Wonderland, making me a babysitter of dust bunnies and smelly pixies. Now you want I should endanger my life by showing you . . ."—he studies the passengers behind me, his crisscrossed mandibles trembling—"*her private memories.*" There's a clicking sound surrounding his whisper, like snapping fingers.

I grind my teeth. "Since when do netherlings respect anyone's privacy? That's not in your code of ethics. In fact, most of you don't know what ethics are."

"I know all I need to know. I know that she's not forgiving, that one." He's avoiding her name, keeping her anonymous.

I follow his lead. "She'll never know you showed me."

The conductor flips pages on his clipboard and scribbles something with his pen, stalling. "There's another issue of concern," he says louder this time. "The memories are repudiates."

"What does that mean?"

"She wasn't forced to forget. She *chose* to. Took a forgetting potion."

"Even better," I say. "She's afraid of them for some reason. That's to my advantage."

The clicking sound grows as his mandibles quiver. "Ideally, you could use them as a weapon. Repudiated memories are tainted with volatile emotional magic. They want revenge against the one who made and discarded them. But you would have to carry them to her, keeping them dormant in your mind. Being a half-blood, you aren't strong enough."

I bristle at his condescension. "Mortals have their own way of making memories dormant. They write them down so the past doesn't preoccupy their thoughts. All I need is a journal."

He holds his pen an inch from my nose. "That won't work with enchanted memories, lessen your book is filled with enchanted paper to bind them. Sadly, I've ne'er heard of such a magic journal. You?"

I glare in silence.

"I thought not." The beetle taps my nose with the pen's tip.

Snarling, I snatch it away and shove it in my pocket, daring him to get it back.

"Fool girl. When repudiated memories nest inside a mind, they become like earworms, playing over and over to a painful degree. Best-case scenario, they cause you to sympathize with your prey so you're worthless against them. Worst case, you're driven to madness. Are you willing to risk losing so much?"

I rub my hands along my bent knees, then tuck the excess material of my hospital gown under my hips. No matter how terrifying it is to imagine someone else's hostile memories eating away my mind, finding Red's weakness is the only way to defeat her.

"I've already lost everything and I've already gone mad." I meet his bulbous gaze. "Need a demonstration?"

Multiple eyelids flick across his compound eyes. Bugs aren't supposed to have eyelids or lashes, but this isn't a typical bug. He's a looking-glass insect, or *reject*, depending on if you choose Carroll's terminology or the carpet beetle's.

The beetle was swallowed by tulgey wood and turned away at

AnyElsewhere's gate. He was then coughed back up as a mutant. Which is exactly what almost happened to Jeb and Morpheus. Thankfully, they were accepted into the looking-glass world, although the thought of them alone there opens a whole new level of horror. Morpheus won't be able to use his magic because of the iron dome, and Jeb is only human. How does either of them stand a chance in a land of murderous, exiled netherlings?

A silent scream of frustration burns inside my lungs.

I lower my voice so only the conductor can hear. "I used to collect insects. I'd pin them to corkboards. Had them plastered all over my walls. I've been thinking of taking it up again. Maybe you'd like to be my first piece."

The conductor either grimaces or frowns—a tough call with all those moving facial features. He motions toward the aisle. "This way, madam."

We head toward the private rooms. Two doors down from Dad's, the beetle stops, looks over his shoulder to assure we weren't followed, and drops a brass nameplate into place: *Queen Red.*

My wing buds tingle, wanting to burst free. A brew of magic and rage simmers just beneath my skin. Ready, waiting.

The conductor starts to unlock the door, then pauses. "I attended a garden party at her palace once." He's whispering again. "Watched her shave the skin off that Door Mouse's friend . . . that hare fellow."

I cringe, remembering when I first saw the hare at the tea party a year ago, how he appeared to be turned inside out. "March Hairless? Red skinned him?"

The beetle nods so frantically his cap nearly falls off. "She caught him nibbling the rose petals. Granted, they'd been planted in honor of her dead father. But still. She used a garden hoe to do it, like a vegetable peeler . . . flayed his hide. Blood spritzed all over the guests. Ruined everyone's best white suits and all the daisies. Ever hear a rabbit scream? You don't forget a sound like that."

I study the bug's blinking eyelids. He's losing his nerve. I sympathize, having been on the receiving end of Red's violence myself. She once used my blood veins like marionette strings—the most physically excruciating experience of my life. She even left behind an imprint on my heart . . . one that I can still feel, a distinct pressure.

Lately, it's more than just pressure. Ever since that fated night when everything went wrong at prom, when I embraced my madness, the press upon my heart has evolved to a recurrent twinge of pain, like something inside is slowly unraveling.

I haven't told Dad. I was busy practicing my magic, concocting my plan. My loved ones need me to win this battle, to be stronger than Red for good this time.

I don't have the luxury of getting a doctor's appointment. And it wouldn't help anyway. Whatever's wrong with me was brought on by magic. *Red's* magic. My gut knows. And I'm going to make her fix it before I end her sorry existence forever.

More determined than before, I reach for the key the conductor's holding.

He tucks it under his hat and then fiddles with the nameplate, trying to get it out of its slot. "I changed my mind," he says through popping mandibles. "A bug is wont to do that, at times."

"No." I grip his twiglike arm. It would be so easy to snap. A fluttering temptation shadows my thoughts—taunting me to be cutthroat—but I pull back and lay a palm across my chest, pledging. "I vow on my life-magic, I'll never tell her you showed me."

"Best you have a seat and wait for your father," the conductor says. Fumbling around beneath the shag that covers his thorax, he pulls out a package of peanuts and hands them to me. "You must be hungry after your journey. Have some lunch."

"I'm not budging until I see her memories, *bug in a rug*." I drop the peanuts at my feet and press my back to the door, blocking the nameplate.

The beetle makes an angry gurgling sound. "Doesn't matter if my body is made of rugs. My mind works just as well as yours."

"Obviously not. You've forgotten what Morpheus told you. I'm royalty."

"Ah, but Morpheus isn't here, is he?"

I struggle to think of a comeback, but the memory of *why* Morpheus isn't here ices through me, making my tongue as ineffective as a slab of frozen beef.

"You're nothing more than a royal *pain*," the conductor taunts. "You are aware we're under an iron bridge? Netherling magic is limited here. It's why we store the lost memories in this place—to keep them safe. So you can't force me to do anything. And I won't get squashed under the thumb of Queen Red for a scrawny, powerless half-blood snippet."

A hot flash of pride pulses through me, defrosting my tongue. "Maybe you should worry more about being trapped than being squashed."

I call upon the firefly chandeliers overhead, envisioning them as giant metal jellyfish. Chains rattle and bolts snap loose from the ceiling. The harnesses pop open, releasing their firefly captives. Thrilled to be free, the glowing insects bounce and spiral around the car like a planetarium show on steroids. The other passengers screech and burrow under their seats.

Yelping, the conductor tries to back away as the chandelier contraptions swim toward us through the air—their metal tentacles propelling them in a graceful yet disturbing display. I duck and the chains capture the bug, knocking off his hat and thrusting him toward a wall. The bolts snap into place and form a giant metal net. He's pinned inside, high enough that his legs dangle off the ground.

The fireflies hover and cast a soft glow.

Teeth clenched, I fish the key from beneath the conductor's fallen hat along with the bag of peanuts. "There's a new queen in town." I glare up at him. "And *because* of my human-tainted blood, my magic is unaffected by iron. So Red's got nothing on me." I start toward Queen Red's door.

"Wait," the beetle pleads. "Forgive my impertinence, Your Majesty. You've made a fair point. But I'm the conductor. I must protect the reserves of lost memories from the stowaways. Let me down, I beg of you!"

I swivel on my heel to face the others. They peer out from under their seats—eyes ogling, tails drooping, hair frizzed—sneezing and trembling in fear.

The conductor whimpers as I toss the bag of peanuts at him. It snags inside one of the chains close to his left arms.

"He's on his lunch break," I tell the passengers. "Anyone who leaves their seats for any reason will have to deal with me. Are we clear?"

The stowaways answer with a collective nod and cautiously settle back into their places. A tendril of satisfaction unfurls within me.

Smirking, I slip the key into place, and open the door to my enemy's past.

DESCENDING

The instant I shut the door behind me, all my confidence wavers.

The room is small and windowless. An ivory tapestry hangs above a cream-colored chaise lounge and a tall lamp stands beside it, casting a glow on the checked floor.

An almond scent drifts from the moonbeam cookies that always seem to be waiting on a plate. As hungry as I am, I can't eat them. Everything is too painfully familiar here.

I hugged Jeb and Mom in this place, felt their love as they embraced me back. My arms ache with longing. On the opposite wall, red velvet curtains wait to open and unveil hidden snippets from the past. I viewed my parents' love story on this train, watched

Jeb's memories, too. I walked in their heads and wore their emotions as if they were mine.

I felt Mom's change of heart when she gave up the ruby crown to give my dad a chance at life . . . even saw Morpheus as he helped her, carrying my dad through the portal into the human realm, despite that it was putting all of his meticulous plans at risk. I experienced Jeb's nobility and courage when he turned his back on his future so I could have one instead.

So many sacrifices have led to this moment. I would do anything to reverse the clock and set things right. But time is merciless.

"Time. You'll have no such constraints in Wonderland. Let that be your silver lining. Now pull yourself together. We must prepare for Red." Those were Morpheus's words on prom night, mere hours before everything fell apart. The message is so resonant, it's as if he were connected to my mind; but that's impossible with the iron dome between us. Still, it makes sense that his insight echoes through my soul when I'm teetering at the edge of insecurity, considering he's Wonderland's wisdom keeper, the custodian of all things mad and daring.

Jeb is an anchor; he holds me grounded to my humanity and compassion. But Morpheus is the wind; he drags me kicking and screaming to the highest precipice, shoves me off, then watches me fly with netherling wings. When Jeb's at my side, the world is a canvas—unblemished and welcoming; when I'm with Morpheus, it's a wanton playground—wicked and addictive.

Each guy occupies a different side of my dual heart. Together, they bridge my netherling and human worlds. What I'm supposed to do with that knowledge, I'm not sure. And unless my dad emerges from his room with memories intact, I might never get the chance to figure it out.

Tears prick my eyes for the first time in weeks. I've become good at hiding my despair. It was part of my crazy act for the asylum—to appear numb and detached. But that's the furthest from how I feel.

Refusing to cry, I lift my chin. Morpheus would say that I'm a queen, and queens don't cry. And Jeb would say, *"You got this, skater girl."*

They're both right.

I turn the dial on the wall to dim the lamp. The stage curtains open, revealing a movie screen. "Picture her face in your mind whilst staring at the empty screen"—I mimic the conductor's instructions from the last time I was here—"and you will experience her past as if it were today."

I'm surprised how easy it is to recall Red's image in the sketches from my mom's *Alice's Adventures in Wonderland* book. Before little Alice fell down the rabbit hole, before the queen's world was shattered by an unfaithful husband . . . before she was betrayed by her king. Back when Red was only a princess.

The screen lights up, and I burst apart into a thousand pieces, reuniting on the screen inside Red's body and point of view.

She's small and young, maybe ten in human years. Although children are different in the netherling realm—wiser and more cynical, lacking innocence and imagination. Her breath rattles in her lungs as she chases a band of pixies. They're dragging a dead body draped in red velvet. The pixies don't stop until they're within the cemetery gate, safe inside the covered gardens.

"Wait! Bring her back!" Red screams.

She almost trips over her gown, but flaps her wings and lifts off the ground. She lands outside the gate just as it slams closed. Standing alone, she peers through the bars. Sister One scuttles out from the labyrinth of shrubbery, her eight shiny spider legs kicking up her skirt's hem. The gardener's humanoid torso leans over Red's mother and coaxes the spirit from her body. It wriggles, rising from the corpse like a fluorescent vine.

Sister One winds the spirit around her wrist and sends the pixies off with the empty body.

"No, you can't have her!" Red shouts, a weight in her chest so heavy it hurts to breathe. The stench of mildew and scorched leaves stings her nostrils. She's never been this close to the garden of souls, having grown up on horror stories of the keepers and the grounds. But tales of scissored hands and trespassers left in bloody shreds hold no sway today. Not with her mother being taken away forever.

Sister One stares back from inside the gate, a frown on her face. "This is hallowed ground, child-queen. Whatever you be thinking, 'tis foolish. You haven't the power here that you wield in your kingdom."

Red scowls. Her entire body glows crimson as she concentrates on the spidery woman's hair. Strands, as shimmery and fine as pencil shavings, flutter around the gardener's face with a breeze, but Red's magic has no effect.

Red looks up and down the tall fence and the thorny branches that stretch over the expanse of the cemetery gardens like a roof. There's no way to breach the defenses.

Sister One smirks haughtily. "It would be a mistake to attempt to find a way in, little princess, lest you wish to know my sister personally. She has a gift for making confetti of delicate little imps like yourself."

A shudder races from Red's spine to the tips of her wings.

With a final glare at Red, Sister One winds the whimpering, glowing spirit through her fingers. In a sweep of skirts and spidery legs, she disappears into the maze of foliage.

Red's kingly father arrives, his face flushed from trying to catch his daughter.

"What's the good of being immortal," Red asks, her nose wedged against the gate and cold from the metal, "if we can't be together eternally?"

"Immortality merely means you reach a point and stop aging . . . and your spirit never dies," he responds between panting. He squeezes her shoulder. "But the body is vulnerable to some things, and can be left but a shell."

Red's arms and legs go numb. Her own body feels like a shell. Empty and brittle, as if it might blow away at the first gust of wind.

She clasps the bars, holding herself steady. "But why can't we bury her in the ground, amongst the begonias and daisies in our palace courtyard? Like the humans do? If she lived in the flowers, we could visit her every day."

Her father frowns, as if considering. "You know our spirits need dreams to satiate them, to keep them from being restless . . . from possessing living bodies. Only the Twidsters can find and supply such things."

"Dreams." Red sniffles. "One day, I'll bring dreams to our kind, Father. They'll be in abundance everywhere, not just in the cemetery. One day, I'll free the spirits, so they can sleep inside our gardens, brushing our windows at night, and bumping against our feet in the day. I'll bring imagination to our world so everyone might always be with those they treasure."

He pats her head, a tender gesture that almost fills the gaping hole in her chest. "That would make you the most beloved queen of all time, scarlet rosebud. But until then we are bound to follow rules like everyone else. We cannot abuse our power and status, or endanger our subjects. No matter how much we love her." He blots his eyes with a handkerchief. "Understand?"

Red nods.

The scene scrambles and blurs. I'm dragged out of the memory and dropped back into my seat, cradled by the darkness around me. A knocking sensation shakes my skull, as if a fist punches it from the inside. I press my hands to my temples until it stops.

It must be the repudiated memory nesting inside my cranium, because I didn't experience anything like that the last time I was here.

The screen flicks on again. A vivid rainbow smears across the room to jerk me back to the stage. My bones settle into Red's, and my skin conforms to hers.

She's older by six years or so. Her father married a widowed netherling after her mother's death, so the Red Court would have a queen to rule until Red was of age. But in just a few more months, Red will have her coronation, and the crown-magic will fill her blood . . .

Red hides behind some bushes in the castle courtyard's garden. The purple-striped zinnias wilt from the anger seeping off of her as she spies on her father and younger stepsister. Grenadine is the daughter from the new queen's prior marriage, and has proven to be a thorn in Red's side.

It isn't enough that her hair shimmers with the sheen of rubies, and her silver eyes dance beneath thick lavender lashes. She's constantly forgetful— a blank slate waiting to be written upon. Her frailty and dependence offer a distraction for the king's grieving heart, one that Red's strength and independence can't.

The king leans down to show Grenadine for the hundredth time how to play croquet, having already reminded her for the thousandth time he's her new father. He points to the U-shaped metal hoops that form a diamond-patterned run in the ground. Pink and gray stakes mark each end, and two sets of balls lie in a box lined with satin.

"We follow the circuit of wickets," the king says gently. "My red color races against your silver. The first side to get their balls through the wickets in order and hit the peg wins."

Grenadine shakes her head, her ruby curls bouncing about her shoulders. "What is a peg, again?"

"The stake, at the end of the run."

"And a wicket . . . is that this?" Grenadine holds up a flamingonecked fae whose body has been magically stiffened to the shape of a hockey stick. The blush-colored feathers ruffle as if the fae is offended by the misnomer.

"That is a mallet, darling. Wickets are the hoops we hit our balls through."

Grenadine's dimples appear like they always do when she's bewildered. "Oh, Father, I simply can't remember."

He smiles, charmed by her mindless grace. "I've found a way around that, I think. Sir Bill?" He waves someone into the scene.

Bill the Lizard—a reptilian netherling with the ability to write without ink—scrambles into view and bows. His red tailcoat and pants shift to green leaves, matching the bush he's beside so convincingly, he appears to be a decapitated head and clawed hands floating in midair.

Grenadine curtsies in return. "Nice to meet you, sir."

The lizard smiles, beguiled by her sweetness like everyone.

"Sir Bill is the Red Court's stenographer. He has the ability to eat whispers," the king explains. "And afterward, he can write them out on any surface, where they'll adhere forever as quiet murmurings, so they can be heard and not seen. Whisper something you wish to remember."

Grenadine mumbles the rules of croquet she heard moments before.

Bill's chameleon-like jaws unhinge, and his tongue snaps out in midair, capturing the echo of her whispers. His bulbous eyes rotate in different directions as he swallows a rather large lump. Next, he takes a velvet ribbon from his pocket and writes on it with a clawed fingertip.

Blinking, he hands the red strip to the king.

"Listen," the king says, holding it to Grenadine's ear.

She waits, then bursts into rosy-cheeked giggles. "It whispered the rules!"

The king ties the ribbon in a bow around her pinky. "Now you'll never forget them. I've asked Sir Bill to be your very own royal consultant. He'll make enchanted ribbons for as long as you need."

Grenadine crinkles her nose. "Bill? I don't believe I've met him."

The king chuckles. "Of course you have. He's right here."

Bill the Lizard takes another bow.

Weary of the spectacle, Red concentrates on the ribbon tied upon her sister's finger. Her body glows crimson as her magic unties the bow. The velvet strip flutters from Grenadine to land in Red's palm. She steps out from her hiding place.

The king's face flushes. He dismisses Bill, sending him with Grenadine into the palace so they can bring more whispers to life.

"Why would you do that?" Red's father asks her, reaching for the stolen ribbon.

Red curls her fingers around it. "Perhaps I should appoint Bill to make ribbons for you, so you might remember you have another daughter. One whom you never spend time with."

The king looks down at his red slippers. "Ribbons wouldn't help. For I haven't forgotten."

Red's chin stiffens. "She's not even yours! I am, by blood."

"Yes, my scarlet rosebud. Every day you look more and more like your mother. And every day I feel the pain of being torn away from her anew. You're braver than me."

"That's why I'm going to be queen," Red says, trying to harden her heart.

"Yes, because you embrace the things that remind you of her. You drink ash in your tea, to remember how she shushed you when you were a babe. You ask Cook for her favorite Tumtum-berry tarts, so you might remember sharing them with her. And you hum her songs."

Red doesn't answer.

"Please understand, dearest daughter. I only avoid you so I won't drag you down. You're too important to the kingdom for me to hinder you. So I watch from afar. I'm a lucky man, to have a daughter who has grown into such a strong young woman."

Red scorns the empty flattery. "Grenadine is the lucky one. Because she has no memory. She can forget any rule that would confine her actions, blot out any failure that would cripple her confidence, misplace any sadness that would inhibit her to love. She has no standards to live by. She's immune—by her own limitations—to everything that would limit her. She views the world with the wide-eyed cheeriness of a slithy tove pup who has never been kicked or strapped to a chain."

The king nudges the croquet-ball box with his toe. "It doesn't make her stronger to forget. You're the one who's strong. For you remember, and yet you go on. That is what will make you a wonderful ruler one day, just like your mother—sympathetic and understanding."

Red's fist tightens around the ribbon. "Emotions born of weakness. I want nothing to do with them."

"Oh?" Her father's stern voice startles her. "Would you disrespect your mother's memory? All for a small seed of jealousy?"

Red grits her teeth, feeling her mother's gaze on her even though she's far away—a crystalline rose inside the garden of souls.

The king narrows his eyes beneath his crown's shadow. "You have the same dark strain as all of the Red royal lineage. Your mother was the first to learn to balance madness with wisdom. Do not forsake that legacy. Make her proud." He holds out his hand.

Tears singe Red's eyes as she drops the whispering ribbon into his palm, an unspoken promise to honor her mother's memory, to never forget her example.

My bones jitter and my head hurts as again I'm thrown into the chaise lounge, only to be jerked back on-screen for the final memory:

Red kneels beside a rosebush, breathing in the sweet scent. The blooms are such a deep red, they look like puddles of fresh blood against the unnaturally bright teal leaves. She planted the bush in the courtyard as a tribute to her father after his death. She yearns for his spirit. She wishes he were here in the ground instead of locked inside the garden of souls, though she's comforted to know he's been reunited with her mother at last.

"I should be with you both in the cemetery," she mumbles to the roses. "Now that my life is over." She rotates a bottle in her hand to reveal the label: Forgetting Potion.

Her shoulders hunch, as in the distance her stepsister's giggle rings out, accompanied by the chortle of Red's husband. Red met him one week after her father died. He had a kind heart like her father's, and proved to be the only man who could reason with her anger, temper her bitterness. His strength was his compassion, and he adored Red. But the queen became obsessed with her pursuit to bring dreams to Wonderland and neglected her marriage, never even taking the time to give her king the children he yearned for. In her absence, her husband was often left alone with Grenadine.

Gradually, Red watched her husband try to befriend her sister, although Grenadine always pushed him away. When Red's king would return to her side like a wounded puppy, his sadness stoked her jealousy. She did the only thing she could: She stole her sister's ribbons to show her husband what a forgetful buffoon Grenadine was.

Every day for months, each time her sister tied bows to her fingers or toes, Red would magically coax them away and send them fluttering into the sky. Soon, they eclipsed the sun like a cloud of glimmering crimson butterflies. Darkness fell upon the kingdom, but Red didn't care. She had no desire to call the ribbons back or to listen to Grenadine's mundane and irrelevant reminders.

Red's ribbon stealing became a game of malice and great satisfaction, until at last Grenadine stopped wearing them altogether. And soon thereafter, she stopped fighting the Red King's advances.

The two fell in love each day, anew, and Red witnessed it over and over again. Furious, she called the ribbons from the sky. They scattered across the castle courtyard in a sweep of crimson rain. Red stood in their midst as hundreds of whispers spun around her, repeating the same words: Keep Red's husband from your heart. She is your sister, a love that's precious. Always be faithful to Red.

Grenadine had been reminding herself daily to do the right thing, and Red had made it impossible for her to remember. The responsibility for her broken marriage was upon her own shoulders. The only way Red could survive was to become like Grenadine and forget her role in everything. Red determined to remember only the betrayals of others, so their wrongs could harden her heart.

Stroking a rose petal, Red whispers one last time: "Mother, Father, I hope you both can forgive me, because unless I forget, I'll never forgive myself." Then she lifts the bottle to her lips.

The image flicks off, the curtains drop, and the lamp snaps on.

Slumped in the chaise lounge, I hold my temples until the drumming inside my skull subsides. I almost choke on the bittersweet tang of roses firmly pressed on my senses. At last I can acknowledge what I've never let myself admit: I'm a descendant of Queen Red. She's an eternal part of me. I can accept it because she did have a heart once. A heart that felt similar losses to mine: the absence of a mother she adored; the fear of losing her father's admiration; the regret of a mistake so monumental, it cost her the love of her life.

Red locked away her most vulnerable moments so she wouldn't hesitate in her quest for vengeance. So she could make the descent into ruthless abandon without remorse.

Empathy pricks my conscience, but I push it away. Mercy has no place on any battlefield . . . magical or otherwise.

If I can contain her scorned memories long enough to reunite them with her mind, they'll rail against her, fill her with regret. Then, while she's vulnerable, I'll swoop in and Wonderland will never have to fear her rage again.

Adrift in a dark swirl of emotions, I stand and smooth the wrinkles from my hospital gown. I'm only a few steps from the door when it flings open to reveal Dad—his brown eyes lit with a fiery light.

"Allie, I remember . . . everything."

PINT-SIZE PREDICAMENTS

Dad tells me his real name is David Skeffington.

"Interesting," I say as we stride down the aisle. "And here I thought we'd end up related to Martin Gardner."

Dad frowns. "Who's that?"

"The guy behind *The Annotated Alice*. Some math wizard." I shrug. "Just shows how preoccupied Mom's thoughts were with Wonderland. When she couldn't find your real name, she gave you one that fit into the Lewis Carroll legacy."

"Little knowing I already did fit," Dad says.

"Why? Who are the Skeffingtons?" I ask.

Noticing the conductor hanging on the wall, Dad doesn't answer.

I help him free the wriggling beetle. "Mr. Bug-in-a-rug wasn't cooperating," I explain, working my captive's tangled fur from the wires and hardware.

"There are other ways to be persuasive." Dad's expression is stern as he lowers the disheveled insect to the floor. "Less violent ways."

I bite my tongue out of respect, though I want to tell him he's oblivious about dealing with netherlings.

After an apology that wins a cautious albeit reverential bow from the conductor and two complimentary bags of peanuts, Dad takes my hand and we step together onto the toy train's platform. The car door shuts behind us with a loud scrape.

I yawn, inhaling the scent of dust and powdery stones in the coolness of the dimly lit tunnel. The whispers of a hundred bugs blend together—a soothing distraction. Red's memories keep nudging me, blurring my mind with disconcerting crimson stains: her flushed face as she tried to hold on to her mother's spirit, the ruby shimmer of her stepsister's hair during a painful croquet lesson as her father slipped away, and the deep bloody hue of whispering ribbons heralding Red's most devastating mistake.

I *can't* sympathize. I have to be strong.

I grip my abdomen, nauseated and unbalanced. I had no idea the earworm effect would be this powerful. I've got to find a way to control it.

Dad notices me rubbing my stomach and holds out a bag of peanuts. "You need to eat."

I pop a few peanuts into my mouth. The salty crunchiness appeases my hunger, but it doesn't quell the splashes of red drizzling in my mind.

"Tell me where your mom is," Dad says abruptly.

I almost strangle.

"Tell me she's not in the looking-glass world."

After swallowing, I answer, "She's in Wonderland."

He lets out a relieved sigh. "Good. There are creatures in AnyElsewhere that no human—" He cuts himself short, as if remembering Mom's the furthest thing from human. "She's one of them. Like that winged boy who carried me through the portal. She's a netherling."

"Partly," I whisper. The *so am I* sits on my tongue, unsaid.

"She's stronger than I ever could've imagined," he mumbles. "She can protect Jeb. They have each other to lean on."

He's halfway right. Mom is strong, and I have to believe she's surviving in Wonderland. If only Jeb *was* with her, he'd be safer, too. I won't tell Dad they're not together yet. First, he needs to digest all he's learned. "They're okay. They all—*both* are."

Dad's struggling enough with the memory of the winged fae helping Mom break him out of Wonderland's garden of souls. He doesn't need to know Morpheus is part of our rescue mission just now. But later, I'll have to explain the huge role Morpheus has played in my life since childhood. Although I can never confess the part he's slated to play in my future, because I made a life-magic vow not to say a word. I can't even tell Morpheus that I've seen what's coming, even though he's seen it himself.

"The problem is," I continue, "the rabbit hole has been filled in. All the portals are tied together. So if the entrance isn't working, neither are the ways out."

"That's why you brought me here for my memories." Dad picks up the dangling threads of my explanation. "To find another way into Wonderland."

I dread telling him the state Wonderland is in. Worst of all, that I'm to blame for it. That my ineptitude in using undernourished and neglected powers caused this entire tragedy. And that to fix it, I'll have to face my biggest fear.

We have a lot to discuss before I toss Red into the mix.

"So what happened between you and the conductor?" Dad changes the subject, much to my relief. "Why did you bully him like that?"

I drop a peanut into my mouth. "He called me a half-blood snippet," I say between crunches. "I thought my solution was pretty creative." My voice is muffled by the sounds of motors and chatty people drifting from the bridge through the vents overhead.

Dad brushes crumbs off his Tom's Sporting Goods polo. "Just like the lies you and your mother came up with were creative."

Ouch. I shove another handful of peanuts in my mouth, wishing things were like they used to be between us. How strange that somehow the lies became the foundation to our relationship. Without them, our bond is shaky . . . precarious.

I ache to reach out and hug him, but the void between us is too vast.

"If we're going to help her and Jeb," Dad continues, "I need honest answers from you. The whole truth. No more sugarcoating."

I study my bare toes, wincing as we step down onto pebbles and broken rock. My soles aren't the only things feeling exposed and tender. "I have no idea where to start, Dad."

He frowns. "I don't expect answers right this minute. We have to find Humphrey's Inn first."

"*Humphrey's* Inn?" I bite my inner cheek. The only Humphrey

I've ever met is the egg-man creature in Wonderland, the one called Humpty Dumpty in the Lewis Carroll novel. "What's that?"

"It's the one clue I have to my family's whereabouts. It was my home here."

"Here, as in London?"

"As in this world. Humphrey's Inn is some kind of halfway house between the magi-kind and mortal realms. It's hidden underground."

His outright acknowledgment of a magical otherworld leaves me reeling. Maybe I was wrong about him being oblivious in dealing with netherlings. Maybe I even suspected as much, but it's still hard to grasp how deeply Wonderland runs through my blood—on *both* sides of my family.

That thought triggers another splash of Red's memories. I waver in place.

Dad steadies me. "You okay?"

"Just a headache," I answer as the sensation subsides. I'll have to make a concerted effort not to think of my great-great-great-grandmother until I can figure out a way to suppress these episodes. "You were telling me about the inn."

"Yeah. It's somewhere in Oxford."

"Seriously? That's where Alice Liddell grew up. Where she met Lewis Carroll."

Dad rubs the stubble on his chin. "Somehow, way down the line, the Skeffingtons were related to the Dodgsons, which was Carroll's surname before he took on a pseudonym. I hope to get more details once we find the inn."

I don't press any further. I can't imagine the information overload he's experiencing.

Off in the distance, the monarchs that provided our rides are hanging on the tunnel walls, wings flapping slow and relaxed. The firefly chandeliers reflect off their orange and black markings. It reminds me of tigers gliding through the silhouettes of jungle trees during a nature show.

The butterflies whisper: *We know the way to Humphrey's Inn. Would you like an escort, little flower queen?*

Goose bumps coat my arms when I think of jostling through another bout of wind and rain. It's not fear. It's electrified anticipation—like standing in line for a favorite roller coaster. My wing buds nudge. The right one isn't fully healed yet. Maybe I can let it out while riding, exercise my wings without the danger of falling.

Yes, please take us. I send the silent answer back to the butterflies.

"Are they talking to you now?" Dad asks when he catches me staring at them.

I swallow. It's hard to get used to not pretending with someone I've been fooling my whole life. "Uh-huh."

He studies me, his complexion almost green in the dim light. I wonder if it's hit him yet, that we allowed Mom to be locked in an asylum for something that was really happening and not a delusion.

"The butterflies know where the inn is," I say.

Dad makes a disgruntled sound. "After we get there, can we please return to our normal size?"

"Sure. I've got just what we'll need." I pat my pocket where the mushrooms wait, surprised to feel the conductor's pen alongside them. I'd forgotten I still have it.

Dad slips out his wallet and sifts through receipts, money, and pictures. He pauses at the family portrait we had made a few months ago and traces Mom's outline with a shaky fingertip. "I can't believe what she did for me," he murmurs, and I wonder if I was supposed to hear, or if it's a private moment. I've never doubted how strong Dad's love is for her, but only recently did I learn how strong hers is for him.

I'm curious how much he's remembered, if he understands that she was going to be queen before she found him.

Dad's jaw clenches as he slides the picture back into its sleeve. "We don't have the right currency. We'll have to use my credit cards. It should be around dinnertime when we arrive. While we eat, we'll discuss things." He looks tired, yet more alert than I've seen him in years. "We'll plan our next move. But it's important we lay low and try not to draw attention to ourselves. Considering my family's profession, they could've made some very dangerous enemies."

An uneasy knot forms in my throat. "What profession?"

He tucks his wallet into his pocket. "Gatekeepers. They're the guardians of AnyElsewhere."

My knees wobble. *"What?"*

"That's enough discussion for now. I'm still processing."

His curtness stings. But what right do I have to feel wounded? I made him wait seventeen years to learn the truth about me.

"Okay." I stifle an apology and study my ragged gown. "It won't be easy to stay under the radar while wearing asylum clothes. You'll need to change, too."

"Any ideas?" Dad asks, then holds up a hand. "And before you say it, we're not stealing something off a clothesline."

It's like he read my mind. "Why not? Motivation always justifies the crime." I clamp down on my tongue. That's Morpheus's reasoning, not mine. It's both frightening and liberating that his illogic is starting to make perfect sense.

Dad narrows his eyes. "Tell me you did not just say that."

I push away the desire to argue my point. Justifying crimes may be the law of the land in the nether-realm, but that doesn't make it lawful to my dad at this moment. "I just meant it would be *borrowing*, if we bought new clothes later and returned the others."

"Too many steps. We need a quick fix. Makeshift clothes."

Makeshift clothes. If only Jenara were here with her designer talents. I miss her more than ever. Over the past month in the asylum, I wasn't allowed any visitors other than Dad. But Jen sent notes, and Dad always saw that I got them. Jen didn't blame me for her missing brother, in spite of the rumors that I was in a cult that victimized him and Mom. She refused to believe I'd be involved in anything that would hurt either of them.

If only I deserved her faith.

I wish she was here. She'd know what to do about the clothes. Jenara can make outfits out of anything. One time, for a mythology project, she transformed a Barbie into Medusa by spray-painting the doll silver and crafting a "stone" gown out of a strip of aluminum foil and white chalk.

Dolls . . .

"Hey!" I shout up at the closest Ferris-wheel-firefly chandelier. "Could you guys give us some light, please?"

They roll across the ceiling and stop overhead, illuminating our surroundings. This place was once an elevator passageway where train passengers would wait for rides up to the village after arriving on the train. Distracted parents and careless children left behind toys which are comparable to our size: wooden blocks that could double as garden sheds, a pinwheel that could pass for a windmill, and a few rubber jacks bigger than the tumbleweeds I've seen bounce alongside the roads in Pleasance, Texas.

A sign hangs over the toys. The words LOST AND FOUND have been marked out and replaced by TRAIN OF THOUGHT.

Past a pile of mildewed picture books, there's a child's round suitcase propped up so the front is visible. The style is retro—pink, cushiony vinyl with a ponytailed girl standing in front of an airplane. Her faded dress was blue at one time. Under the zipper, scribbled in black marker, is a child's handwriting: *Emily's Dress Shoppe*. Sprawled on the ground beside the case is a half-naked vintage Barbie.

"Doll clothes," I whisper.

Dad squints. "We need things that'll fit when we're normal-size, Allie."

"They grow and shrink with you. It's part of the magic."

He glances down at his muddy, torn work uniform. "Oh. Right . . ."

"C'mon." I catch his hand and weave toward the case, suppressing yelps as the rocky terrain jabs my feet. Dad stops long enough to take off his shoes and help me step into them.

They're too big, of course, but the tender gesture reminds me of times when I used to stand on the toes of his shoes so we could dance together. I smile. He smiles back, and I'm his little girl again. Then his expression changes from awe to disappointment, as if he's coming to terms all over again with what I am, what Mom is, and how long we've kept it hidden from him.

My stomach feels like it's caving in. Why did we rob him of such a big part of ourselves? Such an integral part of *him*? "Dad, I'm so sorr—"

"No, Allie. I can't hear that yet." His left eyelid starts to twitch and he looks away, his socked feet cautiously feeling around the debris.

I follow and sniffle, telling myself it's the dust making my eyes water.

When we arrive at the doll-clothing case, it's as tall as a two-story building, and the zipper handle is the length of my leg.

"How are we supposed to open this thing?" I ask.

"Better question: How are you supposed to fit into her clothes?" Dad points to the dust-caked Barbie. "You're barely the size of her head."

The doll's irises are painted as if she's looking off to one side. Paired with her catty makeup, she appears to be sneering at me. Exasperated, I thrust my hands in my apron pockets. My knuckle nudges the conductor's pen. Digging deeper, I hit the mushrooms and an idea forms in my mind. "Let's sit her against the case."

Dad shoots me a puzzled glance but doesn't hesitate. He grabs her shoulders and I take her ankles. A yellowish spider the size of a cocker spaniel scuttles out, grumbling at us for ruining its web. It disappears into the pile of books. Once we have the Barbie seated upright, I settle beside her.

I hand Dad a mushroom and kick off his shoes so he can put them on again. Next, I take a mushroom for myself and nibble the speckled side. I grit my teeth against the discomfort of sinews extending, bones enlarging, and skin and cartilage expanding. The surroundings shrink as I continue to eat until I'm head to head with the doll.

Dad follows my lead, nibbling his mushroom until we're both big enough to unzip the case and wear the 1950s-style Barbie and Ken outfits that slide out.

I shove aside silver bell-bottom pants and a black-and-white striped swimsuit, uncovering a leotard and matching attached tutu the same watery green as Jeb's eyes at times when he's upset. The exact shade they were when he caught me and Morpheus kissing in my room before prom.

Regret gnaws at my stomach. All these weeks, Jeb's been thinking I betrayed him. In the last moment we shared at prom, he grabbed the pendant at my neck—a metal clump that had once been my Wonderland key, his heart locket, and his engagement ring—and kissed me. He promised we were far from over. Even after I'd destroyed his trust, he was still planning to fight for me.

A ticklish sensation brings my attention to my ankle where a spiderweb dangles at the edges of my wing tattoo. I got it months ago to camouflage my netherling birthmark. Here in the shadows, I realize how much the tattoo really does look like a moth, just as Morpheus has always said. I can almost see his lips curl up in smug delight at the acknowledgement.

That strange unraveling pain gnaws in my chest again. It hits most often when I'm teetering between my two worlds.

What did Red do to me?

Red . . .

Her repudiated memories thunder through my skull once more. I groan softly.

"Did you say something, Allie?" Dad looks up from the Ken clothes he's sorting through.

After rubbing my temples, I lift out a sleeveless shirtdress with snaps down the front and a cherry and green-stem print that matches the leotard. "Just that I think I found something." I hold it up for Dad's inspection.

"Looks good. I'll be over here." Dad grabs his bundle and goes to the other side of the case.

I peel off my asylum clothes, careful not to let the remaining mushrooms spill from the apron pocket. I'll have to find another way to carry them.

Before I undress, I search for some lacy lingerie. I've been wearing generic cotton underthings since I've been at the asylum. Something pretty would be nice. Unable to find anything, I settle for what I have on and slip into the green leotard. The ballet outfit's best feature is the open back. It will make it easy to free my wings. The satiny fabric smells of crayons and gumdrops, making me long for my childhood before Mom was committed.

Next, I shrug into the shirtdress and secure the metal snaps along the cherry-print bodice, leaving the skirt open to display the three tiers of green netting that puff out above my knees.

A fuchsia ribbon serves as a belt. Pink stockings complete the outfit. They fit perfectly from my thighs to my calves, but the toes are pointed. I fold the excess under before slipping into a pair of squishy, knee-high red boots.

Red boots. Red's memories bash against my cranium until I feel so much sadness for her I drop onto the pile of leftover clothes. I fist my hands against my head until it passes. When I open my eyes, I'm half-buried in Barbie shoes and accessories, as if I thrashed around half-consciously.

"Everything okay over there?" Dad asks from his side of the case.

I grunt softly, clearing everything off me. "Having trouble with my stockings." Maybe stealing Red's memories was a big mistake after all. I'm going to end up wearing a straitjacket again—this time for real.

As I stand, my foot kicks a Barbie-size diary with a key that must be one quarter the size of a straight pin to a normal human.

The conductor said it would take enchanted paper to contain repudiated memories. A year ago in Wonderland's cemetery, Sister One told me that toys from the human realm were used to trap souls in her twin's lair.

Sister One said that when the most cherished toys are abandoned, they want those things that once filled and warmed them. They become lonely and crave what they had. And if someone gives them those things, they'll hold on to it with every portion of their strength and will.

I flip through the diary. A few of the tiny pages have been written on—hearts and initials and flowers, because writing actual words this size would be difficult for any child. The last two thirds of the pages are bare.

Maybe this diary has missed being written upon.

Morpheus himself said toys harbor the residue of a child's innocent love, the world's most binding magic. If that's true, then maybe these pages are enchanted enough to contain Red's memories, to keep the emotional ties out of my mind.

I bite my lower lip. *Look at that, bug in a rug. I just found a magic journal.*

"Almost done?" Dad moves around on the other side of the case, as if he's pacing.

"Just a sec!" I scramble to find the apron I was wearing earlier and pull the pen from the pocket.

"Netherling logic resides in the hazy border between sense and nonsense." I mouth Morpheus's words so Dad won't hear.

I jot down Red's memories on the remaining pages, writing as fast as I can. The emotions drain from me onto the page, a cathartic experience, like journaling to soften the blow of something tragic.

When I'm done, I close the book. It wriggles in my hands, opening enough to rustle the paper. The memories are trying to break free. Clamping my fingers tight around the covers, I clasp the latch and lock it with the key and the wiggling stops.

My head feels better, my thoughts clearer, and my sympathies are dulled. The transfer must've worked. I can still recall Red's forgotten past, but they feel like events that happened to someone else, not ones I experienced and felt myself. The memories grow distant, silencing the sympathetic thunder in my head.

"Allie, we need to get going."

"I'm looking for something to keep the mushrooms safe," I stall.

As I dig, a pink ballet bag with a drawstring appears. I tuck the diary inside and thread a piece of cording through the diary's key to fashion a necklace. Ever since the prom disaster, I've felt lost without my Wonderland key. This one isn't ruby-tipped and won't open another world. Still, it's a comfort to have it dangling at my collarbone.

Setting aside two mushrooms for me and Dad, I stuff the rest into the bag with the diary, pull the drawstring shut, knot it securely, then hang it over my shoulder.

With a plastic brush, I work the tangles out and braid my hair down both sides. I stare at a crocheted hat and scarf made of soft purple and scarlet yarn, testing to see if Red's memories stay dormant. I have to be sure before we leave. I can't risk losing control when I'm thousands of miles in the air.

When nothing happens, I pull on the scarf and hat.

I step around to the front of the case. Dad's waiting in a Ken outfit: black-and-white plaid jacket, gray flannel pleated pants, and white dress shirt.

I pat the skin under my eyes, worried my netherling markings are showing after all the magic I've performed. "Do I look okay?"

"You look beautiful, Butterfly," he says. His fingertip traces the edges of my eyes, following a phantom pattern that can only mean my markings are in full bloom.

His use of my nickname fills me with gratitude. He's trying to accept me with all my peculiarities, even though he's been dealt a huge shock.

I straighten his collar and brush dust off his jacket. "Best thing about these clothes? We know we're the first people to ever wear them," I tease.

Dad snorts. The sound echoes in the tunnel as we nibble our mushrooms—the smooth sides—until we shrink enough to fit on the butterflies' backs again. We climb atop our winged mounts, flutter through the hole in the bridge's foundation, and take to the sky for Oxford.

FLESH & BLOOD

A cold rain jolts me awake. The scent of moisture fills my nostrils and thunder shakes my eardrums, muffled by a swooping sound. My right cheek nestles against something both soft and bristly.

I shake my head, trying to remember where I am.

The mushroom lair. I'm in Morpheus's arms . . . He's flying me to his manor. I'm terrified to look, but have to know where he's taken Jeb. I push up, expecting to see Wonderland's terrain passing beneath my stratospheric heights. Instead, lightning brightens the haze around me, illuminating Dad as he glides on a butterfly mount up ahead. I'm surrounded by storm clouds, and I'm not being held by Morpheus. I'm riding a monarch.

Sadness snakes through me. Lately, when I sleep, my dreams relive moments in Wonderland with Morpheus, or in Jeb's garage, watching him paint and work on motors, or even making cookies with Mom in our kitchen. One common thread binds them all: Waking up is a dreaded occurrence.

I tighten my grip through the hairy bristles of the butterfly's thorax as we plunge out of one cloud and into another. My vision adjusts through sheets of rain and blinking darkness. The leafy treetops appear closer with each flash of lightning. Our butterflies are descending, which means we're about to reach Oxford and my heart-to-heart with Dad.

What's he going to think when he finds out I'm responsible for this entire nightmare?

Wind skids through us, causing our rides to lurch and catching the drawstring at my shoulder. The ballet bag jostles, hard enough for the diary to bump against my rib cage.

For an instant, I let myself get lost in the flavor of the rain, of skirting in and out of clouds alive with electric light. My wet braids flap around my face and shoulders—driven either by my magic or the wind.

The diary bumps against my ribs again. It's not the ride or the weather causing the movement this time. The strings stretch taut *against* the wind's pull. Something has roused the memories on the pages, made them restless. Maybe by cozying up to my darker side, I reminded Red's memories of their vendetta against her. Or worse, maybe the memories are a part of me now, no matter how much distance I put between us. After all, Red was once a part of my body. And she'll forever be a part of my blood.

Maybe even my heart.

I wrestle the drawstring to subdue the diary. The bag jerks free, slips from my shoulder, and plummets through the darkness and rain along with our chance to return to normal size, and even worse, my leverage against Red.

"Follow that bag!" I demand of my ride.

We are not taxis, the monarch answers. *We stay the course.*

"That's why we have to get it back!" I shout. "To stay the course!"

The monarch ignores my pleas. A daring thrum springs to life inside me, the one that Morpheus has always nurtured, the one I've been honing over the past month.

I rip my snaps apart and shed the shirtdress, leaving only the open-back leotard. The scarf around my neck shields the diary's key hanging beneath.

My discarded dress trails toward Dad. It slaps the back of his head and he looks over his shoulder. "What are you doing?" he yells.

"Saving our one chance to save everyone else." My wings pop free. I groan at the agony shooting through my right shoulder as the wounded one unfurls.

Without risking a look at Dad, I leap off the butterfly. Its antenna slaps my boot's sole as I descend, spread-eagle, caught up on a current of wind.

The hat pops off my head, but the scarf stays secure, its ends flapping in time with my braids.

"Allie!" Dad's desperate scream is snatched away by thunder.

I descend through the rain-streaked sky, terror giving way to awe. My wings provide drag and slow me down, but they're too weak to offer lift. The wind adds another hurdle, buffeting me. I'm invigorated. One thing being crowned a queen in Wonderland has taught me: Power is impotent unless it's cultivated with risks.

This is living . . . a free fall into the unknown.

Rain swirls and pelts me. I force my eyes open and tilt my wings to veer in the direction the bag fell. The pouch comes into blurry view as I gain momentum. An instant before I pass it, I snatch the bag and tuck it into the bodice of my leotard, glad I had the foresight to tie the drawstrings before we left. Everything is still inside.

Lightning slashes my surroundings. Giant trees zoom closer and closer, their leaves appearing deceptively soft. But what waits between the spaces—branches jagged and monstrous—will tear me to shreds. At my size, I may as well be a bug hitting a cracked windshield. There'll be nothing left but blood and tattered wings.

An instant before I collide with the nearest tree, I imagine its branches meshing together, the soft, thick moss rising to coat the domed shape, forming a giant pincushion.

On impact, the breath puffs from my lungs. I slide into the cushioned surface, like a straight pin burrowing through a sawdust filling. The force bends the moss and foliage around me until the top of my head bursts out and slams into the slippery trunk. A sharp pain slices through my skull and spine, and everything goes black.

❦ · I · ❦

When I come to, my muscles and flesh hum with the sensation of being stretched. Something purrs at my ear, then a buzz of wings and a brush of soft fur, all too familiar.

Chessie?

It can't be. I never saw him after the incident in the art studio a month ago. I assumed he'd already returned to Wonderland and was trapped there like Mom. He would've visited me in the asylum otherwise.

My eyes don't want to open. I wriggle my arms and legs beneath the cozy weight of blankets, expecting my head to pound. I heard my skull crack when it hit that tree. Instead, I'm comfortable, serene . . . euphoric, even. A tingling sensation lingers at my ankle. Someone melded their birthmark to mine.

Maybe it *was* Chessie.

I groan.

"She's coming to." It's Dad's voice.

My eyelids refuse to budge. A bitter flavor sits on the back of my tongue and I smack my lips.

"I wasn't sure I got enough down her." Dad strokes my hair soothingly.

"Drinking mushroom tea is five times more potent than eating them." It's a stranger's voice—gruff, as if he's been gargling sand. "She's going to need food soon, to counteract the effects. Perhaps I should bring her something so she can stay hidden. Not all of the castaways are as understanding as this little fellow. In fact, he's the one responsible for keeping them here all these weeks. Most of them wanted to find her so she'd fix the portals. They miss their world and their kin."

So Chessie didn't visit me in the asylum because he didn't want to lead any angry netherlings my way. He's really here!

I force my eyes open.

The scent of melted candle wax warms my nostrils, and the soft glow of firelight blinks against a windowless wall upholstered with royal blue and forest green fabric.

It's a private chamber. I'm on a round, backless couch piled with colorful tasseled throw pillows. The decor reminds me of a circus—wild yet weirdly graceful. Zebra-skin rugs drape the domed ceiling. Other than the candelabras, everything is cushioned, even the floor.

The surroundings are a mixture between the padded cell at the asylum and Sister One's cottage in Wonderland.

Two silhouettes take shape, standing over me.

The stranger looms as tall as my dad. There's something very familiar about him, although I've never seen him before in my life.

A brown-leather cloak swallows his muscular form and suede khaki pants are tucked into his boots. His oversized hood cascades down his shoulders and back. All he needs is a quiver of arrows, and he could be Robin Hood.

Dark hair, flecked with gray, complements his goatee and bushy eyebrows. Eyes the color of root beer study me. "Why, hello at last," he says kindly.

An itch starts at the tip of my nose. I drag a hand from under my blankets to cover my resulting sneeze. I squawk as my nose shrinks to the size of a pea.

"Ah, having a slight reaction to the tea, are you?" the stranger says.

"Slight?" My voice sounds more like a squeak because of my miniscule nose. I throw off the blankets and scramble to sit up.

Dad eases down beside me on the edge of the cushion.

"It's okay, Allie. Just give it a second." Even his calm expression can't settle my nerves. Another sneeze bursts, and my nose returns to normal size, but my right hand inflates and doesn't stop until it's the size of a basketball.

I yelp.

"She has your chin," the stranger says, as if oblivious to my spontaneous deformity. "But the wings and eyes . . ."

"Those are her mother's," Dad says proudly, as if he, too, is blind to what's happening.

Maybe the reaction is that I'm *hallucinating*. I try to lift my swollen hand, but it sits next to me like a boulder. I squeeze it to a fist and give it a hard jerk. It pummels Dad's stomach and sends him rocketing off the couch. He lands in a pile of throw pillows.

Nope. Not hallucinating.

Another sneezing fit overtakes. Once it stops, I sigh, relieved to find my hand is normal and all of my other body parts to scale.

The stranger helps Dad up. Dad brushes off his flannel pants, and they both look down at me with wide brown eyes—as if I were a science experiment.

I pat the top of my head, the one part of me I can't see. "Oh, no. My head's the size of a blimp, isn't it?"

The stranger chortles. "Not at all, child." He slaps Dad's back. "She's definitely got the Skeffington sense of humor, yes?"

Chessie flutters into view, smiling mischievously. I'm so happy to see him I shout his name.

The tiny Barbie ballet bag hangs around his neck and a ragged hole gapes in the bottom. The mushrooms are gone. But thankfully, the outline of the diary still wrinkles the satiny fabric from inside. Red's magical memories survived.

I feel my collarbone to find the necklace still in place, although the key is as big as a regular one after growing with me. Since the book is still toy-size, it must have fallen out of my leotard's bodice before I drank the tea. Maybe it's better that the diary is small. It will be easier to handle if the emotions get unruly again.

Chessie unscrews his head and it rolls toward me along the floor, the bag's strings tangled around his cranium. A silly laugh escapes him as his decapitated body gives chase.

Dad and the stranger smirk.

How can my dad be so comfortable around all this weirdness? And the stranger, too? They're both wearing the same goofy Elvis grins.

In fact, they look so much alike they could be . . .

I swing my legs around. The bright colors of the room disorient me. "Dad? Is this . . . ?"

"Oh, sorry, Butterfly." Dad sits down next to me again, putting his arm around the tutu at my waist to avoid crushing my wings. "This is Bernard."

"Call me Uncle Bernie," the man insists.

Chessie's nose bumps my plastic boot and comes to a stop. I tug the ballet bag's strings, and his head spins like a top. As I wrap my fingers around the diary, the stranger's words register: *Uncle* Bernie.

A smile spreads over my face. There's a knowing behind his eyes, an unconditional affection that I didn't do anything to earn, other than being born.

"You're brothers."

Bernie's grin widens. "That we are. Nice to finally meet you." He places a hand on Dad's shoulder. "Our family . . . they'll be overjoyed. We'd given up hope."

A strangled sound I don't recognize breaks from my throat.

"She needs water," Dad says to his brother.

His brother.

Uncle Bernie nods and promises to return. I watch his back—broader than Dad's—as he steps out into a cushioned hallway lined with dozens of upholstered doors similar to the one in our room.

Chessie screws his head on once more, flitters his wings, and follows my uncle before I can thank him for healing me and watching over the diary.

The door shuts, leaving Dad and me alone with nothing but the popping of lit candles. I can still see the worry lines on his forehead, etched in place by Mom and Jeb's absence over the past few weeks. But there's happiness softening the ones around his eyes.

All my life I thought we had no extended family. Then last year I realized Mom and I were related to magical creatures from Wonderland. Now, I have an uncle. A human uncle who looks like the Prince of Thieves.

I must have other relatives, too. Cousins and aunts, even grandparents.

Which means Dad has nephews and nieces. Parents of his own . . .

"When are we going to meet them?" I ask, not sure he'll pick up on my inference.

"My mom and dad are gone." Regret echoes in his voice, becoming my own. "But I have two sisters, and they have children. As do Bernard and his wife. We'll meet them after we find your mother and Jeb. Other than the netherlings passing through, only members of the Looking-glass Knighthood stay at this inn. My brothers, uncles, male cousins, and nephews. The women and youngest children stay elsewhere in Oxford."

I stare at him, dumbfounded.

Dad catches both my hands. "We're descended from the same lineage as Charles Dodgson. After he discovered the way to Wonderland, and after Alice found her way back out of the rabbit hole—"

"Wait," I interrupt. "*Charles* discovered the way to Wonderland? I thought Alice told him about the rabbit hole. That she inspired his fictionalized account. Are you saying he actually knew the place was real?"

Dad shrugs. "The only history we've retained is that the men in our family were called by Charles to guard the gates of AnyElsewhere. To be appointed as knights. His published works help fund us. It's been our duty for over a century. The boys are tested when they're seven years old. There's usually only one son born with the gene. My brother and I were the exception. We both had it."

"What gene?"

"A second sight like Charles had. An ability to see the weak points in the barrier between the nether-realm and our world. It has to do with infinity mirrors."

The only infinity mirrors I'm aware of are in funhouses at carnivals and county fairs. I swallow hard, wondering how such a childish diversion could be the gateway to a horrific place like the looking-glass world. But then again, maybe that's fitting, considering Wonderland is built upon children's dreams, imagination, and nightmares—considering those things are its very foundation.

"So . . . you had that ability?" I ask.

"*Have* it," Dad corrects. "I forgot after my memories were erased. But it's all come back. I was captured by the spider creature a few months after I started training to be a White knight."

My chin quivers. I should be in awe just imagining him as a knight, but there's sadness in his voice. I lean in to hug him. He wraps his arms around me, careful to avoid smashing my wings.

He regrets missing out on the life he was meant for. Just like Mom missed out on hers.

My birth, my entire existence, has been at the expense of their noble and royal callings. Not to mention, a black stain on the once beautifully bizarre landscapes of Wonderland that are now withering because of me.

"I'm sorry," I say, wishing I could blot out all of my wrongs with an apology. But it's not possible.

I think of the tiny diary in the ballet bag. Red's regrets were so acute, she cast them aside, abandoning the memories that made them. But there's no "forgetting potion" I can take. And even if there were, I wouldn't. Nothing can be erased if I'm going to put things right for everyone. And I will, no matter what it costs me in the end.

EGGS BENEDICT

"Don't be sorry." Dad's breath warms the top of my head. "I do wish I'd known my relatives. But I wouldn't change anything else. If I had been a White knight, I would never have met your mom. We wouldn't have had you. And, for the record, I wouldn't trade my two girls for anything in *any* world." He presses a kiss against my hair.

I snuggle close, struggling to make my voice work. "Thanks, Dad," I whisper, comforted by the waxy-crayon scent of his shirt. Even if he's able to accept the turn his past took, I can't accept the one our present has.

"Okay." His voice deepens to sternness and he eases us apart.

"Let me have a look at you." His brow crinkles as he runs his thumb across the top of my scalp. "That healing trick really worked. You were bleeding so much, I thought you'd at least have a concussion."

He must've been so scared watching me dive into the storm and hit the tree. "How did you know I could be healed?"

"I didn't. I wanted to get you to a hospital. But we were both too small and the mushrooms were gone." A muscle in his jaw feathers. "I asked the butterflies to bring us here. I hoped they would understand, and that someone at the inn would know what to do."

It had to have been terrifying to feel so helpless, to go against the grain of logic and surrender to faith in the senseless. Dad's got more guts than Mom and I ever gave him credit for.

I squeeze his wrists. "You did great."

"That little cat-bird fellow did great." Dad opens my palms and traces the scars there. "That's what your mom was trying to do when you were little and she hurt your hands. That's why she kept saying she could fix you. She wanted to heal you. And I pushed her away." His watery eyes meet mine. "I'm sorry, Allie."

"You didn't know. We never told you."

He frowns and presses his forehead against mine. "Well, you can make it up to me. First off, I don't ever want to see you throw yourself into the sky again."

I smile at him through my tears. "C'mon. I have wings."

He leans back. "Yeah, and they're beautiful. But they weren't working all that great." He looks over my shoulder at the gauzy flaps casting shadows on the couch. "Although they appear to be stronger than they were."

I flutter them. There's no pain. Even the right one feels powerful. Chessie's melding must've healed more than my skull.

I'll be able to fly now, just in time to go to AnyElsewhere.

Dad must see my thoughts on my face, because he cups my chin again. "You're not indestructible, even if you have abilities other girls don't. No more unnecessary chances. Okay?"

I nod to pacify him. He doesn't understand how *necessary* taking chances is to fix things. Even worse, he doesn't understand that I'm starting to crave the risks.

"What else?" I ask to change the subject.

He drops his hand to his knee. "Huh?"

"You said 'first off.' That means something else is coming."

The worry wrinkles reappear on his forehead. "Right. It's time for you to tell me the truth. All of it."

My stomach winds up like a fist. "That's a lot of years to cover. Where should I start?"

"Baby steps. Your mom's history. How Jeb's involved. Does he know what you are? And that winged creature who carried me out of Wonderland's portal—what part does he play?"

"Wow, Dad. Baby steps?"

"Yep."

"Baby brontosaurus, maybe," I tease.

His answering smile encourages me, and I tell him everything. From the moment I first heard a bee and a flower argue in the nurse's office during fifth grade, to my Alice in Wonderland dream that night, to last summer when Jeb and I went through the rabbit hole and I was crowned the Red Queen after finding out who Mom and I are descended from.

Even when Dad's face pales, I go on. Because he has to know about Mom's part, how she once wanted to be queen herself but gave it all up for him. And how Jeb was brainwashed, forgetting our time in Wonderland, but once he remembered, he fought for me and the humans at prom. And that's why he's in the looking-glass world now.

"Oh, no. Not there." Dad's expression fills with dread. "I was so hard on him . . . when he said he hid you after that incident at your school. He was innocent. He was just protecting your secrets."

"It's okay. He knew you didn't mean it."

Dad shakes his head. "He's always been like a son to me. When we find him, I'll set things right. I promise."

"I know, Dad." I appreciate him saying *when* and not *if*. "I have to make things right, too." Though my wrongs against Jeb cut so much deeper.

I inhale a shaky breath before confessing the rest: Morpheus's part in everything. How he helped Mom come up with a way to win the crown but was betrayed when she chose Dad over her quest. How that betrayal drove Morpheus to visit my childhood dreams, to become a child himself so he could lure me into Wonderland without telling me what I was really there to do.

Dad's face darkens—an angry distrust shadowing his features. It's the same look Jeb always gets when Morpheus's name comes up.

Dad opens his mouth, but I interrupt. "Before you condemn him, you need to know that he saved my life in Wonderland. He saved it here in the human realm, too. In fact, he saved Jeb's. He's not pure evil, Dad. He's . . ."

Glory and deprecation—sunlight and shadows—the scuttle of a scorpion and the melody of a nightingale. Sister One's description of him has never seemed more apt. *The breath of the sea and the cannonade of a storm. Can you speak these things with your tongue?*

No. I can't.

"He's what, Allie?" Dad asks.

"He's wicked. He's dangerous. And he's far from trustworthy. But he's devoted to me and Wonderland. In that respect, he's my friend." I stop before the rest can escape: *He's lodged himself inside the netherling half of my heart, no matter how hard I tried to deny him access.*

"How can you say that?" Dad presses. "After all the grief he's brought down on our family?"

"Because we wouldn't be a family if he hadn't carried you out of Wonderland and kept your identity hidden all these years. He didn't have to do that."

Dad's scowl deepens. "I'm not sure I agree with your reasoning."

"There is no reasoning when it comes to Morpheus. You just accept him as he is."

"Well, I *don't* accept him. He caused this to happen. He's to blame for your mother and Jeb being in—"

"You're wrong," I interrupt before shame can intrude on my over-due confession. "*I'm* the one who set everything in motion."

"Allie, no. I get that in some way you had a hand in the rabbit hole being clogged. But I also know it was an accident."

"It's more than that." I grind out the words between clenched teeth. "I unleashed Queen Red but was afraid to face her. I failed to go back to Wonderland, so she came to our world. And now Mom, Jeb, and Morpheus are all victims of my cowardice."

The righteous indignation on Dad's face melts away. A knock at the door causes us both to jump. Uncle Bernie peeks in with the water he promised.

"Bad timing?" he asks.

Dad waves him in, and I take the glass. The drink slides down my throat cold and clean, although it does nothing to calm my stomach. I still haven't told Dad the worst part of all. How I unleashed a power at prom that I knew almost nothing about, and caused Mom to be dragged into the rabbit hole before it caved in on itself.

"You don't look so good," Uncle Bernie says, pressing the back of his hand to my brow. "No doubt a residual effect of the mushroom tea."

I let his explanation hang in the air, though Dad and I both know it's so much more than that. I preoccupy myself with the tiny diary. Taking the drawstring from the torn ballet bag, I thread it through the book's locked latch to form a necklace. Then I drape it over my head so the diary is beside the key that's three times bigger. I'll have to resize one or the other when it's time to open the pages and unleash the volatile memory magic upon an unwitting Red.

"You both need to eat something," Bernie suggests. "And the dining hall is empty enough now that she'll be safe."

My uncle leaves our room and Dad looks pointedly at me. "You shower first. We'll finish our talk over dinner."

⚜ · I · ⚜

The dining hall is carnival gaudy like our chambers, with the addition of a dozen cushioned table and chair sets and the aroma of food. Only one table is occupied, and the guests are netherlings.

They're fixated on the pit a few feet below restaurant level where four human knights are fencing. It reminds me of the staged jousting dinner matches in the human realm, à la Las Vegas.

One set of knights wears red tunics under chain mail mantles, and the other team wears white. Each duo consists of an older man and a boy somewhere between eight and twelve years old. The older knight on the white side is Uncle Bernie. The boys fight as the elders coach them. Their swords bend, and puffs of gray ash sweep up, almost cloaking them at times.

"So, dinner with a show?" I whisper to Dad.

"They're using foils . . . flexible swords with blunted points," Dad says while watching the activity in the ring with a faraway glint in his eyes. "It's part of fine-tuning our concentration, making us perform in front of patrons at a young age. We have to keep a cool head while being aware of the eyes on us, and the scent of food . . . the sounds of voices. We can't get distracted."

"What's with the ash?"

"Ash covers a large portion of AnyElsewhere's terrain. So we learn to move in it without slipping or slowing down." After kissing my brow, he gestures toward an empty table in the corner. "Order something. I want to say hello."

He makes his way down stone stairs toward his relatives. *Our relatives.*

The knights set aside their daggers and swords as he walks over. He fits right in with the white ones, dressed in the same tunic and tan suede pants.

I glance down at my red tunic. The long underwear beneath my pants, although a far cry from the lacy underthings I was hoping for, feels soft against my freshly scrubbed skin. They must've given me a boy's size, because the fit is decent. Best of all, the shoulder seams are torn to make room for my wings. I'm still wearing my Barbie boots, the only shoes that fit.

I look as mismatched and jumbled on the outside as I feel on the inside. Dad's relatives wave, not even fazed by my eye patches and wings.

I wave back, feeling shyer than I'd like.

They all turn their attention to Dad as he shrugs into a chain mail mantle. He takes the sword offered him and walks into the middle of the pit with his brother. They bow; then, in a blink, they're fencing. Ash flies up around them with each lunge and parry.

Dad seems out of his element, his movements jerky and imbalanced. He gets tripped and pinned to the ground by Bernard's sword a few times. But soon, it's like a switch flips on. His thrusts with the sword become fluid and natural. His fingers, wrists, body, and arms settle into a cadence as graceful as a waltz. The clang of swords rings in the air. It's a good thing he's stayed in shape via racquetball and jogging, or he'd never have the stamina for this.

The epiphanies and events of the past twenty-four hours start to spin around me. I stumble toward the empty table Dad pointed out and slide into my seat. The netherling customers I saw earlier still haven't noticed me.

One is a reptilian creature. The other is monkey-faced and woolly. The lizard looks like a floating head and hands. Queen Red's memory of Bill the Lizard resurfaces—the details emotionless and distant. The lizard's body seemed to disappear when his clothes took on the color of leaves around him. It was like his suit was the chameleon instead of him.

Is this Bill? If so, my kingdom is in more danger than I imagined. Grenadine, Red's amnesiac stepsister and my temporary stand-in as queen, doesn't have the royal blood or crown-magic pulsing through her that I do. She'll be hopelessly lost if the lizard isn't showering her with ribbon reminders. By getting Bill stuck here, I've made things even worse.

"It's an optical *delusion*, just so you know."

My attention snaps up to a white, egg-shaped creature standing over me. Parts of his oblong body are studded with colored beads and shimmering ribbon glued in place. He looks like a giant Fabergé egg that escaped from a museum.

He sets down a glass of water, plops a basket of steaming rolls on the middle of the table, then slides a menu toward me. "My customer you keep gaping at. His suit is hooded and made of simulacrum silk. Comes from enchanted telepathic silkworms. It's transparent when pulled over other clothes. It connects with the wearer's mind and reflects their surroundings. Observers are deluded into seeing only the body parts that are bared. Tricky, aye? Comes in handier than you'd think."

His yolk-yellow eyes, red nose and wide mouth remind me so much of the egg-man I met in Wonderland, I can't help but blurt the name. "Humphrey?"

"*Hardly,*" comes the sour answer. "Name's Hubert. Didn't anyone ever teach you how to make a proper acquaintance?"

Wow. He even sounds like Humphrey. I squint. "Uhhh . . ."

"Well, are you going to sit there with your brain idling, or are you going to order some fare?" One praying-mantis arm straightens the collar beneath his chin, while the other balances a tray with a pad and pen as he awaits my answer.

"You're his brother, aren't you?" I ask, pushing aside the menu. The yeasty bread smells too good to resist so I grab a roll and sink my teeth in.

Hubert's cheeks burn red. "Oh, I see. Since we're all the same shape and color, we must all be related, right? An egg by any other name and all that rot."

"Well, no. Since you work here, and the place is named after him." I take another bite of my yeasty roll. "Figured it was a family thing."

"Firstly," he snorts, "I'd ask that you not speak with your mouth so full of bread. And secondly, if you'll take a look at the menu, the inn is called 'Humphrey's and Hubert's.' Centuries of lazy-tongued patrons shortened it. But it's right there in print, so see that *you* don't."

"So you're business partners."

"That would be a *were*."

I wince. "Right. I'm sorry, I just thought—"

"Psssh. I know all about you and your dastardly thoughts." He waves his buglike arm. "You're the one who plugged up the rabbit hole."

My own cheeks grow warm as the latest bite of bread forms a doughy lump, almost too big to swallow. "Th-th-that was an accident."

"An accident." The flush of Hubert's cheeks bleeds into his whole face and body. I worry he might explode, sending his beaded embellishments ricocheting off the cushioned walls and floors like bullets. "An accident like the one that broke Humphrey's shell and caused him to be exiled to the garden of souls? An accident like that?"

Thumping the prongs of my fork against the breadbasket, I frown. "Well, yeah. He fell off a wall. And later he tripped over Chessie's head."

"*Pushed*. He was pushed off that wall. By your great-great-great-grandmother. All so Humphrey would crack atop Rabid White. All so his innards could coddle that little fellow's flesh. Eat it away so Queen Red could 'save' him."

I shake my head. "What happened to Rabid was an evil spell . . ."

"Oh, it was evil. But it was no spell. Our innards are like acid. Unless you possess the curative potion. Which of course Red just happened to have on hand, conveniently." He huffs. "Why did you think Humphrey was in Sister One's keep at the cemetery? Simply for his soul? He had so many cracks after falling twice, he could no longer be patched. He was a danger. It's why everything here is cushioned, so I might not bring the same fate upon my patrons."

Hubert's Fabergé-egg appearance makes sense now. He's patched himself up. At the first appearance of any crack in his shell, he glues something else in place.

"But that's not logical," I say, all the while knowing things rarely are where Wonderland is concerned. "Red manufacturing an accident just to have Rabid in her pocket? Someone that powerful would've had willing subjects left and right."

A loud grunt bursts from the pit below. I glance down to see Dad helping his brother to his feet. The other knights gather around Dad and congratulate him. They're all smiling and laughing, even Uncle Bernie.

Hubert shoves the menu into my fingertips.

"You seem to know a lot about what happened with Queen Red," I stall, glaring up at him.

He scowls. "I heard it from the source. Your great-great-great-grandmother visited my inn. Her compatriot, Rabid, came with her. He told me his story, how she saved him. But I already knew the truth, because Humphrey had told me that she pushed him."

"You're saying Red came *here*. To the human realm. Do you mean after she'd been banished from Wonderland?" Even before the question leaves my lips, I know that can't be right. Red would've been wearing her Alice imprint if it had been after her banishment, living the life of a small human girl.

"She came here while she still ruled," Hubert corrects. "Long before the Alice brat wormed her way into the rabbit hole and caused all the mayhem and Red's downfall."

My tongue dries. I take a gulp of water. "Why would Red have come to the human realm *before* the Alice incident?"

"Are you daft? She visited because she was lonely. Her husband was betraying her. Seemed like she forgot herself after that, along with the kindness her royal parents had once instilled. She even forgot how to make friends of her own kind."

Red's disgruntled and discarded memories shadow my thoughts. Hubert doesn't know how right he is about her forgetfulness, or how deliberate it was.

"The only way she could believe someone was loyal," the egg-man continues, "was if they were indebted to her. Seems that's the only way anyone in your bloodline can secure devotion. Just as you did by closing up the rabbit hole. Now we're all dependent on you to open a way back, so we can't possibly shrink you to bug size and squash you under our shoes as we'd like."

Hubert's voice is shrill and echoing. The lizard creature and his woolly companion snap their gazes to us. The moment they see me, they grimace.

"I'm *nothing* like Red," I growl, surprised at the rage behind the words.

Although, technically, I did bully the carpet beetle conductor to get my way . . . and I did force my dad to eat a mushroom and ride a butterfly across the world to London. But it was for the greater good.

I clamp my jaw. "I'm not a tyrant like her. I'm just . . . determined."

"As was she. Determined to improve our world. She went so far as to study the humans, as if they're better than us somehow. Something *we* should aspire to be." The egg-man looks over my shoulder. "Those wings aren't the only proof of your heritage. You're a traitor, sending us all up river so you could save your petty mortal half. You're nothing short of a—"

"Benedict," I interrupt between clenched teeth.

Hubert's eyes narrow—curious and hate-filled.

"*Eggs* Benedict." I point to a picture on the menu. "Poached eggs. Canadian bacon. Hollandaise sauce and an English muffin. And I'd like a side of fruit."

He snatches the menu, then scribbles my order on his pad.

"Also, for the record," I add, shifting my attention to the glaring netherling patrons, "I'm here to open the portals and the rabbit hole again. The wraiths misunderstood me and sealed up everything." I shudder a little at the thought of the nightmarish phantom creatures and their ear-gutting wails. "I'm going to reverse it all. I'm here to make things better."

"Of course," Hubert scoffs. "Just like Red was going to make Wonderland *better*. But hers was a warped idea of improvement as well. She even took up with a human and started spouting off things better left secret."

A strange intuition pecks at my brain. "What human?"

"His name was Dodgson. Known by most of your kind as that author fellow . . . Lewis Carroll."

I press my spine into my chair and stare at Hubert in disbelief. "You're trying to tell me that Queen Red knew Lewis Carroll. Personally. *Before* Alice Liddell ever found her way to Wonderland."

Hubert's yellow gaze darkens like dried yolks. "As I heard it, Red put on the glamour of a male professor and befriended Dodgson at some fancy university here in Oxford. They had endless philosophical discussions about a magical realm and where there might be an entrance. Red helped Dodgson come up with a mathematical formula to find the longitude and latitude of the gateway. It's how Dodgson discovered this inn. Perchance you should question Rabid, seeing as he was a part of it all and is *your* royal advisor now." The egg-man purses his mouth and taps his lip. "Oh, wait. He's stuck in Wonderland, and there isn't any way there or out, thanks to you. So I guess we'll never know."

He wobbles away on his praying-mantis limbs, leaving my mind reeling.

I don't allow guilt to surface this time. I'm too intent on this new development. Hubert's explanation supports my dad's claim that Charles knew about the entrance to Wonderland *before* Alice fell down the rabbit hole. But why would Red plant the possibility of such a place in Charles Dodgson's mind to begin with? Why would she *want* him to find Wonderland?

Dad's voice breaks through my thoughts and I look up. He's on the restaurant level. Hubert stands between him and Uncle Bernie. The egg-man jots something on his notepad, taking Dad's order. The moment the inn's owner totters to the kitchen, Dad slaps his brother's back. They part ways, Uncle Bernie returning to the pit and Dad headed toward me.

Frowning, I spin my fork on the table. Soft candlelight reflects off the prongs as I try to wrap my head around the Charles Dodgson twist.

"What are you thinking about?" Dad tugs gently on one of my side braids.

"Nothing." Until I can make sense of this information, it's not worth sharing.

Dad drops into his chair and rubs his thumb over the dimple in his freshly shaved chin, as if debating whether to press the subject.

"You were amazing out there," I say to distract him.

He grins and dabs sweat from his face with his napkin. "It all just came back to me. Like riding a bike." He gestures toward the kitchen. "The egg-fellow is putting a rush on our meals. We have to leave within the hour." He casts a side-glance to the netherling guests who are leaving.

"Okay. What's the plan?" I slide the basket of bread to Dad.

He takes a bite of a roll. "It's the changing of the guards this evening. Bernard is going in. He can assure us safe passage through the infinity mirrors, in case I'm rusty at pinpointing the portal. But we'll still have to make it through the gate." The worry lines on his forehead indicate there's something more.

"Did Uncle Bernie tell you what happens if we get turned away?" I venture, letting the *that we'll become mutants* go unspoken.

Dad glances down. "He didn't have to. I remember."

I cringe. He's no doubt witnessed something or someone becoming a looking-glass reject. Skin prickling under my tunic, I slide my half-full glass of water his way.

Dad takes several sips. "If you're worried about mutations, that's only a danger where the passage connects to the tulgey wood. It's a result of being swallowed then forcibly coughed out of a tulgey's throat, and is only a danger to those with magic in their blood.

Humans are immune." A troubled furrow crosses his brow as it hits him that the immunity doesn't apply to me.

"It's okay, Dad. " I pat his hand. "We don't need to take that gate until we leave AnyElsewhere."

"And then we'll be trekking out in reverse, so you'll be safe."

I shouldn't be surprised at how convoluted the rules are. Nothing about Wonderland is simple.

"Now, about the gate that bridges the human world." He taps his fingers on the glass. "It has an eye. My family made a treaty with it, a century ago. The terms are it will let two guards in and two out at each change. Bernard and my cousin Phillip are the two knights going in. They have to smuggle you and me with them. If the gate catches them, it will strike us all dead."

My whole body goes rigid. *Nice.* I've not only endangered my loved ones and all of Wonderland's occupants, but also the uncle I've barely known for two hours and a second cousin I've never met. It seems senseless. "If the gate is so formidable, why are knights even necessary? Why should any of you put yourself in danger?"

Dad takes another gulp of water. "There were once two eyes, one that watched whoever went in, and one that kept track of who tried to get out. But the eyes fought for power instead of working together. The one on the outside managed to kill the other, not realizing it would leave a blind spot inside. That's where we come in. We monitor the looking-glass world for anyone trying to escape."

I raise my eyebrows. It's such a wonder, how humans have been living alongside a magical world for years, yet most have no clue.

"One last thing," Dad says. "My brother says that for the first time, there's someone in AnyElsewhere wielding magic in spite of the iron dome. It's made changing guards complicated over the past month. They usually switch once every two weeks. But the only contact they've had with the knights at the Wonderland gate are messages via their mechanical passenger pigeons. The guards always pack extra supplies as a precaution, but they're about to run out. Whoever's wielding this magic, they're powerful enough to shake up the landscapes and confuse things. Those kinds of theatrics aren't very popular. The prisoners are angry and jealous. We could be going into a battle zone."

My shoulders tense. Even though it's not the first time I've stepped into otherworldly unrest, this news catches me off guard. "I thought I'd be the only one who could use magic."

"Yeah. Me, too." Dad drops a crescent-shaped piece of bread into his mouth and chews while unutterable fears move across his face like storm clouds.

"What if it's Red?" I blurt.

"Using her magic? How?"

"I don't know. But the timing has to be more than a coincidence. Maybe she's immune to the iron since technically she's using the zombie flower's body." I shut my eyes against the image. I won't back down. I'm done running from her, from my destiny and my mistakes. One way or another, her reign of terror is about to come to an end.

Dad grabs my hand. I open my eyes to find his eyelid twitching.

"You still haven't told me why you were in a room on the train with her name etched on a plaque." His fingers tighten around mine. "I don't want you stirring up trouble. She's been dealt justice. She's where she belongs. We're going to go in, get Jeb, and go out the

Wonderland gate. No interactions with anyone or anything other than that. And for sure no getting sidetracked with revenge or old debts. Okay?"

The diary on my neck feels as heavy as a brick in spite of its teensy size. There's more to this mission. We're rescuing someone else, too. I'm not leaving AnyElsewhere without three things: Morpheus, Jeb, and the total annihilation of Red.

Dad swallows the last of the water. "Allie, give me an answer. We need to be straight with one anoth—"

A clatter of dishes stops Dad in mid-statement as Hubert sets down our steaming food along with water and a cup of coffee for Dad. The netherling glares at me before starting toward the kitchen.

"Great tableside manner, *Eggbert*," I say, louder than I should.

Dad grimaces as our host stops mid-step and totters around, his white shell warming to red beneath his beaded bedazzlements.

"Next I see *you*"—Hubert points his tray at me—"you'll either be in a coffin, or be banished from your kingdom for your irresponsible actions. Enjoy your last meal here as the reigning Red Queen, either way."

He leaves Dad and me to eat in the abandoned dining room, the metallic clang of swordplay from the pit hanging between us like a razor-sharp death knell.

CURIOUS CAMOUFLAGE

While Dad goes with Uncle Bernie to collect weapons and practice a few more fencing moves, I wander the halls in search of Chessie.

I'm afraid to call his name aloud, considering Hubert's reaction to me and how so many netherling guests share his prejudice. Instead, I call to Chessie in my mind, hoping I have the ability like Morpheus does. Hoping it's a netherling talent I can master.

A door opens and I duck into the shadows. A maid comes out, pushing a cleaning cart. Ski-shaped runners provide momentum in place of wheels, so the cart moves smoothly over the cushioned floor. A combination of ground pepper and cleaning products stings my nostrils as she passes by.

The maid's profile reminds me of a bulldog—complete with a flat, wet muzzle that causes her to snort with each breath. Her body resembles a pig's, aside from her lobster-claw hands. Tufts of fur speckle her greenish cheeks, elbows, and knees from beneath a short-aproned uniform.

On her cart, three transparent hooded coveralls are crumpled in a pile, revealing subtle folds and pleats that disrupt the atmosphere. It looks like Bill the Lizard is sending his simulacrum suits out for cleaning.

"It connects with the wearer's mind and reflects their surroundings. Observers are deluded into seeing only the body parts that are bared. . . . Comes in handier than you'd think."

Yeah, I bet it does, Hubert. If Dad and I were invisible, it would be easy to smuggle us into AnyElsewhere's gate. And since we're going into a war zone, we could use some camouflage.

I fall into line behind the maid, debating how to get the suits. I might have to resort to magic.

"Excuse me," I say softly.

She turns, snarling. Embossed letters glimmer on her brassy name tag: *Duchess.* Come to think of it, she does favor the duchess sketch from my mom's *Alice's Adventures in Wonderland* book. I'm not sure why a duchess is cleaning rooms at an inn. Unless I got her stuck here, too. In which case it's better not to introduce myself.

"What do you want?" Her question is more of a growl. Her teeth remind me of peppercorns, just like those of the piggish creature I met at the Feast of Beasts last year: the duchess's son. He gave us the pepper to wake the tea party guests. The family resemblance is unmistakable.

"I could use some clean towels," I say. While she's distracted with the lower shelf, I'll snag the suits from the top and run.

"These are velvet robes, not towels. Complimentary to our most valued customers. The boss keeps count of them. If any go missing, they come out of my paycheck." She waves me away with her feather duster.

I catch the feathers and she clamps the handle, engaging in a tug-of-war.

"Your boss wouldn't mind if you give me one," I insist. "We've become fast friends." The lie sounds as stale as it tastes on my tongue, but it doesn't matter because a cloud of orange, glittery mist appears behind the maid's shoulder—silent and stealthy. Before Chessie's body even materializes, I know it's him.

I bite back a smile. He *did* hear me.

I send a silent explanation of what I'm after and Chessie bows, grinning that wide, mischievous smile. He's always ready to leap into the thick of things without question, just for the fun of it. No wonder Morpheus considers him a worthy sidekick.

"About the robes," I say to the piggish maid. "I only need one. You can just tell Hubert it sprouted legs and walked away." I give Chessie a subtle nod. With a swish of orange and gray stripes, he tunnels into the pile of folded velvet robes on the corner of her cart.

"Do I look asleep to you?" the duchess asks me.

"No. Why?"

"Because the saying goes, 'Let sleeping dogs lie.' Well, I'm not asleep, so I don't intend to lie." She jerks the feather duster from my grasp. "Now, off with you."

The instant the "off with you" escapes her mashed-in muzzle, a velvety robe scurries across the floor, long sleeves draped behind. The maid yelps, her orange eyes bouncing from me to the escaping robe.

"Looks like you won't be lying after all," I say.

She throws down her duster and gives chase. The robe floats like a magic carpet with Chessie propelling it underneath. The maid has to get on all fours to catch up.

As soon as they turn a corner, I grab the transparent coveralls and race the opposite direction toward an intersection of three halls. I have a passing thought of Chessie and send him a soundless thank-you. I'm not worried for his welfare. He won't be captured unless he wants to be.

I round a corner and bump into Dad.

"Whoa there." He catches my shoulders. "Where have you been?"

"Trying . . . to find you," I fib between gulps of air. The fabric billows in my arms but can only be felt, not seen.

Dad wouldn't condone stealing. That will change once we're in AnyElsewhere, where his conscience will take a backseat to self-preservation.

Jeb pops into my head. He's like Dad in so many ways. Protective, moral, and kind. Has he lost his strict sense of black-and-white, of right and wrong, to adapt to a world of netherling criminals? He's had to. He's a survivor. His childhood proves that.

I just hope he hasn't forgotten how to forgive. And I hope Morpheus will forgive me, too.

Even if they have, things will still be complicated, because of the vision the Ivory Queen showed me before she went back through the rabbit hole on the day of prom, and what a life with Morpheus could mean to Wonderland.

That puncturing sensation jabs inside my chest, reminding me again of Red. Of what's important *now*. Any decisions about my future will have to wait until Red has corrected whatever she put wrong in me and I destroy her.

"This way." Dad holds my elbow. "Bernard's waiting for us in the mirror room."

Ignoring the sting behind my sternum, I drag the duffel from Dad's shoulder. He's so busy watching room numbers that he doesn't notice me rearrange water bottles, protein packets, trail mix, fruit, first aid supplies, flares, and assorted iron weapons so I can tuck the stolen fabric beneath them.

Borrowed fabric. When I get back, I'll return the enchanted clothes with an apology.

My breath stalls as I realize there's no "when" in our scenario from this point on. Before Dad and I can face the looking-glass world and rescue the guys, or help Mom and repair Wonderland, we have to first make it through the portal and the gate.

Everything—our lives, our loves, our futures—hinges on one word alone: *IF.*

❈ · I · ❈

Dad takes the duffel bag back as we step into room 42.

He's filled me in on what will happen once we enter the gate of AnyElsewhere: how we'll jump into an otherworldly funnel of ash and wind that carries prisoners to the center of the realm and the guards from one gate to another.

First, though, we have to take the mirror portal to the gateway.

I expected the chamber's walls to be covered with mirrors. Instead, it has cushions. The circumference is larger than our private room, and there's no furniture, only a circular, enclosed contraption in the center of the floor. It's so tall, it nearly touches the ceiling.

Bright colors shimmer on the metal exterior, and lines of fat white bulbs dot each separate panel—extinguished and lifeless. It resembles a small version of a Gravitron ride. That was always the first line Jenara, Jeb, and I would hit when the county fair came into town.

A sharp twinge of longing echoes through me with the taste of cotton candy and the smell of corn dogs. It was like magic, the way we'd stand against the inside of a cylinder and the ride would spin fast enough for the floor to drop out, yet we'd stay in place against the walls. I know now it wasn't magic that held us up; it was centrifugal force. I also know now what real magic is—and that it comes with a cost.

The ache for simpler times with my two best friends is so acute, I step forward and run my fingers along the cool, slick panels to distract myself. A loud whirring sound activates as the motor kicks on and the lights start to blink—bright and garish. Dad jerks me back.

"What did I do?" I ask.

"Nothing. It's okay. Right as rain." He's smiling with a faraway look on his face. His eyes glisten with boyhood wonder in the blinking lights.

"Dad, you never told me . . . how did you end up going through the gate that leads to Wonderland?"

His fingertips take over where mine left off, stroking the metal panels. "Uncle William was teaching me how to open it, just the two of us, when he fell to his knees. He was struggling to breathe. I was too small to drag him to a wind funnel, and I knew if I took one for help, he'd be dead before I got back with someone." Dad purses his lips, as if the confession has a distinctive flavor—sour and biting. "He started turning blue. I panicked. I'd heard stories about

Wonderland. That the creatures had healing powers. I let myself through the gate . . . thought I could get help faster that way. I knew they could be evil, but I'd also heard some were kind. Unfortunately, I met with evil first." He presses his forehead to the machine, lights flashing along his skin as he squeezes his eyes shut.

I put my hand on his shoulder, haunted by the image of him trapped inside Sister Two's lair, wrapped in web with glowing roots attached to his head and chest. His dreams were being siphoned away to feed the restless dead. He'd been Sister Two's prized dream-boy for ten years before Mom rescued him. This isn't the time to tell Dad that he might be facing that same evil again once we get to Wonderland. That Sister Two might have Mom in her webby clutches, unless she was able to escape somehow.

"Dad, you were just a kid. You made the only decision you could. You were right, too. If your uncle's skin was blue, he wouldn't have lasted until you got back with someone."

Dad sighs and lifts his head. "He'd had a stroke. Bernie told me they found him dead by the gate, and me missing." Squinting, he eases his thumb into a space between two panels and pushes. He steps back before a door flings open and a set of motorized metal stairs drops down.

Uncle Bernie pokes his head out of the ride's entrance. He's wearing a fresh White knight's uniform. "So, you do remember how to get inside. There's a good sign."

Just like that, Dad's sadness melts away. He smirks and hands up the duffel bag.

I stare at him in disbelief. First, I saw him fence like an expert. Now, he's the master of secret doorways. How can this be the same man who raised me? The man who read picture books in funny voices, who packed my lunches and never forgot that I liked graham crackers with my applesauce?

I thought he was so normal. Yet he'd had an extraordinary life ahead of him, before he was lost in Wonderland.

Dad helps me up the stairs behind him. Inside, we face innumerable images of ourselves amid black-and-white checks reflected off the floor. Mirrors upon mirrors slant along the round interior, covering the walls and domed ceiling and forming reflections that cast other reflections until there's no end and no beginning. The illusion of infinity.

Carousel horses—in vivid colors and wild poses—appear to rise from the checked floor, captured in the reflections, yet none exist where we stand.

"The carousel . . . is it painted on the mirrors?" No sooner do I ask then I realize it's similar to the moth spirits in the mirrored hall at Morpheus's manor in Wonderland, except the horses aren't trapped inside the reflection. They're *behind* it somehow.

"You *see* the carousel?" Dad asks. He and Uncle Bernie exchange surprised glances.

"It would seem your girl is more Skeffington than merely her sense of humor," Uncle Bernie teases, patting the top of my head as he scoots around us in the tight corridor.

Dad takes my hand and leads me through the circular surroundings. "What you're seeing is the other side of the portal, Allie. None of the females in our family have ever had that ability."

Uncle Bernie nods. "Could also be Alison's lineage."

As if sensing my quiver at the mention of Mom, Dad squeezes my hand. "The reflected reflections . . ." He motions around us. "The unending loop of images . . . they're like an optical code. Only those with the gene can make out the two-way mirror effect. The carousel is outside the entrance to the looking-glass world. The Knighthood put it in place decades ago, piece by piece, because the area surrounding the gate is barren. We needed something to aim for on the other side. Now, once we discern which horses are real and not just reflections, we jump astride them through the portal."

"Okay," I say cautiously. "But why can't you use a room of mirrors for the starting point? Why a Gravitron?"

"Well, this isn't how we've always done things," Uncle Bernie answers as he opens a metal breaker box and flips a few switches. "In the earlier years, before such motorized amusements were perfected, our ancestors used to go to carnivals in search of mirrored funhouses. It was risky. They chanced being seen by other thrill seekers. So they began to build their own infinity-mirror rooms. But it's hard to get enough thrust to leap through the portal. Sometime in the 1950s, we started seeing the Rotor rides. They gave us a way to use centripetal force to our advantage."

"I thought it was centrifugal." I'm feeling woozy, and the ride hasn't even started.

"Centrifugal force is reactionary," my uncle says. "It only exists *because* of centripetal. If you spin around and stretch your arm while holding a hammer, you're exerting centripetal force to make the object follow a curved path. But you'll feel the hammer pulling your hand from your body. That is *centrifugal*—a coercion in the opposite direction. Our ride has been adjusted to use both forces against one another so that when the floor drops, your body will lurch forward, like what would happen to the hammer were you to let it go while spinning. It makes entry simpler."

I huff. "Yeah, that sounds . . . anything but simple." I don't stop to consider how we're supposed to land on top of carousel horses without damaging important body parts. The laws of nature are different on the other side, and that has to play a role somehow. Still, I'm taunted by the memory of the mirror I crashed into on prom night. How the glass shattered and sliced my skin. "If you misjudge, that could be painful."

"Painful, but tolerable." Uncle Bernie closes the ride's door. Orangey sparkles seep through spaces in the panels from outside the ride. "That's how one acquires wisdom. By getting a bonk on the noggin, or a bloody nose. We learn through our mistakes, don't we?"

I tap the diary at my neck. *Unless, like Red, you choose to forget your mistakes, in which case you never learn.*

"There's a trick to it," Dad adds. "If you look closely, some of the horses have shadows cast by the carousel's lights. Others don't. The ones with shadows are real."

I focus on the carousel, shocked by how quickly I pick out the real ones. The thought of being thrust toward a plane of glass at high speed makes my pulse kick so fast, I can feel my blood shuttling through my veins. I might've leapt off a butterfly into a stormy sky earlier, but this isn't like flying. I'll have no wind to coast on. I'll have no control at all.

Now I know how Morpheus felt when he was afraid of riding in a car, and it's not so funny from this side.

The Gravitron's motor hums under my feet.

Dad tightens his fingers through mine. "This is the only way to get in and save your mom and Jeb. Just hold on to me and leap when I leap. It's my turn to sprout wings."

A nervous smile lifts one corner of my mouth.

"Speaking of wings." Uncle Bernie gestures to my back. "You should lose yours for now. The portal is small. We don't want you getting stuck."

I frown. I've grown used to my wings being out—to their promise of power. Reabsorbing them is second nature after all my practice at the asylum, although I miss their weight the instant they're gone.

I clench Dad's hand and don't let go as we press ourselves into position against the mirrored wall. Uncle Bernie holds the duffel bag since Dad and I are the newbies. Or, rather, Dad's *adult* body is new to it all.

The whir of the motor grows as we spin, around and around until our backs plaster to the mirror behind us, pinning us in place like the bugs I used to collect. My lungs squeeze, as if they're shrinking. I'm so disoriented I can't make out anything but a blur in the reflections. I gulp against the bile climbing into my esophagus.

Just when I think I'm going to lose my eggs Benedict, Dad yells, "Now!"

There's the sound of a lever being thrown. The floor drops and we're thrust forward, Dad and I linked by a chain of hands and fingers, just like that moment in Wonderland when Jeb and I sailed across the chasm on tea-cart trays.

The glass races toward us. I scream as the mirror bends like a bubble, stretches around us, then bursts so we break through and soar into the other realm.

Dad lets go of my hand. For an instant I'm floating, then I drift into place atop a carousel horse moving in sync with the Gravitron on the other side.

A warm, humid stench surrounds us like a stagnant swamp. Dad wasn't exaggerating when he said everything was barren here.

The only lights come from the carousel. Up close, they're actually bioluminescent bugs in small glass globes. A fuzzy gray firmament shimmers overhead—a haze of nothing.

Black mist cloaks our surroundings, so thick I can't make out the ground beyond the ride's platform. There's no sound anywhere; even the gears of the carousel trundle along in silence.

Dad and Uncle Bernie fall onto their mounts in front of me. Dad's cousin Phillip, dressed in a Red knight's uniform, is already seated on a bench next to Uncle Bernie's horse. I grab the brass rod that holds my mount secure. Tiny triangular mirrors cover the center pole. Through them I can see the inside of the Gravitron. That's where we came out and where the knights must somehow go back in. It looks physically impossible, considering our size in contrast to the narrow bits of shimmering glass.

The adrenaline pumping inside me starts to slow as the ride comes to a stop. Dad takes the duffel from Uncle Bernie and helps me down. My legs waver as if trying to remember how to walk.

Together, the four of us step away from the light and into the nothing. My boots glide as if on air. I'd half expected to feel a sludgy mud sticking to my soles. The strange fog bubbles up around our knees, then falls to our ankles like a boiling, steamy stew, although nothing is wet. The mist has a sound-absorbing quality, eating up every whisper, breath, or shuffle of clothing and feet.

A glowing white gate looms in the distance. The iron dome rises behind it, dark and threatening, like a gargantuan, overturned witch's cauldron.

I pause. The plan my uncle and his cousin came up with—to distract the gate's eye as Dad and I creep through—is too dangerous. With the simulacrum suits, we're all assured safe passage. But we need to get them on before we're close enough for the gate to spot the four of us.

I tug at the duffel bag on Dad's shoulder, making him stop.

"I have to show you something," I attempt to say, but the sound is sucked away before it even leaves my tongue. Uncle Bernie said communication would be being tricky here. I had no idea that meant our words would actually be swallowed by emptiness.

I take the duffel bag and pull on one pair of simulacrum coveralls over my clothes. The transparent fabric hangs off my shoulders and waist. I pull the pant legs' extra length over my feet and tie it in place to cover my boots.

Next, I concentrate on my settings and hold out my arms. The fabric shrinks, fitting my other clothes perfectly. As I keep my thoughts on my surroundings, the background begins to move through me. Only my bare hands can be seen, sticking out from the enchanted cuffs. The rest of my body appears to be gone. By pulling the sleeve cuffs over my fingers, I become nothing but a floating head.

Phillip and Uncle Bernie nod.

Within minutes, Dad has his invisibility gear on. Since he can't speak, he can't question where I got the camo or yell at me for how I went about it. He tucks the duffel under his arm inside the coveralls, so it's hidden from view. The hoods drape our faces so we can see through the fabric, but not be seen.

Our escorts start toward the gate. We follow, spaced far enough apart that we won't accidentally bump elbows or trip over each other's boots. As we get closer, what I thought were bars become scaly tentacles, white and writhing like albino snakes. An unexpected emotion overwhelms me. Not fear. Not trepidation.

It's an all-encompassing sense of loneliness as vast as the nothing around us.

Somewhere inside that gate are my two knights—the dark and the light. Morpheus has to be disappointed in me, for my colossal failure in destroying the entrances and exits to his beloved Wonderland. Then there's Jeb, who believes I threw away the most pure and devoted love I've ever known.

All these weeks I've been concerned for their physical well-being. But what about their emotional states? Jeb thinks I betrayed him. And Morpheus will thrive on feeding that misconception every chance he gets.

Maybe it's not the murderous prisoners or strange wildlife I should be worried about. It would be laughable to think that Morpheus took Jeb under his wings and helped him. All I can hope for is that by some miracle they parted ways without killing one another.

Again, my heart tugs in two directions—a literal, physical sensation that burns. I grit my teeth under my invisible veil, forcing myself to stay in step with our escorts.

We approach the gate. It stands over three stories high. Uncle Bernie strokes the serpentine bars. Even a nest of anacondas couldn't compete with their size. The scales pucker and release, muscles rippling underneath. There's no question how this gate kills its prey. One squeeze would crush anyone who violates the entrance.

These bars could obliterate armies. They probably have.

The image is so gruesome, I whimper—grateful for the sound-absorbing mist. In the gate's center, one snaky appendage pulls free of the others. A white, oblong protrusion resembling a Venus flytrap drops down in front of my uncle and Phillip. It's half the size of a human. As it opens, the jagged edges form eyelashes and a lone eye-ball peers from inside, silver with a slitted black pupil, like a snake's eye. I suppress a shudder.

The lashes blink, slow and studious.

Uncle Bernie and Phillip stand their ground in front of us. The leafy creature hovers across them from head to toe. It lifts high enough to look over their shoulders and I hold my breath, afraid it will somehow sense me or Dad.

It squints before snapping closed and weaving back into the other tentacles. The snaky bars wind together on either side—like curtains being drawn. We step through as a united front, my hair bristling as I jab my elbow into my side to keep from brushing the scales.

I don't suck in a breath until the gate slithers into place behind us.

Dad and I draw back our hoods and share a sigh of relief. His brother and cousin pat my shoulder before stepping up to the top of the stone platform on either side of the threshold next to the knights they'll be relieving. A twister of ash and wind sweeps down in the distance, similar to the white tornadoes I've seen on weather shows.

There's more of the misty nothingness between the platform where we stand and AnyElsewhere's landscape. The vapor glows green, as if radioactive. According to Uncle Bernie's earlier rundown, instead of absorbing sound, it sucks up everything that attempts to cross it.

Both gates are separated from the terrain in such a way. The green glowing vortex holds the prisoners at bay, makes it impossible for them to storm the gates. They would have to control the wind funnels to get across. The other eyeball, the one that used to guard this side of the gate, was mentally connected to the funnels. The knights have formed medallions of the creature's remains and now harness that power to safely travel into and out of AnyElswhere.

After a short discussion with the knights, Uncle Bernie steps down and offers a mechanical pigeon to Dad. "Push the button under its throat." He demonstrates. "When the beak glows, you can record a message. Once you find the boy and make it to the Wonderland gate with the supplies, send us a message to let us know everyone's okay. The pigeon will find us. It's gilded with iron, to deter any of the prisoners from intercepting. You have one day. If we don't hear back within twenty-four hours, we'll follow the pigeon's homing beacon and find you."

Dad takes the iron-gilded bird, tucks it into our bag, and tries to talk. Nothing comes out.

Uncle Bernie nods. "You haven't built up a tolerance to the black mist you inhaled." He speaks loudly over the twister coming our way. "Your vocal cords will stay asleep for a half hour or so." He gestures behind us and we turn to see the funnel hovering close. Winds gust around us, slapping my braids against my face and neck.

"You remember how to do this?" my uncle shouts to my dad.

Dad nods.

"Step in and hold tight to each other," Uncle Bernie directs. He lifts a medallion at his neck, holding it up. An off-white oval shimmers in the center and red strands run through, jagged and fine like blood veins. Tarnished, brassy metal frames the strange stone. "We would give you a medallion of your own, but we can't risk it getting into the wrong hands. Since you have someone to find, I'll have the funnel drop you in the middle of the world, where we release the prisoners. Beware, though. The landscapes are unpredictable lately, and since the twisters are tied to them, they've become unruly. So we can't be sure exactly where you'll end up. We've provided a map. Look for both of the glowing green gates from where you land. They are the north and the south. Use them as the key to the map. Above all else, stay together."

Dad nods. Uncle Bernie hugs us both and nudges us toward the approaching funnel. I watch Dad's hand disappear into his suit as he tightens the duffel on his shoulder. He stares into my eyes. I want to crawl into his hug and hide, like I did as a little girl.

But I'm a woman and a queen now. And I'm the one responsible for all of this. There's no hiding anymore. I tip my chin. *I'm ready.*

We pull down our hoods to keep ash out of our faces, then leap inside together, holding tight as our feet lift and our bodies swirl. Within minutes, the funnel opens to reveal a snow-capped hill coming up fast beneath our feet. Scraggly, leafless trees dot the landscape at the base. I can't see the iron dome overhead. There's a false firmament between it and the ground that looks like an orange sky. A smoky tang stings my nose through the fabric, as if there's a fire somewhere close.

We're ejected onto the top of the peak, and the impact breaks us apart. Dad grabs for me but rolls down the opposite side of the incline, his hood opening so I can see his face and neck. It's a haunting image, as if he's been beheaded. I dig my nails through the fabric cloaking my hands in an effort to clutch the snow. But it's not snow at all. The hill is coated with ash like the funnel we arrived in. The terrain crumbles beneath my fingers and sends me skidding out of sight of Dad.

I remind myself he's been here as a child and survived, and this time he has the advantage of invisibility and a duffel filled with weapons.

My body twists sideways and the hood wraps tighter as I'm dragged along the dusty landslide. My bones clatter with the rough ride until a rock the size of a medicine ball slams into my stomach at the bottom of the hill. The impact knocks the air from my lungs. I struggle to catch my breath.

"Well, bloody holiday. What have we here?" The deep, British accent strokes my eardrums like velvet.

I peer through my hood's fabric. Morpheus stands on the other side of the rock, gaze turned down on me. He glows in the orange dimness, a soft blue light radiating from his hair. A lilac shirt under his navy tapestry jacket complements his alabaster skin. Striped pants hug his streamlined silhouette. He wears a fedora cocked to one side. Although I can't make out the moths clustered around the hatband in this strange lighting, I know they're there.

He holds a cane. The eagle-head handle is so realistic it could be on a plaque at a taxidermy shop. Feathered wings wrap the shaft, and four paws sprout from the base, each one covered with golden fur like lion's feet. Talons splay from the toe-pads in place of claws.

Morpheus is as stylish and eccentric as I remember. Somehow, this place hasn't broken him. I'm so happy, I want to hug him—until I notice the angry red jewels blinking at the tips of his eye markings.

He tucks the walking stick beneath his arm and kneels close, wings drooping. Anger hardens his exquisite features. "Here I'd hoped never to see your face again."

ILLUSIONS

Morpheus's hatred hits me like a fist, an agonizing throb that rivals the bruises where the rock juts into my rib cage.

"Your being here changes nothing," he seethes. "You've made your bed. Now lie in it." He doesn't spare another word, doesn't ask how I got here or even speak my name. He simply shoves the rock aside so it's no longer between us.

I curl into a ball. What did I expect? I destroyed the home he loves, then sent him to the looking-glass world to rot without his magic. It's not like he was going to draw me into his arms and say how much he's missed me.

But it's not as if he didn't play a part in this nightmare himself, either.

An apology tangles with my righteous indignation. Better the words stay locked inside a voice box that's dormant. There'll be time to break through Morpheus's walls later. Right now, I need to find Dad and make sure he's okay. Then we'll search for Jeb—who will most likely have the same reaction to my being here.

I grip the diary and key at my neck to assure they're safely under the clothes. I'm about to stand and trek through the barren trees when Morpheus gets to his feet and turns his back and wings on me.

"I said return to your bed of ash." He prods the rock with his walking stick. "You've no call to chase me down unless I've beckoned you."

I cock my head. Holding out an arm, I stare through it. I'm still invisible. Morpheus doesn't know I'm here. He's been talking to the rock all along. I stand as quietly as I can and stretch my aching muscles.

"We just w-w-wondered"—the rock responds to Morpheus from a mouth that appears beneath the white, dusty surface—"has our most g-gracious king considered our r-request to help us get our eggs back?"

"That's our only question," about thirty smaller rocks pipe in, powdery lips flapping. "If you'll save our eggs."

"Let us put this in perspective." Morpheus lifts his wings over his craggy audience. "You were the ones who carelessly lost your eggs, leaving them unattended so you could take a swim in a temporary ocean. Now, I said I would *consider* helping you. Consideration, by definition, is evaluating facts and meditating on the outcome. That takes time. Even hardheaded scuttlers such as yourselves can under-stand that. I came here today for solitude, a rare commodity when one's own shadow is always at his back. At last I've found a sunless spot, the perfect place for meditation. So, off with you."

The rocks stand their ground. Using the clawed tip of the cane, Morpheus nudges one that has rolled too close.

"Perhaps your brains have fossilized," he grumbles. "Do you truly wish to cross the only one with magic enough to grind your eggs to dust?"

Purple light trembles at the ends of Morpheus's fingers where they meet the cane. The static descends along the shaft and then leaps from the lions' paws to the ground like violet lightning.

I slap a hand over my mouth, too late to muffle my gasp.

Morpheus's muscles tense and he looks over his shoulder, but the rocks catch his attention again.

"Oh, no. We never w-w-want our eggs to be crushed," the largest stony creature answers. "P-p-please." Six lobsterlike legs and two beady eyes burst with a pop from its body. The other rocks follow suit, freeing their limbs and eyes, reminding me of the rock lobster in Carroll's tale.

Whimpering, the rocks scuttle backward in a wave to avoid the magical, crackling glow creeping toward them from Morpheus's hands and cane. Their front pincers snip at the ashes, throwing a white haze across the streaks of violet magic.

I squint. So Morpheus is the one flaunting his powers under the iron dome? That's better than it being Red, but how is he using his magic without being warped by it? Is it the iron that's made his magic purple instead of blue?

"Please!" the rock lobsters plead in unison.

"Well enough," Morpheus says, reeling in the enchanted strands along the walking stick's shaft until they disappear into his finger-tips. "Leave your king to his consideration. Once a decision has been made, I will call for you. Are we clear?"

"Yes, c-c-crystal." The largest rock's color drains away until he's almost transparent, as if he's made of crystal himself. His shell is like a pearl shimmering under the orange sky. The smaller pearlescent rocks follow him, scuttling up the hill and burying themselves in the ash piles until they're as covert as me.

"Cursed realm," Morpheus says. He stands the cane on its four paws and drags some gloves from his pocket to slide them on. "Everyone and everything wants a piece of the royal pie. Even the landscape has an agenda."

I bite back a smile. He's exactly the same as when he was taken—narcissistic, disarmingly snarky, and clever. I'm glad he's found a way to rule the creatures here. Even if his powers have caused unrest among the prisoners and trouble for Dad's relatives, at least they've kept him alive.

He turns to leave, stroking the feathers on his cane as he walks.

I fumble to peel the simulacrum from my face and hands, but it clings to my sweaty skin. I drop my palms to my sides, concentrating on my clothes. Maybe if I envision what I'm wearing underneath, it will reverse the magic that made me invisible.

"Morpheus, wait." My voice is weak and comes out as a whisper. Still, it stops him in his tracks.

Silence . . . all but his sharp intake of breath. Ash sifts under his feet as he swivels on his heel. I hold out my palm to him, transparent with a vaguely discernible outline.

"Someone there?" Morpheus narrows his eyes.

A hand clenches my shoulder from behind. Felt, but not seen. "Allie." Dad's whisper grazes my ear. "Don't show yourself."

I grip his hand back, relieved he's safe. Before I can respond, the ground shakes, coming apart like puzzle pieces. Dad's arm tightens around me and we both teeter in place. In an instant, the terrain has shifted and cracked. Water burbles through the broken seams, filling the rivulets between us. Tiny geysers spurt up—the size of a drinking fountain's stream.

The trees, the hill, Morpheus, me and Dad, we're all afloat on our own miniature islands.

Hot, balmy air blows in gusts, the humidity rising.

"Blast it," Morpheus mumbles, wings splayed low to stabilize the fragment of land under his feet. He lifts his face to the sky as it darkens to gray. "Really?" He yells to no one in particular. "*Geysers?* Is this your idea of a joke?"

I scoot my foot next to Dad's, balancing on our own floating island, trying to make sense of Morpheus's tirade. A mechanical whir stirs overhead as a flock of giant birds comes into view. Instead of using their wings, they hold on to lacy parasols in bright floral prints that spin to give the birds lift. Each one looks like a monstrous Mary Poppins soaring across the sky. On their descent, the parasols invert, and the bird creatures crash into the water. The spray sinks through the simulacrum and my clothes, hot on my skin.

Most of the birds abandon their umbrella contraptions, using their beaks for leverage to drag their steaming, feathery bodies ashore. A few carry their parasols with them.

Though some resemble ducks, others eaglets and ospreys, they're all hideously deformed: the size of gorillas, with four furry arms and hands connected to two sets of wings. Their backs are gnarled and twisted, causing them to gimp when they walk.

Dad draws me closer. Our floating island seesaws as three birds hobble by on ostrichlike legs. The stench of scalded, wet feathers makes me gag. Something tells me they wouldn't notice us even if we were visible, because their sights are set on Morpheus.

He stands his ground as seven of them flap across the moats and surround him, clicking their razor-sharp beaks. Five more climb the hill where the rock lobsters are hiding.

"My, my." Morpheus smiles pleasantly. "If it isn't the doltish dozen. That was quite an entrance. I see you're doing your best to control your mutations. But I'm afraid the real damage is done. I do hope you haven't come for fashion advice. There's no amount of style or suave that can conceal that much ugly."

"Shut up," caws a bird that looks like a kingfisher. "You won't be so cocky once you hear that Manti's found your weakness."

"Yeah, weakness." An eaglet creature snaps his beak close to Morpheus's ear, leaving behind a bloody scratch on his lobe. Morpheus winces but doesn't budge. He performed magic earlier. Why doesn't he take flight and escape? I try to break loose from Dad's grip, but he tightens it.

"This isn't your fight," he whispers, barely audible over the rustling wet feathers and bubbling geysers.

I stifle a growl.

"The jig is up, pretty boy," an osprey says, jerking Morpheus's lapel with one wet, apish hand. The walking stick slips from Morpheus's grasp. "Manti's been spying on you. He knows you disappear after magical stints to recharge. What he wants to know is *how* you recharge, and how you use your magic without it affecting you." The osprey looks at Morpheus's jacket where the fabric he was clenching has disintegrated, leaving a jagged hole. "How did that happen?"

Morpheus snorts. "It would appear my clothes have an aversion to your grimy touch and choose to avoid it at all costs."

My body shakes with an involuntary giggle. Dad squeezes my shoulder again—a warning.

The osprey leans closer to Morpheus's face. "Best to get all that drollery out of your system. Manti doesn't have the sense of humor we do."

Morpheus clucks his tongue. "Well then, perhaps we should try for another afternoon. I'm feeling particularly facetious today. Now, if you'll step aside, I'll just get my walking stick . . ."

"Not happening." The kingfisher mutant closes in. "We sent the rock lobsters to drain you of your magic in exchange for their eggs. You're used up. So you have no choice but to come with us and answer Manti's questions."

Morpheus glances toward the hilltop, where the other five bird creatures are paying the rocks with what appear to be strands of pearls as big as baseballs. His gloved fingers tap his thigh. "Traitorous little crustaceans. Should've known they were up to no good." He turns back to his captors. "So, your boss would like to toss his hat into the ring, aye?"

"You're the one who insisted on rocking the boat and forming a royal dictatorship. We all know the crown belongs to Manti. He's been the queen's knave since before they were even exiled here. Centuries ago. Did you really think you could become king without another candidate stepping up to challenge you?" The osprey kicks Morpheus's walking cane, causing the feathers to flutter. "Nay. The Queen of Hearts has called for a Hallowed Festival day after next, and there's to be a caucus race to elect an *official* king. The one who wins the race will rule by the queen's side. And those who are defeated will lose their beating hearts."

"Them's the rules," a duckbilled bird scoffs, shaking his parasol in Morpheus's face. "Made by the queen herself."

"*Them's* the rules?" Morpheus chuckles, deep and soft. "You need to work on your scare tactics, Ducky. Incorrect grammar wielded by a goon bird who carries a frilly sunshade. Doesn't have quite the effect you're hoping for."

The seven birds tackle him, slamming him to the ground.

I struggle against Dad, but he refuses to relent.

"No eating him!" the duckbilled creature shouts. "The boss man said!"

"He's right," the osprey growls to his companions. "Manti ordered us to bring him in alive. But he didn't give specifics. *Barely* alive work for you gents?"

They all squawk in agreement, attacking Morpheus's prone form. Some pound him with their parasols; others use their multiple fists.

Unable to break free of Dad, I yell until my throat comes fully awake. Hearing me, the birds look over their winged shoulders. I strip off my simulacrum suit just as Morpheus's hand shoves out from the distracted pile of feathers. He snaps a gloved finger and thumb, and the wings along his walking stick open.

The cane transforms into a living griffon—the head and wings of an eagle, with the golden-furred body and paws of a large lion. The beast flies toward the huddle with a roar, dive-bombing the birds.

Morpheus rolls out of the chaos and stands. More gaps mar his jacket now, along with a few in his shirt where his smooth chest peeks through. Even his pant legs have some holes, as if the suit was hung in a moth-infested closet. He picks up his hat and brushes it off. His eyes lock on mine. Heat rushes through my cheeks as he wipes his smudged face with a handkerchief.

The seven birds don't budge under the griffon. Snarling a warning, the mythological creature takes to the sky, chasing the other five birds and the rock lobsters until they disappear over the hill.

As Dad struggles out of his simulacrum suit, Morpheus holds our stare. He tucks away his handkerchief, his expression somewhere between fascination and pride. It's hard to pinpoint, because the jewels under his eyes are flashing through uncountable emotions.

"My Queen," he finally speaks, and his usually strong voice holds the slightest tremor.

"My Footman." I don't even blink, playing along with his nonchalance. "You don't seem surprised that I'm here."

"Oh, I knew you would find your way. It was just a matter of when. You actually made it sooner than I expected." He gestures around him. "Thus, the deplorable state of my house."

"Good help is so hard to find," I tease.

His dark, inky irises sparkle like onyx, and a grin plays at his lips. I can't fight it another second and smile back. The moment shatters as the seven bird mutants rise behind him.

"Look out!" I shout.

Four attack him. The other three fly toward me and Dad.

"Allie, get down!" Dad opens the duffel bag.

One of the birds swoops at Dad's head. The other two collide in midair and flop to the ground. Dad parries, an iron dagger in one hand and a chain mace in the other. Shifting his feet gracefully, he swings the iron-studded ball, taking a chunk out of his attacker's beak.

The two birds on the ground roll into Dad, sending him to his knees. He groans, sprawled next to scattered water bottles and protein packets. Mom's capture flashes through my thoughts in vivid, techno-colored pain.

The madness beneath the surface of my skin awakens. I concentrate on the miniature geysers closest to us, envisioning them as tongues unfurling from water serpents' mouths. The cascades grow until they're big enough to lash in midair and snatch up Dad's attackers, capturing the bird with the wounded beak on the way back. The liquid tongues jerk the giant birds into the moats to immerse them.

Dad teeters at the water's edge with dagger ready. Bubbles rise from the depths, becoming fewer and farther between.

"Alyssa," he prompts.

I don't acknowledge the fact that he used my full name, or the concern in his voice.

Instead, I let the coils of madness creep around my human compassion—caging it so it's oblivious to my actions. Then I stare at the bubbles, willing the air to dissipate, waiting for the birds' lungs to cave in. Craving their deaths.

"You've never murdered anyone, Allie. Be sure it's the only way. Otherwise, it will haunt you . . ." Dad's logic breaks through.

A sick pang roils through my stomach.

He's wrong. I have killed. There were so many bugs in my lifetime, I could fill up a grain elevator with their corpses if I hadn't used them for mosaics. I also contributed to the deaths of countless card guards and juju birds in Wonderland, not to mention an octowalrus.

That's enough. *For now.*

With a silent command, I resurrect the geysers. They rise, carrying the mutant birds atop them. A hot spray spatters across me as I guide the cascading water to the closest tree, imagining the bare branches opening like flower petals. The water plops its passengers inside, and the branches curl closed around them, leaving my dripping, gasping prisoners to glare down at me. The geysers sink back into the moats.

"That's my girl," Dad says.

The power I'm learning to wield scares me, but not enough to make me stop and think things through. And that scares me even more.

I turn to check on Morpheus. The griffon has returned and holds the remaining four birds pinned beneath his giant claws. Blood drizzles from his talons, leaving no question as to what became of the five birds he chased over the hill.

Morpheus stands over the captives. "All it would take is one word for my pet to slice you in twain like he did your accomplices."

The duckbilled creature makes a sound between a sob and a quack as the others shiver beneath the sharp talons indenting their feathers.

Morpheus crouches beside the osprey. "You fellows owe the lady a debt of gratitude." He plucks a feather from the bird's ugly face. "Since I'm trying to impress her, I'm going to follow her example and be merciful. Take a message to Manti, though, won't you? Tell him he doesn't stand a chance to win any races if he can't even fight his own battles." Morpheus traces the osprey's quivering beak with the feather's tip. "Oh, and thank you for the new quill."

Nodding at the griffon, Morpheus stands as the bird mutants are set free. I turn to my prisoners in the tree and release them, too. With defeated squawks and screeches, they scatter into the purplish sky without their parasols, becoming more deformed with every flap of their wings.

Two of them begin to lose their feathers. Their bodies contort in midair until they can no longer stay afloat. They fall from the heights. Plumes of ash puff from the ground in the distance to mark their contact.

"Are they dead?" I ask.

"They are," Morpheus answers nonchalantly. "The ultimate consequence for continuing to use their magic. Their spines curled, and their bodies withered to useless shells."

I press my fingers over the diary beneath my tunic. Red's memories are quiet and calm for now, but their presence brings questions to my mind. "What becomes of their spirits? Will they be looking for bodies to possess?"

Morpheus tucks the feather in his pocket. "That's not how it works in AnyElsewhere. When you're dead, you're gone forever. It's an effect of the iron. Every part of us that held magic turns to ash, from our bodies to our spirits. Our remains are caught within the wind, forming the twisters that funnel prisoners in and out." His face grows somber. "So do not hesitate to kill if it's the only way you can live, Alyssa. Not here."

Dad and I trade uneasy glances.

The griffon rubs Morpheus's leg like a giant cat, then transforms into the cane once more. Morpheus takes it in hand, wiping blood from the talons with his handkerchief.

"Now I see," I say, watching him.

Morpheus's dark lashes turn up, interest glittering in his eyes. "See what?"

"Why you needed a walking stick."

He quirks an eyebrow. "Good that your curiosity is quenched."

"Except for what happened to your clothes."

Looking down at his suit, he grumbles, "Dry-clean only, my arse." He brushes off his jacket, frowning at the holes where his skin shows through.

"Morpheus."

He looks up at me again.

"How are you using your magic unaffected, in spite of the all-powerful dome?"

"I believe I'll keep that one to myself, luv. If I told you all my secrets, there would be no more mystery in our relationship."

"I'm not a big fan of mysteries."

That roguish smile I once hated curls his lips and curls my insides. "Rubbish. You adore them." He steps to the edge of his miniature island and uses the cane's clawed end to drag our floating island close—avoiding the water. "You thrive on the challenge of solving them."

He steps onto our mat and his wings rise, their black, smooth sheen the polar opposite of the opaque bejeweled ones tucked inside my own skin. I catch a whiff of his tobacco scent. It's different than it used to be—less licorice and more earthy-fruity—like charcoal and plums.

"Stop right there," my dad growls when the toes of Morpheus's shoes come to a halt about a foot from my boots.

"Dad, he's my friend and I haven't seen him for a month." I won't admit how much I've missed him. I know better than to give Morpheus the upper hand. "Could you please give us a second?"

Dad runs a scathing glare from Morpheus's head to his wings. "No funny business," he says.

Morpheus's jewels sparkle a mischievous reddish-purple, a precursor to some snarky retort waiting to leap off his tongue. I toss him a pleading glance, and he rolls his eyes in silent resignation.

Satisfied, Dad steps aside and crouches to tuck the simulacrum suits and weapons into the duffel bag.

"Is Jeb alive?" I ask Morpheus.

White bleeds into his jeweled markings—the color of indifference. "I didn't kill him, if that's what you're implying."

"You know it's not. Could you for once just give me a straight answer?"

He gazes up at the smoky gray sky. "Your mortal is alive and well. In fact, you will no doubt be seeing him very soon."

Relieved tears spring into my eyes. "So, that means you know where he is?" Is it possible Morpheus took Jeb under his wings after all?

Dad stops stuffing the fabric in the bag, as if waiting to hear the answer.

Appraising his cane, Morpheus growls. "I *do* know where he is." Before I can respond, he lifts his eyes to mine, jewels now bordering on emerald green. "I suppose I should be grateful his name wasn't the first thing that came out of your mouth."

The jealousy and hurt looking back at me aren't unexpected, but the effect they have on my heart is. It provokes that same ripping, twisty sensation that's becoming all too familiar. I take a measured breath to soothe it. "I've been terrified for *both* of you. Now that I know you're all right, of course I need to know about him."

"You could've at least asked me how my ear is feeling first."

The request is almost comical. Morpheus—Wonderland's most confident and independent netherling—is pouting, and it makes him look like a child . . . like my playmate from all those years ago. More than that, he looks like the son we share in Ivory's vision, which opens a flood of emotions I'm afraid to put a name to.

Dad's footsteps fade as he picks up water bottles and protein packets to give us the privacy I asked for.

I reach up and trace the dried blood on Morpheus's ear.

"Does it hurt?" I whisper.

He leans into my touch. "Stings a bit," he says softly, and studies my mouth so intently, my lips feel weighted. His entire body tenses with restraint. If we were alone, there'd be no holding him back. "You could amend that, you know."

His words knock me off balance. "Amend . . . what?"

He crinkles his forehead beneath his hat's brim. "The pain."

My face warms at the thought of healing him, then blazes when I realize his ear is not the pain he's referring to.

A fluctuation beneath the skin at his collarbone tells me his pulse is flitting just as fast as mine. I start to drop my hand but he catches it, holding my palm to his smooth cheek. The action both surprises and comforts me.

"I thought you'd be furious," I say. "That I sent you here. That I destroyed the rabbit hole and neglected Wonderland. I messed everything up." The confession winds my gut in knots.

He shakes his head. "You made a queen's decision to send for the wraiths. And it was the right one. Even when you do the right thing, sometimes there are dire consequences. Second-guessing every step prevents any forward momentum. Trust yourself, forgive yourself, and move on."

I curl my fingers around his jawline. I've needed to hear those words for so long. "Thank you."

"What's important is you've come to fix things," he says. It's an observation, not a question.

I nod.

Holding my wrist, he tilts his head so his mouth grazes my palm. "I always knew you would," he whispers against my scars, his jewels glistening gold and bright—just as they did over a year ago in Wonderland, the first time he spoke those words to me, right before he dragged me through a crazy game of mayhem and politics that nearly got me killed.

Yet despite how he's drawn to danger, how it thrives within him, or maybe *because* of it, the dark and wicked side of me softens at the feel of his lips on my skin.

Dad's dagger finds its way between us, the tip pressed against Morpheus's jugular. "Time's up."

Morpheus releases my hand.

I squeeze my fingers at my side to stop the tingling along my scars. "Dad, come on. The knife isn't necessary."

Chin hardened to granite, he elbows me behind him. He stands a few inches shorter than Morpheus, but the righteous indignation emanating off him makes up for the size difference.

Morpheus's skin tinges green, an effect of the iron's contact. So why doesn't the dome limit his magic? He definitely has a secret. And I'm going to figure it out.

The thought of the challenge tantalizes me, just like Morpheus said it would. It's more than a little unsettling, how well he knows what lights my fire.

"Do you have any idea what you've done to my family?" Dad seethes, shaking me out of my musings.

Morpheus guides the dagger's tip toward his shoulder in lieu of his bare neck. "I believe I made it possible for you to have a family to begin with, Thomas. A thank-you would suffice."

Dad slides the dagger back to Morpheus's neck. "Here's how this is going to play out. You're going to take us to Jeb then lead us safely across this godforsaken realm to the Wonderland gate, so we can get back to Alison." The metal tip puckers Morpheus's skin. "And then—and only then—will I decide whether I should thank you or '*slice you in twain*,' and leave you in a pile of ash at my feet."

Broken Wings &
Legless Horses

Morpheus and I exchange glances while Dad digs through the duffel. When he opens the map, orange sparkles sift out, snowing into the bag's mouth. A tiny sneeze erupts from inside. Dad jumps back and Morpheus steps forward, wearing an amused half grin.

He scoops his hand inside the bag and lifts out a hummingbird-size ball of orange and gray striped fur. Chessie's teasing smile appears as he unfurls his body and dangles his front feet over the edge of Morpheus's gloved palm. His fluffy tail twitches, a sure indication he's proud of himself.

"Well, look who dragged the cat in," Morpheus says. "Good to see you, old friend." He rubs the feline netherling's tiny head with his thumb.

Chessie arches his back, then turns his impish eyes my way.

"Sneakie-deakie." I can't stop smiling, remembering that moment when Uncle Bernie closed the Gravitron's door and orange sparkles filtered into the chamber. Chessie was planning to hitch a ride all along.

The little netherling attempts to fly, but I stop him, closing my fingers over Morpheus's palm. "Wait. There are rules here. If you use your magic, you'll hurt yourself. It will mutate you . . . kill you even."

"True for most," Morpheus corrects, and lifts my hand away. "But remember, our Chessie is a rare strain. Both spirit and flesh all at once. He can use his magic. He's the one full-blood netherling who can."

"Other than you, you mean?" I goad.

Morpheus intentionally avoids my stare and concentrates on Chessie. "You should refrain from snapping your head off whilst here. With the way the landscape changes, you might risk it getting lost. Now, do you wish to fly, or would you like to hitch a ride?"

Chessie flutters up to Morpheus's one remaining pocket and deposits himself inside, leaving only his head sticking out.

Before Morpheus can move away, I place a hand on his lapel.

Stretching to the tips of my toes, I nuzzle Chessie's fuzzy nose with mine. "Thanks for healing me earlier," I tell him, "and for keeping my necklace safe." Just as I'm about to kiss his head, he ducks into the pocket.

My lips land in the middle of one of the gaps in Morpheus's shirt, smacking his warm, soft skin.

"Sorry." Blushing, I jerk back and lose balance as the ground beneath me totters.

Morpheus catches me around the waist, affection tinting his jewels a pinkish hue. "No apology necessary."

Dad clears his throat. I swallow, stepping away.

"We need to get a move on." Dad gathers the duffel bag and shoves the map at Morpheus. "Where's Jeb, according to this?"

Still intent on me, Morpheus shoves the parchment away without even looking at it. "That scrap won't get you anywhere. The landscape is unpredictable, if you didn't notice. Whoever provided that map should've told you that. Perhaps, having limited human intellect, they can't comprehend the magnitude of said alterations."

My dad frowns. "We were told that the gates' positions never change. I can see their glow, there and there." He motions to the radioactive green waves on the distant horizon to our right and left.

Sighing, Morpheus turns his attention to Dad. "All right. Riddle me this. Which is north and which is south? Do you know from whence direction you arrived? It is impossible to keep from getting turned around in this world without a compass."

"And you have such a compass?" Dad asks.

"I have my walking stick," Morpheus answers cryptically.

Dad clenches his teeth. "So you expect us to just follow you."

Morpheus's lips curl to a spiteful grin. "Alyssa won't have any trouble keeping up. As for you, I can carry you on my shoulder again if need be."

It's a vicious barb, and I send a scowl Morpheus's way.

"Not necessary," Dad says, unfazed. "You'll lead us to Jeb. I have ways of convincing you." He pats the sheathed dagger slung over his left arm.

"Agreed," Morpheus snips. "It's not as if I have a choice in the matter." His retort is edged with frustration. It's got to be more than Dad's iron dagger persuading him. After all, he can take off and fly anytime he wants.

He turns on his heel and starts picking his way through the small floating islands, using the walking stick to bridge the moats like he did earlier. Dad and I follow.

Balancing on the bobbing ground makes the trek difficult until we learn where to step, and fall into a rhythm. Momentary bouts of activity dot the landscape: packs of fluffy rabbits bounding along in the distance that, upon closer inspection, have the same muzzles and sharp canines as wolves; crocodile-like creatures lifting their heads out of the moats—giant jaws yawning to reveal soft white teeth reminiscent of toothbrush bristles; and centipedes scrambling beneath thorny weeds to protect bodies covered with silvery velvet hides and legs studded with tiny green jewels.

Most of the animals and bugs ignore us, which I prefer. I can't hear them or the flowers. But when my tunic catches on a plant with dangling fruits that look like leathery crimson teacups hung upside down, I consider touching it.

"I would not bother those, were I you," Morpheus calls from in front of me, not even sparing a glance my way.

I jerk my hand back. "Is the fruit poisonous?"

"It's not fruit," Dad answers from behind. "Those are egg sacs for AnyElsewhere's amphibious genus of bats."

Bats that live on land *and* in water. *Creepy.*

I give the plants a wide berth so as not to disturb the teacup-shaped flower pods. The poem from Carroll's story echoes in the back of my mind:

Twinkle, twinkle, little bat!

How I wonder what you're at!

Up above the world you fly,

Like a tea tray in the sky.

Twinkle, twinkle, little bat!

How I wonder what you're at!

While trying to remember the rest of the words, I stumble into a large shrub. A confused medley of monarch butterflies stirs from the leaves. Their wings are paper-thin and metallic, like a mix between hammered copper and stained glass. I reach to capture one, but my netherling intuition stops my hand midair.

"What about the butterflies?" I ask.

"They're indigenous to this place," Morpheus answers from a few steps ahead, before Dad can. "And by that, you can expect them to be the opposite of what you'd expect. The crocodiles' teeth are as gentle as a brushstroke, and their temperament the same. They're rather like kittens in this world. But butterflies? One sting, and you're turned to stone. Or, they might choose to slice an artery with a razor-sharp wing. The constant changes in scenery serve to keep the wildlife distracted. Ignore them, and they'll show you the same courtesy."

As the graceful butterflies ride away on a current of air, I notice a shiny, sharp needle protruding from each of their thoraxes, curved and poison-tipped like a scorpion's stinger.

Things quiet down as the wildlife moves on to their usual routines. If you could call anything about teacup-eggs and metal-winged scorpions usual . . .

After discussing a few other weird creatures with Dad, I release my wings and flutter to catch up to Morpheus.

He glances over as I light beside him. A satisfied smile greets me. "What?" I ask.

"You may not be dressed like royalty, but it's good to see you embrace your netherling side so openly."

I study my red boots, suppressing a rush of pride. He doesn't know the half of how easy it's getting to let the madness have free reign. "So, are you going to tell me who this Manti is? Is he dangerous?"

"Bah. He's an ambitious manticorn who's been a lowly knave for far too long. He craves prestige and power. Nothing to concern you."

The fact that there's a real-life half man/half unicorn running around is enough to concern me, and Morpheus's assurance feels forced at best.

"Don't you think we'd get there faster if we flew?" I ask to suppress my jittery nerves. "Dad can use your griffon. You could let him ride him."

Morpheus returns his attention to the landscape. His bejeweled profile sparkles from red to black. "I don't much feel like sharing with your father. I'm sure you can understand."

"Then wait for us, and I'll go back and get one of the parasols the birds left."

"Don't much feel like waiting, either."

I frown. "Stop being so petty." I look back at Dad, who's keeping us in his sight from a few steps behind. "Put yourself in his place. Can you imagine what he's been through? The nightmares he's had to relive and accept as reality over the past few hours?"

Several steps ahead of me now, Morpheus lifts his head, letting the humid breeze ripple the blue fringe at the edges of his hat. "Yes, poor fellow. Must've been unbearable, realizing how much the woman he adores loves him back."

Flapping my wings, I match his swift pace. "You can't possibly compare their romance to . . ."

He appraises my face, wearing a wry smirk. "To whose, Alyssa?"

I nibble the inside of my lip, annoyed with myself for almost showing my hand. "Wait." I study him, from head to toe. Yes, he still appears to be the same Morpheus I've always known. But there is one discernible difference: His wings trail behind him like drizzles of ink, whereas mine flap, lifting me inches above the ground. "This isn't you holding a grudge. This is you changing the subject. You're stalling."

Morpheus scoffs as he drags another mat of drifting land close enough for us to step on without getting wet. "Ludicrous. Why would I do that?"

I jump lightly across. "Because *you* need the griffon. You can't fly any more than my dad can."

While we wait for Dad to catch up, Morpheus holds the adjoining island in place with the walking stick. The only sound is the geysers burbling all around. His silence speaks volumes.

I grasp his hand where he clutches his cane. Through his thin glove, I feel his muscles tense. "I haven't seen you use your wings. Not once since I've been here. That bird thing . . . he said you have to recharge. You're out of magic. Which means you're not immune to the dome. Are you going to tell me what's going on?"

His other hand closes over mine—making me the captive instead of the captor—as he meets my gaze. "Of course. As soon as you tell me what's in the teensy diary around your neck."

My heartbeat hammers the tiny book where it rests atop my sternum. It's still under my tunic, so there's no way he's seen it. "How did you—?"

"Chessie speaks through his eyes. All you have to do is look, and listen."

Chessie's tail slips over the edge of Morpheus's pocket and squirms as if to taunt me.

"Actually," I say, almost to myself, "we have been learning to communicate lately."

"Good." Morpheus nods. "A queen's top priority should be an open rapport with her subjects. Now, back to my question."

I press my lips together, not ready to share the diary's secret. Bringing up my plan to vanquish Red will open the subject of the life-magic vow I made to Morpheus a month ago, that I'd spend twenty-four hours with him after I defeated her. This isn't the time or place to discuss that.

Dad crosses to where we are, obviously distracted by our joined hands. "What are we stopping for?"

Morpheus scowls. "Simply waiting for the human to catch up, whilst knowing that he never truly will," he quips, cool as always. Yet there's a worried crease between his eyebrows—a subconscious tic he can't hide from me. He never answered my question about his wings. The invincible Morpheus is crippled. And that saddens me.

We start walking again, Dad trailing behind. I want to press Morpheus more about his weaknesses here, but his pride won't let him answer. So I change the subject. "I'm feeling curious again."

He twirls his walking stick. "Ah, of course. It *is* your most endearing quality."

I shake my head at his teasing. "The birds mentioned the Queen of Hearts earlier. Is that Red's pseudonym here?"

Morpheus tilts his chin. "The Queen of Hearts is not in fact Queen Red. Your mum often confused them, though I tried to set her straight. Hart was a queen of the Red Court centuries ago. She is distantly related to you. She had barbaric tendencies, murdering her subjects for the most inane reasons. Taking a bite off a tart and leaving it on a plate, or spilling her finger paints. For this, she inherited the sobriquet of Hart*less*. In a twisted bid for respect, she began to collect the one thing her subjects said she was missing."

"Hearts?" I ask, almost gagging at the thought. "That's what the goon meant earlier, when he said those who don't win the caucus race will lose their beating hearts?"

"Precisely. Netherling hearts are unique. They can be harvested so they continue to beat forever even after their bodily cage is gone. The queen has mastered this technique. She can also sense a heart's quality. She uses the organs for everything from clothing embellishments to paperweights. She was banned from the kingdom for that practice, and sent here after she became too violent and murderous to contain. Unfortunately, now she is harboring Red's spirit. Two queens for the price of one. It's quite a bargain."

My throat clenches. "But you said spirits can't possess other bodies here . . ."

"Unless said 'body' is willing, and of the same bloodline. In the absence of magic, lineage becomes the strongest bind. The flower fae that Red arrived in was damaged. In fact, when I last saw her, I thought she was as good as dead—fodder for the goon birds. But she convinced them to carry her to Hart's castle and worked out some sort of bargain with her ancestor to share her body. Although I have yet to hear what the terms were."

Dread chills my bones. If Red is inside another queen's body, a queen who is just as malicious and savage as she is, the memories in my diary could be useless. I need something else to bargain with. Maybe if I figure out Red's ultimate plan . . . "I heard something earlier, from Humphrey's friend, Hubert. We stopped at his inn."

Morpheus practically beams. "Ah, Hubert. How is the old sot?"

"Glittery." I furrow my brow. "And grumpy."

A deep laugh rumbles in Morpheus's chest. "I've always enjoyed his company."

"Yeah." I scowl. "He's a real good egg."

Morpheus laughs again, and I can't contain an answering smirk.

"Anyway," I continue, "he said something unbelievable about Red and Lewis Carroll. That they knew each other before Alice came into the picture." Morpheus looks genuinely surprised but waits for me to finish. "Red *wanted* Lewis to find Wonderland, according to the egghead. Do you know anything about that?"

Morpheus doesn't have a chance to respond before the sun rips through the clouds overhead, a blinding flash that makes us shield our eyes. The sky fades to a peachy sheen and the ground shakes. Morpheus grabs on to my elbow. Water drains from the moats and the puzzle pieces clack together once more. The barren trees that surround us sprout green shimmery leaves and white flowers; in the same instant, grass forms a fringe around our feet.

When everything stabilizes, including the ground, Morpheus lets me go and Dad catches up to us. I squint. It's bright enough that we each cast a shadow, and the tall, leafy foliage forms dappled shade on the ground. Even the smells have changed, from stagnant and smoky to fragrant and flowery, carried on a temperate breeze. It's like springtime in Texas. A pang of homesickness chases that thought. I'm about to mention it to Dad, when a green-tinged sparkly light—no bigger than a grasshopper—drifts down from the sky.

As it descends, the lima-bean-colored skin, glittery scales curved around breasts and torso, and pointed ears, come into view. The sprite's wings flutter, milky white and furred with fuzz, and her hair glistens like strands of spun brown sugar. She drops onto Morpheus's shoulder, burrowing beneath his hat. As he lifts a pinky to pet her foot, she peeks out from behind his blue curtain of hair, metallic eyes shimmering like copper sunglasses.

"So, my lovely little Nikki," Morpheus says to her tenderly. "I suppose you're here to warn me that my ride is coming."

She speaks so softly into his ear, all I can hear is tinkling music like a wind chime.

"Wait," I say. "Why can she fly without mutating? That doesn't make sense."

"You'll have all the answers you seek soon enough." Morpheus hands me his walking stick. The gesture is mechanical, almost resigned. "And you shall be reunited with Jebediah, as well. But beware. He's not the same boy you once knew."

"Huh?" I ask.

"Simply tell the cane to fly," Morpheus says, sidestepping my question. "Above all, don't get it wet." Then he turns his back on me.

The hair at my nape prickles when I notice his shadow doesn't turn with him. Instead, it faces him head-to-head, more like a blotted reflection than an eclipsed outline on the ground. Sighing, Morpheus grasps hands with the dark silhouette and is lifted into the sky on ghostly echoes of his own wings. The tiny sprite looks me over once before following them.

I gape, unmoving.

Dad places a hand on my back. "We have to go. He's our only ticket to Jeb and out of here." His voice is tremulous, and I know he's as freaked as I am.

I hand him the griffon staff.

Arranging the duffel bag on his shoulder over his dagger, he straddles the cane like a child atop a stick horse. "Fly," he half whispers, and—with a rustle of feathers and fur—the creature comes to life. Its beak opens with a roar. The eaglelike wings thrash, rustling my hair, as the griffon ascends with Dad holding tight to its mane.

I suppress the questions spinning in my head, flap my wings, and soar up-up-up, keeping both Dad and Morpheus in my sights as we cut through fluffy clouds, headed toward the white-capped waves of an ocean that glistens in the distance.

❋·l·❋

A mountain rises from the water upon our descent as if it were waiting for us. The sprite and Morpheus, along with his shadow, plummet toward the boulders on the slope. The mountain opens and swallows them before the entrance closes again.

The moment Dad hits solid ground, the griffon transforms into the cane. I land beside them. My wings weigh heavy at my shoulder blades, weary from the workout. I wipe sweat from my brow.

"What now?" Dad asks.

I try to find a crevice or crack that might be the key to opening the mountain. "Could I borrow that?" I reach for Morpheus's walking stick and use the talons to dig at some pebbles. When nothing happens, I stomp my feet along jagged outcroppings.

"Stop it!" A voice—grinding, like stones clacking together. "Stop it at once!"

My chin drops.

"That's no way to make a first impression," the voice speaks again.

"Yes, to make an impression, you really should have a chisel," a second, less peevish voice, adds.

Two faces appear on the mountainside, one of them made of soil, the other of stone. The stony face is the cranky one and has large bulging eyes. The other—the dusty face—has a squinty, almost humorous demeanor.

Dad drops the duffel bag and takes a seat on it. His left eyelid is twitching as fast as the second hand on a clock.

"It's okay, Dad. I got this."

Nodding, he rubs a hand through his hair.

Stepping across some loose pebbles, I make my way over to the squinty-eyed face. "We need to get inside."

"Ohhhh, sorry," says the stony, grumpy voice from behind me. "Only the master can open the door."

"Yep, sorry." Squinty-eyes looks at me sympathetically. "So sorry, in fact, my heart sinks for you."

The ground beneath us quakes and we start to sink into the ocean. Dad gathers the duffel bag, and together we climb as fast as the ocean rises around us. All the times I went rock climbing with Jeb come back to me, and I have the added advantage of wings. Dad does, too, with the griffon cane.

"We're going to have to fly!" I yell. "Before the peak is submerged!"

Dad gets knocked off balance when the duffel bag and dagger slide from his shoulder. He catches them at the last minute but loses the cane. It shuttles down the moving mountainside and plops into the rising waves. When it surfaces, it's the griffon. It screeches, wings flapping as it flails, then melts bit by bit until it's an oily puddle of floating colors.

Dad and I stare in disbelief, oblivious to the waves ebbing at our ankles.

"Allie, go!" Dad shouts, the first one to remember that the mountain is dropping.

Climbing in time with him, I try to coax out my magic. My mind is racing so fast, my imagination can't catch up. I draw a blank. "Stop!" I screech to the mountain out of desperation.

The movement pauses. White froth laps my shins. "Your master would want you to help us," I say, hoping to coax the faces back into view.

"Is that so?" The dirt one appears at the mountain's tip. "Well, there *is* another way in."

Panting, Dad and I exchange hopeful glances.

"Okay. What would that be?" I ask.

"A horse. A special horse. He can get you inside. All you need is to shout his name at the top of your lungs."

Something tells me I'm going to regret asking, but I do anyway. "So . . . what's his name?"

"I can't say it *for* you, bony fool."

I scowl, holding back the urge to stomp on the dirt clods making up the face's lips. "Then give me a hint. The letters of the name . . . an anagram. Something!"

"All's I can say is it's a horse."

The other face appears on the edge of a golf ball-size stone, the features scrunched up to fit the smaller surface. "A horse without legs that can move up and down and forward and backward . . . A horse without a saddle that can cradle the most fragile rider . . . A horse without wings that can sail with the grace of a bird."

I slide my palm down my face. "Are you kidding me? Another stupid riddle?"

The stony speaker curls his mouth to a frown. "I'd rather tread water than listen to your bellyaching. You have only one guess, so be sure you're right!" Then, rocking back and forth until his stone loosens, he rolls into the water with a *kerplunk*.

Squinty-eyes looks up at me and crinkles the sprig of grass that makes up his nose. "Best you figure it out fast. Because your ingratitude has me feeling very low."

The mountain starts to sink again. Within moments, the waves lick our thighs.

I groan. "Dad, what do you think?"

He rubs his twitching eyelid. "Not sure. Maybe a rocking horse?"

I consider the clues. It does seem to match, *mostly*. "What about the sailing part? Rocking horses don't sail. Maybe a carousel horse. They're suspended on a pole, so that could count. They move up and down. But they don't move back and forth, really. And they have legs . . ."

The water reaches Dad's abdomen. "Allie." His expression is the one he gives me when he's about to lay down the law. I don't want to hear what he's thinking, because I already know.

"You're going to have to fly," he says as the water laps at my sternum. "Go while we still have ground to stand on."

"No! I'm not going to let you get hurt!" *Not like I did Mom.*

Her face comes back to me, the desperation in her eyes as the mome wraiths snatched her away and dragged her into the crumbling rabbit hole along with Sister Two and all her soul-filled toys. I couldn't hold on, no matter how I tried. Tears burn along the edges of my lashes.

"Dad, I summoned the creatures that took Mom away. I'm responsible for the danger she's in. If she's gone forev—"

"Alyssa Victoria Gardner." Dad catches my hands in his. "Don't even say it. Whatever you did, it was because you had to. Mom knows that. She's strong, and she's okay. And we're going to find her."

We. I teeter inwardly, my emotions rocking. "You promise you'll be with me?"

"To the very end. You can get us out of this."

"How?" If only I were strong enough to carry him.

"I know how to swim," he answers. "I can backstroke long enough for you to get one of those automated parasols the birds left, or even a piece of driftwood I can cling to."

It's like last year in Wonderland, when I couldn't carry Jeb across the chasm. I was supposed to find a way to come back for him, but I failed him, just like I failed Mom.

My teeth clamp tight. I can't let my doubts win.

I nod to Dad.

He drops the duffel so he can lie back in the water. The bag trails bubbles as it submerges. I scan the distance, unable to see land anywhere. I've no idea how far we've come, or if the parasols disappeared when the landscape changed last.

Still, I have to try.

Hugging Dad tight, I press a kiss to his cheek, tasting salt from the ocean's spray. "I won't let you down."

"I know you won't," he says, and nuzzles the top of my head.

He binds his fingers together for a step to lift me from the water.

Taking a deep breath, I push up and spread my wings high, rivulets drizzling from them as I rise.

"When you're ready, I'll launch you." Dad forces his lips into his famous Elvis half smile. His fake confidence has the opposite effect, reminding me of all the times he put up a front when Mom was in the asylum, and during these past weeks she's been gone. He's doing it again, even though he's as confused and scared as I am.

It's time for me to be the strong one.

Preparing for liftoff, I shake my wings. They're heavy on my back, not just from being soaked, but from the moss wrapped around them like sea creatures.

Sea creatures.

The waves creep to Dad's chin. "Allie, hurry." He spouts water from his mouth. His fingers tense under my boot's sole.

"Wait," I plead. *A horse without legs that can move up and down, forward and backward . . . A horse without a saddle that can cradle the most fragile rider . . . A horse without wings that can sail with the grace of a bird.*

"A *sea horse* . . . ," I whisper. They use their tails to maneuver in any direction, carry their babies in pouches, glide gracefully through the water as if sailing.

"No more time!" Dad yells, and thrusts me up into the sky—just before his head disappears beneath the water.

"Sea horse!" I shout loud enough to make my lungs ache, spreading my wings and flapping so I hover in place.

Dad resurfaces, doing the backstroke. The water bulges as something giant rises behind him. An armored hump bursts out, covered with bony plates, clear like glass. Water streams off to reveal the curve of a spine beneath the transparent armor. The graceful neck of a sea horse—as big as the Loch Ness Monster's—emerges. Sun glistens off the creature. It's beautiful, and looks more like a glass statue than a living counterpart: a sea horse's body with the head of a wild stallion.

Its belly pouch opens, and a funnel of water drags Dad toward it. I dive to join him. We slip into the translucent pocket. The opening cinches closed before the creature submerges once more. The cavity is damp, but comfortable. Dad and I sit and hold on to one another, watching underwater plants and confused fish dart past as we descend toward the sunken mountain. An entrance appears—just as it did with Morpheus—and held safe within our living submarine, we glide into a dark tunnel as the mountain closes around us, shutting out the light.

MIND'S EYE

As we surface, a muted, purplish glow casts shadows all around. The sea horse bends its spine back and forth, squeezing its pouch until we burst free into the shallows.

I cough and shove myself to my hands and knees. Behind me, my wings drape, as soggy and muddy as my clothes. The sea horse snorts, blows froth from its equestrian muzzle, then sinks back into the depths.

Weak from physical exertion, I force myself to stand in the ankle-deep water. Dad gets up, offers his hand, and we wade to a cement embankment to sit and catch our breath.

"Any idea where this is?" I ask, wringing out my tunic. "Did you visit here as a child? Do you remember?"

His brows furrow. "This world is so different than I remember, Allie. It keeps changing. It's as if we're in a picture book and the pages are flipping in the wind."

When I glance over my shoulder for a closer look at the dim tunnel, my breath catches: Graffiti stretches for what seems like miles—words like *love*, *death*, *anarchy*, *peace*, and pictures of broken hearts, stars, and faces are painted in fluorescent colors.

It's a replica of the storm drain Jeb and I almost drowned in over a month ago, the one we used to go to as kids. It even sounds the same, with water dripping all around. But there's one huge difference: The images on these walls are moving.

The broken hearts stitch themselves together, beat several times, then break and bleed. The stars shoot from one end to the other, leaving sparkles in their wake that catch fire and snuff out with the scent of scorched leaves. And the faces glare at us, as if angry. I muffle a whimper.

"Do you see that?" I ask Dad.

"It's not possible."

"Anything is possible here," I correct, then stand, facing the ultraviolet images. My legs tremble, but I step forward. "You realize what this means?"

Dad doesn't respond.

Of course he doesn't. He can't see inside my past.

"These are from Jeb's memories," I explain. "*Our* memories." The thought that I'm about to see him makes every muscle in my body leap. I take off for the far end of the tunnel.

"Allie, we need to be careful." Dad catches up, gripping my shoulder.

I shake him off. "We have to find him!" But with each step, the tunnel shrinks, and so do we. Either that, or it's an illusion—because I don't feel like I'm shrinking. I've done that enough to have the sensation memorized.

No. We're not getting smaller. The images are growing, elongating. They lift from their places on the walls and scrape our skin as we pass. The stars singe my sleeves; the hearts drizzle wet blood. The faces nibble at me—their teeth cold and prickly like straight pins.

I shiver as Dad and I move faster.

A sketch stands guard at the tunnel's end—a neon orange fairy whose wings spread behind her in pinks, blues, and whites.

It's me. The one Jeb painted on the tunnel wall in our world. But this is not a part of the wall. She's facing us, an ominous barricade . . .

"Stay behind me." Dad draws the dagger, waving it as he faces her. Bright colors reflect off the shiny blade and the iron bypasses her lines. Dad steps through without any trouble. "Come on, Butterfly. It's just an illusion." He holds out a hand.

I reach for him, but something jerks his shoulder from the shadows behind. The dagger falls from his grasp and hits the floor with a clang. "Run, Allie!" he yelps as he's dragged away out of my sight.

Terror ices my spine. "Dad!"

My fluorescent double steps back into place, blocking me. "You should be in pieces like the others," she whispers. Her breath smells of sadness, lost dreams, and abandoned hopes—like stale, dust-covered keepsakes in a forgotten attic.

I grit my teeth against revulsion and fear. Dad walked right through her. That's proof she's not real.

I lunge.

My body meets a prickly barrier, each sketched line piercing like barbed wire. I yell and my attacker echoes me. I rip free from her barbs and hit the ground. My bones rattle even with my wings cushioning the impact.

The drawing drifts toward me, her body and face warping as she gets closer. Her mouth stretches cavernously wide and she screeches, "Shred her!"

Her thorny fingers scrape my neck. I shield my face, trying to use magic to recruit the other graffiti along the walls to help. Either I'm too panicked or they're under someone else's spell, because they refuse to obey.

I roll and snatch the dagger Dad dropped in the adjoining passage. In the same move, I whip the blade through the fairy's fluorescent lines, but it has no effect. She attacks again, along with the other graffiti now pulled away from the walls. They surround me: glowing, barbed wire artwork.

I toss away the dagger and hold my hands over my head like we did in school during tornado drills. The diary at my neck trembles and shakes. I brave a look at the sensation of warmth at my chest. Light radiates from under my tunic, as if the words on the pages are infrared.

The drawings shudder and back up, each of them whimpering, even the fairy sketch. They reattach to the walls and settle into place, leaving the adjoining tunnel unguarded.

I scoop up Dad's dagger and plunge after him, using the red glow from the diary to guide me. It's the first time I've seen the tiny book react in such a way, as if the magic inside is burning to come out. I'm not sure what caused it, but I'm grateful. It saved my life.

Absorbing my wet, weighted wings into my skin, I maneuver down the narrow corridors. The sound of dripping water fades. My plastic boots splat on the stone floor. Every nerve in my body skitters at what the sketches planned to do to me and what might be happening to my dad.

You should be in pieces like the others . . . Shred her!

What did the fairy sketch mean, *the others*? I squirm in my damp clothes.

The ceiling drops gradually, as if I'm growing again. The sensation is dizzying, but also gives me a sense of security. The bigger I am, the stronger I feel.

Masculine voices echo through the corridor and lure me to a passageway on my right, where soft slivers of light filter from behind a heavy-looking door that's ajar. I sneak toward it, in hopes one of the voices belongs to Dad.

"You've no inkling what you've done in your desperation to keep me under your thumb." *It's Morpheus.* "No idea what you caused me to leave behind."

"It wasn't desperation," Jeb answers.

An all-encompassing relief swarms through me at the sound of his voice. I inch closer to the door's opening.

"The sprites told me Manti was after you," Jeb continues from the other side. "That he'd sent some goon birds your way. And this is the thanks I get. For saving your ass for the thousandth time since we've been here."

"Bloody hell, *my* arse," Morpheus speaks. "*Your* arse is on a blasted power trip, as always. But you crossed a line. And once I tell you what you've done, you'll never forgive yourself."

Jeb huffs. "Uh-huh. Sit up here so I can fix your ear. I have a painting to finish."

The domestic undertone of their interaction is so fascinating it makes me pause. I wonder how long they've been holed up here together. For the entire time they've been trapped in this realm? I peer inside.

My breath hitches as I see Jeb's back. He's shirtless, wearing faded, ripped jeans in a room lit with a pinkish-orange sunset. The light streams through a glass ceiling. It's like a greenhouse—a carbon copy of the art studio in the human realm where he was trapped a month ago. There's the pattern again: Everything here is born and built of Jeb's memories.

Paint glistens in wet smudges on his toned arms. I hold my breath, wishing for a glimpse of his face, but he won't turn. His hair is longer now, the dark, unkempt waves just shy of touching his shoulders.

Morpheus misled me. Jeb *hasn't* changed. He even has the same passions.

There are easels everywhere. Some untouched, others filled with landscapes, a few of which match the changing terrains we experienced in the midst of the looking-glass world. My brow crinkles as I try to make sense of it all.

Morpheus sits on a table in front of Jeb, dark wings draped forward and dragging on the floor. His discarded gloves lie in his lap, and he picks at one of the holes in his pant leg.

His little sprite companion, Nikki, flutters around both guys as if unsure where to perch.

Jeb lifts a paintbrush to Morpheus's ear, accidentally stepping on the tip of a wing.

Morpheus winces and slaps Jeb's hand away. "Ouch! Your bedside manner is sorely lacking, pseudo elf."

Nikki hovers at the tip of Jeb's nose, shaking a finger. After gently shooing the sprite away, he leans over Morpheus and lifts his brush again. "If you'd keep those things up on the table, there wouldn't be an issue. Now hold still and stop acting like a little girl."

A pulse of violet light passes from the wet bristles to Morpheus's ear. Like magic, the wound heals. I stifle a surprised moan.

Back still turned, Jeb straightens to appraise his handiwork.

Morpheus smirks—a practiced, acerbic twist of lips. "So, is there any particular *girl* I remind you of?"

Nikki flutters between them, her hands clasped and head tilted in a dramatic gesture. She bats her lashes.

"You're right, Nikki." Dragging a fingertip through the paint on Jeb's chest, Morpheus rubs the smudge between his thumb and finger. "He must be thinking of his girlfriend. Though I daresay, if I were Alyssa, his bedside manner would improve tremendously."

Jeb throws his brush down and grips Morpheus by his holey lapel, every muscle in his back taut. Nikki hovers, her tinkling voice scolding them both.

"She's my *ex*-girlfriend," Jeb says. "And I don't want to hear her name. I don't want her haunting my subconscious." He shoves Morpheus away. "You remember what happened when her face turned up in my paintings. We have to forget her. Just like she's forgotten us."

Ex-girlfriend. All warmth inside me snuffs out. He's never sounded this discouraged, not even after fights with his dad. And it's because he thinks I've abandoned them.

Morpheus swipes the paint from his thumb and finger across one of the dust rags piled next to him on the table. The look he gives Jeb is devilish delight. "A shame you have so little faith in the one you once claimed to love." He slips his fingers into his jacket pocket and coaxes out Chessie. The furry netherling flitters his wings, rising. He smiles at Jeb, sincerely happy to see him.

Jeb totters back two steps. "Where did . . . how did he get here?"

Morpheus shrugs. "You should be asking *who brought him* here. That answer is much more interesting."

Jeb shakes his head as the sprite takes Chessie's paws in her hands so they're dancing in midair. "Al would never . . ."

"She would," Morpheus taunts. "She did. And she'll soon find a way into our refuge. Unless your untimely retrieval of me caused her to be captured. In which case, she's in danger, and it's on your head."

"No," Jeb insists. "She doesn't care enough to come."

I want to storm inside and prove him wrong. He's lost all faith in me. And that fact is more excruciating and unbelievable than anything I've faced since the time I first fell into the rabbit hole.

My limbs go numb and Dad's dagger almost slips from my sweaty hand.

Dad! How could I have forgotten him?

A shuffling sound echoes from the darkness further down the corridor. Holding my breath, I tiptoe along the winding hallway. I haven't made it very far when something clenches my arm from behind. One hand slaps across my mouth and another shoves me against the wall, hard enough my spine grinds into the stone.

My captor's build is masculine. He grips my wrists with his free hand and holds them at my abdomen. My fingers tighten around Dad's dagger, the blade pointed toward the ground.

I try to yell, but my attacker's free hand seals my lips tight. He's taller than me, head tilted like a curious puppy, as if trying to figure me out. There's something so familiar about his height and form. When my eyes adjust to the dimness, I almost collapse.

It's Jeb, from his labret to that body I know so well . . . only now I can see his face.

On the right side, red jeweled dots sparkle in a curved line from his temple to his cheekbone, matching his red labret. A closer look at his ears reveals pointed tips. He resembles an elfin knight of Ivory's court, if not for his unshaved jaw. Even his eyes, vacant and distant, lack emotion.

A scream struggles to break loose as more gruesome details come to light. The skin under his left eye gapes open. Where there should be tissue and bones showing through, there's nothing but a void.

My tongue dries, smothered under his palm.

"*He's not the same boy you once knew,*" Morpheus warned. This is what he meant. Jeb is mutated, because of me.

I strangle on a sob.

Movement catches my attention in the emptiness where his skin gapes. An eyeball bobs to the surface, veined and backward. I gag, trying to shove him off. He's too strong and holds me pinned by my own hands.

He bends his face closer. A set of fingers curls from inside the gaping skin above his cheekbone—a hand trying to reach out and touch me. The fingers are shiny and deep red, the color of blood.

The detached eyeball rolls to look at the fingertips while Jeb's other two eyes continue to study me.

I gasp for breath under the unrelenting palm over my mouth. Heat scalds my chest—as electric as a lightning flash—and the diary under my tunic glows once more. It shocks my sense of self-preservation to life. I bare my teeth and bite his fingers, hard enough to break the skin.

With a feral screech, Jeb releases me. I spit out his blood, faintly aware that it tastes like paint.

I fumble for the slippery dagger in my sweaty fingers and catch it at the last minute, accidentally slicing through his jeans and thigh. He howls—a harrowing, animalistic sound—as the skin on his leg peels back in a six-inch gash.

"I'm sorry!" I cry. "I'm sorry for everything!"

Detached eyes and red disembodied hands spill from the opening, riding on slithering crimson vines with mouths that snap like Venus flytraps.

I drop the dagger. Back pressed to the wall, I slide down to the floor. My screams join his agonized wails. The slimy vines trail around me and I kick at them. Bile gushes into my throat as several constrict my ankle.

The door down the hall flings open. Morpheus rushes out with Nikki and Chessie flying behind.

Salty tears stream down my face—coating my lips as I mutter senseless apologies for so many things. So many irreversible things.

Morpheus peels the vines off and lifts me, cradling me to his chest.

"Get that bloody beast out of here!" he shouts over his shoulder. I look across through blurred eyes to see who he's talking to.

It's Jeb. *My Jeb.* The one who was speaking with Morpheus minutes ago. And the only thing marring his perfect face are spatters of paint.

The other Jeb, the one that attacked me, is crumpled on the floor, wailing—a macabre doppelganger of the human boy I know and trust.

"Why is it wandering around unattended?" Morpheus continues to scold. "I told you . . . you should never have granted it such freedoms."

Jeb's gaze passes over me, his green eyes far from the emotionless stare of an elfin knight. They're rife with shock, bitterness, and agony.

Shivers race from my head to my toes. I need to tell him that I've come to save him. That I still love him. That I'm sorry for everything. But my vocal cords stiffen, as if iced over.

My head feels like ice, too. Heavy and deadened. I'm not even sure I'm awake anymore. Maybe this has all been a nightmare. I hold on to the nape of Morpheus's neck, burying my face in his jacket. Nikki and Chessie burrow into my hair. I inhale Morpheus's scent. It's the only thing I recognize, the only thing that's safe.

He carries me back to the well-lit room and sets me gently on the table. I can't stop trembling. My throat aches from holding back sobs.

"Calm down, Alyssa." Morpheus wraps a heavy canvas drop cloth around my shoulders.

Chessie clambers from my shoulder into my lap, his wide emerald eyes asking if I'm okay. Nikki buzzes around my face, patting my temple with her ladybug-size palm—maternal and kind.

My blood flashes hot and cold.

"You look pallid," Morpheus says, gathering the drop cloth tighter around me. "Are you going to need a bucket?"

I shake my head, fighting off the queasy roil in my gut. "W-w-where's Jeb? What was that thing—" Shuddering coughs shake my body.

"Shh." Morpheus places his hands at either side of my hips on the table. His wings enfold us. "Jebediah's putting it away. He'll be back shortly. Breathe deeply and concentrate on me. You are safe."

I take a shallow breath, but it chokes me.

"Look at me," Morpheus presses. I focus on his complexion, the color of snowy shadows beneath the eclipse of his wings, and he begins to sing. Not inside my mind, since the iron dome prevents it, but aloud . . . a simple, sweet lullaby, carried on his beautiful voice.

"Little blossom so filled with dread, clear the nightmares from your head. Let me wipe away your tears, for in this place you have no fears."

He used to sing those very lyrics when he became a child and took me to Wonderland in my dreams. I would pull one of his satiny wings across me like a blanket, and the scent of licorice and honey, paired with his beautiful lullaby, would lull me to relaxation. As I listen now, his jewels flash a serene blue, like the surface of an ocean.

With a few deep breaths, I suppress the coughing. "Thank you," I say.

Morpheus squeezes my shoulders over the drop cloth. "The creature out there wasn't going to hurt you. It was simply intrigued. It's seen your face before. All the creations down here have."

Remembering the barbed wire sketches, I shake my head. "No. The graffiti acted like I was a contagion. They tried to kill me."

He lifts an eyebrow and trails a fingertip along my neck. "Is that how you got these scratches?"

I nod.

He studies the rips in my sleeves and the burn marks from the shooting stars. "How very curious."

"They're monsters." I clutch the cloth tighter around me.

"Not all of them," Morpheus corrects. "Little Nikki has the same creator and she's quite pleasant." As if to prove his point, Nikki lights next to his hand on my shoulder and strokes my hair.

The same creator. The blood on my tunic's hem left by the broken-heart sketches . . . the stains look like paint. Just like Jeb's doppelganger *tasted* like paint.

Sick awareness tightens my windpipe. The fluorescent fairy and graffiti, Jeb's disfigured elfin look-alike, and the landscapes on his easels—it all reminds me of when I first stumbled upon my powers . . . the time I inadvertently made a mosaic come alive. I animated it on the wall at my house—dead crickets and winterberries dancing and dripping inside their plaster frame.

"Oh, no," I say, my voice airy. "It isn't that Nikki is immune to the consequences of using her magic here. She's *made* of magic. Jeb painted her. He painted his look-alike, too. He's bringing his art-work to life." The explanation sounds like fiction in spite of how my gut knows it's true.

A glint of pride reflects back at me from Morpheus's black eyes. "Splendid deduction. Yes, Jebediah has tapped into netherling gifts. But there's more to it than that."

As if satisfied I'm okay, Chessie prances off my thigh and ducks out from under Morpheus's tented wings. Nikki follows him.

Once they're both gone, I turn back to Morpheus. "What do you mean, there's more?"

"Hmm." His fingers find their way to my neck again, but this time, he catches the strings there and drags out the diary and key before I can stop him. "First, you tell me about this little treasure." The red glow glosses his face. He tries to open the book, but the magic is too powerful and the key's too big.

I yank the strings away, tucking them under my tunic once more.

Morpheus studies me. "What are you hiding on those tiny pages, Alyssa? And why?"

I look at him dead-on. "I finally have a secret of my own. Not so fun being on the other side of one, is it?"

The slow burn of amusement warms his features. He leans in and whispers, "On the contrary, My Queen. I cannot imagine anything more delicious than peeling away your defenses, layer by layer, and baring your precious . . . secret."

Heat climbs my chest and fills my neck and cheeks. It's beyond unsettling, how quickly he can shift between comforter and tormentor.

He watches the blush of my skin, obviously enjoying taunting me. "In fact, I'm willing to bet I get to the bottom of your secret before you do mine. It's like I've always told you: Netherling logic resides between sense and nonsense. When you turn your back on everything that you once thought was real, you will find illumination." He drops his wings.

Warm sunset pours through the glass ceiling.

"I suppose we'll see how much you've learned to rely on your Wonderland side." He singles out the red strip of my hair from my braid and holds it up to the light, then tucks it behind my ear. "Netherling intuition can decipher the illogic of everything you'll encounter while you're here, which will aid you on your grand quest."

I sense this "grand quest" he refers to is more than just Dad's and my attempt to get to Mom.

Dad . . . I forgot him again! "My dad!"

"Glad to see you're concerned," Jeb says from the doorway, and I wonder how long he's been standing there. "No worries. I was just with him, and he's all right."

A long-sleeved black satin shirt hangs over Jeb's broad shoulders and arms, unbuttoned and flowing. His eyes glimmer with a disorienting light that confirms there's something otherworldly flowing through him. Though relieved he hasn't transformed physically, I'm terrified of what's happening inside of him.

His labret glints red in the fading light overhead, reminding me of how the elfin knights pricked their skin to mark their faces with gems made of crystallized blood. With his long, wavy hair, Jeb really does favor the ones I met in Wonderland. His stony expression—giving no emotions away—only adds to the illusion.

"Would you take me to him?" I ask about my dad, feeling like I'm talking to a stranger.

"First, answer a question for me," Jeb says. "If you care so much about him, why would you bring him into the middle of all this?"

Jeb's accusatory tone stings. I've been away from him for weeks and was just attacked by his creatures, yet instead of comforting me or welcoming me, he's raking me over the coals. "My dad is as much a part of this twisted fairy tale as the rest of us."

Jeb meets Morpheus's gaze. "Right. Bug-snot told me all about Thomas's past. But why would you drag him through that pain again? He's better off not remembering."

"I—I had to give him his memories back," I stammer, shaken

at the thought of Jeb and Morpheus sharing confidences. "Do you think *you* would've been better off not getting yours back?"

Jeb looks down at the floor, a thoughtful crease between his eyebrows. "I think I would've been better off not ever making them to begin with."

I struggle not to cry. As razor-sharp as the confession is, I'd be weeping blood. "I needed Dad's help to find a way into the looking-glass world. He wanted you and Mom back. It was time for him to know the truth."

"The truth." Jeb scrubs at the red stains on his palms. "Surprised you know what that is anymore."

I whimper before even realizing it.

"It's not what you think," Jeb says without looking up. He splays his hands, as if they're what made me react. "It's paint. Not blood."

I shake my head. "I don't care what's on your hands. Please look at me. I missed you. I was so worried about you."

"Really? Which one of us are you talking to?" His attention crosses to Morpheus, who smirks conspiratorially.

Even more unsettling than seeing the guys on the same side of anything is having them gang up on me. That sharp pain tears inside my heart again, as if Red is there, antagonizing it, relishing my misery.

I squeeze my eyelids shut, damming up the tears that knock behind them. *Suck it up, Alyssa. You're a queen. Act like one.* I stiffen my shoulders and open my eyes.

"I'll find Dad on my own." I shrug out of the drop cloth and start to slide down from the table.

Morpheus places a palm at my collarbone. "You're not ready to be running any marathons, luv. You're still shaky."

"I have to find him."

"He's already been found, like I said," Jeb answers, his attention on the hand pressed at my neck. He narrows his eyes, and with a subtle flick of his fingers, Morpheus's shadow rises from the floor and wrestles Morpheus away from me.

Growling, Morpheus shoves the dark silhouette aside, then glares at Jeb. "Amateur. Cheap parlor tricks."

Jeb gives him a vicious grin. "A pupil is only as good as his tutor."

I stare at them both, speechless.

Jeb turns back to me. "Your dad just needs to sleep. He's tired."

Morpheus's creepy shadow sniffs at my tangled hair like a dog. I scoot back as Morpheus forces it behind him.

"I want to see for myself," I say to Jeb.

Jeb squints. "Why? Don't you trust me? Do you seriously think I would hurt Thomas? He's the only real father I've ever had. The only one in your family who hasn't stabbed me in the back."

I refuse to let him see how deeply he's cutting me. "It's not you I don't trust. It's that . . . thing you painted."

He steps all the way into the room, head cocked. "You told her."

His gaze and accusation are directed at Morpheus, but I answer. "My dad was captured and dragged away. I'm pretty sure it was that same thing that attacked me in the hallway. Did it show you where it took him? It had to, didn't it? Because you're its creator."

Jeb's lashes lift my direction and in that moment, I see my best friend again. Weary shadows under his eyes reveal the vulnerability he's trying to hide. He's human and unguarded. All I need is to drop to the floor, walk over, and close the space between us. But then he looks away, and I'm hit with the reality that the span of steps from me to him is nothing compared to the walls I'm going to have to climb to get to his heart.

"How does she know so much?" Jeb asks Morpheus. "What have you been telling her?"

Morpheus grimaces. "Put your little novelty away and we'll talk."

Jeb tips his head, and the shadow sinks into the floor again, nothing but a dark shape at Morpheus's feet.

Morpheus leans his hip against the table's edge and drags a corner of the drop cloth over Chessie and Nikki, who are dozing soundly. "As always, you underestimate our Alyssa's ingenuity. She figured it out on her own after being attacked by your graffiti army in the entry tunnel."

Jeb looks my way. "They attacked her?" For an instant, I could swear there's concern in his eyes. Then it's gone. "They're not usually violent toward living things."

Morpheus purses his lips. "Well, since most of your creations are unequipped to leave this mountain, and since we've never had living visitors here, we've not exactly tested that theory. Besides, this isn't just any visitor. Alyssa is the object of your rage."

"That's not true," Jeb murmurs, yet he averts his eyes.

Morpheus sighs. "Much as you'd like to deny it, it's obvious your creations are retaining your anger toward her. Feeding off those negative feelings."

"Jeb?" I ask on a whisper.

He doesn't answer.

"Perhaps it's time for you to erase everything and start anew." Morpheus speaks quietly, gentle helpfulness and measured wisdom, though it's obvious he's egging Jeb on.

Jeb meets his gaze. "I think it's time for *you* to stop talking."

"Why? Alyssa will figure it all out soon enough."

I'm feeling nauseated again. "I want you *both* to stop talking about me like I'm not here. What happened to you, Jeb? Was it when you went through the gate? You mutated?"

Morpheus laughs. "'Mutated.' The word you're looking for is *evolved*, luv. He has shed his monkey mortal state and donned the robes of netherling immortality. That's a step up, not a step down."

Jeb growls from beside one of his easels. "Just shut it, Morpheus. I'll decide how much she needs to know and when to tell her."

"Well, let us hope you decide before she's torn to bits, aye?"

I gulp.

Jeb tugs a drop cloth into place over a painting and moves to cover another. "Your dad is worried about you." He addresses me without even a glance in my direction. "I'm going to take you to him . . . so you can rest together."

It's Jeb I need to be alone with, even if it's for a short walk down a corridor. "Thank you."

Morpheus scoops up Chessie and the sprite and strides across the room. He pauses at the door, his wings and back facing us. "Sleep safely, Alyssa. When you wake, I'll help you strategize your battle plans. Bear in mind, I haven't forgotten the vow you made to me. Nor do I intend to let you forget."

I stare at the empty corridor after he leaves. Help me strategize my battle plans? *He knows I'm going after Red.* His earlier fascination with the diary . . . somehow, he's figured out that I plan to use what's on the pages to destroy her. The war's not even won and he's already collecting on the spoils.

"So, are you going to tell me what kind of deal you made with the cockroach?" Jeb watches me as he buttons the black shirt, covering his circular scars before I can count them. I'm tempted to use my magic to impede his progress, to expose his skin to the evening light around us. My fingers itch to seek out the flawed parts of him . . . the damaged, authentic places that prove he's real—that he's the boy I've trusted and depended on since my fifth-grade summer. That the human I love is still somewhere inside.

After my encounter with his doppelganger and Morpheus's accusations about his pent-up rage, I need some assurance.

"Al."

My name on his tongue shifts my eyes to his. What I wouldn't give to hear him call me skater girl.

"What was Morpheus talking about?" he presses.

"I promised him something," I answer softly. I don't want to admit what he already knows. That there's more going on between me and Morpheus than I ever let on.

"A promise, huh? How romantic." His words slash like knives. He's become a master at wielding more than a brush since he's been here. "So that's why you've crashed our little paradise. To keep your *promise* to Morpheus."

I wince. "No. I came to rescue you both. You have every right not to believe me . . . to be mad at me. I know this has been hell. This place . . . it's broken you."

"I was broken before that." His tortured expression delivers the allegation—*thanks to you and bug-rot*—better than his voice ever could. "But I've taken my life back. I'm the one with magic here. I have the ability to make the world as it should be. As it *always* should've been."

He lifts his right hand, and rolls his sleeve cuff so the tattoo shows on his inner wrist. The Latin words *Vivat Musa* aren't black anymore. They glow with the same violet magic as his brush did earlier, giving new meaning to their translation: *Long live the muse.*

"I understand now," he murmurs. "Why the power seduced you. With just a turn of my hand I can create, kill, maim, and heal." There's a dreamlike quality to his movements and words, as if he's in a trance. Blinking, he drops his arm to his side again. "No one can ever make me, or anyone I care about, a victim again. This place isn't hell. It's heaven. And I . . . *I am a god.*"

The ominous declaration hangs between us. My chest caves in, as if someone punched me.

Jeb's shimmery gaze treks across my face, then he steps out the door.

The moon appears outside the glass ceiling, gilding the surroundings with a silvery haze. Rustles erupt under the drop cloths as the paintings begin to move. They jab at the heavy covers as if trying to break free.

Biting my tongue to keep from screaming, I leap from the table and follow the man responsible for the monsters . . . the man dangerously close to becoming one himself.

Nightmare's Paradise

"Jeb, slow down, please."

Some six feet in front of me, he ignores my request as we plod toward Dad's room. My legs drag as if cement blocks have dried around my boot soles, and it's only partly because I'm tired. Even more, I'm disturbed. This winding, slanted corridor looks too much like Jeb's house and mine, each turn embellished with familiar paintings and mosaics from our own collections. Morbid projections stick out from the walls like disembodied hands.

I hold my breath while passing, in hopes nothing grabs me. I can't stop seeing the red snapping vines, fingers, and eyes that gushed out of Jeb's monstrous double.

"Jeb, that creature in the hallway . . ."

"Yeah, for future reference, he's not a *creature*. His name's CC."

"CC?"

"Carbon Copy. And he doesn't have a tattoo on his arm. In case you need help telling us apart. You know, if the pointed ears and gashes under his eye aren't enough."

The taunting is so unlike Jeb, I don't even know how to respond. "Those things inside him. What was that?"

"C'mon now." He turns a corner and I rush to catch up. "You're an artist. What are our masterpieces made of?"

Exhaustion threatens to overtake. I fight the urge to fall into a heap on the floor, determined to keep up with him on every level. "Bits and pieces of us?"

Jeb glances over his shoulder. His expression changes for an instant, as if he's pleased with the answer. Then his emotionless façade returns, and he looks away. "Bits and pieces of everything we've ever imagined or experienced—good or bad. So if a painting were to somehow become real . . . instead of intestines, organs, blood . . . what would be at its core?"

"Our dreams and nightmares."

"Nailed it," he answers.

I cringe and watch another door go by. Is that what waits inside these rooms? Nightmares?

A spectrum of resentment and anguish colors Jeb's past. And he's chosen to delve into *that* palette to build his ideal world. Where are all the happy memories? The hopes? The love?

After what feels like ten minutes, we stop at a door that's made of diamonds. I'm instantly reminded of the tree on the black sandy beaches of Wonderland. The jewels sparkle even in this low light.

Jeb stalls, his hand on the ruby doorknob. "I didn't know you were out there today. I wouldn't have left you and your dad alone . . . defenseless."

I'm not sure I believe him. I want to, but after the way his creations attacked me?

No. Jeb deserves the benefit of the doubt. This is the first real glimpse of the boy I've grown up with, and I'm going to fight for him.

"Nothing could've stopped us from finding you. We missed you. We love you." I place my hand over his on the doorknob. "*I* love you."

He tenses. My chest touches his side and his body reaches out to me involuntarily as his ribs expand with every breath.

"Remember what you said the last time we were together?" I whisper, my mouth at his shoulder, aching at the proximity and heat radiating there. I want to lift to my tiptoes and press my lips where his hair curls against his nape, want to feel him tremble at my touch like he used to. "You said you don't give up without a fight. That was a promise." I wind my fingers into the spaces between his on the doorknob.

His hand tightens. "I never promised."

"You said it. And your word is as good as a promise. I refuse to believe that's changed."

He relaxes, as if I've gotten through. He turns his head and his scruffy jaw brushes my temple. His breath rustles the top of my hair.

The Barbie diary grows hot at my chest, lit up again under my tunic.

"You're wrong, Al," Jeb mumbles against me, as if the red glow brought him to his senses. "Everything has changed."

The bitterness in his voice shatters me.

"Open," he commands the doorknob. With a flash of purple light, it turns. Jeb drags me inside and shuts the door behind us. Disoriented, I spin around to take it all in.

It's not a room with my dad asleep on a couch or bed. We've stepped into a facsimile of a beach at night. A warm, salty breeze rushes through my hair. The sound of an ocean laps at the edge of a white, sandy bank, and the ceiling is an endless sky. Moonlight shimmers off the waves and stars twinkle, casting soft light on the flower garden at our feet.

"The ocean of tears," I whisper, overwhelmed by thoughts of the first night we spent in Wonderland on a rowboat. Even though we were in a mystical place with death and lunacy at every turn, it was the safest I've ever felt because I fell asleep in Jeb's arms.

Now, following him to the shoreline in silence, all I can think of is how gentle he was then, how he rolled me to face him in the hull of the boat while I slept, how he stroked my hair and promised to watch over me.

He's reconstructed one of the most romantic moments we've ever shared. Maybe that means he's been trying to forgive me all this time.

Unless he considers this a bad memory.

"Jeb, why are we—"

"You'll be going to the island to sleep," he interrupts. A surge of white light sweeps by. In the distance, a plateau looms high in the middle of the ocean. A working lighthouse sits atop the rocky slope. Jeb kneels and digs out a rope hidden in the sand. He tugs, straining the shimmery fabric of his shirt. A rowboat comes into view, closer with each pull. "You'll be out of reach of the others across the water."

Others. His cryptic explanation reminds me of the fairy sketch's threat: *You should be in pieces like the others.*

"What others, Jeb? What else have you made?"

He hesitates, his body stiff.

"Butterfly!" Dad's eager shout startles me. His form takes shape in the dim light, sitting in the hull.

Jeb heaves the boat ashore.

Dad leans forward and shakes his hand. "Thank you for bringing her."

Jeb dips his head in acknowledgment. He steps back, giving me room to climb in.

Dad holds out a palm. I reach for him, but only when my fingers meet his warm and callused skin do I relax and step over the bow. He helps me onto a seat.

"Dad, I thought you were—"

"I'm okay, sweetie," he answers, hugging me. "I'll tell you everything later."

I turn back to Jeb. "You're going to stay with us tonight, aren't you? We have to plan how to get everyone home. Please . . ."

"I'll take the sea horse out to search for your duffel bag," he says, avoiding my gaze. "There are clothes in the lighthouse for tonight. I'll see that you have your own to wear tomorrow. Then we'll discuss getting you both to the Wonderland gate."

"Getting *us* there?" I gape at him in disbelief. "We're not leaving AnyElsewhere without you!"

He scoots the boat into the water. Sand grates along the bottom as we cast off. "You'll find food in the cupboards. There's a yellow flower indigenous to this world. Morpheus saw some wildlife eating it once. It must have all the nutrients we need, because we've been living off of it and the occasional rabbit. There's rainwater to drink. It won't take much to fill you." Having said that, he nods to Dad, a signal for him to row.

"Jebediah, you know you're welcome to come." Dad pauses, waiting to see if Jeb will change his mind. When he doesn't, Dad picks up the oars.

Jeb watches our progress as glistening waves lap at the bow and the paddles dig through the water. The lighthouse's beam sweeps by, illuminating the glint of his green eyes and his glowing tattoo. Then he's gone, back the way he came, headed for the door.

Dad stops rowing long enough to touch my hand. "Allie."

Loneliness cleaves through me in all the places that Jeb has always occupied. "He can't stay here. He has to go back home, Dad."

"It's late. We're all tired. I'm sure tomorrow he'll see things differently. If we give him space, he'll make the right decision. We need to have faith in him."

"He hates me."

Dad sighs. "No, sweetie. If that were true, then why is he still protecting you? He's sending us to the island because he's worried for your safety."

"How is being on some lame island supposed to protect us?"

Dad resumes rowing. "Not sure. I was hoping he would've explained that to you."

I clench my hands on the edges of the boat. "He won't confide in me about anything. He's even closer to *Morpheus* than me." My bones weigh heavy, and my emotions are wrung dry. I lean my head back, closing my eyes so the sound of swirling water can unwind my knotted nerves.

"Well, it makes sense that they're close," Dad says. "Considering

Jeb fused with Morpheus's magic when they came through the gate."

My eyes snap open and I sit up, stunned.

That's why. Jeb's barb to Morpheus about the pupil and the tutor, the strange purple color of the magic . . . how they've overlooked their hatred for each other and learned to coexist. *More* than coexist. Bond. Two guys who once were enemies have learned to rely on each other for survival.

"Allie, you okay?"

"I just . . . I wish he'd told me himself."

"He was closed off with me, too," Dad says. "When he first found me in the empty room where that creature left me. But we talked about my past and your mom's predicament. I apologized for being wrong about him on prom night. He forgave me. He'll do the same for you. Just be honest with him. Deep inside, he understands you didn't mean to send him here."

It's so much worse than that. You don't even know. If only I had the energy to tell Dad everything, but I'm too tired to even try. The light passes over the boat before leaving us in darkness again. I won't fall victim to the pity party gnawing at me. I'll win Jeb's trust back. Till then, I'll take comfort in the fact that he can confide in Dad.

"On the upside," Dad continues, "it looks like Jeb has the lion's share of the powers since he's human and the iron doesn't affect him the same. He rations it out to Morpheus through his creations. That's how Morpheus can perform magic without mutating."

I purse my lips. "Wait. It was the griffon cane that was magic, not Morpheus? That's what needed to recharge?"

Dad nods.

So, without Morpheus's magic, Jeb would be a sitting duck, and without Jeb, Morpheus would be magically impotent—a fate worse than death in his mind. Come to think of it, he won't be pleased when he learns we melted his walking stick.

I lean over the edge to let my palm skim a current. "The cane turned into a puddle of paint. Jeb created it, and the water dissolved it." I frown. "It's the water that will protect us tonight. Not the island. But why is the rowboat still intact? And the sea horse? They're also his creations. Why aren't they melting?" I dry my hand on my pants.

"Jeb didn't paint the sea horse." Dad tows the oars through the sloshing waves. "It's part of the wildlife here. Jeb and Morpheus tamed it. As for the boat. Maybe it has something to do with the answer he gave when I asked about that . . . thing. His image. Why it's marred."

"Yeah?"

"He said something about the boundaries of a painting's reality. That whatever originates on the same canvas can coexist. Most of his paintings are contained within a setting he creates. But the few that aren't—that he paints on blank canvases—when they stumble into another painting's territory, unpredictable things can happen."

I pull apart the threads of his explanation. That explains how Nikki can fly outside in the looking-glass world, and how the elfin doppelganger—CC—could wander the halls. "So, if something is painted in a scene with water, it won't erode. But if it's not . . ."

"Right. And I guess in the case of Jeb's image, it got mixed up with some territorial paintings and its face was ripped to pieces."

Dad's words trigger the graffiti's reaction to me: *You should be in pieces.* Morpheus said that all the creations know my image, and Jeb had mentioned something about my face turning up in his art. Which means he must've painted me.

Maybe the graffiti thought I was a stray painting that didn't belong in their scene. And they were going to shred me for being there. Or maybe it's like Morpheus said, and they were seeking vengeance for their master.

A disturbed shudder trails my spine.

"Allie." Dad's voice changes tone. "There's one more thing you need to know: Jeb hasn't asked about his sister or mother. In fact, he talks about them as if they're here. As if he's spent time with them."

The tears I've been holding back finally break loose, fat droplets running down my face. "It's my fault," I mumble, swiping my cheeks with the back of my hand. "I hurt him so much he'd rather stay here and create a false reality than face a world full of bad memories."

"Why do you keep saying things like that? What aren't you telling me?" Dad pauses rowing. We're only a few yards from the island now. I wish he'd keep moving. I don't want to have this conversation. I feel bad enough without his condemnation.

"Something happened on prom night," I admit reluctantly. "Before the dance."

"Let me guess. It has to do with Morpheus."

I groan. "It was just a kiss! Why is Jeb so hurt over a stupid kiss?"

"Wait a minute." Dad rocks back on his seat, causing the boat to bob. "You kissed that arrogant . . . ? I don't even know how to process that."

"Me neither." He'd be even angrier if he knew the rest. That it wasn't the first time. That Jeb also knows about the other kiss Morpheus and I shared in Wonderland. That I told Jeb it didn't mean anything—a lie—then turned around and did it again . . . even though I hadn't meant for it to go that far. Morpheus twisted the situation to his own end, like he always does.

"Morpheus is a mistake, Alyssa," Dad continues, as if seeing my thoughts. "He's manipulative. He has no scruples. And he's not human."

"Neither is Mom. Neither am I. Or Jeb, for that matter. Not anymore. Does that make you love us any less?"

The lighthouse swathes us in light and my face burns under Dad's scrutiny. "Of course not. But *love*? Is that what you feel for Morpheus?"

I swallow hard. "I'm not sure. It's all wrapped up in my loyalties to Wonderland. But there's something real between us. Something powerful." I sink further into my seat. "It's complicated."

Dad starts rowing again. "Well, I know what you feel for Jeb. And it's simple and pure. You two have been friends since the day you met. And it grew into something more. That's a tangible thing, Butterfly. And so rare. The *best* kind of love. He was planning to ask you to marry him. Did you know that? He asked me for your hand."

My eyes sting. It's just like Jeb to do something so old-fashioned and beautiful. At least, like the Jeb I once knew.

"He did propose," I finally manage. "I didn't get to answer."

"What was your answer going to be?"

"Yes," I say without hesitation. "But that was before . . ."

Dad looks up at the stars. "I know. Before he and Mom were taken."

I consider correcting him, but it would lead to an interrogation I can't face tonight.

"You're the only one who can get through to that boy and help him find his way home," Dad presses. "But you'll have to let Wonderland go to do it."

"No!" I prop my elbows on my knees and hold my head to keep it from exploding. "I'm a queen. I have responsibilities there you can't even imagine. It's wrong to deny that side of myself. To turn my back on a world that's depending on me. I tried to do that . . ." I wave at everything around us. "Well, you can see how great it worked out. I'm never running from my responsibilities again. I have an obligation to the netherlings. I care about them. If Jeb and I are going to have any kind of future, he'll have to make peace with the fact that Wonderland will play a role in every choice I make for the rest of my life." I think of the diary at my neck. "In every choice I make *here*."

Dad sloshes the oars harder, causing water to spritz across us. "You were human first. You have commitments there, too. People who depend on and love you. Don't get so caught up in power and politics that you forget that. Or you'll be doing exactly what Jeb is. Hiding from your humanity."

Red's fingerprint—that splitting sensation behind my sternum— punches me. I clutch my hands in my lap to keep from doubling over. "That's not what I'm doing," I grit out. "I'm trying to find a balance."

"How's that possible?" Dad asks. "Madness is the antithesis to balance. I've seen the other side taking over you. And frankly, it scares me. You're drawn to the darkness, to the lawlessness. Drawn to . . ."

Morpheus.

Even if Dad doesn't say it out loud, I hear the name echo in the silence.

"He has insinuated himself into your life," Dad continues.

"Some could argue that Mom's choices had a hand in that."

The boat slams into the shore, jarring us. Anger radiates off my dad, which only feeds the sense of right rising hot inside of me.

"I didn't mean that like it sounded." I attempt to placate him.

"I'm just saying Morpheus didn't plan to use anyone. Not in the beginning. He and Mom had a deal—mutually beneficial—until she backed out."

Dad tosses the oars into the boat with a *thunk*. "Don't ever accuse her of making a cavalier decision. She did the right thing even when it was difficult. Left behind a world that promised her power and immortality, all because she couldn't stomach stealing human children for their dreams."

"All because she couldn't stomach leaving you as one of the stolen." I regret the words instantly. I know it was so much more than that.

Dad shakes his head. "I'm going to forget this conversation, Allie. You're tired and obviously not thinking before you speak." He climbs out of the boat, wading through the shallows to pull it in.

He's mistaken. I *am* thinking, proven by how I didn't tell him the most inconceivable truth of all: That I can actually put a stop to stolen childhoods. That by having a future with Morpheus and sharing a son, I could fix everything between our worlds.

I couldn't tell him even if I wanted to. I can't afford to lose my powers by reneging on a life-magic vow of silence. To defeat Red, find Mom, and put Wonderland back together, I need my magic intact.

Dad secures the boat to the shore by winding its rope around a post. I clamber out before he can offer to help me.

I hate that there's friction between us. I hate feeling so far from Jeb while he's haunting the rooms in this mountain hideaway, facing his nightmares and heartache alone. I hate how jumbled my emotions are when it comes to Morpheus: hurting for him that he's powerless, angry he holds a vow over my head—yet fascinated by him, endlessly.

Most of all, I hate that Mom and my netherling subjects are trapped in a crumbling Wonderland, wondering if I'll ever come to save them.

Something nudges me on that thought . . . something quiet yet hopeful. I saw how strong Mom's magic was on prom night; I learned how much she already knows about Wonderland's inner workings. She was once almost a queen. She can survive in that world.

I keep my thoughts to myself because they feel like hunches and I have no proof. But still, they comfort me.

Led by starlight, Dad and I climb a steep, winding stairway made of stones that leads to the lighthouse. Inside, hurricane-style lamps float along the ceiling and follow us as we move, casting a soft amber glow. The walls are stone, the floor squares of black-and-white sand—miniature versions of the dunes Jeb and I surfed across in Wonderland over a year ago. I take off my plastic boots and dig my tired toes into cool grittiness. At the top of the tower, there's a turret bedroom with a canopied bed and an open porthole that overlooks the ocean, letting in moonlight, the sound of waves, and salty air.

Dad insists I should sleep there and opts for the couch downstairs. Back in the kitchen, we eat the dried flowers. They're stringy, like beef jerky, but a deep golden color. The taste is sweet and waxy, reminiscent of honeycomb in the human realm. We wash the meal down with rainwater sipped from mugs made of rock-lobster shells. Dad and I are both so drained, not another word passes between us.

I duck into the bathroom to take a shower and wash my long underwear so I can lay them out in my room to dry overnight. There's everything I could possibly need: a toilet, a razor, a toothbrush, and citrus-scented soap. On some level, Jeb is still living a human life, however he tries to deny it.

As I head toward the stairs, I stop where Dad is spreading a quilt out on the couch. Even though we're at odds, we hug before parting ways to sleep.

In the tower, I open a wardrobe against the bedroom wall and find a plaid flannel shirt. I shed the clothes Uncle Bernie provided and think about the guards at the Wonderland gate, hoping they're okay after being there so long without supplies. I also worry about the message we were supposed to send via the metal pigeon. It's doubtful, even if Jeb's sea horse finds our duffel bag, that the mechanical bird will function after being submersed. I don't even know if the beacon feature will work, so Uncle Bernie can find his way to us.

I shrug into the flannel shirt, rolling the cuffs to make the sleeves fit. The hem hangs to my thighs. A pair of sweatpants with a drawstring waist is folded neatly at the bottom of the wardrobe. I set it aside for morning.

I'm about to crawl into bed when a glittering green light perches on the opened porthole.

Nikki curtsies daintily. "From Master Morpheus." The tiny sprite's bell-like voice drifts along the breeze. She offers a white box wrapped with a shiny red ribbon. It's about three times her size. She's stronger than she looks, to carry it all this way.

The instant I take the gift, she flitters up into the night sky without another word. Unlike Gossamer, she's not much for talking.

Inside the box are two exquisite pieces of lingerie: a bra and matching boy shorts made of white cotton beneath a glistening gold lace overlay. The metallic lace looks vaguely familiar.

A blush heats my face as I imagine Morpheus's elegant hands folding the items, and placing them inside. There's a note on black paper, no doubt written by the very quill he plucked off the osprey earlier.

The ink looks like silver foil, shimmery in the starlight:

Dearest Alyssa,

I am sending apologies for not welcoming you properly today. I wanted to lift you above me and swing you in circles until we were both dizzy and laughing. I wanted to kiss your lips and share your breath. And I wanted to dress you in threads befitting a queen. Tonight, I shall settle for the humble beginnings to your royal wardrobe. I imagine what you're wearing beneath your clothes is as unworthy of you as the clothes themselves. But know that I will give you armoires filled with lace, satin, and velvet one day when you reign in Wonderland. All you need do is ask.

Your loyal footman,

Morpheus

His sentiments wind around me, sensual and silky. I drape the lacy underthings on the porthole's ledge and trace the golden overlay, trying to place where I've seen it before. Then it hits me: Morpheus's prom costume had a white cottony shirt and a doublet overlaid in gold lace with hook-and-eye closures, just like on the back of the bra. My lingerie is pieced together from the layers of his clothes. He had to sew them by hand since he doesn't have any powers, which would've taken time. That means he already had them made for me, waiting.

Handwritten love notes, handmade gifts. In the absence of his magic, he's making me more confused than ever. The sharp jolt in my heart revives. It's becoming increasingly familiar and acute—as if there's a seam down the middle and it's stretching beyond its limits.

I rub my sternum to alleviate the sensation, then drag my arms out of Jeb's shirt and slip the lingerie on underneath.

My blush burns hotter to find each item fits perfectly . . . that Morpheus knows my body without ever having run his fingers over it; even more, he knows how I've been craving pretty things since I left the asylum. He knows *me*.

Buttoning Jeb's shirt across my torso, I climb into bed and let the canopy curtains drop, grateful they're heavy enough to eclipse the lighthouse's beam. In the darkness, beneath the covers, I hug myself tight, surrounded by Jeb's scent and Morpheus's homespun lingerie.

I dream I'm a paper doll, a creation of paint and imagination brought to life by Jeb's hand. I rip myself in two, at last relieving the tearing pain of my heart. One half of me plays leapfrog atop mushroom caps, wraps myself inside Morpheus's black wings, and dances with him in the sky beside a full moon . . . The other half skateboards in Underland, rides a motorcycle with Jeb, and steals starlit kisses with him underneath our willow tree. And in spite of the parallels and contrasts—or maybe because of them—it's the most at peace I've been in ages. Both Jeb and Morpheus are happy, and Wonderland and the human realm are thriving.

I jerk awake, wishing I really were that paper doll, so I could split myself right down the middle and give everyone their happy ending, just like in my beautiful dream.

MASKS

Voices from the kitchen nudge me awake a second time. I pull on Jeb's sweatpants and my plastic boots and head downstairs. Jeb and Dad have been there awhile, judging by the empty mugs and the plate spotted with honeycomb-flower crumbs.

I'm thrown off by the distorted sense of time here. Since Jeb painted the ocean as a night scene, it's still dark out, but it must be morning because Dad looks rested.

Jeb, however, doesn't.

The circles under his eyes are more defined, exaggerated by the bright glow within his irises. He's in holey jeans and a white T-shirt smeared with red paint. One look at the matching smudges on his hands, and I know he's been creating something new. I wonder what it might be.

As I take the last step down, Jeb stands and rakes aside some hair that's fallen across his forehead. The action borders on shy and self-conscious, but it doesn't take long for his impassive façade to drop back into place. "Now that you're up, let's get you two some clothes." He offers an apple and a bottle of water from our duffel bag of supplies. Looks like his sea-horse patrol was successful.

"Breakfast," he says, waiting for me to take the food.

I pause. "How did you get here? We have the boat."

"I walked across the ocean," he answers, not missing a beat.

His declaration last night, that he's a god, hits me full force. "You did?"

The flirty tilt to his mouth is as unexpected and lovely as an eclipse. "Actually, I painted more than one boat."

"Oh, right." Grinning, I take the fruit and water he's holding. Our fingers touch. A muscle in his jaw ticks, then he turns to Dad and gestures for us to follow.

I fall into line, munching on the apple, hopeful. Yesterday I thought Jeb was lost to me. But if he still has his sense of humor, I can reach through the barrier of anger.

Once we've crossed the ocean, he leads us back to the greenhouse studio. Overhead, white and black moths cloak most of the glass roof. They pile up and creep across one another, forming a living blanket that looks like a midnight sky specked with stars. The result dims the room to shadows. A sheet of soft daylight filters from the only glass panel left bared—creating the disorienting illusion of night and day all at once.

A palette of various colors waits atop the table. The familiar scent of the paint comforts me. I don't even question where he's getting his ingredients to make it. Even though it smells normal, its origins are probably magic.

The studio appears bigger this morning in the absence of Jeb's landscape masterpieces and easels. The only canvas that remains is a sheet along a wall, draped from ceiling to floor. There's a cheval mirror on one side of the room, and Japanese screens obscure two of the corners. The red cranes embossed atop the panels move as if alive. A moth drops from its place on the ceiling, lands on the farthest screen, and is gobbled up by one of the painted birds with a squishy crunch.

Dad takes it all in with a disturbed frown.

As for me, I'm mesmerized. Last night I was leery of Jeb's handiwork, but today a tickle stirs inside my blood—the resurgence of my madness. Jeb's aberrant creations, their wildness and macabre functions, seem to feed my netherling side.

"First," Jeb says, talking to Dad as he lines his brushes and mechanical pencils along the table, "we have to draw your shadow."

He has Dad take off his shirt and shoes and roll his pants to his knees. Then he poses him in front of the canvas and snaps on a lamp. Bright light imprints Dad's form on the sheet.

"Hold still," Jeb says as he sketches the image. I've missed watching him as he works. And to witness the power brewing beneath his skin as he breathes real life into his creations . . . it adds a dimension we never could've shared in the human realm.

Like he said last night, he understands the allure of magic now, the passion and the freedom that goes along with giving our masterpieces the ability to interact with the world. The darkness in me swells with fascination while the human in me nudges a warning—tiny yet powerful . . . demanding to be heard.

Part of accepting power is acknowledging how intoxicating it can be. Jeb's becoming an addict, just like his dad. I've been drunk on magic and madness myself. The only way to find sobriety is to balance it with the best parts of being human. But it won't be easy to remind someone of humanity's virtues when they've been crushed as many times as Jeb.

"Once I finish the outline," he says, drawing Dad's lower half, "I'll fill it in with paint. Then you'll need to back up into the painting before it dries. It has to be joined with your skin to be able to follow you anywhere. It'll stay intact as long as it doesn't touch water. Since I manipulate the weather and landscapes, that won't be an issue."

I lift an eyebrow. "So, you're basically playing the part of Wendy."

Jeb pauses and glances at me. "Windy?"

"Wendy, from *Peter Pan*. You're stitching Dad's shadow into place." *Peter Pan* was his favorite fairy tale as a child. His mom read it to him every night.

There's the hint of a shy, boyish grin on his face—the one he used to give me when I'd catch him off guard. Then his smile is gone and he's back to concentrating on his work.

His detachment is like a splash of cold water. Dad winks subtly my way, encouraging me to relish the victory, however small it was.

Jeb finishes his sketch on the canvas and starts adding wings. "Unlike Al"—curves and lines flourish flawlessly with a graceful sweep of his hand—"we don't have the equipment built in. The safest way to travel here is to fly, so you'll need wings for our trip to the Wonderland gate."

"We're going to the gate today?" I have mixed feelings about the news. I know that if I leave without facing Red, it will come back to haunt Wonderland and the ones I love again. She's proven that she won't be gone until I *make* her gone. But I also want to get to Mom as quickly as we can, and it's impossible not to be excited when Jeb has decided he's coming. "So you're going to leave with us?"

Dad watches me with contrition in his eyes.

"You misunderstood," Jeb answers, punching holes in my buoyant hopes not only with his clipped response, but the flattened tone of his voice. He returns to the table and mixes paint until he has a black pigment with purplish undertones. "Only your dad and I are going today. His choice."

Dad offers an apologetic frown. "We plan to take the supplies to the guards and feel things out," he explains. "You're staying here. So we can be sure everything is on the up-and-up before you and I try to leave together."

You and I. The room grows gloomier.

I clench my hands to fists. "There's no way I'm sitting here while you two face all the weirdness out there. I'm going."

I want to add one thing more: that if Jeb thinks for one second I'm going to let him stay behind when we leave for Wonderland, he's mistaken. I'll use my magic to force him to come home if I have to.

The thought of his graffiti army stomps through me. I had no power over them. Jeb is my match now, in every way. It would be a difficult fight to win.

"Allie, please," Dad presses.

"What?" I snap. "You still don't think I can hold my own? Even after everything you've seen?"

"That's not it at all. It's your bloodlust I'm worried about. None of us knows where Red is. But it's a given she knows you're here now after our encounter with those birds. I don't want you running into her. Remember our deal? We get in, we get to the gate, we get out."

I can't help but notice he omitted the part about getting Jeb. Frustration burns my eyes. There's nothing I can do about Jeb until I have some time with him. But maybe I can use his and Dad's absence today to my advantage. After they leave, I'll go out on my own and search for Red. I have a feeling the diary will lead me straight to her.

I look up at the moths on the ceiling to maintain an angry facade. If Jeb were to find out about my plan, he could paint a gilded cage around me and I'd be trapped. "So, what am I supposed to do all day while you're gone? Play with bugs?"

Jeb crouches to fill in the sketch's lower half with paint. His lips twist to a cruel sneer. "That's your favorite pastime, right? And you'll have your prince of moths for company."

I keep my expression unreadable. Morpheus staying behind is actually a good thing. He can accompany me to find Red. He knows his way around this world and understands its occupants better than me. The only downside is my vow to him, how determined he is to collect, and how a part of me is starting to crave those twenty-four hours at his side in Wonderland.

"So . . . you're not taking Morpheus?" I manage to sound nonchalant.

"He'd be lost without his griffon." It's impossible to miss the smugness in Jeb's voice. "He can't fly without it, and he needs its homing device to lead him back here if he gets turned around."

"So *that's* his compass."

"Right. All my paintings have the ability to find their way back to this mountain—to me—no matter how far they wander."

"But Morpheus can use his shadow." I attempt to reason with him.

"I took it away. It needs some repairs," Jeb says—an answer for everything.

Unable to hide my annoyance, I blurt, "Well, that seems like a pretty stupid move. There's safety in numbers, you know." I bite my tongue so they won't know I'm the one needing a safety net.

"We're taking reserves." Jeb motions toward one of the Japanese screens in the corner. The crane flaps its wings and pecks at the panel it's stuck to.

"What, the *cranes?*"

Preoccupied and silent, Jeb guides Dad to back up into the painting, then seals them together with a flash of magic from his brush.

Dad steps away and the painting peels off the canvas—a quiescent, fluid trail along the floor—looking like an ordinary shadow with the addition of wings.

I wander over to the Japanese screen Jeb pointed to, curious.

"Al, wait," Jeb warns, dropping his brush in some water and rushing my direction.

Before he can reach me, I peer behind the screen. A drop cloth hangs in place atop something shaped like a hat rack. I tug the covering away.

CC screeches and scrambles out, almost knocking me over in its haste to escape.

I scream.

"Hey!" Dad starts toward the creature.

Jeb catches it before it can run out the door. "It's okay. I've forbidden him to ever touch either of you again." He pats his doppelganger's shoulder. "Show them, CC," he urges—his voice tender, as if speaking to a child or a pet.

The creature turns and I steel myself for the macabre fissures in its face. Instead, a red heart-shaped patch covers its eye along with the gaping holes I saw yesterday. There's a slit in the middle for CC to see out. The other perfect eye and cheek are uncovered, and the elfin markings sparkle in the daylight. It's easier now to make out the creature's porcelain coloring—somewhat lighter than Jeb's olive complexion. With the heart over its eye, CC resembles a harlequin from a pantomime. All that's missing is a diamond-patterned costume instead of jeans and a T-shirt.

Considering the red smudges on Jeb's clothes and hands, this is the project he was working on before coming to the island.

"You made a mask for CC this morning?" I ask.

"I made it for you. Last night. I didn't want his grotesque appearance scaring you again."

The kindness of the gesture touches me. No wonder the circles under Jeb's eyes seem so much darker today. I wonder if he slept at all.

He sends the creature out and avoids looking at me. "I'll coax your shadow out when it's time to fly," he says to Dad.

Dad nods and watches the dark shape move with him along the floor.

"Clothes are next," Jeb says, rinsing his brush. "They'll be removable once they're dry, and you can wear them multiple times. But the paint has to touch as much of your bare skin as possible to make them fit."

Dad stalls. "As much as possible?"

"You'll wear a loincloth. That's how I make roach-boy's clothes."

Imagining Jeb and Morpheus in such an intimate position is both sexy and comical. As vain as Morpheus is, a lot of bickering about fashion choices must've taken place.

"What about Allie?" Dad asks, a paternal defensiveness raising the pitch of his voice.

Jeb concentrates on the paint he's mixing. "Unless she wants to wear my clothes, we don't have any other option."

I shrug, accentuating the size of his shirt. "These are about to fall off. They won't work for traveling."

"She's not going to wear just a loincloth while you paint on her," Dad insists.

"Of course not." Jeb tosses two rolls of elastic bandages my way. "I found these in your duffel bag. They'll adhere to the paint to become part of the outfit. Cover your underclothes. Leave your arms, stomach, and legs bare. It'll be no worse than wearing a bikini. And there's a clip for you to pin up your hair."

His curtness stings. Four weeks ago, he wouldn't have suggested me wearing something like that without anticipation in his eyes. In fact, before all of Wonderland broke loose at prom, we were talking about taking the next physical step in our relationship. The biggest step. It's excruciating to know I've lost the power to move him on a human level.

I slip behind the closest screen and strip down, then pin up my hair.

Dad comes out from his screen first. While Jeb works on his clothes, I take my time so I don't have to see my dad in a loincloth. Of all the horrifying things I've witnessed, that would rank up at the top.

I wind the bandages around Morpheus's lingerie and craft a

swimsuit any mummy would be proud of. After I check to be sure Dad and Jeb are done, I step out, using the flannel shirt like a robe.

Dad takes a quick look at me and seems satisfied I'm properly covered.

My jaw drops. He's cloaked in feathers, has four wings, and reminds me of the goon birds we encountered yesterday. "What is that?"

"We'll blend in better if we look like Manti's lynch mob," Jeb explains, rinsing his brushes. "They run surveillance across the sky. I have a goon costume of my own. It's the perfect camouflage."

The word *camouflage* reminds me of the simulacrum. "Wouldn't the best camouflage be invisibility?" I kneel next to the duffel bag opened on the floor.

"Jeb and I looked for the suits," Dad answers. "They weren't in there."

I frown and dig through the other items. The metallic messenger pigeon turns up, but when I press the button on its throat, its beak no longer glows. I return to my search for the simulacrum.

"It doesn't make sense," I say to myself aloud after giving up. "Everything else is here."

Jeb shrugs. "Maybe enchanted silk isn't waterproof."

Dad starts for the door. "I think I'll go back and clean up the kitchen at the lighthouse. I need to practice moving around in feathers."

He either feels as awkward seeing me half-dressed as I did him, or he's giving me time alone with Jeb. Either way, I'm grateful.

"Thanks, Dad."

He nods and shuts the door. He's only been gone two minutes

when it reopens and Morpheus storms in, facing Jeb at the table, unaware I'm in the opposite corner.

He's in new clothes today: a satiny silver jacket over a white T-shirt and sleek black pants. Without a hat to contain them, his glowing waves match perfectly with the silky blue tie hung loosely around his neck. Yet in spite of his change of wardrobe, his wings droop, a sure sign he's miserable.

"You know, you're being entirely unreasonable," he growls to Jeb. When Jeb doesn't respond, Morpheus slams a palm next to the paintbrushes, causing them to jump. "I'm merely asking for another walking stick—" His voice cuts off as Jeb looks over at me. Morpheus turns.

A flush creeps into my face. I tug the shirt plackets together to hide the miniature diary at my neck, and shuffle my feet to cover the tattoo on my left ankle before he can tease me about it. Then, remembering I'm naked from the thighs down, I step behind my screen again and peer out.

Morpheus scowls. "Alyssa, what is that under your robe?" He turns to Jeb. "This is our lady queen. And you're dressing her in bandages?"

Jeb doesn't even look up from his preparations. "What she wears under her clothes is of no concern to you."

"Bah." Morpheus snags a paintbrush. "She should be draped in starlight and clouds, lace and softness. Nothing less should touch her skin." He points the bristles at Jeb. "I saw what you put Thomas in. You are not painting her into one of those goon suits. She is royalty. *Dress* her like royalty. Give her some glitter . . . some glitz. And a crown."

"Go back to your room, Morpheus." Jeb takes the paintbrush. "The grown-ups have work to do."

Morpheus tilts his head to meet my gaze from behind the frame. "Aw, shy little blossom. You should've seen the atrocities he tried to put me in those first few days. He didn't let me have a say until I walked around naked for a few hours. Should you decide to employ that strategy, I'll be behind you one hundred percent. Or in front of you. Lady's choice." He winks.

An unexpected spark of amusement jolts through me. I wait for his suggestive teasing to send Jeb into a jealous rage. Instead, Jeb calmly organizes his paint.

"Jeb wouldn't be here to see it even if I did," I grumble to Morpheus. An unspoken *And he wouldn't notice anyway* echoes in my head. "The bird costumes are for him and my dad's expedition. I'm not invited and neither are you. We're under house arrest."

Morpheus takes in my dour expression and turns back to Jeb. "My word. You're leaving her in *my* care? How very mature and trusting of you, pseudo elf." He grips Jeb's shoulder. "If you'd like to get an early start, you can forgo the new clothes. She won't be wearing them once you're gone, anyway. Consider it my contribution to the cause."

Jeb slams Morpheus against the wall so fast I almost miss the move.

Triggered by the activity, the moths along the ceiling descend like bits of falling ash. They cling to the wall next to Morpheus's wings, outlining him. Bright yellow sun gushes through the abandoned glass panels.

Jeb and Morpheus stare at one another—eye to eye. Purple light pulses between their bodies.

"What you have to ask yourself, Alyssa"—Morpheus addresses me, but keeps his focus on Jeb—"is who he's most jealous of." He drags his fingertips through Jeb's wavy hair. "Me, or you."

Jeb doesn't even flinch. "Guess you'll never know." He studies Morpheus's unchanging expression and his muscles start to relax. "And nice try. But no dice. You're both staying behind."

He releases Morpheus, who casts me a rueful glance. "Sorry, luv. Now that he has netherling acumen, he's not so easily manipulated. I've decided to find it charming. No worries, though. You and I, we'll think of some way to occupy ourselves." He sweeps his wings high and the moths flutter around him in tiny tornadoes.

With a flick of his hand, Jeb beckons the insects over. They hover in front of him, forming a human shape as if mirroring his image.

"Escort Mothra back to his room," Jeb charges them. "And keep him busy while I'm gone."

Morpheus smirks and steps across the threshold as the faceless moth-guard shoves him on his way.

The door closes by itself

I step from behind the screen and frown at Jeb. "Why did you do that?"

"Because we should get started, and if I leave it open we'll just have more distractions." Tucking his thumb inside the hole on the palette, he points me to the place where Dad stood for his fitting.

I don't budge. "You know I'm not talking about the door. I can't stand the way you're treating him. Flaunting the fact that he's pow- erless . . . that you hold all the magic."

"Oh, right. Because he's *never* done that to me."

I look down at my bare feet. Clenching the paintbrush's handle between his teeth, Jeb cups my elbow and positions me atop a drop cloth.

He lifts my chin with a fingertip, then takes the brush from his mouth. "Look straight ahead."

My body remains stationary, but my opinion leaps for a chance to be heard. "You know, I expect that kind of cruelty from Morpheus. His sense of right and wrong is skewed." I study Jeb's face. "But yours isn't. Bullying? I thought those days ended with Boy Scouts in seventh grade. You're a man now. And you're not that kind of man. Not like your—" I stop short and bite my tongue, hard enough to draw blood.

Jeb's expression hardens. "My *father*? Damn right I'm not like him. I'm stronger than he ever was." His voice is low and controlled. "I'm beyond what he thought I could be. Beyond what he said I was capable of. You know how he felt about my art. Wonder what he'd say if he could see me now."

He holds my gaze long enough to register my unspoken acknowledgement. Then, without touching me, he parts my shirt's plackets. My skin reacts to his hands' proximity—remembering what it's like to be stroked by them. The shirt slides off my shoulders, free of my wrists, and puddles on the floor behind me, baring my bandaged breasts, waist, and naked stomach to the light. I'm exposed, on every level.

Jeb inhales a sharp breath. We stand there, blinking at each other in the brightness. The scent of paint and citrus soap lingers on his skin. Wet smudges glisten in patches on his arms and neck, spotlighting taut muscles.

On impulse, I trail my forefinger through a blue streak next to his collarbone.

He grimaces and jerks away. I drop my hand, defeated.

Intent on his palette, Jeb swishes the paintbrush through a black tincture. He smooths it across my left arm, from the shoulder to the top of my bicep. Defined lines form a cap sleeve. The bristles tickle and the paint is cold, but it's Jeb's ability to disconnect his emotions that gives me goose bumps. I don't even know him anymore.

He steps back and reloads the brush, then moves to the right arm. Absently, he runs his tongue across the inside of his lower lip, nudging his labret. "Do you remember when I got this?"

The unexpected question unbalances me. I hold still in spite of the blossoming heat beneath my skin. "Two hours after your dad's funeral," I answer hoarsely.

"And you know how long I'd wanted to do it before that, but every time I'd bring it up . . ." He flips over his forearm.

The tattoo glows, yet it's the cigarette burns that hold my attention. "Yeah."

"Well, it was about more than proving his reign of terror was over." Jeb's voice is aloof, as if he's reading from someone else's life pages. "It was a reminder. That *I* was in control of my choices, of my body and my life. That I had a say in what happened to my sister and mom." He circles around to my back, leaving my chest and stomach unpainted. After he finishes the backs of my sleeves, the bristles trail a line down my spine and stop a few inches above my waist, making a stripe from one side of my ribs to the other.

I suppress any reaction to the tickling sensations.

"Funny," Jeb continues, "how I thought something so insignificant could put a dent in what that drunk bastard did." He laughs. Not the heartwarming laugh he used to have. It's deep, brittle, and mirthless. "Now . . . now I can paint a piercing anywhere on my body, or a tattoo, and they become real. Alive. Powerful." He sweeps the cool, creamy liquid across my back, creating a cropped T-shirt. "Anything I make will fight for me. My labret could be as deadly as a samurai sword. All I have to do is paint it and command it. If I'd had that in our world, I could've stopped him from hurting Mom and Jen. I could've made their lives better. I can do that here." He pauses. "I have, you know. Those scenes play out as they should've. Every time, my old man is the one beaten to a pulp. And Jen and Mom are untouched and happy."

I shiver, terrified at how detached he's become from reality. "Jeb, that's not your sister and mom. These are all just paintings. You know that, right?"

His brush resumes its journey across my back, but he says nothing.

"You have to let go of the guilt," I say. "You were only a kid. If you let it fester, it will kill everything good inside you. You're not like him. Even when he hurt you, you weren't violent. That's what made you a better person. Not the power to hurt him back, but the power to rise above and help your sister and mom have a good life in spite of it. You found a way to do that peacefully, through your art."

"I've found an even better way now." The danger edging his voice makes the hair along my neck stand up.

Tears singe my eyes. A few slip free and run down my face. They hang at my jawline before dripping down and spattering on my chest.

Jeb finishes the back of my shirt—leaving slits at my shoulder blades for wings—and moves to my front. He studies my face. "You're going to have to stop crying. You'll smear the paint."

"Jeb, please."

"It's not worth the tears," he assures me, though a tremor shakes his voice as he notices the wetness on my chest. He drags a horizontal strip of paint along the bottom of my rib cage and above my navel to form the shirt's front hem. "You're looking at this all wrong. To be able to create your own scenes and landscapes. That means you get to reign over them. Hell, I've given myself wings with my shadow. I can fly with you. Together, we could rule this world and build our own happy endings. I have everything to offer you that Morpheus has." He juts out his chin in thought. "*Had*," he corrects with a smug smile.

My lungs ache, as if he's knocked the breath from me. "I don't want those things from you. I love your faults and imperfections. Your kind heart. The scars that match mine, and the struggles to find ourselves. I want your humanness. Nothing else."

He frowns. What I wouldn't give to witness his lips break into a genuine smile. The one with those dimples I love. My throat hurts, clogged with emotions I'm afraid to unleash.

"I would've followed you anywhere," he mumbles, his voice raw with agony. "All I ever wanted was to spend forever with my best friend. With the girl who gave life to my paintings. But I'm not the one who inspired your mosaics, am I? It was always Wonderland. That's why you chose him."

"*Chose* him? It was a kiss, that's all—"

"It's not the kiss. Sometimes words are louder than actions."

"Words . . . ? What words?"

"The promise you gave him that you couldn't give me."

I growl to keep from crying again. "You're not making sense. Please, tell me what you mean." Maybe Morpheus told him about my vow. If he's been taunting Jeb this whole time about our day together, that would explain some of this animosity. But not all of it.

"No more talking. I need to concentrate." Jeb fills in the lower half of my shirt. He layers paint along the skin beneath my bust line, avoiding where my necklaces hang. I should take them off . . . get them out of his way, but I can't move because the brush is riding the curve of my right breast, coating it so no bandage peeks through.

Jeb's breath catches at the same time as mine. I know his body language, how the muscles work in his jaw when he's struggling to stay in control.

The brush becomes an extension of his hand. It doesn't matter that bristles and a handle stand between us. Even through the bandages, I can feel our connection. There's no heat, or warmth, or pressure. It's a deeper bond, born of friendship and hard-won trust: a summoning beneath the skin, as if my spirit calls to him.

I sip slivers of air with each movement of his brush . . . afraid to breathe too loud, afraid to move. Afraid if I disturb the atmosphere in any way, I'll break the spell he's under. Maybe I *can* bring him back, help him remember the good parts of his human life. Maybe, if I can get him to reach out and hold me, it will remind him of everything we meant to each other.

His hand starts to shake the moment he finishes painting my left breast.

"Jeb." I venture a whispered plea. "All those weeks I was in the asylum, I gave in to my madness, faced those fears. But I never forgot you. Or us. Please, show me you remember, too."

His gaze intensifies on mine. My body aches with longing, familiar with that look from the past.

The palette and brush clatter at my feet as he grabs my face, careful not to smear the paint on my chest. His thumb traces the trails my tears made on my cheek and then nudges the dimple in my chin. His breath cloaks my face, warm and sweetened by the honeycomb-flower he ate earlier.

I run my palm across his chest and lower, seeking his scars through the thin fabric of his T-shirt. Seeking the Jeb I've grown up with. My solid rock in spite of his own brokenness.

He groans. His fingers thread through the hair bunched at the base of my neck. I clutch his shirt, tip my face to kiss the labret at the edge of his lower lip.

With a surprised sound, he breaks my hold and jerks back. Red light reflects off his face. We look down at my neck simultaneously. The diary's pages are glowing.

"What is that thing?" His voice is thick with emotion. The red light flickers in his eyes like candles' flames. His expression changes from curious to mesmerized. He uses his pinky to lift the two strings grazing my collarbone, managing not to touch the dip between my breasts.

"Are those real pages?" he asks.

I push my heartbeat from my throat with a gulp. "It's nothing." I lift the tiny book along with the key over my head and hide them in my fist.

Don't slip away again . . . Please, stay with me . . . Hold me, hold me, hold me.

My silent mantra shatters as he catches and flips my wrist to drop the necklaces onto his waiting palm. The moment they make contact, he curses and flings them across the room. Eyes widened in shock, he opens his fingers.

The diary left an imprint—a red, fiery brand—in the center of his hand.

ROOMS

Jeb pries his palm away as I try to assess the severity of his wound. His mood shifts to accusatory in the blink of an eye. "What do you have inside that book? Why did it burn me?"

"I don't know," I mutter, as much to myself as anyone.

The diary has protected me at least twice while I've been inside this mountain. Does it think Jeb is a danger to me, too?

Is he?

"It's just words," I add. "Magical words. Nothing to do with you." I can't be any more specific, or he'll figure out that I'm planning to search for Red while he and Dad are gone.

Jeb narrows his eyes, as if he doesn't buy it. I'm bewildered, wondering once more where all this animosity and suspicion is coming from.

Dad chooses that instant to step back into the room. He notices my half-painted state and quickly looks away. "Everything okay with you two?"

"Never better," Jeb says.

Dad picks up the duffel and carries it to the table to sift through the supplies with his back turned, an obvious ploy to give us privacy.

Not that we need it. Jeb makes additions—a panel of lace flowing out from my T-shirt's hem to cover my navel and lower back, and fingerless gloves that match—so removed from the motions, I feel as if I am a one-dimensional doll after all, and he's folding paper clothes around me.

When he's done, he leads me to the cheval mirror so I can watch as he taps each painted piece with the brush's tip, now lit with violet sorcery.

The golden pigment on my legs transforms to glittery, footless tights that end at my ankles. They bend and stretch, like spandex. The two flaps of red, ivory, and green plaid he painted from my waist to midthigh form a front and back seam on a miniskirt, and the black cropped T-shirt loosens to a comfortable fit. The ivory skull and gold vines on front puff out as if embroidered with metallic thread.

He takes down my hair, then whisks the paintbrush through my platinum blond waves. I reach up to touch a tiara-like headband of white roses and glistening rubies that match my crimson streak.

For the first time in a month, I feel like me again. Part netherling and part human—and a touch regal.

Jeb's reflection appears behind mine, his chin above my head. He drops the diary and key necklaces into place, careful to touch only the strings. "I can't stress this enough," he says. *"Don't get the clothes wet."*

I turn to thank him for giving me such beautiful things, but he's already across the room, discussing the Wonderland gate mission with Dad.

Back behind my screen, I check under my clothes. The bandages have bonded with the painted outfit, leaving only Morpheus's lacy gifts intact. I pull my Barbie boots over my tights. We decided it was better I have waterproof shoes. As soon as I step out, Dad and Jeb escort me to the lighthouse.

Dad gives me a hug and strict instructions not to budge till they return. Together, they head back to the boat. I'm gloating to myself, laughing at how they've forgotten I can fly, when Jeb stops halfway down the stone stairs, says something to my dad, and returns to where I'm standing.

He grips the doorframe above my head, leaning over me, his strong features lit up by the moon. "I know you're planning to leave," he says.

I stifle a denial, furious he can anticipate my every move when I can't even peel away one layer of his thoughts.

"There are only two ways to get out of this refuge," he continues. "One, the way you came in. I've commanded the graffiti not to hurt you, but also not to let you into that tunnel. You don't have enough rainwater here to erase them all. And if you try to take water from this ocean, it will evaporate as soon as you carry it out of the scene. The other way is the mountain passage, and I'm the only one who controls it."

The netherling in me is impressed by his new role as master manipulator. But the human side, the one who knows this isn't the real Jeb, is afraid of what he's become.

"Take advantage of this time," he insists. "Rest and preserve your strength for Wonderland. It isn't going to be a picnic for you or your dad." The old Jeb flashes into view as he looks hesitant, and I wonder if he's considered what it will mean for us if he stays in AnyElsewhere. That it will be good-bye forever.

He drops his burned hand and squints at the fresh scar. "You never told me what was in that book."

I cradle the diary between my fingers. "I told you it was words."

He huffs. "Well, it looks like words will always stand between us then, huh?" With that, he leaves. "*Sometimes words are louder than actions*" echoes in the scrape of his boot soles on the stone steps.

What could I have said the last time we were together that was so treasonous it tore his faith in us apart?

Gritting my teeth, I slam the door. Despite what Morpheus would have me believe, there's something other than rage, jealousy, and regret eating away at the Jeb I know. Maybe netherling magic is too much for any mortal to harness without going crazy.

I sit on the bed in the tower. Worried about Jeb and Dad's excursion, and disoriented by the perpetual darkness, I leave the canopy curtains open and lie on my side to watch the starry sky through the porthole. I breathe in the salty air, and plan my escape: Once Jeb and Dad have time to leave, I'll seek out Morpheus in the underground rooms. He's bound to know of another exit from the mountain. We'll use the diary to lead us to Red. Although I'm not sure how we'll find our way back afterward.

My eyelids grow heavy and I fall asleep . . .

Somewhere in my dreams, I see glimpses of Mom. Her hair is long now, far past her shoulders and shimmering with a soft, pinkish tint. She looks healthy, aglow with magic. She's with Grenadine in the Red castle, replacing my substitute queen's whispering ribbons in the absence of Bill the Lizard. Each day, Mom gently reminds Grenadine of the things she needs to remember. For that, she's respected and revered by the court's subjects.

But there's a darkness encroaching that respects no one . . . a dusky dread that creeps along the castle walls and seeps into the crevices.

Before it can overtake the palace, Ivory and her knights arrive. Ivory blows a silvery mist that freezes everything it touches, including the card guards. Then she leads Mom and Grenadine somewhere safe. A place of light and glistening hope.

The dream ends, leaving their location a mystery. All I know is Mom has found sanctuary.

Unsure how long I slept, I scramble out of bed and sprint through the door. The moment the night air hits me, I free my wings. Half flying and half hopping, I race down the steps toward the shore. I leap at the last minute. My boots skim the water, then I'm airborne.

I'm reminded of how Mom flew alongside me on prom night. Morpheus once told me that she and I have an unusual bond. That he was able to use her dreams as a conduit into mine. Maybe she's found some way to reverse that power and communicate with me. Maybe by having me here in AnyElsewhere, so close to Wonderland, she's able to break through—because the dream I had feels like a premonition.

My body lightens and I rise higher as if the thoughts of her are giving me lift. The waves shrink, farther and farther below. The whitecaps look like foam on a cappuccino, the water as dark as coffee with only the starlight to see by.

Once inside the mountain hallways, I absorb my wings and head straight to Jeb's studio—the only door that's ajar. The sun is shining, so maybe I didn't sleep too long. I glance at the table and paintbrushes. The one he used on my clothes still glimmers with violet magic.

I take the brush and follow the direction Morpheus turned when escorted by the moths. Five doors line the twisting hallway. I jiggle each knob in passing, not surprised to find them locked.

The first door is fashioned entirely of marbles. The next one's wooden face is marred with cigarette burns. Another is crafted of gnarled bark with a draping of willow leaves. Velvety red rose petals form the next to last one. I stroke the soft flowers and breathe in their delicate fragrance, thoughtful.

"Morpheus!" I call out. Hearing nothing, I decide to open them all—find him by process of elimination. There aren't any keyholes. Come to think of it, each time Jeb unlocks the diamond door, he simply commands the ruby knob to open.

"Open," I say to the door of marbles, but nothing happens. I lift the glowing paintbrush and tap the knob with the bristles. Still nothing. Then I notice the diary necklace is glowing. Not only that, it's reaching toward the doorknob, pulling the string tight around my neck, as if magnetized.

Crinkling my brow, I lean down so it can touch the metal handle. There's a spark and a click. Setting the brush aside, I open the door and step into an exact replica of the entryway at Jenara and Jeb's house.

"Al?" Jenara greets me.

I gasp. Her eyes are dull and emotionless, like Jeb's elfin doppelganger. Her pink hair is pulled up and she wears a funky pair of black-and-white checked leggings with a metallic silver tunic.

"What brings you here?" She acts like it's the most natural thing to see me.

Emotions lodge in my throat. I want to throw myself into her arms. But this isn't Jen. She's nothing more than a hollow reflection of my best friend.

"Mom!" Jen calls. "Al's here! Make us some cookies or something equally Martha Stewart–ish." Linking our arms, Jen leads the way into the shadowy living room.

My skin prickles. She sounds like Jenara. She acts like Jenara. But, in my experience with some of Jeb's creations, she's not to be trusted.

"Hey there, Alyssa." A man's voice originates in the darkest corner of the room, from behind a wooden platform designed with wheels and pulleys. "Is Jeb with you?"

"Um . . . ," I answer, recognizing the voice vaguely.

Jenara flicks on a floor lamp, illuminating the wooden contraption and the JABBERLOCKY'S MOUSETRAP painted on front.

"No," I mumble in disbelief. It's the same device that was at the bottom of the rabbit hole when Jeb and I fell inside the first time. The one that opened the doorway to the flower garden and the madness.

The one that started it all . . .

Jeb's dad stands up behind the wooden maze, tinkering with one of the pulleys. His profile looks young and kind—nothing like the bitter, weathered man he was before he died.

Nausea hits me. Jeb brought him back to life in this kinder version, to relive his ideal family moments. It's sweet, sad, and disturbing.

"Well, he has to be on his way," Mr. Holt says, and faces me full-on. I stifle a moan. His eyes glow orange, flickering like the lit end of a cigarette. When he blinks, ash falls, tumbling down his face and leaving gray streaks. "This is his favorite game, after all." He drops marbles into place on one of the ramps. "And he owes me a rematch."

"You're just hoping he lets you win this time, Dad." Jenara giggles. He winks at her, causing embers to crumble down his cheek.

I shudder. "Uh, I have to go." I back up with both Jen and her dad following.

"But you just got here," Jen says, her voice more threatening than friendly now.

I bump into something soft and mushy and turn on my heel.

"Cookie?" Jeb's plump mom smiles up at me and offers a plate piled with treats. Chocolate chip, bloody razor blade, and broken glass appear to be the flavor of the day.

"I don't belong here," I whisper, unable to tear my gaze from the deadly snacks.

"No, you don't," Mrs. Holt says. "Because we're here to make him happy. And you've made him sad. But we're going to fix that. Eat a cookie."

My gut twists. I sidle toward the center of the room as they surround me, the request becoming a hiss: "Yesssss, we insissst. Jussst one cookie . . ."

The diary at my neck releases a blazing red light. Jeb's pseudo-family leaps away screaming. They land on the floor, a tangled mess of limbs. Pulse hammering, I exit the room and shut them inside, thankful Jeb painted them in their own setting so they can't cross the threshold.

I press my back against the door. Its glassy chill seeps through the slits in my shirt. The marbles must represent making marble ramps with his father, one of Jeb's happiest memories. If that was a pleasant scene, I'm terrified to find what's behind the cigarette-burned door around the next bend.

I'm not sure if it's determination to find Morpheus or my dark side's desire to delve deeper into Jeb's mind, but I move forward.

Using the diary to trigger the latch, I peek inside. A gym with weights, a stationary bike, and a treadmill sit beneath blinking, dim fluorescent lights. There are no occupants, so I step in. A punching bag shaped like an egg hangs a few feet away from a wall of broken mirrors. The front faces me with painted eyes, round cheeks, and a mouth—a creeped-out, nursery rhyme version of Humpty Dumpty.

A hiss comes from the back of the bag. Trembling, I watch as it makes a slow revolution and somehow locks into place in spite of the twisted ropes that wait to unwind.

My breath gusts out of me. It's Mr. Holt's face on the other side. Not a flat drawing, but a flesh-and-bone, three-dimensional face, snarling. *This* is the Mr. Holt I knew: his once handsome features sharpened by anger and discontent, his cheeks hollowed out by too much alcohol and lack of proper nutrition.

His eyes, like the other Mr. Holt's, are formed of lit cigarette butts.

He scowls. "Trip me again. I dare you, worthless little punk. Make me spill my beer. That's what you get. Stop crying, dammit. That's what happens when you leave your toys out. No! Your mom shouldn't have to pick them up for you. It only makes her share your punishment. It's your fault she's bleeding. *Your fault.*"

The childhood pictures I've seen of Jeb's agonized gaze burn into my brain. This is what he suffered every day. I'm amazed he survived at all. No wonder he always blamed himself for what happened to his mom and sister.

Mr. Holt's tongue continues to flap, the words degrading and hate-filled.

Something snaps inside me—the part that wants revenge for all he did to the boy I love. I lash out and slap his lips so hard the sound echoes sharply and my hand stings.

The bag spins around slowly. "Hahaha! Was that supposed to hurt? Your baby sister hits harder than you." Mr. Holt spits out a tooth, some blood, and a stream of obscenities.

I can't move. I actually left a mark on him . . . I cut his lip and broke a tooth. How many times has Jeb been here, pounding his father's face? Judging by the bruises and gashes on this bag, he probably lost count. If he felt as unfulfilled as I do right now, it didn't do him any good.

I rush from the room, my spirit heavy and dismal as I shut the cruel taunts of Mr. Holt behind the door.

Jeb, what have you done to yourself? He's fallen so far into despair and bitterness, it's as if he were dead. A vast hopelessness lodges in my soul and strangles all hope.

Legs heavy, I stumble around another twisting curve in the tunnel and reach the third doorway.

"Morpheus!" I shout again, voice cracking. I don't want to see any more. Jeb's not the boy I once knew, and I don't know how to get him back . . .

Worse, I don't have time to figure it out.

A motorized sound draws me to the door made of bark and willow leaves.

I hesitate. If each door symbolizes what's behind it, this one has something to do with the willow tree that joins my and Jeb's backyards. We used to play chess under it as kids. Then when we became a couple, we'd go there to be alone.

It doesn't make sense that he'd put Morpheus in here, but the vibrating sound hasn't stopped. "Morpheus?" The hum intensifies. I take a breath, tap the knob with the diary, and peer inside.

Snowflakes fall from the rafters. It smells like real snow, though it's not cold on the skin, only glistening. Black lights and fog complement the dreamy atmosphere. Unlike the other two rooms, this one's not demented or disturbing.

It's beautiful.

I step inside, cautious. The front half is decked out like a prom scene: silver pillars wrapped in greenery, an arch swathed in purple velvet, and white tulle draped around a wicker bench. Shiny Mardi Gras masks hang from rafters on varied lengths of string—purple, black, and silver.

A replica of the dress Jenara made me for prom is arranged atop the bench—white lace, pearls, and airbrushed shadows. I inch closer, intrigued by the wrist corsage in a clear plastic box. Upon spotting the ring nestled inside one of the roses—tiny diamonds forming a heart with wings—I drop to the seat, my body weak. It looks exactly like the one Jeb gave me when he proposed. The one I wore on my neck that fused with my Wonderland key and heart locket beneath the press of Morpheus's magic.

I trace the box's lid where a gold ribbon binds it. With one tug, the bow poofs into a golden, glittering fall of letters that form a message in midair—

Things I once hoped to give you:
1. A magical wedding . . .

Choking back tears, I take out the ring and loop it onto the string alongside the diary's key at my neck, tucking it under my shirt to keep it safe.

A picnic basket sits at my feet beneath the bench. There's another ribbon, and when I untie it, more letters form a glimmering parade through the air:

2. Picnics at the lake with your mom and dad . . .

I sniffle and make my way to the middle of the room, where reproductions of my mosaics float next to Sold signs. I tug a ribbon loose and free another message:

3. A lifetime of shared successes and laughter . . .

Overcome with emotion, I turn toward the humming noise along the back wall. A motorcycle idles high up in the rafters, amid strands of white Christmas lights. A bow is tied on the handlebars. I free my wings and rise. Snowflakes and a soft breeze wind around me as I settle atop the seat, returning me to all the times I rode behind Jeb, my arms wrapped around his sturdy form. Completely at ease, yet so unbalanced. So perfectly, erringly human.

I stiffen my chin against a quiver and slip the ribbon loose from the handlebars:

4. Midnight rides across the stars . . .

The lovely words glisten all around me, feeding my need for more. There are too many ribbons and objects to count. I fly from one to another, unwinding more wishes: for little girls with my hair and eyes, and boys who have their mother's stubborn streak; for the safety of one another's arms every night; for growing old together and cherishing every wrinkle, age spot, and gray hair; and on and on and on.

My chest swells—so full it could burst. The room is a shrine to everything I've ever hoped for. Things Jeb wanted to give me. His heart shines in all he created here; his selflessness, his nobility and devotion, the desire to make others happy. His true character hasn't been destroyed. It's just been shelved, suppressed.

My Jeb *is* alive.

I flutter to the ground and reabsorb my wings. I don't want to leave. But before I can help mend Jeb, find Mom, and fix Wonderland, I have to get Morpheus and face Red.

"I'll be back," I whisper, and lock the door behind me.

Two rooms left to explore.

I stop at the rose-petal door. I don't even hesitate this time. One tap of the diary, and I'm inside.

The walls, also lined with red roses, curl overhead and meet in the middle, forming a dome. Tiny clear globes float above me, tin-kling as they bump into one another. They each harbor vivid moving scenes—like miniature silent films.

One in particular catches my attention. Inside, an ashen funnel drops from the sky. Out falls Queen Red in her giant zombie-flower form, along with Jeb and Morpheus. It's the moment they first got to AnyElsewhere. The guys are still wearing their prom clothes, and Jeb has on a half mask.

I capture the globe to watch the scene unfold up close. Red looms over Jeb and Morpheus, casting a long blue shadow. A dis-torted, snarling mouth widens in the midst of her flowery head, and rows of eyes blink on every petal. Her ivy tangles around the guys as they wrestle, trying to escape. Jeb breaks one arm free and digs in his pants pocket, dragging out a knife. Morpheus distracts Red—strong-arming the vines until she slips several more around him to keep control. Jeb saws through his restraints—just like he did when we faced the garden of monstrous flowers on our trip to Wonderland.

Once he's loose, he grabs the severed ivy, using it to bind Red's other limbs and help Morpheus.

Red teeters, then hits the ground, helpless.

As the dust clears, Jeb and Morpheus glare at each other. Still clutching a vine, Jeb rips off his prom mask, shouts something, then turns to walk away. Morpheus jumps him from behind. They fight on the ground and Morpheus ends up on top, wings enfolding them in a tent. The outline of Jeb's face presses against the black, satiny membrane from the other side. He's suffocating. Anger boils up inside me.

The scene ends. Ivory told me weeks ago that Morpheus's actions are where the truth lies. Last year when he used that smothering trick on Jeb, he was knocking him unconscious to be alone with me. So he had to have a reason to want Jeb unconscious this time. And there's only one way to find out what it was.

The moment I turn to go, the remaining globes drop down, insisting I look inside. An uneasy tremor quakes through me with each glimpse. One is an image of Queen Red's mother when Red was young; there are also moments between Red and both her parents—drinking tea, laughing . . . planting flowers; and Red dancing with her father as her mother claps from a distance.

These are all things Jeb can't possibly know. Things only *Red* would know.

Before I can piece together what that means, an image of Charles Dodgson takes shape inside a globe that's floating away. I stretch up to grab it.

He's walking on a flower-strewn path alongside an older, distinguished gentleman. As they stroll beneath some shady trees, the older man's appearance shifts and I see—so clearly—Red wearing the professor's imprint. Just like Hubert said, at the inn.

My heartbeat thunders.

Charles carries a journal filled with handwritten equations and longitude/latitude directions. Together, Charles and Red's professor-imprint step through some shrubbery, coming to stop at the little-boy sundial statue—the gateway to the rabbit hole—that once hid Wonderland's entrance before I destroyed everything.

The image goes dark. I'm about to release the globe when it lights up once more to another scene and a group of people having a picnic. Several children, a mother and a father, and Charles. Alice Liddell's face comes into view. She looks just like the seven-year-old in the picture Mom had hidden in Dad's recliner. This family must be hers . . . the Liddells, close friends with Charles.

Alice's face is alight with excitement as she scampers alone through a haze of vintage spectators. Scones, teacups on lace doilies, and parasols abound. She circles a familiar set of shrubs. Eyes wide with wonder, she stands head-to-head with the sundial statue. It's been pushed aside, exposing the hole underneath.

Two fuzzy white ears appear from within, and a bunny face complete with wriggling nose and endearing whiskers comes into view. Alice gapes as the bunny motions with a pink, padded paw for her to follow. What she doesn't see is the shift of the imprint, and Rabid White's bony hand, old man's face, and white antlers.

The white rabbit disappears back into the hole. Looking around her, Alice hesitates. But the curious light in her eyes burns brighter than her fear, and she plunges in. Queen Red creeps from behind a rosebush and coaxes the sundial statue back into place over the hole, locking it. She's gone before Charles and Alice's father appear, looking for the missing child.

Neither one knows there's a hole beneath the statue, apparent by the bewilderment on their faces. Charles had found the gateway, but never figured out how to open it.

I know the rest of the tale by heart: Alice was missing for days. Then later, after she returned, Charles, a.k.a. Lewis Carroll, wrote her story out on paper. But it wasn't Alice who returned at all. It was Red.

The globe goes dark again and I release it.

I stand in place, numb.

All this time I thought Alice accidentally stumbled into Wonderland. But Red planted the possibility of the nether-realm in Charles

Dodgson's mind as his colleague. When Charles found the sundial statue and nothing more, he figured his calculations were wrong. So instead, the tale blossomed to fiction within his storyteller's imagination. He filled Alice and her siblings' heads with fanciful notions and fairy-tale enticements, made the mistake of mentioning the statue, even took the family to see it during a picnic, never realizing the repercussions.

Red *wanted* Alice to go down the rabbit hole. She arranged for it.

An uncomfortable warmth niggles in my skull—my netherling intuition waking . . . nudging. Either because Red's spirit once shared my body, or because her memories are still on the back burner of my mind, I know that this epiphany is fact, not speculation.

Hubert said Red wanted to improve the netherling lineage. That she thought the humans were better somehow.

What makes human children better? Why does Sister Two steal them and string them up in the garden of souls?

Dreams and imagination . . .

The diary wriggles at my neck, further validation. The forgotten memories on these pages shaped Red's motivations long before she chose to forget them. But the problem is, she did choose to forget. She forgot *why* she wanted to bring dreams into Wonderland.

"I'll bring dreams to our kind, Father. They'll be in abundance everywhere, not just in the cemetery. One day, I'll free the spirits, so they can sleep inside our gardens, brushing our windows at night, and bumping against our feet in the day. I'll bring imagination to our world so everyone might always be with those they treasure."

The only things Red remembered after killing her memories were that she wanted to bring dreams to the nether-realm, and she wanted power and revenge. Somehow, they became one in her mind.

After her husband betrayed her, she had nothing to lose by playing the part of a careless queen, to have herself banished from the kingdom so no one would notice when she disappeared into the human realm.

She trapped a human child in Wonderland and wore her imprint as camouflage so she could breed with a mortal and bring back halfling heirs. Those descendants were supposed to introduce dreams and imagination into the netherling world. But how was setting Wonderland to rights supposed to satisfy her need for revenge and power?

My head feels foggy and bloated. I'm still missing something. A crucial part of her plan.

I look around for more scenes. Up at the center of the domed ceiling, the globes are being crafted by a green, leafy vine, just like the one Jeb had in his hand when Morpheus attacked him after they escaped Red. The vine is suspended in midair without anyone guiding it, giving life to each scene with a glimmer of crimson magic that drips from its tip.

Crimson magic. That was the color of Red's magic in her memories. Morpheus's is blue. Jeb's is *purple*.

I lean against the wall, short of breath from the overpowering scent of roses.

How could I have missed it? When Jeb fell into this world wrapped in those vines, he absorbed a part of Red's magic, along with a part of Morpheus's—who was also trapped. And I'd bet my life Morpheus already knows. It explains why the images in this room belong to Red, and why the graffiti attacked me. It explains why Jeb seems like someone else . . . and why Red's forgotten memories scorched him through the diary.

The carpet beetle's words echo in my mind: *Repudiated memories . . . want revenge against the one who made and discarded them.*

The memories on the diary's pages sensed Red's remnants inside Jeb and his creations, and wanted revenge. It was never about protecting me at all.

Nearly tripping over my boots, I back out of the door. It slams shut behind me.

Red is a part of Jeb. So how can I destroy Red's spirit and end her forever without killing him, too?

ARMOR

The final door is free of embellishments or design. Of course Jeb would craft a plain entrance for Morpheus's room.

I rush inside and tuck the diary necklace under my shirt next to the key and the ring, expecting Jeb's moths to be standing guard. Instead, I'm hit by hookah tobacco, scented of charcoal and plums and carried by a gentle breeze. An ultraviolet mushroom the size of a truck tire sits in the distance. The cloud of smoke settles across it like heavy fog over a village.

A circle of trees twines together to form a domed roof. A lavender sky peeks through the canopy, casting moving shadows. Tiny lights bedeck the branches.

Morpheus's lair looks just as it did when Jeb and I visited Wonderland, and when I visited during childhood dreams, learning how to be a queen.

Speckled with lime green moss and bright yellow lichen, the ground feels springy under my plastic soles. Happy memories of playing childish games with Morpheus nearly overwhelm me, entangled with all the confusing adult emotions he's awakened over the past year.

Sprites drop down from the trees, luminous and temperamental. They shake their fists at me, intolerant of my presence like most of Jeb's creations. When they start darting at me like marble-size hail, hard enough to leave welts, Nikki comes to my rescue with Chessie close behind. They round up the others and herd them toward the hookah haze. The sprites' grumbles clang like silverware being tossed in a drawer as they retreat into the cloud.

"Carousing Cap!" Morpheus shouts from inside.

Chessie and Nikki dart out and disappear through the trees in search of Morpheus's missing hat.

"You sent them after the wrong one," I protest. "We won't be doing any celebrating."

"There's a pity." Morpheus's voice floats out from the cloud, as sultry as the smoke that carries it. "You're certainly dressed for it. Your mortal has outdone himself." He puffs and a wisp of smoke drifts toward me. "I suppose, though, since we shan't be showing off your stunning ensemble, we could find a waterfall to play in. I'd like a peek at those gifts I sent you last night."

The skin under my lingerie tingles. I stiffen my chin, determined not to let him see his effect on me. "I saw the rooms."

"Ah," comes his disembodied answer without a hint of surprise.

"Well, before you rain down all the usual accusations, I should clarify that I wasn't going to let you kill Red. Not until we flush her from your mortal toy's system."

I fake a laugh. "Right. You want Jeb dead as much as her. Two birds with one stone."

"If that were true, he wouldn't be here now. When we landed, the goon birds started swarming overhead. They prefer live food, so I faked killing Jebediah. I hid him to protect him, just as I've been doing ever since."

Taking a few steps closer, I stub the toe of my boot on a baseball-size rock. I pick it up, rolling its smooth surface between my lacy gloves. "You're not protecting him. You're hoarding him. He's your crown jewel. With the magic he rations out to you, everyone treats you like a king—" I stop myself short because it's a role Morpheus will play again for real, if I pledge my eternal future to him one day.

His deep chuckle curls up on a tail of smoke. "Does it ever disarm you, Alyssa . . . how well we see through one another? It does me." His voice softens on the admission—a depth of vulnerability he doesn't often use.

Of course it disarms me; everything about him does. I toss the rock from one hand to another. "Birds of a feather. Yada yada yada. The cliché is kind of boring."

"I rather like to think of us more as moths of a flame. And trying to predict which of us might get burned first is far from boring, luv."

A trickle of excitement drizzles through me at the underlying challenge. "You realized Jeb had been touched by magic. That's why you saved him."

Another chuckle thickens the smoke around the mushroom cap. "I saw crimson dribbling from the end of the vine and the purple light under his shirtsleeve. Somehow, the iron dome caused a magnetic reaction, merging my and Red's magic into him. Yes."

"So, that's when you came to the mountain?" I press.

"Jebediah did a sketch with some mud out in the open. His creation came alive. So we made a makeshift paintbrush and paints. With those, he hollowed out the mountain and tamed the ocean and its inhabitants by altering the existing world. It's how his landscapes work: He reshapes the water into lakes and moats . . . molds the terrain to mountains, hills, or valleys. Each time I venture out, he changes my surroundings to keep the wildlife confused and clear of my path. But this ability has emotional limitations. Though he has no trouble conjuring landscapes and crafting creatures, when it comes to his more personal paintings, he's plagued by an artist's block. And the less satisfied he is with the results, the deeper he falls into despair, which gives Red's magic a tighter hold on his muse."

My eyes water, either from the smoke or my fear for Jeb's sanity. His warning to Morpheus when I first saw them together in the studio makes sense now: *Remember what happened when her face turned up in my paintings.* "Something went wrong when he tried to paint me."

"He could never get you right. You were missing legs and arms. Gaping holes in your face. Just like the self-portrait he made."

My stomach knots. "But I thought the other paintings attacked CC."

"Sometimes the paintings attack one another. But that one was Jebediah's doing. He can't see past the broken image that his father trained him to see. So he cannot paint himself whole. It's why he finally painted it as an elfin knight, in a last-ditch attempt. Same was true of you. His confusion and anger kept getting in the way of perfection. He hid in that willow-tree room, trying to get you right . . . trying to make an image 'worthy of your memory.' The only way I could get him to come out, to live again, was to abduct each of your facsimiles. I led them to the water and watched them dissolve to nothing. They were so horribly disfigured it was inhumane to keep them alive, but our tortured artist didn't have the strength to destroy them. So I did it for him. I convinced him the best way to be free was to stay out of the willow room. To avoid reminders of you, and embrace his anger."

I lean against a tree and press the cool rock against the ring hanging under my shirt, to ease the pricking sensation in my chest behind it. No wonder rage and violence are ruling Jeb's heart. He's subsisting on powers siphoned from two of the most potent, brilliant, and manipulative Wonderland denizens. He's at war with himself trying to contain it. Just like I used to be. Yet his struggle is greater, because he's two parts netherling to one part human.

I close my eyes. "He must've felt so alone."

There's a grunt inside the cloud. "Truly, Alyssa. You wound me. I'm grand company."

My eyes snap open. "You *lied* to him. You didn't want him to know it was Red's magic that was making him hate me. How did you pull that off? He had to see those memories in the rose-petal room."

"In spite of the magic he wields, your mortal is out of his element here. He's had no one to trust but me. No one to confide in but the source of his power. So when I told him the images in the rose-petal room were my memories, of times I'd spent with the royal family, he had no reason to question my sincerity."

I tighten my fingers around the rock. "*Sincerity.* Like you know what that is. You let him get eaten up by her hatred just to drive a wedge between us."

Morpheus clucks his tongue from inside his clouded veil. "Had he known about Red, he would've turned her magic against me. Killed me with a flick of his wrist. It was self-preservation. The fact that it put distance between the two of you, that was simply a fringe benefit." A tendril of smoke lifts free and breaks into vaporous shapes: hearts, rings, music notes.

I growl. "Yeah. Anything that gives you an advantage." I wave away a smoky heart, breaking it in half.

A large, dark wing cuts the smoke and disappears again, enveloped in the haze. "You've driven me to it. You have that boy on such a high pedestal. It's far too slippery up there for one so unprincipled as a solitary fae. It's not as if I haven't tried to drag him down. I looked inside his soul. Hoped to find his weaknesses. Only to discover that even those could be considered strengths under the right circumstances."

"Wait. *What?*" I glare at the cloud, wishing he would come out and face me. "What do you mean, you looked inside his soul?"

"I rode the memory train a few months after you left Wonderland. Before you and Jebediah visited on the day of your prom. How's that for sincerity?"

Hot fury blossoms in my face. "You spied on his lost memories? You had no right!" The branches overhead start to shake, as if triggered by my outburst. The diary heats up against my shirt, becoming effulgent.

"Oh, please," Morpheus taunts. "Save your righteous indignation for someone who has not stood eye to eye with your manipulative side. You did no less, viewing your mum's memories. Your father's.

Red's. By the by, using a toy diary enchanted by a child's love-magic to hold repudiated memories at a safe distance . . . bloody brilliant. If I weren't already head over heels for you, that stunt would've pulled the rug out from under me and left me flailing flat on my back."

I clench the diary under my clothes. "How did you know it was her forgotten memories inside?"

"The same way you know Red has poisoned your mortal toy's muse. Netherling intuition and superior reasoning. Proving once again that you and I are alike in more ways than you care to admit."

"We're nothing alike." A lie, and I know it. Even worse, he does. "My motivations are honorable. I stole Red's memories to stop her from ruining anyone else's life."

"A queenly enterprise indeed. But it all comes down to this one truth: You are a lady of *action*, and I am a man of same. We excel at risks and trickery, and won't hesitate to use them if it's the only way to preserve what we love. Which is why, in spite of my ethical shortcomings when compared to your cardboard-cutout prince, you will ultimately choose *me*."

His certainty seeps into my brain, making a mockery of my own irresolution. "It's more than that. It's choosing which side of me to embrace, and which one to turn my back on. I *will* fix Wonderland. And I'll be there each time the nether-realm needs me." I'm almost woozy from the burn in my heart, as if it's been scored down the middle with a hot knife. Red's fingerprint is getting deeper by the hour. "But I can't choose beyond that yet." *Not without falling to my knees from the pain.*

"And that, my plum, is where your selfishness comes full circle, and it's confirmed without a doubt that you are a malicious queen of the Red Court through and through."

"Enough!" Control snapping, I chuck the rock into the hookah smoke. It sails straight through without stopping and clunks to the ground on the other side of the mushroom. Morpheus's mocking laughter spurs me to toss another one, but two holes in the cloud offer little satisfaction. I want to launch every rock in my path as a missile until Morpheus is a piece of Swiss cheese.

My magic has proven useless against Jeb's creations, but Red's memories can affect them. Maybe I can coax out the power on the diary's pages, pit it against my magic. Like the Gravitron ride, use two forces against one another to elicit a volatile reaction.

The harder I concentrate, the hotter the book gets against my skin. The red glow gushes through my sternum and into my veins. I breathe it in until it boils my blood and bubbles over, then redirect the force to lift the rocks from the ground. Overhead, the branches on the trees snap down and hit my makeshift ammunition with a satisfying *thwack*, sending it shuttling through the haze to leave ragged holes. The cloud begins to dissipate.

"*At last*," Morpheus says in an overly exhausted tone. "Must it always take my goading for you to realize you have no limitations other than what you place on yourself?"

I can't see him yet, but the sprites are there, bouncing in mid-air and snickering. They stick out their tongues, then flitter away between branches, wandering off in the direction Chessie and Nikki took.

The remainder of smoke dissolves like cotton shredding into the sky, fully exposing the mushroom. Balanced flat across the top is a large moth, dark wings flapping low and wide. Its proboscis sips from the hookah pipe and releases another chain of stars and hearts.

"Wait," I say, anger melting away to confusion. "You can't be in moth form. You can't use your magic. It's all illusions."

"That it is, My Queen." His voice tickles the cusp of my right ear, even though I'm still staring at him on the mushroom. "Just like you, using Red's repudiated memories to give the illusion of power against our pseudo elf's paintings. Well done, by the way."

I twist but can't find anyone around me. "This isn't real."

"It is as real as you want it to be." His whisper teases the left side now, a flourish of tantalizing heat along my neck.

I turn, but he's nowhere to be seen.

The moth flaps its wings, slow and lazy on its perch. At the same time, the feel of soft lips trails down the nape of my neck. Unwelcome pleasure blooms through me at his touch. "How are you in two places at once?"

"Optical delusion," answers his voice from behind. He draws me close with invisible hands around my waist.

Invisible hands . . .

"The simulacrum." I trail my fingers along his unseeable arms. "That's why the suits weren't in the duffel bag. You stole them."

"And you made it all possible by stealing them first. You wise and wicked girl."

As much as I try to fight it, the netherling in me glows at his praise. My skin sparkles like starlight, reflected in tiny prisms on the ground and trees.

Morpheus coaxes me to face him and slips the simulacrum hood off his head. His wild hair moves in the breeze, the jewels tipping his eye markings glimmer a passionate purple, and the smile that greets me is both savage and playful. The rest of him comes into view as reality bleeds through the simulacrum's mirage—silver jacket over a T-shirt, black pants, blue tie, and magnificent wings folded against his back.

I rest my palm on his chest to ensure he's not a hallucination. "You took the suits so we could sneak past the graffiti guards after Jeb left."

He steps back, peels off the enchanted fabric, and bows with a flourish.

"It was a good plan," I admit as he straightens his clothes and preens his wings. "But we don't have a means for you to fly, or to find our way back."

He smirks again. "Of course we do, silly truffle. Don't you know I always think of everything?" Hands on my shoulders, he turns me to the giant moth at rest on the mushroom. "Look through your netherling lenses."

I refocus and find it's not one single moth. It's a hundred or more, clasped together to mimic a larger one. These are the moths that escorted Morpheus here under Jeb's direction. And the mushroom isn't typical, either. Its top is hollowed out, with a small door in its side and a harness connected to the moth.

"That was going to be your ride?" I ask on a whisper.

"*Our* ride." Morpheus claps his hands. Giant wings beat gusts all around us as the moth tugs the mushroom free from the ground. Together they rise, like a hot air balloon and its basket—graceful and majestic. The tree branches open to let the contraption escape far, far up into the sky.

I gawk at its ascent.

"And," Morpheus says, "we have tea service planned for the trip. The spritelings have gone to fetch us some victuals."

"But . . . how? The mushroom can't exist outside of Jeb's setting here. Right?"

Morpheus pulls slick blue gloves onto his hands. "It can now that I've reassigned it."

"What?"

"Jebediah's creations are one-half magic, the other half artistic vision. So although I cannot change his masterpieces to another form, they are *convincible*, if one but imagines them a new purpose. Granted, it works better on the paintings that have no specific command from him. The mushrooms here have no assignments other than to look pretty. And his instruction for the moths to keep me busy was too open-ended. They accepted whatever scenario I imagined, so long as I was in fact keeping busy."

I shake my head. The master of word manipulation strikes again.

The moth carrier bounces atop the air currents, carrying my curiosity to new heights. "But you're a full-blood netherling. You don't know how to use your imagination."

"On the contrary. I do. Thanks to you. I followed your example in our childhood. I absorbed it without even realizing. Then, when I was stuck here deprived of my magic, I had to find something to while away those weeks and hours. Perhaps that was the silver lining to this entire debacle. The lack of magic is what leads humans to fantasize in the first place. And Alyssa, what a wonderfully powerful force an imagination can be."

His expression is awestruck, exactly the way he used to look at me during our childhood escapades. How inconceivable, that I was his teacher, too. He once told me I was, but I never grasped what he meant until now.

Ivory's words about Wonderland from weeks ago rise and bounce on the wind, much like Morpheus's flying apparatus: *For so long, innocence and imagination have had no place there . . . Morpheus experienced those things via you . . . Through your child . . . our offspring will become true children once more; they will learn to dream again. And all will be right with our world.*

Morpheus has always had dream manipulation; he's different from any other netherling in that respect. Now that he's learned to harness imagination, too, it makes him the only full-blood netherling who could father a dream-child.

The diary warms against my chest. Such a child would fall right into Red's plan. Discomfort itches my throat as it hits me: She's had so many pawns lined up on her chessboard. Her husband, her sister. Rabid White, Carroll, Alice, Mom, me. And Morpheus. Most of all, Morpheus.

"Do you want her for your own?" Queen Red's words resurface in my memory from that agonizing moment over a year ago, when Red inhabited my body and tried to make Morpheus help her break my will.

"So very much—" he had said.

"Then do my bidding. She'll be yours physically, and there the heart and soul will follow in time. You can romance your way into her good graces. You shall have forever to win her."

Red was using Morpheus even then. She was holding all the cards. He didn't know about the child at that point. Not until he saw Ivory's vision just a few months ago. Ivory specified that, and out of all the netherlings, I believe in her honesty the most.

But how can a child that Morpheus and I share give *Red* power?

"Alyssa?"

I must be gaping again, because he taps my chin, nudging my mouth closed.

"Where did your mind wander just now?" he asks.

I need to tell him that I've seen the vision of our son. I need his input on how this could tie into Red's revenge. But I have to analyze the wording of my vow to Ivory. There must some way around it . . . some way to tell Morpheus without *telling* him.

The tinkling sprites return and drop a silky cloth on top of my head. Morpheus drags it off and holds up what appears to be a garment bag. He scowls at the sprites. They clap and twirl in midair, as if they've discovered buried treasure.

"Naughty little spritelings," Morpheus admonishes. "That's not what I told you to fetch. I sent for a picnic basket, yes?"

They flitter around my head, pointing at me, their cheeks growing fat and red as they throw aerial temper tantrums.

"Well, I suppose this *is* the time to give it to her," he concedes. "But I should be the one to open it."

The sprites unite in a wave and shove the bag toward me.

"Fine." With a sigh, Morpheus hands it over.

"What is this?" I ask.

"Just be careful," he instructs.

I loosen the drawstring and thousands of thin, shimmery monarch wings billow out from the opening. It's a hoard of scorpion flies!

A scream erupts from my throat.

Morpheus takes the bag back as the sprites' laughter rings in my ears—a melody of mocking jingle bells.

"I told you to be careful," he scolds, and peels off the bag. The wings aren't attached to bugs at all; they're part of a gown, each wing meticulously hand sewn to form tiers. Jeweled centipede legs are embroidered along their razor-sharp edges to make them safe to the touch. The fringe adds a green, glitzy glimmer to the red, orange, and black display. The bodice is sleeveless and fitted, while the skirt poufs out to a knee-length hem.

The tiers shimmy in the breeze and produce a metallic jangle like a hundred tiny chains.

I can't believe my eyes. "You *made* this? For me?"

Morpheus rakes a hand through his hair, leaving several blue strands reaching up like the tree branches around us. "I knew you'd be coming to end Red. I rather hoped you'd wear it to face her. It is the only coat of armor worthy of your dangerous beauty."

"Armor?" I can't stop looking at his rumpled hair. "This is incredible. How many times did you risk your life to make it?"

"Oh, come, Alyssa. I know my way around a needle and thread. Sewing is hardly fatal."

I laugh, reminded of our childhoods when he would string moth corpses onto threads and fasten the morbid strands to his hats for decoration. An eccentric habit he practices to this very day. "Seriously. You could've ended up a stone statue. Or sliced to pieces. How many wings did it take?"

He shrugs. "I lost count after one thousand seven hundred and twenty-two." A sideways smirk curls his lips.

I grin. There's still something in the bag. I drag out a pair of crimson knee boots made of leathery material, along with shoulder-length gloves and leggings to match. "Are these painted?"

"Oh, they're very real. Made entirely of a bat's hide. The creatures are quite huge once full-grown. I had my griffon round one up for me." He puts everything away then cinches the garment bag closed and hands it off to the sprites.

I wind my hands in my miniskirt as the tinkling little netherlings disappear through the trees again. "You always keep me on my toes."

He surprises me by catching me around my waist. "Then I shall have to amend my strategy. My intent was to sweep you off your feet."

Before I know what he's doing, he lifts me, my boots dangling at his shins. He spins us both, wrapping us in his wings until I'm dazed and giggling.

"I wanted to lift you above me and swing you in circles until we were both dizzy and laughing," he murmurs against my neck as we tumble to the ground, trapped beneath his tented wings.

My body aches on impact—but it's a delicious ache. I can hardly breathe with the weight of his ribs covering mine, with the scent of his tobacco surrounding me, smothering and intoxicating. The curve of his smiling mouth glides along my collarbone and I gasp at the velvety sensation. I force his head up so I can look at him . . . break the spell.

He slips the bejeweled headband from my hair, sweeping stray strands from my face. The slickness of his gloves grazes my eye markings.

"I wanted to kiss your lips and share your breath," he says softly as he leans close.

It hits me that he's fulfilling the desires listed in the note he sent with the lingerie.

I remember the last kiss we shared—the taste of his tongue, the way it made my spirit soar but trampled Jeb's into the ground.

Jeb—who's out there with Dad, trying to pave the way so we can get to Mom. Even with Red's hatred seeping through him, he's still endangering his life to help me.

I push against Morpheus's shoulders. "I—I'm not ready—"

He lifts my hands over my head and holds them against the itchy, phosphorescent grass, pinning me in place. His grasp is gentle enough that I could break free at anytime.

"You came here to destroy Red," he says. "Which means you *are* ready . . . ready to claim your throne because you've embraced your love for Wonderland. And lest you forget, *I* am Wonderland. As are you." Even in the eclipse of his wings, the sparkle from my skin lights up his face. He drags me into that inky gaze framed within long lashes, sets me adrift in the madness and beauty there.

"Jebediah has given up on you, but I never will. I can offer you the security you desire. If you'll but be mine, your heart will forever be sheltered in my care. Yes, we will quarrel incessantly and fight for dominance. And yes, there will be ravishes of passion, but there will also be gentle lulls. That is who we are together. You'll never need fear that your love is not reciprocated. For although you've made me feel things I am not equipped for . . . I cannot *stop* feeling them." His chin quavers. "You opened Pandora's box within me. Set loose the imaginings and emotions of a mortal man. And there is no closing it ever again." The jewels under his eyes twitch between dark purple and blue. "As much as I abhor being anything akin to human, Alyssa, I wouldn't dare try to close it. Because that would mean losing you."

The confession is lovely and brutal—laced with honesty that I not only hear in the rasp of his voice, but feel in the quaking of his muscles as he holds my hands over my head.

"You think me egocentric and incapable of sincerity," he continues, entwining our fingers so the scars beneath my lace are pressed to his gloved palms. "'Tis true. Your mortal knight was willing to die for you with no way out, selfless to a fault. I had the vorpal sword when I let the bandersnatch take me in your place; I knew I had a means of escape. Perhaps that made Jebediah's sacrifice greater. But I have made sacrifices, too. I stayed away so many years after our childhood, after your mum went to the asylum, so you could live your life."

"Because you'd made a life-magic vow to her; you didn't have a choice . . ." I stop short of telling him that I know only too well how binding those vows can be.

"Yes. But I let you leave again, last year after you were crowned. And all those nights I brought you to Wonderland in your dreams, even though it pained me for you to abandon our dreamscapes and return to the mortal realm, I let you go each morning to live your reality there. It may not seem much when compared to your mortal's gallantry. But for me—self-seeking, arrogant prig that I am—that is the sincerest form of sacrifice. Letting you go. Do you not see that?"

Empathy claws through me. I struggle to find some word of gratitude or apology, but nothing seems sufficient. All I can do is nod.

As if waiting for that signal, he releases my hands, cups my face, and whispers in my ear. "My precious Alyssa, share reality with me. Give me forever. We will wreak such beautiful havoc together."

Temptation shimmers through my blood, a taste of eternal power and pandemonium. His soft lips glide across my jaw. I'm dazzled by his touch, drugged by his promises, falling deeper and deeper into him. Before he reaches my mouth, I catch his hands and roll him off until he's the one on his back, his wings no longer a hiding place but silky black pools along the ground.

I prop my top half over his so I'm in control. "I can't think," I whisper. "You're making me crazy."

"Insanity is the most pristine clarity." He winds a leg around my hips and topples me onto him. "Let the lunacy in. Let it be your guide." One corner of his mouth lifts to a boyish grin.

I push myself up on my elbows. I haven't seen him this relaxed since we were playmates: bits of grass strewn through his hair, clothes messy and wrinkled. Even his T-shirt has come untucked. He stretches languorously under me, and the silvery scar on his abdomen catches the light, that telltale mark from Sister Two when he fought her inside Butterfly Threads just weeks ago. When he almost died to help me and Jeb escape. But I didn't let him die, because I couldn't imagine a world without him.

I can't imagine a future without him, either. Not anymore.

Following a dark instinct and a darker desire, I touch the scar. His taut skin twitches and he catches a breath.

I jerk my hand away.

He snatches my arm and drags me back down so our noses touch. "It's beautiful," he says, his breath fragrant and fruited. "The mark left by your love when you saved my life. It matches the ones on your palms, from the first time you saved me. Again and again, your actions pay tribute to your true feelings. But I want to hear the words." His lips caress my jaw and stop at my ear. *"Say them."*

His low, purring voice electrifies my skin. The Wonderland queen thrashes to life. She shines light on the sentiment hidden inside the blackest corners of my heart, until I can no longer deny it.

I seek out his eyes, entranced by the depth of emotion there. "I care about you . . ." It's a shallow, inadequate reply. The deepest truth freezes on my tongue: *The netherling in me loves you, passionately.*

Those words are too chilling, fragile, and extraordinarily unique to release; they might vanish like snowflakes if exposed to the heat of reality too soon.

But Morpheus is done waiting. He drags me closer, pressing my lips to his and kissing me in warm, exquisite strokes.

It happened too fast. I never saw it coming.

Oh, but my netherling side did, and she casts my human armor aside.

She guides my hands, knots my fingers through his hair, teases his tongue with hers. She won't let me pull away, because she wants to be there again. In Wonderland, where his tobacco-flavored kisses always take us . . .

Because the things I loathe are the things she adores: His snark, his infuriating condescension. His menacing mastery of half-truths and riddles. The way he shoves me into the face of danger, forces me to look beyond my fears and reach for my full potential.

Most of all, because he encourages me to believe in the madness . . . in *her* . . . the darker side of myself: the queen who was born to reign over the Red kingdom and to give Wonderland a legacy of dreams and imagination.

His gloved palms seek the bend of my waist, the bow of my hips. He moves me on top of him, so close there's not enough space for a blade of grass between us. His kisses grow insistent, desperate. His flavor winds through me, fruit and smoke and earth, and other things born of shadows and storms . . . things I can't put a name to.

I'm carried far away where flames lap at my skin, blinding orange and yellow and white. Heat singes my nostrils.

I'm on the sun. Not an earthly sun, but Wonderland's. Morpheus is with me, wearing a ruby crown. Together, we're waltzing barefoot inside the fiery core, unaffected by the inferno swirling around us, aware only of our dance. Glowing embers gild our wings. My red gown, made of roses and netting and lace, catches a spark and burns away. His beautiful crimson suit does the same, dispersing like ash. Our spirits mirror our flesh, all secrets and desires laid bare. We're free, face-to-face, on equal ground . . . with nowhere left to hide but inside each other. He opens his arms and I go to him, no hint of reservation.

The image fades. I'm on top of Morpheus again, fully clothed on the grass. It must have been a vision, like the one Ivory had of a banquet and a child, a glimpse of a future bequeathed to me by my crown-magic.

The profoundness courses through me, yet I can't forget my humanness and my love for a mortal man who painted a room filled with beautiful dreams, a man who's lost his way and needs me now more than ever.

That pressure on my heart scores through my chest, stealing my breath. I push free and gulp for oxygen as I scramble to stand.

"*Jeb*," I mumble.

Morpheus snarls and gets to his feet, tucking in his shirt. He sweeps grass from his pant legs and straightens the tie at his neck. "That was a sorely disappointing proclamation of love. Perhaps you'd do better writing a sonnet, preferably with the omission of the letters *J*, *E*, and *B*."

"I'm sorry." I grind a knuckle into my sternum to ease the burning sting. "I have to do the right thing, for everyone. I just don't know what it is. All I know, is everyone needs something different.

You, Jeb, my parents, Wonderland. I want to rip myself apart . . . be two beings altogether."

Morpheus frowns. "Don't ever say that, Alyssa. It is dangerous to wish for such things."

"Why? I can't change that I have two sides to my heart. No matter how much I wish it."

"You should ne'er even think it. The only way you will ever find peace is if your two sides learn to coexist. You would not be the girl I shared a childhood with, without them both."

His touching admission makes me consider something I haven't yet. "The girl you helped shape to be a queen." I look to the sky ceiling, drowning in my own indecision. "You always told me I was the best of both worlds. Taught me to embrace both my magic and my imagination. Now, I have two inner voices to follow. Each one is drawn to a different life in a different world. I'm hurting everyone because I'm confused. And I *hate* it." I turn to him. "Maybe that's what makes me want to hate you."

He studies my features, silent and stoic, and I wonder if at last he regrets everything he taught me, everything he brought me into.

I skim my fingertips over the jewels flashing through gloomy hues across his face. "But hate is the furthest thing from what I feel for you. The very furthest thing."

He captures my hand and presses my lace-covered palm to his chest, trailing his thumb across my knuckles.

I shove the tender moment aside to give my mind's wheels freedom to turn. "You said we're going to flush Queen Red out of Jeb so I can destroy her, forever. How are we supposed to do that without hurting him?"

Morpheus bends to pick up my tiara, returning it to my hair

and smoothing away wispy locks. "That, luv, will require the biggest sacrifice of all." His thumb follows the strings at my neck. "And you're the one who will have to make it."

He doesn't get the chance to explain before the door to the room flings open, revealing Jeb at the threshold. Even though he's insisted that we're over, déjà vu echoes through my conscience, as if I've been caught betraying him again.

That worry fades once his appearance registers: dripping blood, wild hair, pale face, and anxious expression. The feathers on his costume have fallen out—a bird that barely survived a cyclone. Worst of all, Dad's not with him.

"Jeb, where . . . ?"

His gaze pierces us with otherworldly light. "Both of you. Come with me. Hurry."

WATER & STONE

We sprint to the art studio. I'm one step behind the guys, trailing alongside Chessie and Nikki, who fling Morpheus's requested cap at him as we rush down the corridor.

When we arrive, agonized groans greet us, and dread clenches my chest. The studio is shadowed. Hazy indigo light streams through the glass roof, remnants of dusk. A figure lies on the table, writhing in pain.

"Dad!" I shove past Morpheus where he's stalled in the doorway, cap clenched to his sternum.

Jeb's already at the table, giving Dad his hand to squeeze.

Tears strangle me. For weeks I've been worried about Mom, when it was Dad who was in danger all along. Why couldn't my visions have shown me that?

I press my palm to his chest. His ticklish, feathery costume muffles his rapid heartbeat. "Wh-wh-what happened?" I ask.

Jeb concentrates on Dad's face. "I couldn't stop them."

"Stop who?" I press.

Instead of answering, Jeb growls—a guttural sound tangled with rage and remorse. I want to comfort him, but I also want to shake him. For letting my dad get hurt, for going without me.

Morpheus steps between us. "Patience, luv. Our elfin knight finally realizes he's not the god he thought he was."

My brain clutters with little-girl fears. "Daddy." I lean over him, sniffling. "Daddy, look at me."

His eyes flutter, but don't open.

"We followed the glow, landed close to the abyss of nothing," Jeb mumbles, his voice quavering and husky from his earlier outburst. "The knights at the Wonderland gate could see us. They used their medallion and sent a wind tunnel. We were waiting to be picked up . . . but we were attacked. The queen's guards shook up a cage filled with scorpion flies and released a swarm. I tried to get out my sketchpad, to draw nets to capture them . . . like the ones I make for you." He shoots a glance to Morpheus.

"Your magic failed," Morpheus suggests.

"*I* failed," Jeb says, eyes on Dad again. "The sound got into my head. Louder than a million locusts trapped inside a concert hall."

Dad wails, rocking his head back and forth, trying to cover his ears. "Make it stop!"

"What's he talking about?" I ask.

"He's been saying that since he was stung," Jeb answers. "It's like he still hears them buzzing."

"He was *stung*?" Is it me who asks the question? I'm not sure. Everyone's voices are distant, and my body feels compressed, like I'm swimming through sludge at the bottom of the ocean.

"CC was able to kill most of them, and I came out of it enough to capture the others . . . but a couple got loose. I'm sorry, Al." Jeb still won't look at me.

Morpheus strips off his jacket, drags a sloshing bucket from beneath the table, and fills a sponge. "Where did they sting him?"

"His left leg, I think," Jeb mutters.

"No. It isn't true." I push between them, gripping one of Morpheus's biceps. "You said those things turn people to stone. He's not stone, see?"

He peels my hand away. "We need to get him out of this costume, to assure he's only been stung in one place."

"This can't be happening!" I shout.

Morpheus forces me to face him. "If he was stung only on his leg, it buys us time since it's farther from his heart. Now get something to keep him warm. He's about to be very wet."

Chessie lights on my shoulder, patting my neck in a comforting gesture. Nikki takes me by my pinky and leads me to a peg where a drop cloth hangs. I lift it off. I'm no longer underwater. I'm flittering somewhere far away, tethered by a bungee cord that keeps snapping me back to something I don't want to be a part of. Filmy twilight seeps through the glass ceiling, magnifying my disorientation.

I hand off the cloth to Jeb. "This can't be happening. It can't."

Neither guy answers. They cover Dad to his shoulders, then use sopping sponges to melt off his costume underneath.

Strange, stupid conjecturing fills my head. The drop cloth isn't melting. And what about the table? Won't the water destroy it, and Dad fall crashing through? Maybe it's not a painting; maybe it's like the honeycomb-flowers, bat hide, rabbit meat, and rainwater. Something derived from the raw resources in this place.

All questions fade as I see the serious expressions on Jeb and Morpheus's faces.

I move to the front end of the table and nuzzle the top of Dad's hair, my fingers curled around his ears. "You're going to be okay, Dad. Mom needs you to be okay. We both need you." The scents of maple syrup, laundry detergent, and lemon cleaner surround me. It makes no sense he'd smell that way. My brain must be playing tricks because he's always been home, safety, and comfort to me.

Dad pummels the back of his head against the table, his face screwed up in pain.

I shove my hands under the nape of his neck to protect his skull from the hard wood. "Do something!" I shout.

Jeb finally looks my way. "Al, we're trying."

For the first time, I get a glimpse at his face. He looks just like the little boy in the pictures at his house. Lost, tortured, haunted. The only difference is the blood on his cheek and the labret glistening beneath his lip.

I'm about to ask him if he's hurt, too, when I catch sight of my dad's ankle sticking out from the edge of the cloth. His skin is white, dry, and powdery like cement. The hair has fallen off. A thousand minuscule lights glint off his skin, like a sidewalk under an evening sky.

He *is* turning to stone.

My windpipe nearly closes. "Use your magic!" My voice sounds like a boiling teapot—airy and whistling. "The paintbrush. Heal him like you did Morpheus's ear." I grab Jeb's arm. "Please."

He and Morpheus exchange guarded glances.

"It only works on Morpheus because we share magic," Jeb answers, his expression filled with so much regret it reaches beyond his enchanted state, making him appear raw and human. "Wait." He furrows his brow. "Your dream-magic. Thomas is a human. He can slip into dreams."

Morpheus nods, catching on where I'm oblivious. "The poison spreads through the bloodstream, spurred by the victim's agitation. If we can subdue him to a REM state—send his mind where he cannot hear the buzzing—we can calm him. Hold the venom at bay."

"The Queen of Hearts," Jeb takes up again. "She has a remedy for this. Otherwise, her idiot guards wouldn't be handling the insects."

I look back and forth between them. "Yes. Do it. Please . . ." I don't notice that my face is wet until Chessie blots my cheeks with his tail.

Jeb starts to touch Dad's head, but Morpheus stops him. "You don't know how to harness dream-magic. You need guidance."

I tighten my jaw, suspecting the real reason for Morpheus's intervention. If he were to let Jeb unleash his full power, Red's strain would also seep into my dad. And who knows what the result would be?

Jeb shrugs and I stand back, completely useless in spite of all my magic.

Morpheus cups his bared palms around Dad's temples and Jeb nudges aside a wing to stand shoulder to shoulder beside him, his hands pressed to Morpheus's. Though Jeb's tattoo glows purple, the light that they radiate is pristine blue—strictly Morpheus's—as if they've practiced bypassing Red's magic many times before. Morpheus looks at Jeb incredulously, seemingly surprised by the purity of the force.

The light pulsates through Dad's body, from head to toe, just like when Morpheus unleashed his dream-magic on Jeb the day of prom.

Dad's body goes limp and his facial muscles relax.

I slump across his head, exhausted even though I've done nothing.

"Now, we see to you," Morpheus instructs Jeb, and motions for him to sit. He rewets a sponge. "You're bleeding."

Jeb scoots onto the table's edge. "No." He runs his hands across the red smudges on his costume. "It's paint," he explains, dreamlike. "A residue from CC. His palms were sliced following my command to keep the guards from hijacking the funnel."

Morpheus frowns and stops blotting Jeb's face. "Where is CC now?"

"He was running interference so I could escape with Thomas," Jeb answers. "The guards captured him."

Mumbling an oath, Morpheus throws the sponge into the bucket. After drying his hands on the drop cloth, he drags his jacket on and paces toward the entrance where he set aside his hat. He positions it atop his head, wings drooping behind him.

"We need a plan to get the antidote." He works his gloves into place. "Any hope for the element of surprise is ruined. Red knows Alyssa is in AnyElsewhere. Now they have CC, who knows the way to our mountain."

Jeb digs his fisted knuckles into the table. "I'll go tonight, before they can try to find us. I'll get CC back, and the antidote. We'll heal

Thomas and send him and Al through the gate before anything else happens."

I shake my head. "We're not leaving without both of you. Got it?"

"How would you get inside, pray tell?" Morpheus asks Jeb, ignoring my attempt at a command.

Jeb drops to the floor and strips off the bird suit. A navy blue T-shirt and faded jeans cling to him, wrinkled and popping with static from being underneath the costume. "Maybe I can shake things up. Crumble a few turrets and knock down a wall or two."

"We've already tried that once," Morpheus contradicts. "Your magic is limited to the natural terrain. Things built at the hands of others, they're beyond your capacity to alter." He adjusts his cap, and the orange moths along the brim sway. He looks at me. "Hart has arranged a caucus race tomorrow to elect an official king. We wear the simulacrum . . . go first thing in the morning when the gates are open."

"All the prisoners will be preoccupied," I reason, rubbing Dad's hand.

Jeb slants his head in thought. "It would help if we had a floor plan. We'd know exactly where to go for the curative, no detours."

Morpheus nods. "We could send someone tonight, someone small enough to slip through existing holes in the wall. While they're exploring, we can rest, prepare, and plan."

Nikki looks up from the other side of the room where she and Chessie have been teasing the cranes that occupy the Japanese screens. She flitters over to us. "Send me," she insists, her voice tinkling as she points to herself.

I'm touched by her bravery. "Nikki is strong. She could carry the antidote back herself if she finds it."

"I don't know," Jeb says. "She's so tiny. What if—"

"Nikki is ideal," Morpheus interjects. "You designed her to have free run of this world. She's small and swift. And on good terms with your paintings. If CC is sent to lead the guards here, she can distract him. Chessie and I can accompany her as far as the castle gates, wait in hiding for her to finish the expedition."

Jeb runs a hand through his hair, leaving it disheveled. He's obviously still worried for his sprite. "Okay. But I'm the one who screwed up. If she's not able to get the cure, I should go to this race thing tomorrow. Not you and Al."

I start to object, but Morpheus beats me to it. "You're needed here. You command the creations. You're better equipped to protect Thomas should the mountain be attacked. Chessie will be our runner if something goes wrong on our end."

Jeb nods, resigned.

Morpheus wraps the drop cloth around Dad and lifts him to a sitting position. "He needs to be somewhere safe, on the chance the mountain is breached."

"I'll take him to the lighthouse," Jeb offers. "Al, you can stay with him through the night."

"Okay," I whisper. I'm scared to be alone, even though it's my own father. I don't know what I'll do if he gets worse. "What if he wakes?"

"He shan't wake. The spell he's under will last until Jebediah and I release it."

I remind myself a queen is supposed to be brave, and agree.

Jeb balances Dad over his shoulder. Moving aside to let him by, Morpheus grabs my arm before I can follow them into the corridor.

He waits until Jeb is out of earshot and looks down at me. "Jebediah cannot go to that castle under any circumstances." He watches the door. "It's too dangerous for him."

I'm not sure I believe in his concern. "Why?"

"He's a vessel we can all pour our magic into, in a land of powerless fae. Such a rare commodity is priceless. A weapon to be feared and coveted by everyone. It's almost destroyed him trying to harness just mine and Red's powers. The inhabitants of this place—the Queen of Hearts, Manti and his goons—they are soulless and merciless. Were they ever to realize what he is, they would fill him to the brim with their magic. Eat him up like a cancer until there's nothing left. There would be no getting your mortal back after they finish."

The logic of his words weighs on my already heavy head. "So, you really were protecting him all this time? By keeping him holed up here?"

His hand slides down to my wrist in unspoken affirmation.

"Thank you." I squeeze his fingers in mine.

Morpheus gestures to Chessie and Nikki, directing them into the hall to watch for Jeb. "Don't get sentimental. I did not do it for him. I did it because I couldn't have you tortured by guilt had he come to such an end. You would've blamed your choices on prom night for the tragedy. It would have ruined your faith in your ability to rule. You'd be a worthless queen if you couldn't trust your own judgment."

The jaded explanation falls in line with the reasoning of a solitary fae. Of course it's for the greater good of the realm he loves. But he still did the right thing, and Jeb's alive because of it. I won't forget that. "So, what do you propose we do? Tell Jeb about Red's part in his magic?"

"Absolutely not. He'll get some cockamamie idea to stand up to her if we do that. We have to get him out of this realm before they discover him."

"But he doesn't want to leave," I mumble, unable to mask the defeat in my voice. "How do you protect someone who doesn't want to be protected?"

"He will leave if you take away his source of power. We'll make a bargain with Red for the antidote. She abhors this place. So we offer her an escape route. She may share Hart's body, but Red is the most cunning, have no doubt. We get the cure for your father, and in exchange, take Red out of AnyElsewhere. Jebediah will be forced to follow us, to stay tied to the magic he's become dependent on. He'll feel the draw, instinctively. Just as he feels one to me. Once we're back in Wonderland, the iron's magnetic effect will reverse. The magic will return to its proper vessels. And Jebediah will be human again."

Why would Morpheus make such a sacrifice? Drag not only Red back to his beloved world, but another queen bent on destruction, just to help two mortals?

I shift on the balls of my feet and suppress my suspicion, trying to take him at his word. "The guards . . . they won't let the Queen of Hearts through the gate. Even if my dad is well enough, he won't be able to convince them. Red's inside her, and Hart's a prisoner. They both belong here."

Morpheus taps the diary at my neck. "Which is why the Queen of Hearts must stay behind. We shall smuggle Red out under the guards' noses."

"It's not like we can wrap her up in simulacrum. She's a spirit—"

The horror hits me even before I finish rolling the reasoning off my tongue. Morpheus's cryptic statement earlier when I asked how we would flush Red from Jeb's system: *That, luv, will require the biggest sacrifice of all. And you're the one who will have to make it.*

This is what he was intending all along. When he formed a majestic moth ride to carry us, when he said he'd help me strategize my plan.

It was never my plan. It was *his*. For me to go to the castle, let Red's spirit inhabit me, and carry her out of this realm.

"No," I say, pulse hammering so hard in my wrists I can see the movement beneath my skin in the dim light. "I came here to finish her. Not to give her access to my—" I can't even say it aloud. She already did something to my heart that needs repair. I won't let her in again.

Everything that's happened today . . . the rooms, my epiphanies, Morpheus's seduction, Dad's life-threatening state—all of it stifles me like smoke, making it hard to breathe. Woozy and overwarm, I sway. Morpheus backs me to the table.

"Now, we'll have none of that." He draws me into a hug and strokes my hair—a tender gesture that feels out of place with his scolding words. "This is the perfect plan." His voice rumbles in his chest next to my ear—soft and melodic. "It's the least dangerous to everyone, most of all Jebediah." I shut my eyes, letting his steady heartbeat knock against my cheek. "The hardest part will be tricking Hart into letting Red's spirit go. But as for Red herself, we won't even have to bargain. It's all she's ever wanted, to be part of you."

To be part of you. Bile burns the back of my throat. What if it was Red that Ivory saw in the vision . . . Red living vicariously inside my body? What if it's *her* future with Morpheus, not mine? If that's true, my and Morpheus's child will belong to her. She'll be his mother.

I clench Morpheus's jacket lapels. Doesn't he realize what could happen if I can't defeat her once she's inside me? Doesn't he understand the danger? Not just for him, but for our future child?

"I'm not letting her use me as a vessel," I say against him. "Not ever again."

He eases back and drags a gloved thumb along my temple. "Not even for your mortal? And for the father who needs you? You have her memories to vanquish her the moment we step across the border and Jebediah is cleansed of her power."

I grip the tiny diary like a lifeline, but still feel myself sinking. "It can't be the only way."

"It is. The only way to salvage what we love."

My nerves prickle. "*We* love? You don't care about Jeb. You said so yourself."

His lips tighten. "He has his merits. Enough that he deserves to live. Just like your father did all those years ago." He almost looks sincere. But the fluctuation in the color of his jewels gives him away. I've finally learned to read him.

My strength rallies. "No. You're lying. This isn't the only way to get Jeb out."

Morpheus presses both hands on the table behind me, penning me in. "As you said. He has no desire to leave."

I shove him back. "I can convince him."

"What? By seducing him?" Morpheus scoffs. "I have half a mind to let you try. Whatever it takes to get the boy out of your system once and for all."

An angry throb pulses in my temples. "You're right. You do only have half a mind if you think your 'letting' me has anything to do with anything."

His cocky grin answers. "Go ahead then. I'll swipe the memory of his touch away. And I shan't need a forgetting potion to do it. I've every faith in my abilities to o'ershadow anything that mortal can do for or *to* you." He drags his fingertip along my waist, reminding me of what happened between us in his room earlier. "Why are we arguing, hmm?" he croons. "It's a moot point. You had the morning together. He painted your half-naked body, the lucky sod. Had that been my job, your pretty clothes would ne'er have been crafted. He doesn't want you anymore."

That truth scores through me. But I won't let a wounded ego derail my resolve. "There's something else to this Red thing. And if you don't tell me, I'll wear a simulacrum suit and go alone tonight to get Dad's cure and put an end to her for good."

His alabaster complexion pales. "Don't be a fool. To get into that castle, it will take teamwork. And we must be armed with an escape plan. Most importantly, you need to sleep first. You can hardly stand."

I step from between him and the table, inching toward the door. "Why would I need to stand? I can fly. And neither you nor Jeb can stop me." With a snap of my shoulder blades, my wings release, rushing another surge of power through my veins.

Morpheus's gaze tracks my wings. Filaments of moonlight stream down from above, illuminating his enthralled expression. "That is a breathtaking display, luv. But dare not mistake my veneration for surrender."

He starts toward me, his expression fading to a scowl. I've triggered one of his dark, combative moods. It doesn't matter, because my imagination is more refined than his, and he's given me the secret to manipulating Jeb's paintings.

Before he passes the Japanese screens, I mentally beckon the cranes. They cease pecking their beaks against their rice-paper prison and turn their attention to me. I assign them a new role: lace spinners, with the moonlight as their thread.

Bugle-like squawks burst from their throats as they step out of their screens and plop in front of Morpheus in full 3-D form. Wavering on scaly gray legs, the duo clacks and slides along the floor, learning to balance for the first time. Then, wings spread, they lift their elegant necks to full height, reaching Morpheus's chin.

He backs up, his jewels flashing a yellow-green—cautious fascination.

The cranes capture moonlight in their beaks as if it were tangible threads. Pulling it taut from the ceiling, they weave it into a network of glistening lace with otherworldly speed. One blink, and the panel is already down to Morpheus's chest.

He tries to duck underneath, but the birds adjust their trajectory, looping, twisting, and braiding the mesh so it reaches his shins. He hardly has time to retreat before the barrier hems him into the back corner of the room . . . a gauzy fence from ceiling to floor. As soon as they finish the first panel, they start on another, beaks clacking.

"Well played," Morpheus says from the other side, curling his fingertips through the unbreakable threads. Admiration glistens in his dark eyes. "I am your prisoner. Although I always have been."

We watch each other in silence. The one thing innate in both of us is our fear of being held captive. I remember his beautiful, agonized confession weeks ago: *Nothing can break the chains you have on my heart.* In the vision I had, when we danced upon the sun, we were free and equal in every way. That's what I wish for him. For us both.

"I never wanted you to be my prisoner," I insist.

He flourishes his arms in a grand gesture. "Yet here I am in a cage of your making."

"If you could learn to be honest, the walls would come down."

He clenches his jaw.

"You're using Jeb to influence my choices. Again. I'm not falling for it this time. Why do you want to free Red? Is there something between the two of you?" I pause at the threshold, waiting.

"No! I hate the wretch." His face, crisscrossed with lacework shadows, grows somber. "I hate her with the same changeless passion with which I love you."

The confession is sweet in its simplicity, reminding me the emotions he feels are foreign to him; being a solitary creature, he doesn't understand how deeply interwoven love is with trust. "You want me to believe in your love? Then no more secrets. If we're going to be equals, we have to work together. You're so used to being on your own, you don't know how to trust anyone but yourself. That has to change. The human in me, she *needs* trust. Have faith that I'll understand and won't judge you. That I can find a way to help you. Maybe a better way."

His stubborn silence mocks me, so I turn to leave.

"There is no better way!" The desperation in his voice causes me to spin and face him. "If there was, I would never ask this of you. Red put the spell upon Wonderland's terrain. Only her magic can reverse the decay and return its original splendor. Without her, the nether-realm will fall to ruin, and nothing will redeem our world. Our home. *Your* kingdom. That's why we have to smuggle her out . . . and the only way is inside you. You are her lineage, and the only one strong enough to harness her magic and use it for good once we cross the border."

Icy tendrils of frost gather around my backbone. "You expect me to let her live inside me forever?"

He grips the lace again. "Of course not. Only until reparations are made. Then we rid ourselves of her blighted existence once and for all."

Chessie and Nikki burst into the room, stirring tiny gusts across my hair as they head toward the lacy prison. They swoop at the cranes in an effort to distract them.

Jeb brushes past me at the door. His arm scrapes my wing, and a tingle radiates from its tip to my spine. He must've made it all the way to the diamond door then realized I wasn't in tow. Before I can ask, he motions to the hall, where Dad is propped in a sitting position—sleeping soundly.

Jeb studies the spectacle of the hissing cranes, Chessie, and Nikki, all tangled in the lacework. He turns to me.

I give a halfhearted shrug.

He flicks his hand and the gauzy wall dissipates, returning to strands of moonlight and freeing all its prisoners. Jeb commands his birds back into place on their screens. They squawk, step inside, and flatten to embellishments once more.

Nikki flitters over and tunnels into Jeb's hair, offering a jingling thank-you and twirling the silky waves around her like a dress.

Chessie perches on Morpheus's shoulder as he starts toward me. "Alyssa, you must see how crucial this is."

Jeb stops him, his palm on Morpheus's chest. "Hold up there, moth-nugget. When I was coming back down the hall, I heard that you expect Al to let that monster possess her again. No way that's happening."

Morpheus growls. "This does not concern you. You would rather break Alyssa's heart than give up the power you crave and face the real world. So you have no say. It's her choice to make. Her kingdom at risk." He looks pointedly at me. "*More* than her kingdom."

Jeb shoves him and their bickering escalates. Nikki buzzes around, trying to referee.

I look at my surroundings: the twisted magic everywhere, rooms filled with nightmares, my father propped against a wall, rendered comatose so he won't turn to stone.

Jeb wants to stay here?

No. This place is poison. We have to get out. All of us; even if the only way to convince Jeb is to capitalize on his addiction to the power . . .

Chessie catches my gaze, floating over Morpheus and Jeb's tirade like a ball of glittery orange and gray ashes. His wide, wise eyes speak to me, forcing me to face what will become of him, of the whimsical and strange netherlings stuck inside the memory train in the human realm, of those in Wonderland. Forcing me to reconcile what will happen to them all, once their beautifully bizarre home rots beneath them. How lost they'll be.

A sliver of pain slides through the frost encasing my courage and cuts it with precision. There's no question what has to be done.

"I'll do it." Though my voice sounds like little more than a squeak, it stamps out Morpheus and Jeb's yelling match.

They both turn to me, deathly quiet.

I lift my shoulders so my wings spread tall. "I'll do anything to save Wonderland"—*to save everyone I love*—"because I'm responsible. I was weak. I won't be again."

Joining hands to paws, Chessie and Nikki take to the air in celebratory spins.

"Alyssa . . ." Morpheus's demeanor is pure reverence. "I always knew you had the heart of a queen."

Jeb grips Morpheus's T-shirt, gritting his teeth. "If you love her the way you claim, you'd let that witch possess *you*."

Morpheus glares at him. "We're not of the same bloodline. And even if I could, only Alyssa has ever managed to overpower Red. It is fated that she carries her out and defeats her once and for all."

"Jeb, please. I've made my decision." My throat hurts, even though I'm almost whispering. I'm so tired. "Dad needs some clothes, and a place to lie down."

Jeb releases Morpheus and heads toward the hall. His expression is contained fury as he lifts Dad onto his shoulder. "I assume you're coming this time," he grumbles, then starts down the long corridor once more.

Trembling at the threshold, I cast a glance toward Morpheus. "She nearly tore my insides out once. Her mark is still there. I feel it." I don't tell him the rest: that it's as if the strands of my heart are splitting, that I'm convinced it's a magical effect from her possession, and each day it seems to rupture a little further. "I'm not sure I have the strength to rip her out again. Not without killing her and me both."

His expression shifts to something so close to worry, it freezes my breath. He looks down at the diary. "You have a weapon now. Her memories give you an advantage she'll never expect. That will weaken her."

"We don't even know that it will work," I whisper.

"It will," he says. "It must." The concern echoing in the fathomless depths of his eyes belies the confidence of the words. For the first time ever, he shares my doubts.

We stay like that for countless seconds, staring at each other.

When he reaches out to comfort me, I step backward into the hall. Without another word, I fall into line behind Jeb, unable to shake the dread that has wrapped itself around my neck in the form of a diary: a child's toy that will either save my life, or bring it crashing to an end.

TIDES OF DESTINY

Once we arrive at the lighthouse, Jeb carries Dad to the tower. He dresses him and calls me up. I cover Dad's sleeping form with blankets then sit on the edge of the mattress beside him, taking off my boots.

I've only been in the looking-glass world a little over a day, yet it feels like weeks. I can't keep up with the passage of time here. And tonight promises to be the worst stretch of all as we wait to see if we'll get Dad's cure, or have to face the Queen of Hearts's deadly caucus race.

I stroke Dad's head, expecting Jeb to try to discourage me from going along with Morpheus's plan. Instead, he watches me silently as the moonlight and the lighthouse's beam take turns illuminating the walls.

"I checked his leg and the venom hasn't spread," Jeb finally says, his deep voice velvet-sweet like it was in the human realm, before Red's magic infiltrated him. How ironic, that my heart isn't the only one she's tainted. It makes me hate her even more.

"He's going to be okay," Jeb continues. "He's the strongest man I've ever known."

The glimpse of the boy from my past is so vivid, I fall into old habits and spill my soul. "I had a vision about Mom, that she's alive and safe. I think she's sending messages through my dreams."

Jeb leans against the wall, not even questioning me. He's seen and worked enough magic at this point to believe in the unbelievable.

"What am I going to tell her if . . . ?" My voice trails off.

"No, Al. He'll get through this because he's the one dreaming now."

I nod. "I hope he's dreaming about being safe. About the things that make him happy."

"He's probably fishing," Jeb adds from beside the porthole. "Just like he used to take us." He forces a short laugh, more sorrowful than happy. "Remember that time you dumped out a whole box of bait?"

I almost smile. It was the summer before eighth grade. Dad bought crickets at the bait shop. "They were screaming for help."

There's a thumping sound, and I don't have to look to know it's Jeb's knuckles against the stone wall. "That's when I first started falling for you."

I glance at him over my shoulder. With his tousled hair gilded in silvery starlight, he's as lovely as any mystical sight I've ever seen. "You never told me that."

He turns his back to look outside. "You were so worried about those bugs. The same girl who stuck pins in them every day for her art. Yet you couldn't shove a hook through them to catch a fish."

"Because they were already dead when I used them for mosaics. I didn't have to hear their suffering."

"I didn't know that. All I knew was there was so much more to you under the surface. So I started sketching you—trying to make it come through, to read between the lines."

He always drew me as a fairy, as if he really was deciphering my secrets. I'm heartsick that he's lost the ability to paint me while he's been here, that it almost broke him to try.

"And your dad," Jeb continues. "He didn't get mad that you turned the bugs loose. He just pulled out the aluminum lures, and that's what we used from then on. I never knew a father could be like that. Forgiving. Kind. He's the best guy I know. Pretty sure he saved my life a time or two."

I sniffle and swipe my nose with the back of my hand, then tuck the blanket under Dad's chin, studying his serene face. "He was supposed to be a knight." My vocal cords constrict. "Instead, when Mom was committed, he had to be both parents. I used to think he was boring because of that. But that made him the biggest hero of all." To keep from crying, I bury my face in Dad's shoulder, taking comfort in the rush of his breath at my temple. His skin smells of the paint that earlier coated his body.

I barely notice the weight settling beside me on the bed's edge.

"Al," Jeb whispers, closer than he's been since I first arrived at the mountain. His fingertips trace the edge of my wings.

"I want my family back. I want you and Morpheus safe, and I want to fix Wonderland."

"I know."

His empathy strips away my defenses and I lift my face to unleash my darkest fear. "But I'm terrified to let Red inside me again." I stop short of telling him why—that my heart feels like it's breaking, literally—because he looks away.

The mattress shifts as he stands. "I should go guard the entrances."

Though it's not the pep talk or comforting hug I was hoping for, I try not to be disappointed.

He heads toward the door. "Get some sleep, okay?"

I nod. My body, heavy with exhaustion, wants to do just that: curl up beside Dad. But as Jeb's boots clomp down the staircase, it dawns on me why he didn't try to talk me out of going through with Morpheus's plan. Jeb feels responsible for Dad's plight. He thinks he can get the cure himself so I won't have to face Red's possession at all.

Wonderland's repair isn't Jeb's priority. Getting Dad and me to Mom safely is all he's thinking about. But if he's captured in that castle, they'll use him as a vessel for their magic until there's nothing left, just like Morpheus said . . .

I close the curtains around Dad and race down the stairs. When I pass through the empty kitchen, dread comes to a rolling boil inside my veins.

I shove through the door. "Jeb!"

He's already at the lower quarter of the winding stairs, silhouetted by shadows and headed toward the shore and the rowboat.

"Jeb, wait!"

I spur my wings to fly and land in the same instant he drops from the last step. Sand grits under my bare soles as I plant myself between him and the boat, out of range of the lighthouse's beam. "Don't do this."

He tenses, his T-shirt tightening around his muscles. "It's my place."

"It's *not* your fault."

"It's not about whose fault it is. It's about destinies. I'm the one who has the best chance against Red."

I frown. "What are you talking about?"

"Give me some credit. We're artists. We know colors, how they combine. Red's magic and Morpheus's." He holds up his wrist where his tattoo glows. "There had to be a reason mine was purple."

My jaw drops. "You knew?" I'm so astonished I don't even move as he steps around me.

"I've known all along. When did you figure it out?" he asks, unwinding the anchor rope from the post.

"When I saw inside your rooms."

He pauses. Exhaling loudly, he sits on the boat's bow. Elbows propped against his knees, he winds the rope between his fingers. "So you understand why I can't leave now. My creations, they need me." His misplaced devotion makes me ache. "Besides that, this . . . hatred. It's become too big for the human world. I could hurt someone. Jen, Mom. You. I'd be just like my old man."

I tell myself the sting in my eyes is from the salty air. "No. You'll never be like your dad. You've made conscious choices not to be. Even with Red's venom feeding your soul, you're still gentle with me."

"According to Morpheus, I almost strangled you a month ago in our world. When I was strung out on Tumtum juice at the art studio. You were so desperate to hide it from me, you made an irrevocable deal with the devil."

Anger crashes through me. So Morpheus did tell him. All

because I wasn't crafty enough to make him vow never to speak of it to Jeb. Well, I'm done being naive and careless with my words. From now on, I make life-magic vows that work to my advantage.

This is why Jeb couldn't paint my portraits. It wasn't Red's hatred, but his own guilt for almost choking me. My insides shrink, empathy causing the feeling instead of an enchanted bottle inside a rabbit hole.

I watch the rope slide through Jeb's fingers, his movements graceful despite his hands' masculine shape.

"I didn't want you to have to struggle with what happened," I say. "I was wrong."

He shrugs. "I'm not so sure, judging by the things I've created."

"No. It's this place. Red's influence. We just need to get you through the gate. Cleansed of her power. Then you'll be yourself again."

He shakes his head. "I've suppressed this rage for years. Coming here and hiding in this mountain, it gave me an outlet, brought it all to the surface. Now that I've given it free reign, I don't know if I can control it anymore."

His face changes to that of the wounded little boy again. Morpheus was wrong. It isn't me Jeb has given up on. It's himself.

I step closer, sand sifting under my feet, as I realize another truth. "Wait . . . if you've known all along about Red's magic, you've been playing Morpheus, letting him think he was playing you."

"Yeah." He smirks. "I tricked the trickster. Ironic, right?" A hint of pride shines through, making his eyes glimmer the color of spring leaves.

"You could've turned her power against him. Hurt him. But you didn't. Why?"

"Because hurting him would've hurt you."

The confession buckles my knees. I sink down beside him on the bow. My wings hang limp inside the hull of the boat and warm sand fills the spaces between my toes. "I don't understand how you can't see it."

"See what?"

"I'm the priority, over your own feelings. You have complete control over your anger. So much so, you *chose* not to hurt Morpheus because he's my friend."

Jeb's back stiffens. "It's more than that. You want to be with him. To live with him in Wonderland. Forever." He taps the rope against his thigh in a lighthearted manner, but there's no hiding the heaviness in his shoulders.

A lump rises in my throat. "What are you talking about? That vow I made was just for twenty-four hours."

"Prom night," Jeb says, getting to his feet. "After I helped your mom with your dad. When I came back to your bedroom." He nudges me off the boat.

I stand and rub my arms, chilled by the direction the conversation's taking. "Jeb, that kiss wasn't supposed to happen. I didn't mean for it to."

"Yet when I got back today, you were in his room. Your clothes were wrinkled, your face flushed."

My cheeks burn. So he did notice. "I'm so sorry." *And I'm so tired of lame apologies.* "I can't seem to balance this. My two sides . . . they're always at war. I'm not trying to lead you on. Or him, either."

Jeb's frown deepens. "I know you're not playing games. I also know you're not the kind of girl who kisses a guy for no reason."

"You're right. The first time was to get my wish back. And the second . . . it was supposed to be a peck on the cheek. He changed it to something more."

"Oh, come on!" Jeb shouts, causing me to flinch. "This is what makes me crazy. That you can't admit it to me or yourself. You kissed him because you have feelings for him."

Feelings . . . such a simple word, except to a half-blood netherling queen whose life is not only unraveling, but her heart, too. I tighten my lips.

My silence triggers an unsettling expression across Jeb's face . . . like a storm slowly building.

The boat behind him starts to rattle, a physical manifestation of his emotional turmoil. I jump as a loud pop splits the wood's seams. The panels snap open so it's nothing but an emaciated skeleton.

"I tried to tell you," he says in an unsettling monotone. "I can't trust myself."

I square my shoulders. "The anger wasn't directed at me. And it never will be."

"Doesn't matter. Because we're over."

"I don't believe you." From beneath my shirt, I drag out the ring he painted in the willow room. "I saw all the beautiful dreams you have for us."

Clenching his jaw, he takes my shoulders—carefully, as if I'm made of glass—and maneuvers me so I'm a few inches from the boat, close enough to the ocean for the warm tide to lick my toes.

"*Had*," he corrects. "Past tense."

Gaze turned to the ground, he waves his palm above the sand. Each grain sparks with red light and two holes open, sucking me down to my ankles. They close over my feet. I try to move, but I'm stuck.

Confusion creeps through me. "Jeb?"

"Another thing your moth prince doesn't know. I've learned how to separate the two strains of magic. I put your dad into his dream trance earlier. Morpheus was just a prop. Too bad I didn't control his powers on prom night. Maybe you would've chosen me instead. Then I could've given you all the things I wanted to, instead of only dreaming about them." He slips the necklace with his ring off my head and dips it in the water until the beautiful band of diamonds and silver disintegrates to a puddle of paint. Only the diary's key remains.

Rooted like an unwanted weed, I can't do anything but watch.

He drops the necklace back into place over my head and returns the boat to its former glory with a flourish of his hands.

I recover my voice. "I *did* choose you!"

Back turned, he clears off the seat. A breeze scrambles his hair, making the tangles even messier.

I thrust out a hand and snag his back jeans pocket. "Jeb, don't do this."

He pries my fingers free and moves out of reach. "Do what? Help you get what you wanted?" He coils the rope in the hull. "When your fae boyfriend had his wings around you in your room, you told him all you were asking for was a little while. You said forever was worth that."

A breath shunts out of me.

I had no idea he was listening in the hallway before the kiss. I had touched my lips to Morpheus's cheek, keeping it innocent. Jeb didn't see that, because Morpheus's wings dropped only when he made that kiss into something more. Jeb saw what Morpheus *wanted* him to see. But worse than what Jeb saw, was what he heard. What came out of my own mouth.

Sometimes words are louder than actions.

Understanding ticks through my mind, as vicious and cutting as a razor-sharp second hand on a clock.

"You needed time to break up with me," Jeb says. "After I'd just asked you to marry me. I was hoping for forever, but you were already planning it with him." Jeb heaves the boat into the water and quickly steps inside the hull to keep his clothes dry. He sits, facing me, oars in hand.

The foamy tide laps at my ankles, melting my leggings until my shins are exposed. I tense my thigh muscles, twist my calves. But I might as well be standing in cement. He's about to end his life, give up everything, all for the sake of what he *thinks* I want.

The diary at my chest glows, yet I can't slow my racing thoughts enough to use it. My mind is as useless as my body.

"Wait!" I grapple for the bow, but it slips under my fingertips as the tide pulls the boat into the ocean. "It's all out of context, okay? I didn't say I wanted to break up with you!"

Jeb drifts out of my reach. "What else would you have been asking time for, if not to let me down easy? I get it. I tried to choke you. I'm not worthy of trust." He drags the oars through the water until he's several feet away.

No. I can't let him believe that. The only arsenal I have is the truth. My vow to Ivory stated I wouldn't tell anyone about the vision of my and Morpheus's child. But the prospect of my immortality is fair game.

"I can have two futures. One with you in the mortal realm. Then, later, as a netherling queen. What you heard on prom night was me asking Morpheus to give me and you space. To wait for my human life to end."

Jeb pauses rowing. Water sloshes around the hull, towing the boat out further. The lighthouse flashes across him and his labret sparkles as he watches me. "How is that even possible?"

I attempt to explain it, that I'll age in the mortal realm, but won't die. That when I'm old and frail, I can fake my death and go to Wonderland. That once my crown is placed on my head, I'll return to the age I was when I first became queen.

What I don't say is how much it hurts to consider outliving the people I love, to leave my human family behind. I can't say it, because Jeb's pain concerns me more.

"So, after everyone dies, you'll go to Wonderland and be perpetually sixteen?" The bitter bite in his voice punctures like thorns. "I'll be gone. And you'll spend forever with *him*. What am I supposed to do with that, Al?"

I fist my hands, worried he might split the boat again and fall into the water. "I don't know."

"Well, I do. I'll go to the castle, get your dad his cure, and send you and Morpheus off on your merry way. So you can skip the whole aging-in-the-real-world thing and be eternally young now. I mean, who wouldn't want that, right?"

"Jeb, no!" My vocal cords strain and it registers how far he's drifted from the shore. We've been shouting at each other without my realizing it.

In fact, he's been moving farther out without even rowing.

A red glimmer undulates through the water, lighting the depths with pulses, as if there were a living heart underneath. On each vibration, Jeb's boat rides a wave closer to the opposing shore and the exit. He's controlling the ocean, just like he does everything here.

"The sands will release you when I'm gone, and you can stay with your dad," he calls over the distance. "By tomorrow morning, you'll be on your way to Wonderland with Morpheus."

Frustrated tears singe my lower lashes. Here we are again, in a mystical hostile world, battling each other instead of the dangers lying in wait. "You have no idea what they can do to you!"

I simultaneously tug on my legs and flap my wings until my ligaments feel like they'll snap. The harder I fight, the hotter the diary gets. Determined to stop him, I recall step-by-step how I used the tiny book as a catapult for my powers in Morpheus's room.

When the crimson glow seeps into my veins, I redirect the flow, hurling it at the ocean. It works, rolling a wave that reverses the rowboat back my way. The lighthouse blinks, illuminating Jeb as he stands up in the hull. Balanced gracefully like a surfer, he chucks the oars down. Despite the span between us, I swear I can see him sneer.

It stokes my darker side. She relishes the challenge.

"Want to play, do you?" I whisper.

His hair whips around his head. He raises his tattooed wrist—glowing purple like a beacon—and coerces another wave, higher than mine. The water heaves him toward the opposite shore. In turn, I do the same, dragging him back to me. Our aquatic tug-of-war escalates, our drunken determination dancing on some sentient level, until the ocean sputters and snarls.

Gusts whip through our hair and clothes. A splash melts my leggings to mid-thigh and leaves my skirt's hem a jagged fray. A stray upsurge splatters across Jeb's shirt, rendering him half-naked.

A spark rides the air between us—not visible, but *visceral*, like all those times we played chess while fighting our feelings for each other. That's what collides and teases the ocean to a raging, frothy roar—even more than our magic.

I notice the giant red bubble in the depths too late to stop it, an accumulation of our power that bulges until it erupts into a tidal wave. Jeb slams into the water. His head bobs for an instant in the lighthouse's glare before the boat capsizes and pounds him, then he disappears in the swell.

I've killed him.

"Jeb!" I scream. The wall of water shifts my direction, blocking the starlit ceiling. The ground shakes and hauls me down until the sand swallows my knees, embedding me even deeper.

I bend at the waist, digging until my fingertips sting and bleed. It's futile. The wave curls and arcs—two stories above me. I wrap my wings around myself, my arms over my head, and brace for impact.

The water crashes down—sweeping me under and knocking the air in my lungs loose. A silent scream erupts from my mouth in bubbles. My wings snap open and flail, scraping my body. I fight the urge to breathe as my spine contorts and twists.

The murky water blinds me. Warm brininess seeps into my nostrils and the seam of my lips. Grappling for the diary and key at my neck, I'm relieved to find them still there, though I can't remember why. My arms, legs, and wings go limp and I fold.

A warm pressure grips around my waist, startling me to alertness. The sands release my legs. Jeb holds me in his arms and we surface together. I gulp air and cough up salt water.

After dragging us to shore, Jeb collapses beside me, sputtering. The ocean laps gently under his instruction, as if it wasn't trying to tear us apart seconds ago.

My wings wrinkle beneath my back and I absorb them, skin prickling against the sand. All my clothes are gone—everything but my lingerie, sopping wet and clinging to me. My pulse spikes as I realize Jeb's clothes have vanished, too, other than a soaked pair of periwinkle boxers that look a lot like the fabric of his tuxedo shirt.

Propped on his elbows, he turns me to face him and rakes wet snarls of hair off my face. He loops the diary and key behind my neck so they're no longer between us.

Water beads along his whiskered jaw and gathers around the edges of his labret. "Didn't I tell you never to scare me like that again?"

My mind clears instantly: That's what he said when we weathered the original ocean of tears in Wonderland.

"You came back for me." I press myself to him, fill the words with as much awe and gratitude as when I used them to respond a year ago.

His hands cradle my head. "I'll always come back for you, Al," he whispers.

I hold his wrists and our heartbeats slam between us. "And that's why you'll always be a better man than your dad."

His features soften to a poignant frown and he leans in to skim his mouth along mine, leaving a warm imprint of salt so illusory it could be a teardrop. The moment I start to respond, he breaks contact and pushes away.

I bite back a sigh.

He sits on his knees, appearing far too pensive for my liking. I've seen that look before. He's about to scold me for taking risks.

"I won't apologize for being reckless." My defensive rebuttal leaps out before he can even open his mouth. "The more I think like a netherling, the more conniving and strong I become. How's that a bad thing here?"

"You're right." His confession shocks me. "Listening to your darker instincts is the only way to survive and master these worlds. I get it now."

Of course he does. He's been around since I was an awkward kid in middle school. He knows the human side of me better than anyone. And now, after becoming a netherling in his own right, it's given him new insight into the Wonderland side of me, too.

Goose bumps coat my arms as a breeze blows over me.

He stands. His bared skin glistens in the starlight, each chiseled line brushed with water and sugared with sand. "You're cold. Let's get you some clothes."

As I start to take his hand, his eyes pass over my lingerie slowly.

"Where the hell did you get those?" He obviously recognizes the fabric. "How does that cockroach know your measurements, huh?"

I frown and drop my arm. "I could ask the same thing about your boxers. You can't even sew a button onto a shirt. You've always had Jen around for that."

He pauses, jaw clenched. Thankfully, the diary at my neck flickers and distracts him. He lifts its string. "This book . . . it has something to do with your great-great-great-grandmother, doesn't it?"

"How do you know that?"

"You used it against her magic inside me. I saw it glowing red from across the ocean. It caused the surge. I—I even feel different."

"You do?" I flip his wrist to study where his tattoo glows.

"Yeah. I still feel her power. It's just . . . tamed."

I furrow my brow. "These are memories she forced herself to forget. They're enchanted. They hate her and want revenge."

We both look at his palm where the diary left its imprint. He drops the string so the tiny book dangles at my neck again.

"Al, do you know what this means? You don't have to let Red inside you to fix Wonderland. Maybe Morpheus hasn't realized it yet—or maybe he's too big of a jerk to care—but you have the key to reversing her destruction right there. And you've already learned how to master it."

I inhale a sharp breath. Why didn't I think of that? I can pit her memories against her damaging spell over Wonderland, use them to put everything back the way it was.

There's a nudge inside my chest, a reminder that I have to face Red, fix my heart, and end this thing between us. But my top priority is healing Dad and leading him, Morpheus, and Jeb into Wonderland to help Mom. I'll reverse Red's spell on the landscapes, then come back and finish things here.

"Okay"—I sort out the new plan aloud—"all we have to do is get Dad's cure, then we can get out of here."

Jeb looks down on me. "*You* can get out."

"Jeb, please."

"I've got nothing to go back for."

I want to scream *ME!* but it won't make a dent. "You can just forget your mom and Jen? They need you."

There's no masking the sadness in his eyes at the mention of his family. "They're better off with me here. I can still take care of them . . . be a liaison for the guards at the gates, protect the human realm from the inside."

"So your plan is to stay and siphon magic off of Red forever?"

A muscle in his jaw spasms. "At least that way I *get* a forever." He holds out his hand, unspoken insistence we head to the lighthouse.

A sense of enormity overwhelms me: Dad was spot-on. I'm the

only one who can convince Jeb to leave this place. I have to show him that life is worth living outside this horrible realm, even if it comes with mortal limitations.

I lace my fingers through his and tug him down so we're face-to-face. The gritty terrain jabs my naked knees.

He digs a fist into the sand. "What are you doing?"

"Reminding you that I'm still human enough to need you." I rake my hands across his biceps and down his pecs. Water and sand crumble to shimmery, granular trails along his chest hair in my wake. As I touch him, his breath catches and his long, dark eyelashes close in exquisite agony.

I splay my fingertips and open my palm to match his cigarette burns to my scars. His muscles answer with tiny twitches, every part of him strong where I'm soft.

"Jeb."

He opens his eyes and we lock gazes.

"*This* is why we fit. Because we're both damaged, in a way that can't be healed. Even by magic."

His gaze holds steady.

"I love you," I whisper. "Do you still love me?"

He leans closer, bracing his knuckles on the ground beside my hips. "I'll never stop."

My stomach somersaults. "Then come home."

"What good will it do?" His mouth is inches away and the question scalds my lips. "Things can never go back to the way they were."

My chin tightens. "You're right. Because we've both grown and changed. Because we understand each other on every level now. I've seen all your secrets. You've seen mine. We can live for today. Not think about forever."

He lifts a sand-covered hand and traces the red streak of my hair. "You're being naive. Morpheus won't let us. He'll dangle your magical eternity in front of me, knowing it's something I can never give you. Knowing, as a human, I have nothing to offer that compares to that."

He starts to draw back, but I grasp the waistband of his boxers where it hugs his abs. I hear the husky intake of air as he looks down at my hand, then back up at my face.

"You're wrong. There's something you *already* offered that's every bit as magical and rare as forever. You offered to grow old with me. That's something Morpheus can't do." I stroke my fingertips over his whisker-rough jaw. "I didn't get to answer that yes, I want to marry you."

For an instant, Jeb's eyes sparkle with a hopeful light.

"Do you still want that?" I ask.

His fingers weave through my hair, so tight they pinch my scalp. "There's no one I'd rather spend my life with. Make a family with. But you made a vow to Morpheus. Twenty-four hours alone together. He'll do anything to keep you from coming back to the human realm." He presses our foreheads together. "I would fight for you, Al. Until the day I die. I just don't know how to fight magic without magic. Not anymore."

So *I'm* the reason Jeb doesn't want to leave or give up his power. It's been me all along.

His agonized expression scores my insides raw. Morpheus's promise on the day I made that vow dances along the edge of my psyche: *I'll show you the wonders of Wonderland, and when you're drunk on the beauty and chaos that your heart so yearns to know, I will take you under my wings and make you forget the human realm ever existed. You'll never want to leave Wonderland or me again.*

It's not that Jeb doesn't have faith in me. It's that he's seen the writing on the wall. Morpheus always finds a way to win. He's the most manipulative and brilliant strategist I've ever known.

But he's met his match. Or, rather, he's *created* her.

"You don't have to fight for us." I trace Jeb's tattooed wrist. "I can fix it so Morpheus will leave us alone."

Jeb frowns. "You're kidding, right?"

"No." My voice is resolute and strong, almost as strong as Morpheus's when he told me the secret to getting the upper hand: *Once you know someone's weakness, they're easy to manipulate.*

Jeb touches my face, as if shaken by the seriousness of my tone.

I could argue that Morpheus brought this on himself by forcing Jeb to live with the knowledge that he almost choked me in spite of our arrangement . . . by always manipulating every word, action, and promise to his advantage. I could say he's taught me well and I'm finally thinking like a netherling. *Like him.*

But this isn't for revenge. This is for leverage. Morpheus and I have forever to make things right between us, but Jeb only has one lifetime. He's been dealt enough misery already. I'm what makes him happy, and he does the same for me. So we should spend Jeb's one life together.

"Jebediah Holt," I say, my palm covering my chest in pledge form. "I vow on my life-magic that you'll be my first in every way . . . in marriage and everything that goes with it."

His face opens with wonder and astonishment, as if I've offered him the Milky Way and all the undiscovered galaxies beyond. "Wait, did you just—?"

Before he finishes, there's a spasm behind my sternum that sucks my breath away. My heartbeat staggers for an instant, like a fish flopping behind my rib cage. I wail and draw my knees to my chest.

Jeb rubs my arms. "Al, are you okay?"

Cringing, I uncurl my body slowly. My fingers dig into the sand to fight the harsh sting. "I'm fine. It—it's just a muscle cramp." The lie tastes sour, like blood.

What if Red put a spell on my heart to control me? To bend me to her will? Every time I stray from her path toward Wonderland, I'm punished with agonizing pain. Just like she used my veins as puppet strings when she shared my body last year.

I can't let her win. Tomorrow will be here too soon, and I have to convince Jeb to leave with us. If I don't, he *will* die.

I grasp his hand, ignoring the pain. "Only you can release me of the vow's binds. Morpheus will never ask me to break it. I need my magic, to be the queen he's always trained me to be. Wonderland's best interest is the one thing in the world he would put above his own desires."

Jeb's jaw falls. He half laughs. "Using your role as the Red Queen for a bargaining chip. That's ingenious."

I push aside his dark bangs. "I have great potential as a diplomat, yeah?" The teasing is a hollow ploy to cover that I'm struggling to breathe without my chest hurting. I have to get to Red. Make her undo everything she's done.

Jeb smiles—a genuine Jebediah Holt grin, complete with dimples. Such a beautiful distraction. "I love you, skater girl."

The nickname winds through me, comforting and sweet. I smooth my palm across his shoulder. "Say it again."

"I love you."

"No . . . the other part," I plead.

He pulls my body to his, so our mouths come together in a warm, soft kiss. "*Skater girl*," he whispers against me, brushing hair from my face.

We kiss again—his touch no longer illusory but confident and urgent. He lays me back, covering my body with his delicious weight as he teases my mouth open. I hold his face to savor the movements of his jaw, the flavor of his skin captured in droplets left by the ocean, the feel of his crooked incisor against my tongue, reacquainting my favorite parts of him.

"I missed you, Al." His kisses trail my chin, my neck, and down the center of my collarbone, following traces of dried water. The splitting fire behind my sternum soothes to tolerable under his lips. I sigh and arch into him, but he freezes.

"Shh. Do you hear that?" he murmurs.

A cacophony builds from somewhere in the distance across the ocean's lapping tide: thrashing wings and screeching wails. I lift my head as a flock of condor-size flying beasts soars toward us. Goon birds are straddled atop their backs, wearing diving helmets that look like brass gumball machines with glass viewing holes.

"Bats!" Jeb shouts, rolling off. "Get to the lighthouse, now!"

DEADLY CAUCUS RACE

Carroll's rendition of *Twinkle, Twinkle* blinks through my mind, but the giant creatures flying toward us are the antithesis to all things whimsical and little. And they look nothing like tea trays.

Fierce gusts rip through our hair. I choke on a puff of blowing sand. Jeb pushes me behind him the instant a bat swoops down. Sleek as crimson leather, the mutant creature lifts off, carrying Jeb into the sky with its talons.

An eagle-faced goon opens the glass window on his helmet and laughs from his seat atop the bat's back. "Easy as catching sunning snails."

"You fool. It's the girl Manti wants!" another one shouts from his winged perch. "And remember, she's to be kept intact!"

"Then I'd say we got here in the nick of time," blurts a chicken-beaked goon crudely. His compatriots howl with laughter before turning their airborne mounts toward me.

"Jeb!" I scream.

"Get to the lighthouse!" he yells from up high as he wrestles the claws curled around him.

No way. I release my wings. As I launch toward Jeb, three bats swoop at me from different directions. So tuned in to their target, their goon riders don't notice each other. The closest bat dips a swanlike neck. The center of its starfish-shaped muzzle opens, thrusting out a cluster of six-foot long, slimy tentacles lined with sharp fangs. One of the teeth snatches my diary necklace and breaks the cord.

Shrieking, I toss out my hand to pry the string off the bat's fanged tongue, but the bat swallows the tiny book. The other two goon birds veer deathly close. I dive at the last minute. The bats collide and plunge into the ocean with their riders. Flattening out my wings along a current of wind, I skim over the water and ascend.

Silhouetted against the starry sky, Jeb breaks free of his captor and hangs on to a talon while calling upon a wave. The water lifts high enough for him to drop into place. He slides down a slanted plane of foam toward me, catches me around the waist, and skates us both to the lighthouse's entrance.

We rush inside and slam the door, locking it behind us.

Upstairs, Dad is still sleeping. Jeb and I inch toward the porthole. Amid screeches and thundering wings, our tower shakes. Bits of the wall crumble away, forming a wide crack. More bats gather at the opening, trying to dig through the rock. The sky thickens as they circle overhead, taking turns attacking our sanctuary.

The beacon flashes across them in intervals, spotlighting hideous tentacles and veined wings. More and more holes appear in the tower as the walls fail to withstand the collisions.

Gusts from giant wings filter through the openings. The curtains swirl around Dad's canopied bed and my bare skin chills.

Another bat hammers the tower. I struggle to keep balance. "We're outnumbered!"

"Not even close," Jeb answers calmly. His eyes sparkle with netherling sorcery. With a sweep of his fingers through the porthole, grainy cyclones stir up from the ground surrounding the lighthouse. "We have regiments as innumerable as the sands."

Inspired by his ingenuity, I try my hand. "And arsenals as uncountable as the stars." Using the trick Morpheus taught me, I reassign Jeb's night sky a new task: guided missiles.

The stars careen in the direction of our attackers like giant flaming rocks, herding them toward Jeb's sand funnels. Several goons avoid the cyclones by diving off their bats. They flap deteriorated wings across the ocean in hopes of escape. My star missiles catch them, ripping through feathered chests and knocking off helmeted heads. All that's left are their corpses—bright orange cinders and black ash afloat atop the frothy waves.

The sand cyclones carry the bats away through the room's exit.

As the dust settles, we survey the mess around us.

I snort, a bemused and nonsensical sound that's completely out of place with what just happened.

Jeb glances over at me, grinning. "We still make a great team," he says, his hair catching a breeze.

"Just like in Wonderland, when you didn't have any magic at all."

He doesn't answer, only studies me thoughtfully. He looks away to wave his hand across the cluttered floor. The tower repairs itself, holes sealing up bit by bit, until only a powdery residue remains.

"Will there be more of those bat things?" I ask.

"They're harmless without their riders," Jeb answers. "I've got to see how the break-in happened. The graffiti army should've stopped it. I also need to make sure the other rooms are okay."

The concern in his voice touches me. He's worried about his creations.

"We should both get some clothes on first," I remind him.

He pauses, his gaze traversing my body. My arms cross self-consciously, though such modesty seems unnecessary after all I've promised him. The key at my neck meets my inner wrist and I remember the lost diary.

As if sensing my thoughts, Jeb frowns. "What happened to the book?"

"One of the bats swallowed it. Red's memories are gone."

He curses.

Dread and nausea make my head swim. I glance over my shoulder at the bed. The curtains are tangled around the posts, exposing Dad's peaceful, sleeping face.

"It's going to be okay, skater girl." Jeb's voice is close and soft. He runs a fingertip along my left wing, sending a thousand titillating sparks through my spine.

"I hope so."

He pulls me into a hug, stroking my frizzed-out hair. "It will. Because you're not just a girl anymore. You're powerful and brave. A better queen than Red could ever hope to be." The heat from his bare torso seeps into my chest, warming me all the way to my toes.

A hissing sound erupts outside the porthole. Jeb breaks our embrace to face the cloud of orange, glittery mist seeping in.

I sigh in relief. "Chessie."

Jeb holds out his hand for the hovering embers.

The little netherling's smile appears, although it's actually a frown because as he materializes on Jeb's palm, he's upside down, his tail skewed like a question mark. Tied to his paw is a corked vial. The label reads *Stone Counteractant*, just above a black-and-white drawing of a scorpion fly.

"You got the cure," Jeb says, incredulous.

"Thank you!" I take the vial, so relieved I can't contain a smile.

The furry netherling flips upright but his whiskers droop further downward.

"What is it?" I concentrate on his whirling eyes. "Wait. *Morpheus* got the cure?" I translate for Jeb. "He went into the castle? But he had a plan for tomorrow."

He would never do something so spontaneous. Unless he really was convinced I wouldn't survive another encounter with Red. I'm the only one he would put himself at risk for, because I'm a queen and Wonderland is his utmost priority. But even beyond that . . . because he loves me.

My soul sinks, acutely aware of how I've hurt him tonight. And he doesn't even know. "Where is he?" I ask.

When the answer surfaces within Chessie's pupils, I drop to my knees.

"Al." Jeb kneels beside me and forces me to look at him. "What did he say?"

I grind my teeth to keep from screaming. "Morpheus has been

captured. He's scheduled to be the entertainment at the Hallowed Festival tomorrow. The queen is going to harvest his beating heart."

❄·I·❄

We pour the curative down Dad's throat and Jeb releases him from his dream state. Then we take turns showering, getting dressed, and explaining to Dad everything that happened while he was out. Neither Jeb nor I mention our engagement. It feels wrong, to give my dad reason to celebrate while Morpheus's life hangs in the balance.

Our plan is back on for first thing in the morning when the gates open. We choose our clothes wisely. It would be a mistake to have the added vulnerability of water-soluble outfits on such a precarious mission.

Dad and I will wear the tunic and trousers from Uncle Bernie, while Jeb dons all that's left of his prom tuxedo: navy blue flocked velvet vest and navy pants. Paired with a navy T-shirt from his painted wardrobe, his outfit is complete.

I've yet to fill Dad in on the small detail of Red's pending possession. Now that I've lost the diary, it's the only way to save Wonderland. He would never go along with the plan if he knew. I'm back to lying to him for his own good.

While Jeb and Chessie search the mountain rooms, Dad soaks in a hot tub. Although the curative dissolved the stone, the muscles and bones in his leg sustained some damage.

He limps out of the bathroom fully dressed, rubbing a towel over his wet hair.

"Anything to eat? I'm starving."

Jeb told me this would happen. It's a side effect of the dream state. I load up a plate with the honeycomb-flower and rabbit jerky and take a couple of pieces for myself. The floating lanterns cast amber light and shadows around us as I silently watch him wolf the rest down. I wonder if he was this ravenous when Mom rescued him from Wonderland. After all, he'd been sleeping for years that time.

Dad has started on his third helping when Chessie and Jeb return.

Jeb carries Dad's duffel and the garment bag that contains my scorpion-winged dress. I can't stop replaying Morpheus's reaction when I loosened the drawstring. How he teased and joked to make light of the incredibly sweet gesture. How he dismissed all the cuts from the razor-sharp edges he must've endured before he finally had the centipede legs sewn in place as protective fringe.

"Are the simulacrum suits in the duffel?" I ask, trying to hide the tremor in my voice.

"We could only find two." Jeb wipes paint from his hands on a towel. "Morpheus's room was a wreck. All of them were. There were a couple of bats tangled in the graffiti. That's how the goons got through the entrance. They came up through the ocean and sacrificed some of their rides for a distraction. I'm not sure how they found their way to the mountain in the first place. I never saw any signs of CC. Also not sure how they knew to use rainwater on the doors and rooms to melt everything away." He tries to appear nonchalant, but his face is pale.

I know too well what it's like to watch something you created die. A month ago, I breathed life into flames, then had to be the one to douse them to save my peers at school. It hurt, like losing a piece of myself.

Maybe it's for the best. Maybe those dark and damaged parts of Jeb's soul will at last be put to rest, and he can abandon this world and all the bitterness and doubts . . . leave everything behind without a second thought. With the exception of the dreams in the willow room. I hope he holds on to those.

"The only other thing left in Morpheus's room was this garment bag," Jeb says, stirring me from my thoughts. "Do you know about the dress inside?"

"Armor," I whisper, feeling numb as Morpheus's words taunt me: *I rather hoped you'd wear it to face Red. It is the only coat of armor worthy of your dangerous beauty.*

My netherling intuition rouses, a theory taking shape. It's no coincidence that only one invisible suit is gone, that the goons knew how to destroy Jeb's artwork, or that when everything melted away, the duffel and the garment bag were the two things that remained . . . because they're real, not painted. It's also no coincidence the goons had been sent for me.

I bite my lip.

"Al, what are you thinking?" Jeb presses.

Dad stands up from the table, favoring his left leg.

I drag my fingers though my damp hair to hide that they're trembling. "Morpheus always has an escape plan. That's why he took a simulacrum suit. For him to be captured, he had to *let* himself be captured. Something made him alter the original plan. Maybe he even let a few things slip on purpose. Everything that's happened in this mountain tonight has been a strategic move to get us to come after him. For some reason, it's important that we go to that castle tomorrow, and that one of us . . . me . . . is fully visible."

Dad slams his fist on the table, rattling the plate. "That's suicide! We should head straight to the Wonderland gate while everyone is preoccupied at this monster fest."

"I'm going." I scoop up the garment bag. "It doesn't matter why he was captured. Intentional or not, he's been captured, which means his suit has been confiscated, too. He's put himself in real danger. I won't leave him there. And he's counting on it."

I don't finish my explanation . . . that I have to save him because the netherling side of me has fallen in love with him. I don't have time to deal with the fallout of admitting that aloud.

Dad slaps his gimp leg. "We should at least try to get real backup. Without a suit for me, I'm worthless. We weren't able to send the pigeon back, so Bernard is probably halfway here, looking for us. We could find him, enlist his help."

"That could take a full day," Jeb says.

I shake my head. "Morpheus doesn't have that much time."

Dad's eyelid twitches. "You are not putting your neck out for that manipulative—"

"Dad!" I try to overlook his prejudice. He didn't see firsthand how Morpheus assisted when he'd been stung, or any of the other courageous things Morpheus has done in the past—all incredible feats for a solitary, selfish fae.

He also can't see that deep inside, my netherling instincts are telling me the reason Morpheus has arranged this is somehow related to Wonderland's best interests. Though I still don't completely trust his methods, I understand his motives. And one thing I will never doubt is his loyalty to his beloved home.

Our home.

"I agree with Al," Jeb says, shocking me and Dad both. "You know I'm the last person to jump on the Bugs'R'Us bandwagon." He casts me a dark scowl, ensuring me of his everlasting disdain for Morpheus. "I don't like his tactics, but he's protected me while we've been here. He could've exploited me for prestige and power.

For whatever reason, he did the right thing. Because of that, we owe it to him to see him back to Wonderland."

Earlier, I explained to Jeb what Morpheus said about him being a vessel, and he's still not backing out. He trusts my strength and judgment that much.

"Thank you," I whisper.

Something flickers in his eyes before he tears his gaze from mine: *anguish*. It cuts as deftly as a blade. I know it's because of my unspoken feelings for Morpheus. Even with all that's settled between us, I'm starting to understand that asking Jeb to live a life with me, while knowing I'll have a future with another, might be too much for any mortal man to endure. I only hope it doesn't keep him from walking through the Wonderland gate when it's time, no matter what it means for us.

That intense tearing sensation digs deeper into my heart. I turn my back to mask my wince and press my thumb to my sternum, starting toward the stairs.

"You can't be serious about this," Dad says from behind.

I inhale a few shallow breaths. "It's time for me to face Red. No more hiding." I'm resigned to the fight ahead, knowing she's the only one who can fix all the things that are wrong—in me and Wonderland. There's relief in acknowledging that.

"It's a trap!" Dad shouts. I hear him shuffling awkwardly on his wounded leg. "What's your advantage once you're captured?"

I twirl to face him. Jeb has resurrected Dad's shadow. The dark creature cups Dad's elbows from behind to help him balance.

"Our advantage," I answer, "is that Jeb, Chessie, and I are the only three beings in this world who can use magic. Which is the same reason you can't stop me. So you can either go along and hide outside the castle as backup, or wait here until it's over. I love you, Dad, but it's my kingdom at risk, so it's my call as queen."

Jeb studies his boots. Dad clenches his jaw so hard I could swear the scorpion fly's poison has seeped into his chin. Yet he doesn't say another word.

Up in the tower, I take out the gown and admire how the winged tiers shimmer in the soft starlight—the orange, red, and black contrasting like shadows to flames. It almost seems sacrilegious to loosen the glittery green centipede legs so meticulously sewn into place, to leave each fringe weakened. But Morpheus would applaud the choice. In fact, I sense that I'm doing exactly what he expects me to.

Once I'm done, I take the diary key off my neck. It's useless now. I carefully slide the dress into place over my skin. It fits as if painted on, hugging my curves and flaring at my knees. The lining is made of rabbit's fur. I'm wrapped in a shell of comfort, while on the outside, all it will take is my magical coaxing to lift away the centipede hems and expose the wings' razor-sharp edges, rendering me untouchable.

I can't think of a better coat of arms. I won't be standing in the presence of Red or Hart wearing a knight's tunic and baggy pants. In this dress, I'll be playing the part of Medusa, turning my evil ancestors to stone with a brash baring of terrible beauty. If the sting-ers hadn't been removed, I could change Hart to a literal statue, which would make her surrender of Red's spirit so much simpler. Instead, I have a gown with bite enough to make the heartless queen think twice about dismissing me or my demands.

I slip into my red leathery shoulder gloves to protect my arms, then pull on the leggings and boots—which, of course, are the per-fect fit. Perfect for walking straight into the wisdom keeper's web.

I'm not going in blind. I know Morpheus has an agenda. All I can do is hope it's for the greater good, and that his plan is foolproof this time.

Otherwise, I'm the biggest fool of all, for leading the two humans I love most to their deaths.

⁂

We decide a few hours of sleep are more important than Jeb altering the landscape to our benefit. When morning arrives, it's cloudy and cold, but at least we're rested and ready for battle.

We fly toward the castle—Jeb and Dad carried by their shadows, and me soaring high on a chilly updraft of wind. Morpheus's shadow follows behind at Jeb's command so we'll all have a way to escape once our business at the castle is done.

Sunrise streaks the horizon in tendrils of bloody red splashed across a stone gray sky; I try to convince myself it's not an omen. Our destination is a cliff far enough from the castle to avoid being seen by the goon birds and their bats patrolling the turrets, yet close enough to scope out the entrance.

We arrive at an outcropping of rocks that form a cave. I land gracefully behind some trees, wishing Morpheus were here to see. *"It's all in the ankles,"* I mumble.

Chessie tucks himself beneath my loose bun, tickling the nape of my neck. Jeb and Dad alight beside me and we peer through the thickly clustered trunks. In lieu of water, the moat surrounding the outer walls contains ash—the remains of the dead. A school of giant eels, appearing prehistoric with bony obtrusions jutting from their backs like shark fins, swim through the powdered carnage.

They're nothing like my pets at home.

A motley crowd of mutants are gathered on the outer banks of the moat, waiting, just like us, for the drawbridge to drop and invite them in.

Though *invite* isn't quite the right word. There's nothing welcoming about this place. Giant fanged skulls sit atop the turrets as if in effigy, along with skeletal tails that wind around the towers in coils. It's as if a legion of dragons wrapped around the stone to die, then petrified. The outer walls slump inward on an unnatural slant, giving the impression they could fall and crush everyone inside at any moment.

A loud creaking howl accompanies the lowering drawbridge and tugs at my gut.

"We need to get down there," Jeb says.

I turn to Dad. "Please don't be angry."

He sighs. "How could I be? Your mom would've done the same thing. Sacrificed everything to save someone she cared about. She did, in fact."

I hug him, breathing in all the scents of home. When I was a little girl, snuggled against his shoulder, I always felt safe. That will never change. "Thanks, Dad."

"Sure," he mumbles against my head. "I understand. But I don't have to like it."

He'll like it even less when he sees who I'm bringing back in addition to Morpheus.

"I love you, Butterfly," he whispers.

"I love you, too." He holds me so long, I have to break free.

Sighing, he turns to Jeb to clap his shoulder and hand off his iron dagger. "Take care of my girl."

Jeb secures the weapon. "She's the one with all the moves. I'm hoping she'll take care of me."

Before Dad can delay us another second, we're on our way.

We wind through the trees to the end of the cliff and coast down behind a craggy outcropping. Jeb sends his shadow back to stay with Dad.

While waiting to slip into line, Jeb studies my face, as if memorizing every feature. I glide my gloved fingers across his cheek, brushing aside some dark wavy strands.

His gaze intensifies, full of unnameable emotions. "Let's get you ready, foxy lady."

I manage a grin as he takes out a furry foxlike mask from inside his jacket and slides it into place over my eyes. He painted it for me, custom-designed the eye slits and muzzle to fit the top half of my face. Feathers form the ears, and he even added a butterfly's antennae. With the addition of my wings and dress, I almost look the part of the insects I once killed so thoughtlessly.

I straighten the simulacrum suit over his tux and T-shirt. He has the other suit along with his painting items inside the duffel bag he's slung across his shoulder, ready for Morpheus once he finds him. I know he's secretly hoping to find his doppelganger, too, although he hasn't said it aloud.

"Time to blend in," Jeb says, tucking Chessie's dangling tail into my bun.

I nod, but I'm not ready to stop looking at him yet. He's the only thing giving my legs the strength to stand.

"Just remember," he says. "We stick to the plan. Get Hart alone, convince her to hand Red over, and I'll search the dungeon. Once you get Red, hightail it out. Don't worry about us. We'll be invisible, and you can fly. Everything's going to be all right. Send Chessie if something goes wrong, and we'll find you."

I nod again. There's so much I want to say to him: *Thank you for your faith in me, for always putting yourself on the line for this crazy half life of mine—I love you and don't want to lose you . . .* But all I can manage is, "Be safe."

"Back at ya." He tucks the duffel bag under his arm to keep it hidden under the simulacrum and starts to gather the hood over his head.

As if rethinking, he stops and laces his fingertips through my gloved hand, pulling me close. "In case I don't get another chance to tell you . . . One, you look amazing." He traces my eye markings where they curl out from under the fuzzy edges of my mask. "And two . . ." He turns my hand to kiss my covered palm. "You got this, fairy queen."

Sucking in a sharp breath, I throw my arms around his neck. He hugs me tight, presses his lips to the top of my head, then steps back and pulls his hood into place, vanishing from sight.

His invisible fingertips touch my leather ones, leading me out to follow the current of creatures great and small. With the comforting pressure of his hand driving me, I trail the end of the line.

My dress jangles softly as we tromp across the wooden bridge, a mellifluous undercurrent at odds with the ominous swishing of the eels some twenty feet beneath us. A shiver races through my spine as Chessie burrows deeper into my hair.

Gurgles, snorts, and murmurs drift from the guests, shifting my attention from what's below to what's ahead. In appearance, they're similar to the netherlings I encountered in Wonderland at the Feast of Beasts a year ago . . . more bestial than humanoid, some with living plants growing out of their skin. Though these creatures are twisted and gnarled, mutated from using their magic.

It's a hard habit to break, as proven by Jeb's struggle to walk away from the power. Maybe that's an upside to my letting Red possess me. It will give Jeb even more incentive to leave, in case my vow for a future isn't enough.

As we step off the bridge, we filter through a small covered portico, then the courtyard opens up—some three acres wide. Rising high in the center are two thirty-story skeletal frames, tall and loopy, like twin roller coasters made of giant bones, eerily similar to the petrified dragon remnants on the castle towers. So mesmerized by the sight, I nearly trip over a reptilian tail in front of me. A snarling mouth travels along its scales, sliding from the creature's face to the end of its tail, and yaps at me like a disgruntled puppy.

Apologizing, I take a few steps back.

Jeb steadies me from behind and I focus on our surroundings again.

When I was ten, Dad and I went to a circus in the human realm. Ultraviolet settings, disturbing neon costumes—a black-light nightmare so rich with atmosphere and characters, it took on a life of its own. I didn't understand at the time why I felt so comfortable amid the bizarre grandeur of it all. Not until last year, when I started remembering that Wonderland's landscapes have the same qualities and how many dreams I spent there with Morpheus.

Now, surrounded by the denizens of AnyElsewhere inside the courtyard, I can't help but fall back into those memories. With the overcast sky and low-hanging walls folded in on us, the darkened background magnifies the fluorescent color scheme of water fountains, festival tents, and statues.

Jeb squeezes my hand three times, our signal. Since I can't watch him go, I glance across the way where several reptilian guards escort a mutant with a grizzly's head and a monkey's body off the grounds in cuffs. They start down some stone steps set into the wall of the castle. It's a safe bet they're going to the dungeon.

"Be careful," I whisper, though I know he's already gone. Chessie's warmth under my hair offers a small comfort.

I pass a cluster of fountains. An odd assortment of creatures play handcrafted musical instruments, composing haunting songs on pumpkin drums, celery guitars, and flutes made of river reeds. Glowing sprites spin in the air and perform aerial ballets, using the spouting water to propel them upward. They screech as the water changes to a haze of steam that boils their bare flesh. Breaking free, they scramble for the edges of the fountains and whimper, nursing their blisters. The bestial spectators beside me laugh and shout slurred encouragements, as if intoxicated by the violence. The steam turns back to liquid, and the sprites mount the water sprays once more. The tiny netherlings must be driven by a compulsion to seek out pain, for they continue until their bodies are so damaged, they die and turn to piles of ash.

I fight my fascination and turn away.

Everywhere I look, similar gruesome sports and sadistic games take place. In one corner, inside an open tent, feline creatures covered in scales with serpentine faces and forked tongues walk on all fours along high wires strung over a flaming pit. Their tender paws sizzle across the searing metal and the noxious scent of scorched scales fills the air. Again, I notice piles of ash where prior participants died.

"Faster!" a woolly creature with moss sprouting from his ears yells from below. "No pussyfooting! Give us a show!" The participants yowl and cry, yet still limp back into line to go again as soon as they leap down.

Inside another tent, contenders take turns crawling through a trench filled with beetles whose exoskeletons are shiny, silver, and as sharp as double-edged razor blades. Though each player is sliced and bleeding by the end, they don't hesitate to return for another bout.

Clenching my teeth against an unsettling urge to walk barefoot through the trench myself, I make my way toward the center of the yard, where reptilian guards roll in two clear, glassy balls—each one big enough to house a garden shed—and hoist them with ropes and pulleys onto the skeletal roller-coaster frames I saw earlier. The guards lock them in place on steep inclines that will launch the spheres into the thirty-story drops. The image reminds me of the marble runs Jeb used to make with his dad, only these are to scale.

A crowd gathers and grows restless for the event. I stay in the back, curious, but keep my eyes open for any sign of the Queen of Hearts. With a glance to assure no one's looking, I tug on Chessie's tail, the signal for him to set off on his search for Nikki. He's supposed to find her and come back to me. He flitters away, using the shadows for cover.

A tall man, built like a Greek god and wearing only black satiny pants that hug every muscle, climbs a ladder to the top of the wooden incline. He steps to the edge of the giant frame. Instead of bare feet, he has silvery hooves, although his hands are humanoid.

His smooth skin shines like copper—a severe contrast to his pale blue eyes. Thick white hair grows from his head, along the nape of his neck, and down between his shoulder blades like a horse's mane. A swirling nine-inch silver horn curves out above the bridge of his aquiline nose, centered between white eyebrows.

He's gorgeous. And he's obviously in charge.

Manti. I edge closer to the noisy crowd. He's the best lead to find Hart and Red.

"Any one of you who wishes to challenge me for the king's throne . . ." His voice, deep and dulcet, silences the murmurings. "This is your chance." He holds up a golden crown and smiles, teeth canine-sharp and blinding white.

Someone stirs in the crowd. A lion creature, walking on two legs like a man, raises his fisted paw in the air. "I challenge thee!" he roars. His golden fur glistens in the soft light as two lantern-bearing guards escort him toward the ladder.

Once they've scaled to the top, the guards snap open transparent doors on the glass orbs so Manti and his opponent can climb into their spheres. Each guard drops in a small, fluffy creature from a box.

Although the animals look as adorable and benign as Pomeranian puppies, manticorn and lion alike bristle and back up, keeping a wary eye on their companions.

"Let the caucus race begin!" one of the guards shouts as the doors slam shut.

The crowd howls as the ramps click open, propelling the balls into play along the twisted run with a sound as loud as thunder. It doesn't take long to realize why Manti and his opponent feared the addition of the tiny animals. The creatures have the ability to turn themselves wrong-side out and become nothing but teeth. Spatters of red appear on the insides of the orb, smearing as the occupants try to avoid the snapping torture. They're stuck in a rotary fish tank with furry piranhas.

My netherling sensibility holds me captive, makes me hungry to watch. Each participant tries to stay balanced enough—in spite of being eaten alive and slipping in his own blood—to increase the momentum of his rolling ball and be the first to the end of the run.

Manti's orb reaches the finish line, and he's quickly dragged free while the still snapping inside-out puppy—saturated with blood—is shoved back into its box. Two guards help Manti stand, pouring something down his throat from a bottle. The gouges in his skin miraculously heal, leaving no scars.

The lion's sphere comes to a stop and two other guards drag him free. He's been gnawed so much, his fur is gone—leaving his whole body a raw gaping wound.

The spectators start to chant: *"Take him apart! Show us the heart!"*

With a fluid stride, Manti leads the way. The guards drag the unconscious lion fae to a round, deep puddle of water, set into the ground and edged by flat stones.

"Into the pool of fears!" Manti shouts.

The guards dump the lion in. He awakens and flails at the surface, howling in terror as bubbles churn and the water runs red. What's left of his skin is eaten away by an acidic reaction until something drags him down inside the depths. A few seconds later, a meaty object bobs to the surface. Manti picks it up tenderly and lays it on a gold, satin pillow, showcasing the still-beating heart for all to see.

I should be terrified. Instead, I'm furious. The thought that the queen plans to do the same to Morpheus's heart triggers a murderous compulsion inside me. Wonderland is violent and bizarre, but charming in its way. AnyElsewhere is a whole new level of cruelty. Bedlam on steroids.

The cheers grow deafening as an exquisite woman strides gracefully onto the scene. Her hair is parted down the middle, one side dark burgundy and the other a fiery crimson. Her dress is at once startling and beautiful, just like her. Red and burgundy ruffles cascade over a black tulle underskirt. It creates the effect of zebra stripes, flaring out to a full, lovely shape that drags on the floor. Pulsing, shimmery red beads the size of lima beans embellish the elbow-length sleeves. But they aren't beads at all. She's wearing the hearts of sprites on her sleeves.

Her wings mirror mine: opaque and jeweled. That, with the addition of matching eye patches, glistening skin, and a small gold tiara, leaves no question as to her identity. She might be centuries old, but she looks young enough to be my mom's sister.

Manti holds up the pillow for Hart and kneels on one knee. "For you, O Majestic One."

She places a gold crown on his head and takes the heart. Blood drizzles between her fingers as she holds the throbbing organ high.

"Any other challengers feeling *lionhearted* today?" she asks, her melodious voice a blend of two octaves, as if she were singing a duet with herself. Or maybe it's her voice combined with Red's.

I waver in midair, reminded of how Red used me for a mouthpiece a year ago, how it felt to have her vines burrow through my blood veins and manipulate me like a puppet.

"Any of you wish to challenge the king?" the queen taunts once more.

My throat dries. It's now or never. Grimacing, I slip off my fox mask and drop it. I flap my wings to lift myself above the crowd, high enough to be seen in the lantern lights yet out of reach of any hands or claws.

"I wish to challenge the *queen!*" I shout.

The Queen of Hearts places her bleeding, macabre prize on the pillow, frowning up at me as she wipes the blood from her hands onto Manti's white mane. Several of the guards shove aside the spectators below me and aim arrows at my wings.

The burgundy side of the queen's hair turns crimson, strand by strand. *"Weapons down! I command you."* Red's voice breaks from Hart's mouth on a gust of air. A vinelike appendage unfurls from the queen's forearm—a physical manifestation of Red's possession. The ivy snaps at the guards. *"I said weapons down!"*

They lower their bows and back up.

"No! I am the one in charge," Hart shouts, her voice rising an octave. She wrestles Red's tentacle protrusion, her burgundy locks overtaking once more. "Capture the girl and bring me her life-clock! It is special. It will be the pride of my collection."

Confused by her command, I beat my wings harder to stay adrift and out of reach.

The queen motions to her guards. Two new ivy appendages slip free from her sleeves and latch onto both her wrists.

"The girl is to be left intact," Red hisses, wrapping her vines around Hart's arms until they're bound to her waist.

The queen fights with the vines and her hair flashes—from bright red to burgundy. The guards shuffle their feet, unsure which queen to listen to. Even Manti appears confused. It's as if they've learned the hard way that whichever queen gains control of the body should have their loyalty.

"The girl came of her own volition," Red reasons, *"just as Morpheus predicted she would. Her body is not to be harmed. She's here for the ceremony, and this grim assemblage will serve as witnesses."* At this, all of the queen's hair changes to crimson.

Ceremony. Morpheus must've laid out our proposition for Red to inhabit my body and leave this world. I'm assuming they've talked Hart into it somehow.

But what's a ceremony have to do with it?

"I wasn't aware we'd need witnesses," I shout, hovering higher.

Movement stirs behind the queen. Her subjects and attendants part to make way and Morpheus steps through. At first glance, I'm thrilled to see him unchained and unhurt. Then I notice how he's dressed, and how at home he seems standing in the midst of the royal party.

Looking up at me, he takes off a tall, checkered red and burgundy top hat that complements his burgundy pinstriped suit, black shirt, and red tie. His jeweled eye markings blink darkest purple, and he offers his most scintillating smile. "Come down, luv. Don't be shy. Every wedding ceremony needs witnesses. Why should mine and yours be any different?"

MATTERS OF
THE HEART

The Queen of Hearts's hair flip-flops from one shade to the other as she accompanies us to a room in the castle. Three of her guards follow behind. It reminds me of when I was forced to stroll down a corridor in the Red castle with Morpheus a year ago, only minutes away from sure death at the snarling mouth of a bandersnatch.

A death he saved me from, I remind myself.

I clench my jaw as he holds my hand, fingers woven through mine. I've postponed unleashing my magic and the deadly dress. I'm going along with the engagement charade for three reasons:

One: Jeb is somewhere in this castle, and I have to keep my cool long enough to locate him.

Two: I'm so relieved that Morpheus's heart isn't on the chopping block, I can't find it in my own heart to strangle him yet.

And three: Morpheus's expression promises answers and begs cooperation. There's more to this than he's letting on.

I'll finesse the truth out of him once he and I are alone, which must be what he had in mind when he requested we have a moment to ourselves before the ceremony. Red agreed, but each step I take becomes more weighted. I suspect she was compliant because we're going somewhere private to transfer her spirit.

Without the lifeline of the diary, I may as well be drowning. I tighten my fingers through Morpheus's as waves of insecurity roll over me. Holding my gaze, he lifts my hand and kisses my gloved knuckles. He's genuinely glad to see me.

That would change in a blink, were he to hear about my life-magic vow to Jeb. Even though the human side of me has always belonged to Jeb, even though somewhere in Morpheus's heart he's always known it, he's going to be furious. Both guys may have learned to coexist in this world, but if Jeb stands in the way of some master plan, things could change in a heartbeat. I won't tell Morpheus while we're in this castle. His jealous, feral side is too unpredictable when it comes to Wonderland or me.

After climbing two flights of winding stairs, we walk through a marble hallway. Hundreds of shadow boxes line the walls, boasting a selection of hearts—different sizes and shapes—that pump wildly in their compartments. With each thump, blurs of red smear the glass lids, as if the organs are knocking on the doors of their prisons. A coppery, meaty stench curdles my stomach.

I try not to compare the bugs I killed and hung on the walls at home to what Hart has done, but the parallel is striking. Collecting must be in my blood. I don't dare speculate what else might be . . .

The guards open a set of double doors and usher us into a chamber with black shag carpet and burgundy tiled walls. The queen accompanies us inside against her will. It's apparent by her crimson hair that Red has taken over again. After we're safely inside, the guards step out into the hall and close the door behind them.

"Welcome to Hart's playroom." Red's breathy murmur slithers into my personal space.

Her presence pricks that frangible place behind my sternum where she left her mark. I crush my fur-lined bodice against my skin in an effort not to be paralyzed by the climate of terror and oppression that surrounds her in any form. I have to be stronger than her.

I familiarize myself with the room, seeking out possible weapons. An assortment of gold velvet parlor chairs and chaise lounges lines the walls. Stolen hearts provide the decor: picture and mirror frames utilize the throbbing organs in grisly albeit creative ways; throw rugs ornament the carpet, tasseled with sprite-size thumping beads like the ones on the queen's sleeves.

The most intricate and morbid display is a giant brass chandelier at the center of the domed ceiling, tipped with the pulsating organs. Impaled with light bulbs, they glow from within, casting veined luminaries along the white ceiling. The contractions of hollow muscles and the rush of blood circulate in an eternal loop, as if projected onto a screen. With the discordant vibration of heartbeats and the strange, pulsing lights, the room feels like a conscious thing—and we are the prey, trapped inside its rib cage.

Is this what Morpheus felt like, being swallowed by the bandersnatch?

Disoriented, I catch his elbow. In response, one of his wings enfolds both of mine, snuggling me into his side in unwavering support. His scent surrounds me.

"*The one thing Hart asks,*" Red says, her vines wrestling the queen's hands to maintain control, "*is that you not touch her paints or her tarts.*"

A table is set with pastries along with a glass of white liquid that looks like milk. On the wall above it hangs an easel filled with blank papers held in place by a clip. A set of finger paints in small containers waits to be used. The sight of them makes me think of Jeb, and I gasp against the shortness of breath that has come to accompany the knifelike stab behind my breastbone. Dizziness blurs my vision.

As if sensing my distress, Morpheus takes a seat on a parlor chair and draws me into his lap—my wings draped to one side of his legs and my calves along the other. He folds his arms around me, completely at ease.

"You see. It's as I told you," he speaks to Red, his voice a deep rumble close to my ear. "We're utterly in love, and planning our future." He settles our joined hands in my lap, causing the dress's tiers to jingle softly. I struggle not to stiffen as I wait for the ripping inside my heart to subside. The backs of my thighs are flush against his lithe, muscular ones, a distraction and a comfort. "She wore the wedding dress I told you of. Is that not proof enough? Now, as per your side of the bargain—"

"*Oh no,*" Red intones. "*Not until we are married. That is the bargain. You've tricked me once. It won't happen again.*"

"*We* are married? What do you mean, we?" I look over my shoulder at Morpheus, who offers a pleading wince from beneath his hat's brim. It's infuriating to have the iron dome overhead. Without it, he could send me his thoughts instead of me playing this game blind.

"*We, as in us three. The wicked trinity.*" Red smirks at her cleverness, and a stray strand of ivy pulls the red streak free from my bun. The hearts on her gown's sleeves begin thumping so wildly, they make a wet smacking sound. Her dark blue gaze falls on mine as my hair comes alive, wrapping around her vine affectionately. It's my magic causing the contact, not hers, which scares me even more.

"You and I are to reclaim the throne for our bloodline once and for all," Red continues. *"And to prove to me that you are serious about your royal duties, that living as queen in Wonderland is your one priority, and to ensure there are no more mortal distractions, you will marry Morpheus, today. He told me you love one another, that you will rule the Red kingdom together. I want to see it for myself. I will not leave this place until you've forsaken your other life and the boy who's been such a distraction for you. Or, if you prefer, I can rid you of him permanently and give our predecessor the human heart she's been craving for her collection."*

Fear for Jeb's safety resurrects my courage. I yank my treasonous hair away, forcing it behind my ear. "Keep making threats like that and I won't take you out of here at all, wretch. You can stay and rot."

"Your beloved betrothed wants me to repair Wonderland far too much to allow your stubbornness to stand in his way. Isn't that right?"

I glare over my shoulder at Morpheus. He glares back, unreadable.

"Looks like the only rotting will be your free spirit under my command," Red baits, as one of her vines slithers toward me on the floor.

Still riding my surge of anger, I concentrate on the carpet beneath her, imagining the pile as the tentacles of a sea anemone. The fibers stretch tall and tubular, capturing her advancing appendage.

I smile as she looks up at me, shocked. "I've been practicing.

Want to try again? I have an entire sea of carpet to play with. And the way I remember it, your spirit withered under *my* command, just like now."

Morpheus's fingers tighten through mine—a squeeze of encouragement or of warning, I'm not sure. Either way, I ignore him and engage in a stare-down with her poisonous eyes.

"Oh, but I've taken measures to assure that won't happen again. Haven't you noticed yet?" Red lifts Hart's inanimate hand and points it at my chest, triggering the tearing pain anew.

My concentration wavers. The vine I captured escapes the shrinking filaments of carpet.

In the same moment, Red topples, flung to the floor by Hart's resurgence in their shared body. They roll around, looking like a mutated mental patient, scratching and tearing at their ever-changing hair with fingers and snarls of ivy.

I leap to my feet, ready to liberate my dress's razor edges and rip her to shreds while I have some leverage.

Morpheus tugs me back into his lap and whispers in my ear, "You would only damage the shell and turn both spirits to ash." It's amazing how he reads my mind without any magic at all. "We need Red to fix Wonderland. Bide your time, luv. Bide. Your. Time."

Always the voice of reason, even when madness drives his every action. Red holds all the cards, along with my heart. She admitted she's tainted me, confirmed my suspicion that I need her not only to fix Wonderland but to fix my insides.

There's a loud thud as the queen's spinning body busts into the table's legs and spills the milk. Red manages to get the upper hand again. She stands, entwines the queen's arms, and smooths her crimson hair with a shaky vine. "*Get your betrothed in hand, or the bargain is off,*" she says to Morpheus. *"And you know what that will mean for your precious home."*

I start to offer a nasty retort, but Morpheus tightens his hold around my waist—an unspoken plea.

Red's attention shifts to me. "*Today, you will welcome my spirit within your body. We will wed Morpheus, leave AnyElsewhere, and take our rightful place on the Red throne. Your betrothed has voiced a particular eagerness to begin your honeymoon.*" She rustles to the door in a flowing cascade of netting, satin, and tentacle-like vines. *"Prepare for the ceremony. I'll return before the hour is out."*

She leaves Morpheus and me behind the closed door with nothing but the pounding of a hundred hearts—those that are disembodied and rocking the room, and the two wrestling within our own chests.

I leap off his lap and face him. "Eagerness to begin our honeymoon? Really?"

"Oh, don't be so coy, my blossom," he purrs, his flawless face the embodiment of temptation beneath the chandelier's throbbing glow. "You know we can hardly keep our hands off one another."

The netherling inside me fidgets, tantalized by his teasing. "What I know is that you always kiss and tell."

Instead of the pompous grin or snide comeback I'm expecting, he shushes me with a finger to his lips and mimes: "The walls have ears."

I don't dare assume he's being figurative. Standing slowly, he keeps a wary eye on our surroundings. He takes off his hat and gloves, then places them in the chair.

I bide my time as he lifts a cloth napkin from the table and runs his fingers across the burgundy wall tiles. He's on the last quarter of the room when he scoops something into his hand and beckons me close. Five pea-size creatures scuttle over the lines of his palm. They resemble tiny human ears with crab legs and wings that seem too small to lift them.

Wrapping them in the napkin, Morpheus squashes them and shoves the wadded cloth under the door. "Ear mites. They would've recorded anything we said and reported it to the queen." He leads me to the center of the room. "Now we can talk freely."

I remind myself not to overreact . . . to give him a chance to explain. "So, this is a wedding dress?"

The smug smirk I expected earlier makes a belated appearance. "Perhaps not what I originally intended you to wear for our union, but it will do in a pinch. Aren't you glad you had the foresight to put it on?"

I take down the bun at the back of my nape, giving my hands something to do other than punch him. "You made it clear I should wear it," I say, weaving my red streak back into the rest of my platinum waves.

Morpheus watches my every move, momentarily distracted as I pin up my hair again, piece by piece.

"I thought the dress was meant to be a weapon." I slip the last bobby pin into place.

"Oh, with the way it fits you, it very well is," Morpheus says, his voice gruff. The spilled milk on the table has started an annoying *drip-drip-drip* onto the carpet. He backs me up to a chaise lounge out of the way of the mess.

I sit on the edge of the center cushion, my wings strewn behind me. "Tell me what's going on, and this had better be good."

He shakes out a cloth napkin. "Still don't trust me, aye?"

"I trust that you don't want to face my wrath."

He snorts. "I'm game for anything. Will you pelt me with falling hearts in a symbolic rain of our unrequited love? Or perhaps chain me to a wall in lace made of moonlight and have your way with me?" His jeweled markings blink through a rhapsody of colors: flirtatious, taunting, and malicious.

"Would you be serious? You have a lot of explaining to do."

His jewels coalesce to emerald green. "As do you. Let us start with why you were rolling about with Jebediah half-naked on the sands of a beach whilst I was putting myself in danger for your father's antidote."

I resist my jaw's temptation to drop. He doesn't get to guilt me. There's only one way he could know that, and it doesn't bode well for his own nocturnal activities.

"You're working with Manti . . ." My vocal cords grate against one another—as if made of sandpaper.

Morpheus sops up milk with the napkin to silence the dripping. "We'll get to that. But first, you need to be apprised of what took place while you were playing peek-a-boo with our pseudo elf's crowning attribute. Two of your father's relatives were captured by the queen's guards last night. When I was accompanying Nikki to the castle, I saw them being escorted through the gate. I didn't know who they were, only that they were knights and that one shared your father's eyes."

I twine my hands nervously. "Uncle Bernard."

"He's all right."

"I can't believe we dragged him into this . . ."

Morpheus sits on the arm of the lounge, his wings cascading down behind him. The pulsing chandelier lights shimmer along his black lacy cuff as he picks off some lint. "You have Jebediah to thank for that, actually. Before his scenic transformations confused the wind tunnels, the knights never had a reason to journey across the looking-glass world on foot. Your ex's interference has endangered the fragile inner workings of this world."

"But he did it to protect you," I defend. "You told me yourself that he changed the landscapes to confuse the wildlife."

Morpheus grips his thigh. "Why are you still so infatuated with that mortal? After how he's hurt you?"

I glare up at him. "Something that you've *never* done."

Glancing down at his whitening knuckles, Morpheus grinds his teeth. "I've never given up on you."

The sincere rasp to his voice softens me. "I know." I lace my fingers through his, and his muscles contract in response. "But Jeb didn't give up on me, either. He gave up on himself. And you had a hand in that."

Morpheus rolls his eyes. "We're straying off track. You're not embracing the seriousness of the situation. For centuries, Hart has been looking for a way to attack the Wonderland gate, to hijack a wind tunnel and get across the abyss of nothing. Can you imagine the chaos she could wield with access to a knight's medallion?"

It's strange, but on some level, I'm relieved at his words. "I was right . . . I knew Wonderland had to be in danger." The fact that I put my faith in him and he didn't let me down lifts the weight from my shoulders. I didn't endanger Jeb and Dad needlessly.

"More than Wonderland, actually," Morpheus says, interrupting my thoughts. "The Queen of Hearts agreed to keep Red's spirit alive only because Red convinced her you'd be coming here to rescue me, and Jebediah, had she not thought him dead. It's why Red captured us and dragged us into AnyElsewhere in the first place. As collateral. The two queens planned to use you to find a way back to Wonderland, where Hart would have access to the portals into the mortal realm and could harvest human life-clocks for her collection."

"Life-clocks?" I twine the words around on my tongue, tasting the syllables. When she first saw me, the queen said she wanted mine.

Morpheus gestures to the room's decor. "Her pet name for stolen hearts. Life-clocks."

Shivering, I dig my fist into my chest to ease the pain. Hart said she sensed mine was special. She must know it's damaged. Maybe she can tell me what Red has done to it.

"Alyssa. Why are you so pale?" Morpheus slides down the chaise's arm to settle next to me. He presses the back of his hand to my cheek, checking my temperature. "You're positively glacial."

His hand scorches my skin and I push it away. "I'm just worried." *About more than I can say.* How can my body be so cold, while a line of lit gasoline burns down the back of my sternum? I clench the edge of the cushions, determined to hold myself together. "We have to get the medallions back . . . and get my uncle and the other knight out of here."

Pursing his lips, Morpheus catches my wrist and peels off a glove to rest his thumb on my pulse. He frowns, but seems satisfied enough to smooth the glove into place and settle my palm in my lap. "It's already been handled. Due to my swift thinking, and no thanks to you and your faithlessness."

"Would you stop that? I wasn't faithless. You and I aren't committed to each other yet."

"*Yet.*" His face lights up. "So you *have* envisioned a future with me."

I fight a wave of tenderness. How can this ageless fae creature be so wise about war and strategies and politics, yet so like a child about relationships and love? "Give me the details of your plan, because I know you have one."

His chin twitches. "It isn't exactly a plan. 'Tis more a bargain."

"That involves me without my consent." I narrow my eyes. "Strange how often that happens."

He loosens his tie and clears his throat. "First, let me assure you your relatives are fine. Manti used CC to stage an uprising in the dungeon."

"Wait . . . so Manti has Jeb's doppelganger?"

"Yes, the queen gave it to him as a gift. Manti was eager to accept, as elfin knights make the best soldiers. And this one, being a painting, is even more a robot than most. During the confusion in the dungeon, Manti helped your uncle and his comrade escape before the queen could cut out their hearts. Fortunately, they harbored only one medallion between them. Unfortunately, Hart had already confiscated it. She gave it to her guards and told them to hide it, so even she doesn't know which one hid it or where it is. That way, Red doesn't know, either. So Hart no longer needs anyone's help to cross the border to Wonderland. But Red controls half her body and is willing to outsmart her and get the medallion in exchange for certain . . . demands."

The jewels along Morpheus's eyes flash to a pale tea green, the color of satisfaction. No surprise, since the demands apparently involve a wedding. Yet I'm still in the dark as to if the ceremony is fake or real.

"Details, Morpheus."

He leans close to the table and takes the plate of diamond-shaped tarts, offering me one topped with dripping red fruit that resemble pomegranate seeds. "You should eat. You still look too anemic for my liking."

I groan at his stalling tactics. "We were told not to bother the tarts."

Morpheus takes a delicate bite and chews. "Pilfered pastries," he says between swallows, "are the least of Hart's worries at the moment." He sets the plate aside and dabs his lips with a napkin. "She has a traitor in her midst."

"Manti." I frown. "I'm confused. I thought you two were enemies."

"Enemies make the most loyal compatriots, if they share a common goal." He touches my bottom lip, leaving behind a smear of fruity glaze. He watches as I suck away the bittersweet residue, then he licks the rest of the glaze from his fingertip. At the appearance of his tongue, heat blossoms in my face.

He smirks. "Look at that. I revived the color in your cheeks."

I scowl. "Can you dial back the seduction? This isn't the time for romance."

His answering grin is irrepressible. "On the contrary, any hope for escape hinges on romance. I've been watching Manti since I fell into this hellhole. He's terribly in love with Hart. He had wooed her for centuries, unsuccessfully, until they both landed here. In this world, he has no interference from royal suitors. Not only that, she can be herself . . . Her cruel obsessions, her degradation, they're embraced by the barbaric denizens. She's revered for the very actions that resulted in her being shunned from our world. Manti believes it would break her spirit if she went back. And he fears he'd lose her to another king. He won't let that happen, even if it means tricking her."

I glare at him. "The parallels are striking."

Morpheus blinks at me, unfazed. "Aren't they? Since I know how the lovesick fool thinks, he was easy to manipulate."

"Which means you were behind the raid on the mountain." *Just like I suspected.*

"For the most part," Morpheus admits. "I told Manti how to get there, what to take, and what to leave standing. You and Jebediah managed to thwart my plan to have you hand-delivered. But I knew . . ." His dark eyes glitter and he caresses my cheek. "I knew you wouldn't leave me to die. So I told Chessie the queen was planning to gut out my chest."

My entire body bristles with a mix of frustration and fury. I start to stand, but Morpheus holds me down.

"For the record," he says, "I was at death's door. Red was debating whether to kill me herself or feed me to the eels beneath the drawbridge. It took some fast talking to convince her I had anything to offer in exchange for my pitiful life. And had you not come to fulfill that trade, I would be eel fodder as we speak."

I shake my head. "So, the antidote for my dad. That was insurance."

"Your human conscience wouldn't let you leave me here after saving Thomas, even if it managed to overpower your darker side's love for me."

I'm about to berate his tactics, to deny any feelings for him, when he cups the nape of my neck and presses his lips to mine, velvety soft. It's nothing but a peck, yet the flavor of the tart he sampled lingers like a warm, savory bruise—an irresistible torment to the netherling within.

He draws back and my skin glistens, radiant prisms reflected off his face and the cushions. I'm gripping his jacket lapels, yet I don't even remember reaching for him.

"No more denials," he says as he presses his left hand over one of mine. "I've seen the love in your eyes and in your actions. I felt it yesterday when I held you in my arms, and today, when you came to save me. Which is why my arrangement with Red for the medallion should not be thought of as a ploy or a bargain, but as the next logical step of our relationship."

I release his lapels. "Logical? A *wedding*? So we're going to fake it, right?"

"How can we fake it if Red is inside of you? No, it must be authentic. And eternal." He smiles blissfully—all boyish naiveté and worldly charm in one exquisite being.

I must have a pained expression on my face, because he trails his thumb across my eye markings.

"Alyssa, we are going to have the most glorious future. You'll see."

It can't happen, for so many reasons. One of them is my vow to Jeb. But there's another obvious reason. "It's too soon. We're only starting to know each other."

Morpheus's brow furrows. "We shared a childhood."

I knit my fingers nervously. "It was all innocent . . . playing . . . training. It takes time for a human to grow into that kind of commitment. It takes a trial by fire."

"Ah. We will have our trial by fire. 'Tis a netherling tradition for the couple to walk through a circle of flames, to burn away the tethers of their past and start life anew, pristine. Like purifying precious metal."

The image of us in the midst of Wonderland's sun revisits: waltzing barefoot as our clothes catch sparks and burn away, embracing one another with no reservations.

A tingle of anticipation races through me, but I suppress it. "No. Not literal, *symbolic*. Giving and taking. Learning to understand and trust one another through any situation. I've had that with Jeb, for six years. I'm only starting to have it with you."

Morpheus grunts, low in his chest. "I am not going to wait around and play second fiddle to Jebediah while your mortal side grows to understand and trust me."

"You're not second best. You and I get to have forever. *Forever*. Jeb has one life. It's only fair I spend it with him." I dance around the truth, as close as I'm willing to get.

"*Fair?* All this time, he's been with you during your waking hours. I've ever only had you in your dreams. I want you in reality. I've waited for what feels like a thousand years already. It is time for our forever to begin."

He's not thinking this through. "Do you really want to start our life together while I'm harboring Red's spirit?"

"We both knew you'd be carrying her out of this world." The statement is matter-of-fact, but compassion softens his voice. "And you will *still* defeat her. The only thing that's changed is she wants assurance you aren't to abandon your royal responsibilities again. She knows if we're wed, you'll ne'er leave Wonderland. It was the one way I could get her to agree to hand over the medallion. And she refuses to make the exchange until the marriage is official. Surely you can see I had no choice."

Ivory's vision clambers through my mind with the sound of a toddler's footfalls, knocking my worst fear loose: Red's found a way to get everything she ever wanted. To have me marry the only neth-erling who can give her access to a dream-child, and to be ringside in my body as it happens. She's planning to use our offspring for her revenge. But how?

I get to my feet and back away. "I thought that for once you had no ulterior motives. You're no longer under Deathspeak. No longer trying to prevent Red's destructive tide across the nether-realm. Your only motivation was to leave AnyElsewhere, repair Wonder-land, and have me beside you there."

"That *is* my only motivation." His bejeweled eye markings are the sincerest shade of crystal, like human tears.

I back up more, my boots dragging on the shag carpet.

He stands cautiously, as if I were a wild animal he's trying not to spook. "Alyssa, we're shut inside a room with four walls. It's not as if you can run from me, or whatever this is you're accusing me of."

I groan. "The reason Red lured Alice into the rabbit hole was to change the very foundation on which Wonderland is built. She wanted to introduce dreams and imagination into the bloodline, so netherlings would no longer have to depend on the human realm for them."

By his shocked expression, it's obvious this is the first he's heard of her plan. "That's a far nobler quest than I ever thought her capable of."

"Not noble. There's no way she'll let the dreams be free, let them be accessible to everyone. She wants to control that power so she'll be the most feared and dreaded queen of all time. Yes. Yes, that's got to be it." I shiver from head to toe, too horrified to even consider what I'm saying next. "I won't let her use him like that."

"Him?" The question slips from Morpheus's mouth on a shaky breath.

Panic sluices through me—a rush of cold and hot. It's too late to take back what I said. I hold my breath, waiting to see if I feel different . . . if there's a physical drain as my powers fade away.

But nothing happens. With just a thought, I coax the papers on the easel to flip and flutter in place. It hits me that I haven't broken the vow; I didn't specify our child in my statement. *Him* is anonymous. Netherling vows are all about technicalities in the wording.

In fact, come to think of it, I promised Ivory never to *tell* anyone about the vision she shared, but I didn't say I wouldn't *show* anyone.

I stop beside the easel. We've already ruined the Queen of Hearts' pastries. What's a few opened paint containers?

Morpheus moves behind me to look over my wings, close enough that his clothes snag on my dress's tiers with tiny popping sounds. I can feel the tension coming off him.

I remove my gloves. After opening three colors—red, blue, and black—I plunge my finger into one, letting the cold goo cover the tip. I work in mosaics. It's not easy to portray what I've seen in my head using paint and paper. I don't have Jeb's skill, his light strokes, the ability to translate inner shapes and lines of gravity. But I do my best, sketching a rough image of me in my monarch dress, Morpheus in his suit, and a tiny boy with my eyes, his daddy's blue hair, and wings.

Before I've even drawn the finishing touch of crowns on our heads, Morpheus backs up and drops into the chair where he laid his hat and gloves, crushing them. For the first time, he doesn't seem to care.

The gems on his temples and cheeks glimmer a deep royal blue, as if he's moonstruck. "You've seen him," he whispers.

I don't answer.

"When? How?" he asks.

I tighten my lips more.

By the resigned set of his jaw, it's clear he understands I'm teetering on the slippery slope of a life-magic vow.

"Oh, Alyssa," he murmurs. "I've wanted to tell you for so long. I feared it would frighten you. He's the most special of all children. He's going to save our world. Going to teach everyone how to imagine and dream." That whimsical countenance returns to his face—a glow of euphoria. "I've a list of names for him. And there are so many games we can use to guide his skills."

"I want him to be happy, Morpheus. Above everything else. To have a childhood."

His features soften to an acute tenderness. "Of course. I'll sing him lullabies every night. You . . . you can teach him to view the world through the lenses of innocence. We'll love him. Dote on him. It would be impossible not to. I cannot stop seeing his beauty— the perfect blend of me and you." Morpheus catches my smeared hands and laces our fingers. The trio of paint smudges his skin so it matches mine as he holds our fingers side by side. "All the shades of us, in one brilliant rainbow."

The room grows hazy, or maybe it's the weird lighting.

Morpheus urges me into his lap and snuggles my head under his chin, securing me within his tobacco-scented embrace. It's the gentlest gesture we've ever shared. "Now you know where you belong, Alyssa. With me and our child."

Red's vicious imprint tugs behind my breastbone, gouges into my heart. I pull back to meet his dreamy gaze, cupping his face in my hands and leaving smudges of paint on his jaw.

"That's what you're not seeing," I say, my voice airy. "He won't be *ours*. Yes, you'll be bringing a halfling child into the nether-realm. Maybe that's all that matters. Even if it's Red who'll share that life, not me. As long as Wonderland thrives."

"No." He startles me by standing us both up. He swipes his crushed hat and gloves to the floor, sets me in the chair again, then kneels at my feet, taking my hands. "You are my only queen. We will cast her out the moment we repair Wonderland. Before a child is ever conceived. I *swear* this to you."

I truly believe he wants that, but he doesn't know I've lost my ace or how tired and depleted my body's feeling. "The diary's gone. My one chance to defeat her." I almost tell him it's his fault for sending Manti's goons, but what would guilting him accomplish at this point?

Morpheus shakes his head. "That solution was temporary at best. Those memories are still within you, dormant. You can awaken them, weaken her. I believe in your strength. Will you never do the same?"

I tense up. "My heart . . . it's not strong enough. When she was inside me. She did something to me. I'm sure of it."

He glides my knuckles along his jaw, smearing the shades of red, blue, and black I left on his skin moments ago. It's obvious he thinks I'm being hysterical. "You're frightened. But now that you know how special our son will be, now that you adore him as I do, that gives you even more reason to be brave. And even more reason to accept our union."

I jerk my hands away. He's not hearing me. "I can't marry you today."

He grinds his teeth and stands, looking down on me. "So, your petty human insecurities are once again more important than an entire world's well-being? *Two* worlds'? You'll allow Hart's special brand of ornamentation to be stamped upon every wall in the human realm? You'll let Wonderland's landscapes die?"

"I'm just saying we have to figure out another way to get that medallion, and another way to smuggle Red out of here."

The pulsing lights shimmer off the paint smudged on his face . . . coloring him with an eerie and dangerous camouflage. "You and your damnable other ways. This isn't at all about what we do or don't have between us, is it? There's something else preventing this marriage . . . something you're afraid to tell me."

I hesitate.

"Alyssa!" He clasps my shoulders and draws me to my feet, losing all patience.

My confession tumbles out. "I made a life-magic vow to marry Jeb first. If I marry you instead, I'll lose all my powers . . . forever."

CHRYSALIS

With a caress more sinister than comforting, Morpheus drags his hands from my shoulders to my wrists, streaking my skin with paint.

Then, unspeaking, he takes out a handkerchief from his jacket and wipes the smudges clean. His delicate touch leaves chill bumps on my arms. After scrubbing his face and hands, he tucks away the handkerchief and lifts his crumpled hat from the floor.

In a sweep of black wings, he turns his back and paces, pounding the dents from the red and burgundy topper in time with his steps. His lean muscles move in fluid, powerful lines beneath his tailored suit, exaggerated by the pulsating lights.

He's precise and controlled, but his mind is spinning. Underneath all that grace and restraint, a savage prepares to strike—a pupa, waiting to emerge as a scorpion fly and turn Jeb to stone.

I take stock of the room once more, sizing it up for nets. There are limitless possibilities, yet I'm not in any hurry to imprison him again. Not when he's spent all these weeks trapped and humiliated without his own magic.

"How could you use a life-magic vow so flippantly?" His snarling voice breaks through my silent scheming. The question scores like a venomous barb, making my breastbone burn as if hot wax drizzles down the center.

I study the wet paint on my palms and fingertips, then turn them, moved by the colorful fingerprints he stamped on the backs of my hands when we discussed our child. "There was nothing flippant about it. It was the one way to ensure you'd let me share Jeb's mortal life . . . to give him hope, so he would leave this world."

Morpheus stops in his tracks. I have his full attention. "So, you manipulated us both with one vow." His long black lashes tremble, and admiration shimmers behind his wounded gaze—the same look I've received throughout my life each time I please him. Although the dark, angry crimson of his blinking jewels belies any true pleasure. "Bitterest irony. It would appear I trained you too well—"

A small buzzing sound interrupts him, out of sync with the hearts' rhythmic pounding in the room. We both see it: a minute disruption in front of my face where an ear mite stutters in midair.

Morpheus tries to trap it in his hat, but it zigzags between us, throwing my voice out in perfect mimicry: *"I made a life-magic vow to marry Jeb first. If I marry you instead, I'll lose all my powers."*

The bug parrots my confession once more before I take a swipe at it. It dips low and flies for the door. Morpheus leaps too late. The ear mite skitters under the space at the threshold, escaping.

Placing his hat on his head, Morpheus casts me a scathing glare. "I assume Jebediah is in this castle somewhere. He would ne'er let you come alone now that you belong to him again."

I seek Morpheus's gaze beneath the shadow of the hat's brim. "Your intentions?"

"He's about to be in grave danger if that ear mite gets to Red before me."

I can't argue that Morpheus is the lesser of two evils where Jeb's well-being is concerned. "He's in a simulacrum suit, looking for you in the dungeon."

Morpheus's face darkens. "Don't dare leave this room. All I need is you running about and mucking things up more than you already have."

Before I can respond, he flings the door open and slams it behind him. He scuffles with the guards, then talks his way out of being taken into custody by suggesting they "lock the blasted door to contain their magical ward, considering she's the biggest threat to AnyElsewhere."

Then he makes up an excuse about needing to find the queen.

His determined footsteps fade down the hallway and I mentally hurry him along. He has to catch the ear mite before it reports to Red, and even more pressing, has to find Jeb before anything happens to him.

I tell myself that's why he left in such a hurry . . . to protect Jeb. Not because he's jealous and wants to eliminate him, rendering my vow null and void. The two have forged an understanding over the past month. They'll never like each other, but they've spared one another countless times, and have learned to work together, because they both love me.

I have to believe that Morpheus isn't acting on his desire for our future to start today. That he's not being driven by his romantic ideals: a tapestry of emotions and actions as fierce and unpredictable as the wildness of Wonderland itself. I've seen his compassion and how he struggles to do the right thing.

"Have faith in him," I whisper to no one but me. "He'll one day be your king."

He told me to stay put. Little does he realize, I have no choice. I'm too weak and woozy to leave my prison.

I return to the easel and swipe my fingers across the drying paint to blur it beyond recognition. It's bad enough that Red is hoping for a child between us. Once she's possessed my body and sees him for herself, it's only going to make getting rid of her that much harder.

When my fingers glide across the image of our little boy, smudging him to an indiscernible blob, that stitch in my heart ruptures another agonizing degree. A coppery taste stings my tongue. I cough, cupping my mouth with my palm. As I pull my hand away, fresh blood spatters the paint between my fingers. I double over, struggling for breath.

The room shakes to the beat of a thousand pulses. Streaks of burgundy and black mingle with shivering light. My arms and legs ache. I absorb my wings to lighten the load, but my spine curls and I lower myself to my knees as darkness swarms my vision. I shut my eyes, focused on breathing. Rolling to my stomach, I let the shag carpet cushion my cheek as I drift toward unconsciousness, into the hazy, numb warmth of a vision . . .

My body is light as air, free of pain. A black oily sludge drips from the walls and seeps across the floor toward me. The puddles rise into phantom shapes like smoke.

Mome wraiths.

They engulf me, sniffing my hair, wailing in my ears until my bones clatter. Oily marks stamp my skin where they grip my arms, fingers of shadow and illusion biting into me. They drag me to the top of the castle's tower and toss me down. My stomach leaps into my throat.

Far below, the rabbit hole opens—a black, spiraling tunnel. I fall fast, racing past open wardrobes, stacks of floating books, pantries, and jars of canned goods pinned to the tunnel's sides with thick ivy curls. I clutch at a wall, knocking into furniture and tearing at vines until my descent slows.

Below in the darkness, a struggle takes place. Sister Two wrestles in midair with my mom, who's strung up by webs. Mom uses her magic, animating wayward books and pinned-up furniture to bombard Sister Two's head and torso. The grave keeper's eight legs and poisonous, scissored hands are preoccupied deflecting the attack, which buys Mom time to break free. She slips out of the spider's thrall and starts falling.

"Mom!" I shout.

She looks up. "Allie!" she calls back and reaches for me.

The wraiths wail overhead and pull the rabbit hole closed, shuttling us all out of the tunnel and propelling us into Wonderland on a landslide of dirt.

I dig myself out into the flower garden. Lightning slashes the sky, casting fluorescent hues across the landscape. A pungent, charred scent carries on a loud and melancholy wind. Dark purple clouds fill the sky.

Mom is just within my reach, surrounded by vicious zombie flowers as tall as trees. Sister Two scuttles toward her with an army of undead toys.

I clamber up to help Mom, but my hand passes through her. I'm noth-

ing but a ghost here, and I realize I'm reliving her entry into Wonderland that fated night.

A white swan swoops down, transforming into Ivory. Landing on the ground, she glitters from wing tips to toes. Her magic radiates in the purest strains of silver. She twirls like a crystalline ballerina and white mist streams from her mouth. Frost cloaks the ruthless flowers, slowing their movements.

A man breaks through the trunklike stems. I recognize him as Finley, the mortal Morpheus used as an imprint when he was in the human realm. Finley's dressed as an elfin knight and commands Ivory's army. With a collective shout, the elves attack the flowers, their swords clanging against the iced stems, cutting through in one sweep. The flowers scream and fall, writhing on the ground. Sister Two hisses and herds her undead toys into the heart of Wonderland, retreating to the garden of souls.

Ivory turns and offers a hand to my mom.

Mom takes it, then looks back at me. "I'm safe and we're surviving. But the heart of Wonderland is dying. The doldrums are closing in. Come soon. We'll hold them off as long as we can."

I try to make sense of her warning, picking my mind apart for the definition of doldrums, *but it escapes me.*

"Allie!" Mom screams. "Wake up . . . wake up!"

Lightning streaks across the sky and splits into my chest, slamming me back into my broken body and the reality of unquenchable pain.

Someone has propped my back against what feels like cool tiles. I'm too weak to even lift my eyelids. I inhale and strangle on the liquid filling my lungs.

"*She's dying,*" Red says, somewhere beyond my closed eyes.

"As she should be," Hart responds. "Just look at the mess she made of my paints! And she nibbled on a tart. Confounded little mouse."

Judging by Hart's tirade, we're still in the playroom. The scent of her perfume suffocates me, even more potent with my eyes closed. It's the stench of death—wilted flowers and rotted flesh.

"*Let me out so I can preserve her vessel*," Red hisses.

"Don't be cross with me!" Hart scolds. "You had to know this would be the result when you put the spell upon her."

"*No. Once the netherling side fully awoke to madness, it was supposed to absorb the human one, transform it. I could never have predicted the mortal half of her heart would put up such a fight. That it would be strong enough to hold on for so long and endanger them both.*"

A whimper lodges within my throat and a bitter metallic flavor gags me. I want to clench Red's neck, to choke her. Instead, I'm the one choking . . . on my own blood.

"It's your spell. Simply reverse it," the queen suggests, ignoring my struggle.

"*Now that the heart is splitting in two, I know of no magic that can save her. Nothing for me to do other than pull her together from the inside.*"

I moan.

"*Hurry, you fool*," Red prompts the queen, desperation in her voice. "*Set my spirit free.*"

"I need collateral," Hart counters. "For the trade of the medallion. I want more than one measly human life-clock. I want them all."

One human life-clock? Who could they be talking about? Jeb? My dad? Did they catch Uncle Bernie again?

Whoever it is, one of my loved ones is in danger.

I try to move, but agony slices through me, a metal stake splitting and gouging my breastbone. To keep from crying out, I freeze in place. My eyelids seal tighter.

"I already told you you'll get more. My bargain with Morpheus is to hand over the medallion once the marriage is official. I said nothing about leaving you here."

"You don't think your king will have something to say about my following you through the gate?"

"Once Morpheus realizes I'm the only thing keeping his cherished Alyssa alive, he will do whatever I command."

I inhale a sharp breath. The air scalds and scrapes my lungs, as if sprouting thorns on the way in. The sensation dulls my reasoning; still, I try to piece things together. Red plans to trick Morpheus. He must already suspect this. He's a mastermind. The wise and cryptic caterpillar, emerged from his chrysalis in the form of a beautiful winged fae.

But he doesn't know what she has for leverage. He's unaware of my dying heart, or Red's spell on me.

Other than Wonderland, I'm his only weakness. And she's using both.

How can he refuse her?

I'm the only one who can stop this. I open my eyes to slits and groan, trying to concentrate enough to unleash my magic. Black fog crowds my peripheral vision . . . makes it impossible to focus.

The Queen of Hearts crouches in front of me, one half of her hair bright crimson and the other side burgundy. "This is all moot," she says to Red. "You heard what the ear mite said. The dullard girl has made a vow to the mortal. There will be no marriage betwixt her and Morpheus."

"Everything will fall in place once we find the boy. The vow is bind-

ing only for as long as he lives. We kill him, you have the start to your human collection, and I have my royal wedding."

"No." I try to speak over the blood gurgling in my throat. I've done it again. I've endangered Jeb's life more than it already was. "I . . . won't let . . . you."

I attempt to slap Hart's face, but my hand falls limply to my lap.

The queen's clammy palm cups my chin. "How remarkable. Her life-clock is split in twain, hanging by mere threads. Yet still, she has fight in her." Her expression grows intense. "I already have the medallion. I have my own way into Wonderland. There's no reason I should do anything you ask, Red. I'm going to let her die and take her specimen. I've never seen another like it."

"There will be another, one day," Red insists, frantic. *"Morpheus and I will have children through her. I'll spare you one of their hearts. But not hers. Hers belongs to me. It doesn't matter if you get into Wonderland. You won't have access to the humans without the portals. Alyssa is the only one who can reopen them. And my plan for her and Morpheus reaches beyond your petty ideals. I am giving their firstborn—the first netherling capable of dreams—to Sister Two. She abhors chasing down human children. For centuries she's complained about how tedious it is. So in exchange for an immortal child that will forever supply the souls in her lair, she and her disgruntled toys will aid me in overthrowing Ivory. Once I have the magic of both crowns, my control over all of Wonderland will be absolute. And you and every inhabitant of AnyElsewhere will be welcomed upon our borders to come and go and plunder the human realm as you please."*

I sob, at last face-to-face with Red's horrific plan yet physically unable to intervene.

Hart clucks her tongue. "You've made a fair point. We have an accord. But the girl is barricading the transfer of your spirit by sheer will." The queen draws her hand back, fingers dripping with my bloody saliva. "She's the one who needs convincing now."

"Let me in, Alyssa." Red's entreaty is eerily tender. *"You're bleeding to death. What good will such a loss be to anyone? It will endanger both the human boy and Morpheus. Not to mention all of Wonderland."*

Tears trickle down my face.

Her argument is sound. As terrified as I am for my future child, he'll never exist if I don't save everyone today. The only way is to let Red's spirit hold me together, then hijack her magic to fix Wonderland. I know her strategy now. If I can be stronger than her long enough, I'll defeat Hart and cast Red out once and for all. I can't let myself consider what will happen to my heart after that.

I slump forward in surrender.

My lungs shrink and my veins wither, depleted of oxygen. My eyelids droop, unable to resist the welcoming darkness that waits there.

"Hurry, hag. Release my spirit before she fades to ash and neither of us gets what we want."

Hart groans in resignation and her clammy hand presses my forehead. A bright light bursts behind my eyes.

White-hot tendrils shoot from my skull into my spine, forcing my body to straighten. To awaken.

I remember this feeling . . .

My eyes flutter open. The colored streak of my hair pulls loose, dancing. Bit by bit, my bobby pins drop to the floor until all of my hair matches the enchanted strands, free and flowing around my shoulders in vivid crimson waves.

The intrusion migrates to my arms and legs, filling my limbs with power.

My veins illuminate under my skin. Each one grows, expands to the form of a living, breathing plant that blossoms out of me like a snake.

Red inhabits me, and I welcome her, because she's making me strong.

The splitting agony in my heart yields to the sensation of needles stitching it back together. All the pain soothes away and the beat is unified and solid. I fill my lungs, drinking the air.

I wrap my arms around my chest, hugging myself, embracing Red's vitality.

"*Yes, my child.*" Her voice forces its way from my mouth on a breath. "*Together, We shall be unstoppable.*" She addresses us as a collective *We*, as if We are one being. The possibility appeals to my madness in ways I never imagined.

The leafy tendrils sprouting from my skin lash at the Queen of Hearts. She takes a step back, cautious. Red uses the connection between her ivy strands and my veins to move me, as if I were a marionette. This time, there's no pain, no cracking of bones or ripping of muscles and veins, because I don't fight her. I move gracefully, as if I'm floating. I look down to find my body propelled by the vines, a creeping plant. My feet aren't even touching the floor.

However wrong it looks and feels, all dread and fear vanish.

What's so bad, really? The power coursing through us? The horror on Hart's face as We wrap her in our deadly ivy? Her eyes bugging out like a guppy's as We tighten our clasp on her neck?

No. Nothing bad here. On the contrary, the brutality is rapturous.

"Please," Hart murmurs, her voice no more than a whistle of compressed air. "Our bargain . . . the medallion."

Right. We still don't know which of her guards hid the medallion. My and Red's thoughts intertwine as one. *Let her live. She yet has a part to play.*

Before We release the queen, several guards enter the room, their reptilian faces reflections of terror. "Y-y-your Majesties," the one in charge stutters. "Manti has captured the human boy."

We unwind our tendrils and drop Hart. She flops to the floor and gasps for breath. Her guards help her move a safe distance from us.

"*Tell Morpheus the transfer is complete*," We say, our voices merging. "*Bring the boy to the courtyard, and let the ceremony begin.*"

ASHES, ASHES . . .
THEY ALL FALL DOWN

Clouds darken the sky and a chill wind rustles our crimson locks, flicking them across our shoulders like unmanageable flames.

The courtyard has been stripped of the colorful carnival tents, all but an awning of canvas stretched over the stage where the ceremony will take place. The eight-foot stage rises alongside the pool of fears. Thick black ropes drape from the tops of the inwardly slanted castle walls to a wide pole standing in the center. Red ribbons are tied in bows along the ropes, reminiscent of that fool Grenadine's forgetful and traitorous ways.

We bite back a snarl of envy. Soon, We'll have our kingdom once more, and our first order of business will be to banish that faithless wretch into Wonderland's wilds, forever.

The Queen of Hearts waits upon the stage with a shadow box cradled in her arms. She faces a priest in burgundy robes and a tall rectangular hat. His froglike form is secured by a harness to the center pole so he can sleep upright. His fat chins bubble with quiet snores. A small swarm of lightning bugs hovers around his head, waiting.

Behind Hart, at ground level, hundreds of witnesses are seated— those same guests who earlier played sadistic games in hopes of killing themselves. *Imbeciles.*

We wait behind the audience for Morpheus to arrive and walk us down the aisle. Outside the awning, up high on the skeletal platform where the caucus race commenced, sits one giant sphere. An inferno burns inside, licking the glass in hot oranges, yellows, and reds. At the end of the ceremony, We will walk in the midst of those flames with our groom, initiating our trial by fire. After that, We'll be forever joined to him.

On the far end of the courtyard, the musician drags a bow across a cello. The strings are strung from the eviscerated gut of a half-living beast. The vibrations harmonize with the wounded creature's wails and carry over the expanse to create a morbid wedding march.

Upon the third note, Morpheus steps from the shadows of the far tower. His shoes clomp, a sound barely audible beneath the keening acoustics. His wings drag lower to the ground as he sees our altered appearance.

At his arrival, the audience stands and applauds.

Our vines strike at the tiny sprite and that meddlesome cat where they flutter around Morpheus's head. They cower and dive beneath his hat.

The audience applauds louder.

Jaw clenched, Morpheus offers a palm. Our ivy reaches for him, but he slaps it away.

The guests grow silent. Even the music stalls. Only the priest's snoring, the lightning bugs' buzzing, and the inferno crackling within the sphere can be heard.

Morpheus opens his glove once more. "Give me Alyssa's hand. I will touch *only* her."

We guide our limp fingers to join with his powerful ones. He bends his head to kiss our knuckles. Warmth sparks at the contact, sending a distantly familiar hum of pleasure through our human body. Our fingers jerk in response.

Morpheus tips his chin up, his jeweled markings a passionate purple. "Alyssa, can you hear me, little plum? She's made you forget your humanness. But I know you're still in there."

"Of course We're in here," We answer. *"But there's room for one more."* We smile seductively, roaming our leafy tendrils along his black shirt and winding them through the spaces between buttons to stroke his bare chest underneath.

The affection on Morpheus's face shifts to a tortured scowl as he drags our vines from the fabric, pushing them away.

We sneer. His comfort and happiness are irrelevant. He is a means to an end, a beautiful pawn on the chessboard of our life. We will relish using him up.

A tendon in his neck twitches as he starts us down the aisle to the beat of the macabre song that echoes once more in the courtyard. The monarch wings jingle on our dress with our movements.

He squeezes our fingers. "Why aren't you wearing your gloves?" he mumbles from the side of his mouth.

The question is pointless, but his covertness amuses us, so We answer. *"We thought you admired our naked palms. The battle scars won for you in our lesser form."*

He flashes us a sullen glare, as if We have no right to speak of such things. As if they're sacred somehow.

We savor his torment. Our heart beats in unified vindication. One pulse . . . one purpose. To give us our vengeance. To at last reap the rewards of the scheme that began so long ago with a curious little girl named Alice.

To the left of the stage, a troop of goons siphons in. Manti appears behind them with the captured human boy. The prisoner wears tuxedo pants and a vest. A black cloth bag covers his head. His hands are bound behind his back with chains wrapped around a large rock. Manti struggles with the rock's weight, carrying it so the boy can walk.

The harlequin doppelganger brings up the rear, wearing a T-shirt and worn jeans. The line of red jewels sparkles on one side of its face. On the other, its heart-shaped eye patch is torn, and there's movement in the black emptiness where the skin gapes. The back of an eyeball bobs to the surface, slimy with veins and optic nerve. It rolls around, then disappears into the hole.

The gruesome display tickles us and We laugh out loud, shrill and gleeful like a child with a new toy. Our cackle wakes the sleeping priest for all of two seconds before his bulbous eyes grow heavy and he's snoring even louder.

Morpheus dips his head low and pulls us along by our hand. We drift beside him, proud, propelled by our vines.

The doppelganger climbs the stage and takes his place next to the queen. A breeze coaxes its hair away from an ear, revealing the pointed tip. Manti shoves the mortal to his knees on the stage's edge, closest to the pool of fears, and drops the rock beside him with a loud *thunk*.

We skim up the stairs and observe the human captive with remorse. Not for his life, but for all the delicious sport he could've given us. He's alluring, for a lesser being. We would've enjoyed using him up, too.

We take our spot in front of the priest, our groom to the left between us and the chained mortal; Hart is on the right, holding her box. Manti and the doppelganger stand on her other side.

We're moments from victory. Moments from Wonderland, our crown, and our throne.

Morpheus lifts the bag from the mortal boy's head and steps back, cursing.

A strip of cloth cinches across the human's eyes and another across his mouth. His olive complexion is flawless, aside from fine lines of blood drizzling down his cheeks, bridging the blindfold to the gag. Another line of red runs down his chin.

"Why is he bound like this . . . and *bleeding*?" Morpheus demands.

"My question precisely!" Hart grouses from her place between us and Manti. "I want to see the fear in his eyes and hear his screams as we retrieve his life-clock."

"I had no choice, O Majestic One," Manti answers his queen. "I confiscated his paints, but he improvised. He painted in his cell with mud made of dirt and saliva, hid everything he made in the shadows. Forgeries of the walls and prison bars came alive and turned against us as we tried to bring him here. We lost a dozen of your devoted guards to violent deaths at the hands of his creations. The only way to stop his magic was by gouging out his eyes so he could no longer see to bring new things into being . . . and cutting out his tongue so he could no longer speak to command them."

Morpheus pales, as if even he can't stomach what's become of the mortal.

Something twists in the core of our being, a pricking pain, rousing an unexpected and unwelcome voice . . .

Jebediah Holt, it sobs.

Our heart skips a beat, then falls back into rhythm. We won't be swayed by a name. We stand taller beside our groom, blotting out everything except the impending triumph flowing through our veins—a high unlike any other.

But there's more . . . The broken voice won't relent. *There's more to him than a name . . . more to them both.*

No. We refuse to listen. *They are stepping-stones. And soon, all of Wonderland will be pebbles beneath our feet. We will rule over both king-doms and everyone will worship us.*

"You fools!" Morpheus shouts, reminding us where We are, what's at stake. "I could've convinced the mortal to release Alyssa of the vow. I could've—" His voice cracks.

"Ha." Hart snorts. "Well, he can no longer do that, can he? He's forever lost the ability to speak. Only one way to release it now."

In an explosive flurry of wings and rage, Morpheus lunges at Manti, catching the manticorn by his horn and dragging him to his knees. He holds a knife at the base of Manti's horn. "Stay back," he yells to the guards.

Hart yelps and the audience leaps up and cheers, some climbing into their seats for a better view, the anticipation of bloodshed working them to a frenzy.

Since Morpheus has the upper hand on stage, the guards and goons descend the stairs in an effort to contain the crowd.

Through it all, the priest sleeps beneath the humming lightning-bug cloud.

"You betrayed me," Morpheus seethes next to Manti's humanoid ear. "I gave you his whereabouts with the condition he would not be harmed."

Manti struggles, but his horn is his Achilles' heel, the source of both his strength and weakness. He's at Morpheus's mercy. "I had to prove my loyalty to my queen. To make up for the human knights who escaped the dungeon under my watch."

"Savage!" Morpheus growls and forces the manticorn to stand. The doppelganger rushes forward, breaking them up.

Morpheus loses the knife and Hart grabs it as Manti moves back into place between her and the doppelganger.

"Enough delays," Hart threatens, giving Manti the knife. "The wedding goes on as planned, Morpheus. Try anything else like that, and you'll be swimming with the eels before the day is out."

We wrap our vines around Morpheus's arm and pull him toward us as Manti and Hart turn to the audience, calling out commands to silence them.

Morpheus studies the mutilated mortal. Profound misery darkens his features. He peels our tendrils away, curses under his breath, and throws down his hat.

The little sprite and Chessie flitter out, carrying a miniature hookah. We watch them, suspicious.

As if spurred by the activity, the human prisoner contracts his muscles in a futile effort to break free of his chains. He makes a guttural choking sound—animalistic and gut-wrenching without his tongue.

His agony fascinates us, demands our attention. That sense of knowing twists inside, sharper this time, like a knife. The unwelcome voice revisits:

This isn't the first time he's bled for you, it prods. *And he has painted with more than mud. How could you forget the room of starlight and snow, ribbons, wishes, and dreams? How could you forget all he's sacrificed for you?*

Chessie appears in front of our face. He sucks on the hookah pipe and blows a puff of smoke. The scented cloud permeates the air and coats our tongue, triggering images: licorice tobacco and a seductive fae with an agenda, ocean salt and a mortal boy's sweat, maple syrup and a father's love, a mother's sacrifice and a lunar garden rich with lilies and honeysuckle.

The human within us dances for an instant, awakened by her senses. Her emotions are overwhelming . . . frightening.

We writhe in place, our vines whipping out to chase Chessie away. But it's too late. The knife of knowing saws back and forth across the tethers We've secured around our heart.

We won't allow it. It will hurt if the seams are broken.

Concentrate. Concentrate only on the man who will be our king.

Our attention shifts to Morpheus, then to Hart as she and Manti face the priest once more, having placated the bloodthirsty guests.

The guards and goons barricade the stairs, forming a line between the wedding party and the audience.

"Wake up, you buffoon," Hart says to the priest, and the lightning bugs strike him with electrical charges until he giggles so hard his bulging eyes open. "Begin the ceremony."

The priest smacks his fat, slimy lips. "Do you come into this union free of all binds?" The croaking question bulges from his greenish throat.

Morpheus's head hangs so low his hair cascades across the left side of his face. His bejeweled profile fades to the color of tears through spaces in the blue curtain. "A life-magic vow stands between us."

"Then it must be broken, or forfeit the union," the frogman says, and yawns loudly.

Silence wreathes the courtyard. We look at the flames in the sphere overhead. The brightness burns an imprint on our mind, cauterizing the human emotions trying to weaken us.

"It is time, Morpheus," Hart presses. "Prove your loyalty to your brides and your world, and you will be rewarded with the key to the gate. Bring me the boy's heart."

Morpheus snarls. "First, you show me the medallion. I want to see it."

Hart offers the shadow box to Manti. She opens the lid to reveal five pulsing life-clocks. With a squishing sound, Hart plunges her fingers into the fattest one, then drags out the medallion. She lays it across her palm, dripping with blood. "Proof enough? Now kill him."

Morpheus takes our unresponsive hand and holds it close to his lips. His breath cloaks our fingertips, another disarming sensation. "Remember: Memories are your greatest weapons," he whispers.

We turn back to the suffering mortal. Pictures blink through our mind: the same boy in cargo shorts and a dark tee beneath his Underland vest, black lights highlighting his toned arms with bluish flashes; the boy in his feather-duster mask for the junior prom masquerade; *Jeb* sand surfing with *me* on tea carts, then pouring out his blood to save my life over and over and over; Jeb kissing me after I broke his heart, and fighting at prom for me and every other human.

One of the threads on our heart breaks loose with a visceral twang, reviving the voice:

His tongue said beautiful words to you . . . His eyes held you in their gentle gaze. Never again. Unless you stop this. He might still be healed with magic, just as he once healed Morpheus.

It's *my* voice—my reasoning—quiet and still, desperate to be heard. But my vocal cords lie dormant as if I've swallowed the black mist outside of AnyElsewhere's gate. Like my body, my words are held captive by Red's vines.

Still, she can hear my liberated thoughts.

Jeb is wounded . . . but he can be saved. Morpheus will do the right thing.

Morpheus will show no mercy, Red contradicts in my mind. *He'll do anything for Wonderland. That is his priority. That is why I chose him to be our king. That, and the fact that because of his childhood with you, he can father a dream-child. What a profoundly perfect twist of fate that turned out to be.*

Another thread snaps loose from my heart, the pain precise and acute. I embrace it, because it reminds me I'm still here. I'm alive. I'm empowered.

Determination boils in my blood, scalding my skin. I concentrate on my fingers, forcing them to squeeze Morpheus's hand.

His eyes widen. He looks from me to the medallion Hart's holding. A muscle in his jaw twitches.

"Make a choice," Hart seethes. "Either the human gives his life, or Wonderland belongs to the denizens of the looking-glass world."

Morpheus looks at the crowd of deranged guests salivating and brutal, then down at Jeb's kneeling form. The blood on Jeb's chin has dribbled to the T-shirt under his tuxedo vest, bright red against the white fabric.

My feet twitch . . . My legs ache . . . My stomach knots. Every part of me slowly wakes, but my vocal cords shrivel under Red's clutches. I fight for the use of my limbs. Her vines hold me too high; I can't get my feet on the ground. A grinding sensation shuttles through my bones as punishment for even trying. Red winds my arms within her ivy and pins them to my sides.

A whimper dies in my throat.

Memory nudges beneath the pain. A reminder that I overpowered her once before. I move, ignoring the splitting sensation inside me, and clamp my fingers around a vine. I tug it. Rivulets of blood spurt from where the ivy stretches my skin.

Another one of my heart's seams snap . . . then another and

another. I yelp from the excruciating burn. I can't tear her out without ripping my own heart in half.

Defeated, I go limp.

"*Hurry,*" Red says aloud, using me as her mouthpiece, desperate now. "*Kill the boy, and she'll be your queen forever, Morpheus. Simple as that.*"

"Give me his life-clock!" Hart shouts to Morpheus. She holds the medallion high, swinging it like a pendulum to tempt him.

Morpheus grips Jeb's vest and forces him to stand. Jeb wavers, unbalanced by the inability to see. He strains against the cuffs binding his hands. He kicks his legs blindly in self-defense.

Morpheus turns his gaze to me, the black depths filled with so much remorse I know what he's going to say before he even says it. "Alyssa, forgive me. But I will always do what's best for Wonderland."

"No!" I shout, freeing my vocal cords at last.

The crowd surges, provoking the guards and goon birds to strengthen their barricade.

Still holding Jeb's vest, Morpheus glances over his shoulder at the chaos. "Now!" he shouts.

Chessie and Nikki appear from out of nowhere, hovering over Hart. Nikki distracts the queen as Chessie dips down and snags the medallion, taking off toward the gate. Manti sends the doppelganger after the feline fae. The crowd's fervor reaches manic intensity as they turn on the royal party and the stage.

Hart screams and Manti drags her toward the castle for safety.

Red screeches in my head. The sound guts my inner ears like a chain saw set loose, sending me in a vertigo tailspin.

The surroundings blur as if I were riding a spinning top. I can make out snippets: Red's vines whipping out and slapping Morpheus and Jeb off balance; Morpheus tumbling over his wings and hitting his head, his eyes lolling shut; Jeb, tripping over the rock behind him and sending it over the edge.

The chains attached to the rock jerk his body from the stage. He plummets toward the pool. Nikki dives after him, trying to wrangle the chains, then plunges into the water behind him.

My twirling vision comes to a stop as Jeb flails at the surface. The depths suck him down, swallowing him—my best friend, my devoted love, the guy who has given up everything for me, more times than I can count.

The water churns with acidic, red bubbles.

I look away, sobbing, too weak to watch what's left of him rise to the top. I keep hearing his voice in my head from a year ago, the first time we kissed. We were in Wonderland and I asked him not to break my heart. And his answer was, *"I'd cut mine out first."*

He can't be gone. This can't be real. This is all a nightmare.

Everything moves around me in slow motion: Morpheus lying unconscious on the stage, the crazed guests closing in, overpowering the guards and goons.

All the good in me dies. All the compassion and mercy sink into the darkest part of my soul. The color of blood replaces them, a swirling, snarling tide I want to swim in forever.

The guests press through to the stage and the guards and goon birds retreat.

Cowards . . .

In a surge of drooling, vicious single-mindedness, the mutants pass over Morpheus's unconscious form without touching him, their sights set on me, drawn by my royal heritage.

"You've lost everything," Red prods from somewhere in my head. *"Your memories failed because you belong to me now. Surrender to my control, and I'll save us both."*

But it wasn't only my memories that Morpheus wanted me to use.

"Take her apart! Show us the heart!" the mutant mob chants as it closes in. Red's tentacle-like vines multiply, holding them all at bay.

I let her defend us, let her distraction serve as my opportunity. I dig inside myself, in search of the crimson-stained moments the diary helped me suppress. I drag them to the surface: Red's flushed young face as a child when she tried to hold on to her mother's spirit, the ruby shimmer of her stepsister's hair during a painful croquet lesson as she felt her father slip away, and the deep crimson hue of whispering ribbons heralding Red's most devastating mistake, when she sent her husband into another woman's arms through her own selfish insecurities.

Red shrieks, defenseless against the shock of her regrets. Her vengeful memories hone in and impale her. Her vines withdraw into me, my skin closing up around them as if they were never there. My feet meet the stage.

I conjure my imagination, picturing her as a spider pierced through the thorax with a pin, until she curls up in my chest, helpless as a bug nailed to a plaster backing. Pain spears through me, ripping me down the middle as she succumbs to her sorrow and my heart begins to split in two. I strangle on the taste of copper.

But I won't die. Not until I've dealt out revenge.

Concentrating on Red's listless tendrils inside me, I coax them to cinch the organ back together.

She no longer owns me. *I own her.*

The mutant mob overpowers me in a surge of fur, drool, and

claws. They rip at my hair, snarl in my ears, and tie my arms back. Then they lift me, carrying me toward the edge of the stage where Jeb fell.

"Take her apart! Show us the heart!" The morbid chanting grows frenetic.

I'm passed overhead from creature to creature, crowd surfing toward the pool of fears. Rage rises in me, fiery hot and blistering. It strips the color from my hair and twists it into platinum dreadlocks, alive with fierce magic—feeding my own dark power.

The flaming sphere on the track catches my eye. I envision the skeletal platform as a centipede, the track becoming the exoskeleton and the support structure the legs. With little coaxing, it rearranges its position. The inclines click open and release the massive inferno of glass. It thunders along the twisted run, then leaps off, flying toward the pool. It lands in place and plugs up the opening, preventing the creatures from tossing me in.

The track continues to move, snakelike, tangling in the ropes and the awning attached to the pole at the center of the stage. The awning rips in half and the ropes draw tighter and tighter until the castle's outside walls fall inward, crushing half the crowd. Ash puffs out as the stone hits the courtyard.

What's left of the mob drops me in their midst, as if stunned by my magic. They grunt, growl, and mumble among themselves. Gathering my bearings, I stand, my arms still bound at my back.

"Cover her eyes!" an apish beast shouts. "Her magic is limited to her vision!" One of them drops the bag Jeb was wearing over my head, ties it in place, and shoves me to the ground, knocking the wind from my lungs.

"Now, burn her to ash!"

I inhale, hungry for air, swept under by the smells of paint and citrus soap. The scent of Jeb.

His death replays in my mind. He'll never see his family, never hold me, never call me skater girl again. His beautiful art will live on in the human realm, yet he'll never see how it touches people's lives, or realize he was already the man he always tried so hard to be.

The creatures snarl and paw at my prone form—hot breath and ripping claws—as they scoot me toward the inferno in the ball.

I'm too deep in the mire of emotions to look for a way out, slammed with the idea of Jeb's heart floating in the pool, somewhere beneath the flaming sphere.

Desolation gouges me, harsher than the punches and fists jarring my bones as I'm dragged toward a flaming death. I curl into a fetal position.

Tears singe my eyes and I scream until my lungs draw up inside me like dried rosebuds, small and useless.

Then, beneath the echo of my despair, the small and quiet jingle of butterfly wings makes me remember: Morpheus's armor.

I have to live . . . I *will* live. For my loved ones and for Wonderland. And to avenge Jeb's death.

All it takes is one thought, and the protective fringe releases from my dress's razor-sharp tiers. Too many claws hold me down, so I wiggle like a worm. Warm wetness splatters my skin, followed by the scent of blood as the winged blades slice my captors, one by one. Even in my blindness, I can sense them pulling back, though they won't retreat, too excited by the prospect of watching one another get mutilated.

The moment there's room enough I roll, around and around.

Agonized cries intersperse with dark laughter as the creatures keep coming back for more.

Rolling, faster and faster, I coax the wind to pick me up and rise like a cyclone. I plow blindly through everyone around me, shredding everything to pieces.

I am wind.

I am fury.

I am *pandemonium*.

I spin and spin and spin like the Gravitron ride, until no more sound is left. Until every last cry and sick cackle is silenced.

When my revolutions slow, I land lightly on my feet, head still cloaked and arms tied. I stand in place as the sound of footsteps sloughing through sediment stirs behind me. I know who it is, even before his gentle fingers, now free of gloves, work at the bindings on my wrists and lift the bag from my head.

Morpheus stays at my back, as if giving me time to absorb the destruction my madness has wrought.

A soft mist coats the air, a precursor to a storm. I blink in the gray light. Nothing and no one is left standing in the courtyard. No walls, no stage, not even the skeletal track. Morpheus must've roused in time to seek shelter in one of the towers during my rampage, because only the castle itself still stands, along with the covered portico that opens to the drawbridge. I've leveled everything else to ash and dust.

Hart peers out from one of the tower's highest windows.

I glare up at her. "I am the reigning Red Queen!" I shout. "You are a has-been. And you'll be a dead one, if I ever see you again!" It's a promise and a dare.

She lets a curtain fall, retreating behind its black folds.

Manti and the guards and goon birds look out from other openings to survey the damage, but it's obvious they want nothing to do with me or my rage.

As Morpheus turns me to face him, my attackers' powdery remains swallow my boots and sift on the wind. Bright red streaks cover my arms, but it's not the blood of my victims. It's mine.

I realize now why he asked where my gloves were earlier. He knew it would come to this.

So many emotions flicker over him—astonishment, concern, remorse . . . and the always-present adoration. I raise my hand toward his face and he winces, as if anticipating a slap. Instead, I stroke his cheek and those beautifully expressive jewels under his eyes, then lift to my toes and press my lips to his. His flavor and warmth envelop me. He moans and cups my face on either side, kissing me deeper, but I pull back.

"I love you," I whisper, because he has a right to know the truth before I kill him.

His jaw goes slack, delicate features sparkling with the mist and the reflection of the soft blue glow of his hair. The fathoms of his eyes open to me, maelstroms of passion and hope and unbridled happiness. I see Wonderland's wilds in them . . . a panoramic view of the kingdom I was born to rule. Another time, I would have been drawn inside those mesmerizing depths, set adrift with him. Now, those tender emotions are out of my reach.

When he opens his mouth to speak, I place a finger on his lips.

"It's my love for you that makes this hurt so much," I say, my voice strong and resolved. "I had faith in you and you betrayed me."

His face falls and indignation courses through my body, so overpowering I can't contain it. I siphon off of Red's dormant state, conjuring her vines out from my skin, commanding they obey *me* now.

I snap a tendril out and catch Morpheus by his throat, lifting him high. His legs swing and his wings flap helplessly. "I was gullible enough to tell you where he was."

"Alyssa, wait." He hisses and struggles to loosen the vine wrapped around his windpipe and carotid artery.

"You just handed him over. You knew better than to trust them. You gambled with his life, after he put it on the line to save yours." My tears start anew—angry and anguished. As if sympathizing, the sky opens and a cold rain sweeps in to wash the hot saltiness down my face. I lick it from my lips.

I waver, thrown off balance by Morpheus's weight. My pulse separates into two distinctive strains and it hurts to breathe. Red's temporary hold on my dual heart is as fragile as she is now, the strands stretching because I'm usurping her power.

I ignore the physical warnings, tighten my noose until Morpheus's throat bulges and he claws at the ivy strangling him, desperate to breathe. I see our son in his eyes and my compassion surfaces, threatening to soften me, but the queen has tasted vengeance and is intoxicated.

"There's nothing you can say to fix this," I murmur darkly. "Not one thing that will merit my mercy."

Morpheus's fingernails gouge at the vine and he sips enough air to rasp three words: "You . . . are . . . *Wonderland.*"

WONDERLAND

I slacken my hold on Morpheus's neck enough to let him breathe.

He gulps air hungrily. "I"—he coughs—"will always"—another breath—"do what's best for *you*."

I blink rain and tears from my lashes. "Jeb is dead!" My shout strains my throat and the tendrils holding my heart together. Dizziness rushes in and I wobble. I gather my bearings and drag Morpheus closer. More vines erupt from my skin, wrapping him from his waist to his chest. "How can that be what's best for me? Answer me!"

"Skater girl."

The voice comes from behind, not from Morpheus's compressed

vocal cords. I drop the vine from his neck, but the others hold posi-tion. I can't turn around, afraid I'm imagining things.

"Look, I get that he's a pain in the ass." A strong, familiar hand touches my bare elbow and the heat stings my cuts. "But it'd be more sporting with a king-size flyswatter. Set him down, huh?"

Morpheus holds my gaze, a smug smirk quivering at his lips. "Told you." Then he glances over my head and takes another gulp of air. "About bloody time you got back."

My limbs tremble and I lower Morpheus to the ground. The vines retract into my body as I spin on my heel.

It's CC facing me. The harlequin doppelganger now wears a knight's tunic and pants. Chessie sits on his shoulder, smiling from ear to ear. Two of Jeb's shadow creatures stand under the portico next to the drawbridge to stay dry, their wings at rest as they await further commands.

I watch in wonder as CC transforms in the rain.

The sleeves of his tunic are rolled up, and a glowing purple tattoo begins to appear on his right inner wrist, a sheet of flesh-colored paint rinsing away. The points of his ears, the heart-shaped eye patch, and the mutilations under his left eye melt away, too. His porcelain coloring vanishes as rivulets of black, red, and white track down to reveal Jeb's clear, olive complexion. Everything—the gashes and the dislocated eyeball, the elfin jewels and ear tips—were painted on . . . made alive at Jeb's command.

He and Morpheus managed a trade somehow: Jeb for his cre-ation.

They tricked everyone. Including me.

I shake my head. Chessie launches from Jeb's shoulder and flutters in front of me. His whirling, all-knowing eyes recount everything: Morpheus finding Jeb in the dungeon; the two of them in private, coming up with the plan and sneaking into Manti's chamber in simulacrum suits; Manti agreeing to everything as long as he got to play the loyal king to salvage his reputation in his queen's eyes; Jeb painting and animating the miniature hookah that triggered my human memories; and last of all, Jeb touching up his doppelganger's face to flawless perfection before painting bloody streams under the blindfold and gag, then masking his own ears and face with elfin features, harlequin face paint, eye patch, and gaping holes.

Chessie smiles again, tiny teeth glinting. I open my palm for him and he rolls to his back so I can rub his tummy. With a contented grunt, he leaps into flight and makes a beeline for Morpheus, who puts him to work looking for his hat in the ashes.

I turn to Jeb, still shaky. "CC's image. His face. I thought you couldn't complete him."

Jeb rubs his labret with his thumb. "Because I couldn't see inside my heart. Ever since I can remember, I measured my worth against who my old man was, or how successful my art was. You've been telling me all along that I chose to be better than my dad. It was a *choice*. It finally hit me that you were right. Every time your life was at stake, my first thought was to help you. Like today, even if I couldn't have painted a way, I would've found another. That's the one good thing that came out of my childhood. Having seen the worst is what helps me choose the best. This place let me face my demons. But you . . . you always had faith I would beat them. And now I have. Thanks for that, Al." His green eyes shimmer with a self-possession they've never had. Complete and total acceptance.

The rain stops, and reality hits full on.

Jeb's alive and whole—in every way. Morpheus didn't betray us. And all the horror I just witnessed was a brilliant, twisted lie.

Jeb twines one of my blond dreadlocks around his finger. "You okay?"

I'm tempted to scream at him for letting me believe such terrible things about both of them. But I'm too happy to have him alive, standing here and talking to me . . . touching me . . .

I want to leap into his arms and hug him tight. Since my dress is a killing machine, I settle for pressing my palm against his chest. His heartbeat thumps from the other side of his clothes. I will never take that rhythm for granted, or the fact that he still has a life-clock.

"Never scare me like that again," I say.

He lifts an eyebrow. "Hey, that's my line." Using my dreadlock, he draws my face close and brushes his lips and labret across my forehead, then down my temple to my mouth in a gentle peck.

Morpheus makes a huffing sound. "Well, that's just jolly beautiful. I'm the one who got a bump on the noggin and half strangled."

Jeb releases me, rolling his eyes.

Morpheus brushes futilely at the ash clumped on his clothes. "Sucking up all her sympathies when you had the easy part. *Follow Chessie out the gate, and lead him to her father and uncle's hiding place.* Oooh, so scary."

Fighting a smile, I study the raw red marks along his neck that look like rope burns.

I take his hand and squeeze it. "I'm sorry. I didn't know."

His thumb rubs raindrops from my knuckles. "You couldn't know. From the moment Red inhabited you, everything you knew, she knew. We had to concoct a plan to get the medallion and make you remember your strength and get angry enough to tame her spirit, all without her knowing. Without you knowing. It was the only way."

The only way . . .

The phrase triggers my dad's advice when we first arrived here: *You've never murdered anyone, Allie. Be sure it's the only way. Otherwise, it will haunt you . . .*

I look again at all the death in my wake. My stomach turns. "It was the only way."

"Yes, it was," Jeb says from beside me.

"Damn right it was," Morpheus agrees. His gaze flicks to the piles of ash, making it clear that he understands I'm talking about so much more than their plan. I'm glad Jeb wasn't here to witness my rampage. It's enough that he saw me in Red's chains.

Chessie erupts from a pile of soot, propelling Morpheus's dust-covered hat like he did the robe at the inn yesterday. The hat zigzags through the air, Chessie refusing to give up his prize. His head peeks out and his mischievous smile spreads when Morpheus scowls.

I purse my lips, one more question niggling. "So Manti . . . you attacking him on stage. That was part of it?"

"Yeah," Jeb says. "About that." He cocks his head at Morpheus. "You laid it on a little thick out there."

Morpheus clucks his tongue. "I performed masterfully," he answers, at last managing to claim his hat from Chessie.

"Right," Jeb scoffs. "Pretty sure my mistreatment wouldn't have sent you into hysterics, drama queen."

Morpheus smirks. "Fair enough. On the other hand, your portrayal of a brainless wind-up numbskull was spot on."

Jeb's lips quiver, as if he's fighting a smile himself. "You know, I still have enough paint to make that flyswatter."

"Tut. No need for violence." Morpheus taps the dust from his hat and places it on his head. "I'm simply giving credit where it's due."

Their eyes glitter with levity, just like when they tease me. They're enjoying the banter. There's even an undercurrent of respect where there used to be little more than tolerance.

My heart swells, both sides of it, so proud of how they worked together, saw past their resentments for the greater good. The sensation is beautiful, but it causes another rip—a visceral pop behind my sternum.

I gasp.

"Al, you're white as a sheet." Jeb throws a concerned glance to Morpheus. "Maybe she's losing too much blood."

"Perhaps." Morpheus catches my left wrist to check my pulse. I can tell by the suspicious crimp of his brow that he's thinking about my anemic spell in Hart's playroom.

I pull away. "I'm fine. Really."

Jeb turns my other arm over to assess the damage. I cringe as my wounded skin stretches.

"I don't share her magic," Jeb says. "I can't heal her."

"I can, once I'm restored. For now we'll staunch the flow." Morpheus takes out his paint-smudged handkerchief, reminding me of our time in Hart's room. I still can't believe I almost choked him. And after professing my love . . . something he's been waiting so long to hear.

With one glance he alleviates my guilt. Even without him being in my head, I know what he's thinking: that he understands my darker side and her vicious kicks; that, in fact, it's those very kicks that challenge him and make him feel alive.

I mime a thank-you. He winks and gingerly presses the hanky along my skin.

A strong gust blows through the leveled courtyard, stirring clumps of wet ash into a frenzied cloud. A wind tunnel appears in the distance, just above the cliff where we landed this morning.

Jeb takes my elbow gently. "We need to get going. Your dad, uncle, and the other knight are inside that grove of trees, waiting. We have a wind tunnel to catch."

"You said *we*," I point out as the three of us walk swiftly toward the portico to retrieve the painted shadows.

Jeb throws one last glimpse over his shoulder at the pool of fears and the giant ball of flames covering it, as if looking for ghosts. "I have nothing left to stay for."

I'm selfish because I'm glad all of his creatures in the mountain were destroyed. How ironic, that I have Morpheus to thank for that, too. Or maybe he planned it all along. It never ceases to amaze me, the far-reaching scope of his machinations.

"Poor Nikki," Jeb says, his voice heavy.

Morpheus offers a sad nod and Chessie hangs limp over his shoulder, his smile turned upside down.

"I thought she was trying to save her creator," I add as we all walk through the portico and onto the bridge. "But she was trying to save her friend."

"She was a brave little spriteling," Morpheus acknowledges. "And speaking of small but fierce females, it's time for you to spread your wings, luv."

I don't feel so fierce. Just the short walk across the courtyard has left me winded. I'm not sure how long I have before Red's power runs dry and the tendrils holding me together give out.

For one second, I consider telling the guys about her spell, share my concerns so I don't have to shoulder them alone. But what good would it do? They would only be tormented because they can't fix this. No one can.

Red herself said there was no magic that could heal me.

My eyes burn at the edges. I've never felt more alone.

"Let's go get your mom." Jeb stands back so my wings can sprout open.

I force a smile, pushing past the tearing sensation behind my breastbone to take flight, eager to see Dad and hug him. With Jeb carried by his shadow on one side and Morpheus and his shadow on the other, we head for the cliff and our transport to the Wonderland gate.

As we fly, the memory of my vision about Mom buffets me like the wind currents. She's safe, but Wonderland's heart is ailing. What will we face when we get there? I only hope I can fix things before my own ailing heart gives up the fight.

I can die happy, if I know Wonderland will live.

❄··I··❄

I have just enough time to absorb my wings, slip out of my deadly dress, and pull an extra tunic over my leather leggings before we're sucked into the wind tunnel and dropped in front of the gate that leads to Wonderland. After I fill everyone in on my vision about Mom and Ivory, Uncle Bernie hugs me and Dad good-bye. We promise to visit once we're back in the human realm.

It's a promise I'm afraid I won't be keeping.

Leaving Uncle with the other knights, we make it through the gate without anyone knowing I'm harboring a fugitive. After that, aside from the horrible rotting stench, traveling through the tulgey's quarter-mile-long throat isn't nearly as terrifying or dangerous as I expected. Partly because Dad has ventured through once before and leads the way, but also because the tulgey is frozen. Literally.

Morpheus expected as much, even prepared us for it. He said according to my vision, Ivory froze things to slow Red's decaying spell. To give us a chance to stop it.

The tree's open mouth comes into view, offering a misty silvery light to see by. Our breaths form clouds of condensation as we maneuver around the giant ice-slicked gray tongue, using the splintery teeth like stepping-stones.

I leap from the unhinged jaw into the heavily wooded thicket behind Dad. Jeb and Morpheus bring up the rear. The neon grass glistens with frost and crunches beneath my boots. A mildewed scent hangs on the air, even though everything is cloaked in winter.

Tangled branches and looking-glass rejects—netherlings that have been spit back out of the tulgey in strange and awful forms—all stand motionless. Morpheus names the creatures: a carpenter ant with a body made of tools; a hornet with a trumpet for a nose; and a grasschomper with a locust's body and a horse's head, sporting a clump of frosty grass sticking out from its muzzle—as if it was suspended mid-chomp.

The scene is uncannily like the frozen tea party Jeb and I encountered on our first trip here. But unlike the tea party, there's no broken watch that has suspended time in its icy thrall. This is something else entirely.

I meet Jeb's gaze and he tips his head, acknowledging the memory.

Morpheus stops beside me. Glowing blue flecks swirl around his hands like fiber-optic mittens. They brighten and dim, then brighten again. His magic is stuttering as it warms up, like a car's motor that has sat too long without use.

"Are you sure you told us everything about the vision?" he asks me as Jeb and Dad search for a path.

"I think so." I rub my forehead. "I was . . . in a weird place when I had it. Why?"

Morpheus purses his lips. "I expected the terrain to be under a perpetual winter. But Ivory froze the residents. I can't understand her motive. It was the landscapes that were in danger of falling into disrepair. Not the netherlings."

I nibble on my lip. Something nudges at the back of my mind. Didn't Mom use a strange word to describe the sickness that had fallen over everything? But I can't remember what it was . . . it started with a *D*.

Frustrated by my amnesia, I trundle over to where Dad and Jeb are clearing away fallen branches from a trail that appears to be the only way out.

Dad stops me as I reach down to help. "Allie, let us do this. I don't want you to reopen your cuts." He turns to Morpheus. "Will you be able to heal her soon?"

Bright orbs of blue light—strong and unfaltering—burst along Morpheus's fingertips. The glow reflects off his face. He smirks like an enchanted schoolboy. "Yes."

Chessie flutters around him in celebratory spins.

Dad nods and takes an iron dagger from the sheath at his shoulder. "All right. Jeb and I are going to see if this trail is safe. We'll be back."

Jeb squeezes my hand before he follows. I hold on to him, surprised to see his tattoo still glowing, though instead of violet, it's pure red. He lifts his eyebrows in a bewildered gesture before rolling down his sleeve, an unspoken request for us to solve the mystery later. He and Dad duck under a mass of low-hanging tulgey branches and vanish from sight.

Chessie's eyes whirl, telling me and Morpheus how much he's missed his home and wants to revisit his favorite haunts.

"First, find Alyssa's mum and Ivory," Morpheus insists. "Let them know we're here. If the mirror passages are working, have them open one for us."

Chessie agrees, then weaves through some closely knit trees, gone before I can blink.

Morpheus lifts his hands, testing his power. Blue electric filaments reach to every branch in the canopy overhead, shaking white billows loose. He stands there—wings arced high—proud and regal as a fluffy downpour showers over him. A hearty laugh rumbles deep in his chest. He's carefree and playful, even more than when he was in his room in AnyElsewhere. He's been without magic for so long, he's drunk on it.

The snow flurries over me, too, cold and refreshing. It reminds me of Texas and the seasonal snowfalls Jeb, Jenara, and I played in as kids. Snowmen, snow ice cream, snow forts. I can't help but laugh with him, in spite of how weak I feel.

"Dance with me, blossom," he coaxes, and when I hesitate, he reels me in with his magic. I snuggle into his chest and let myself savor his vitality, wishing I could absorb it.

He wraps an arm around my waist and clasps my hand with his. Lips pressed to my dreadlocked head, he hums the lullaby's tune while his inner voice fills my head on a frequency only I can hear: *"You dazzled me today. So uninhibited. So filled with malice."*

I smile secretly and follow his graceful steps. His wings cascade around us like swirls of ethereal ink.

"*In fact,*" his mind-speak continues, "*now that I have my magic back*"—he spins me out, then pulls me against him again—"*I expect you to give me another crack at our game.*"

"Game?" I ask.

"I am not averse to roughing it up," he answers, no longer humming. He takes my hand, nips at the knuckles with taunting teeth, then guides my fingers to the red marks on his neck. "Wrathful queen and wayward footman . . . that will be standard fare for our love-play. Sans Red's vines, and we'll both be scantily clad."

I snort. "You're delirious."

"I prefer the term 'mad.'"

I smile up at him, thrilled to see him teasing and content. I press my ear to his chest so I can hear his strong heartbeat. I try to make my dual heart merge to one beat and follow its perfect rhythm. I fail.

"Alyssa, I am whole again," he murmurs as our dance slows to a gentle rocking motion.

"I know."

"Jebediah is whole, too."

I don't answer, because somehow Jeb still harbors Red's magic and I'm not sure what to make of it.

"So, you must convince him to release you of your vow," Morpheus adds, resolute.

I start to pull back, but he hugs me tighter.

"You love me. You admitted it."

"I do love you."

His body trembles in response, as if he can't contain his emotions at my confession. "We both know you made the vow to get your mortal knight out of AnyElsewhere. To give him faith in his humanness and you. Your stratagem saved his life."

I grind my teeth. "That's *not* the only reason I made it." It's important that he accepts my love for Jeb. I'll have to tell Jeb the same thing about Morpheus before I'm gone. I will not leave them with lies hanging between us. "I love you *both*."

Morpheus tenses and waltzes me around the small space again, retracing our dance steps through the snow until our footprints erase themselves. We twirl from one end to the other, as if he thinks he can distract me from my own truth.

At last, we come to a panting stop, face-to-face. All of his earlier playfulness snuffs out like a candle as our breaths form clouds of condensation between us. "I'm done waiting. It is now or never. And dare not forget, our union will ensure what happened to your father never happens to another human. No one else will be trapped by Sister Two, because we will gift Wonderland with our dream-child."

His words punch me with a realization that hasn't yet crossed my mind. Since I'm dying, our son will never be born. Wonderland will have to continue to steal children for their dreams forever. Unless we can find an alternative.

There's a harsh snap behind my sternum and a bitter, metallic flavor coats my throat.

I press my face into his chest, stifling a sob. "I thought we were dancing."

In response, he spins me. I break free and come to a stop in front of a tree trunk. Its expression is locked in an openmouthed morose frown, just like the tree we stepped out of. I stand back and survey all the tulgeys within sight. Every single one has the same expression, as if it was miserable the moment the ice swept over it.

The heart of Wonderland is suffering. The doldrums are closing in. Come soon. We'll hold them off as long as we can.

"Doldrums," I murmur.

"What did you say?" Morpheus asks, coming up behind me.

"*Doldrums.* That's the word Mom used when she said to hurry. She told me the doldrums were closing in."

I look over my shoulder for his reaction. His jaw is clenched, his beautiful face crestfallen. He appraises the trees and the looking-glass rejects. "I thought Red merely cast a spell. But it was a plague . . . an extermination. *Toxic gloom.*"

"I don't understand."

"Doldrums are microscopic creatures. Their destruction is so devastating and complete, they've been in containment for centuries. Each of the castles has a supply of them under lock and key, as a means to keep the peace. To keep both kingdoms in check."

I nod. "Mutual Assured Destruction . . . both sides know that any attack on the other will be devastating to themselves. We have the same thing for nuclear weapons in our world."

Morpheus rubs his temple. "Red must've smuggled them out before she was exiled from the throne. When she launched her revenge against you and me, she didn't simply plan to destroy the beauty here . . . she was going to eradicate everything."

"But why? I thought she wanted her kingdom back?"

"It must have been her alternate plan, in case something went awry with the Alice one. This way, she could level all of Wonderland, then rebuild to her specifications."

"Of course. That fits. She wanted to rule over everything." I'm about to tell him how she intended to use our child as a bargaining chip to defeat Ivory and rule both kingdoms, but he interrupts.

"She must've released the plague after you left for the human realm," he says. "After she found a new body to inhabit. That's when it all started falling apart."

"And that's when you tried to get me to come back." I move to the nearest tree and slide my scarred palm over the glacial bark. I sense Morpheus's closeness, but don't turn around. I'm too ashamed. "I should've listened."

"You had a bit of a learning curve." There's restraint in his voice. He's angry. "What matters is what you do with what you learned."

"But can Red's magic fix this?"

He sighs, placing his hand alongside mine on the tree so his body and wings hedge me in. "It comes down to more than fixing at this point. It is a renewal. Creating the world anew is the only way to stop the infection, and only the power of those who've once experienced crown-magic have that ability. It takes lineage from both kingdoms working together. Ivory couldn't do it alone. That's why she froze everything, to keep the inhabitants from getting infected until you came and could help. Together, you'll re-create the landscapes and then, once they're pure, Ivory can safely release all the netherlings from her suspension spell. It might take every ounce of power Red has left, paired with yours and Ivory's, to address a pandemic so widespread."

My eyes tear up, because my magic is only as strong as I am, and Red's is waning.

Morpheus strokes my hair where it hangs between my shoulder blades. "There is a silver lining, luv. You won't have to cast her out. You'll simply use her up. And then she shall be defeated at last. Gone forever."

He doesn't realize I've already used most of her up. In trying to keep myself alive, I've damned Wonderland to die. I never considered how closely entwined our fates might be.

I crumple, my palm skating along the tree's frozen face as I plop to the ground.

"Alyssa?" Morpheus crouches beside me in an instant. He catches my chin and forces me to look at him. "Are you feeling anemic again?"

I struggle to breathe. It grates inside my chest, like inhaling angry bees. Blood creeps into my throat and gags me.

Morpheus's jeweled markings flash through an anxious kaleidoscope of colors. He whips off his jacket, wraps me in it, and rolls up his shirt cuff. "Take off your boot so I can heal you."

I clench my teeth against moving. The only way to manage the agonizing pain, to keep my heart from ripping any further, is to stay frozen like everything around me.

Morpheus gives up waiting, peels away the boot, and pushes up my legging's hem. He traces the tattoo that he loves to tease me about, then presses our birthmarks together. A spark rushes between us, expanding like a flame through my veins. The power heals his neck and my arms, yet never quite reaches my heart.

During the euphoric rush of warmth, Morpheus's gaze locks on mine and I'm bared to the bone. He sees what's wrong.

"Oh, little plum." His voice is a croak of despair. "Why didn't you tell me?"

I clamp my eyes shut. "I'm sorry." The apology turns into a wheeze.

"No," he snarls. "You did try to tell me. In the mountain. And in Hart's playroom. I was too bloody preoccupied to listen."

No more guilt. He needs to be thinking of our home. "Find a way." I gulp back another rush of blood and saliva. "Save Wonderland."

Morpheus lifts me into his arms, cradling me gently. "That's exactly what I intend to do." Even though I can feel his warmth seeping through our clothes, I shiver.

Through half-lidded eyes, I watch blue lightning zap from his fingertips to the branches overhead. Using it like ropes, he tugs the canopy apart. His wings flap, stirring up snowy gusts. We launch out of the woodland and into the sky. Wonderland's sleeping terrain passes beneath us at dizzying heights—white and glittering. Black fringe dots my peripheral vision.

My stomach kicks once, reminding me I'm alive. Then I close my eyes, and face the darkness waiting there.

Sutures

The sound of chimes wakes me, tinkly and melodious. A flurry of sprites skitters along my body. My dreadlocks are gone and my hair fans my pillow in lustrous, white-blond waves. The sprites sweep makeup brushes and sparkling jeweled clips into place with as much precision and proficiency as an automatic car wash, leaving the scent of perfume and powder in their wake.

One sprite rushes by my nose and tickles the tip. She looks so much like Nikki, I do a double take. The itch she caused evolves to a sneeze, sending all the tiny fairies in a scatter like dandelion seeds.

They chitter in annoyance.

I rub my eyes, sit up, and take stock of my surroundings.

I'm sunken inside a large bed under downy quilts so white and fluffy they look like drifts of snow. The sprites gather up baskets from the white marble floor, four to a handle, and flitter through the half-opened door.

I blink. I've never been here, but I know this place from the sketches Morpheus once drew in the back of Mom's *Alice's Adventures in Wonderland* book. This is Ivory's glass castle and I'm in an ornate chamber: glass walls frosted with ice to give me privacy from the other side, and crystal candleholders with no candles or wicks. Their silver flames float, like glowworms suspended in midair.

A crystallized chaise lounge sits in front of a fireplace where more silver flames crackle. Somehow, they give off heat and light without melting the ice on the walls. Mom and Dad sleep soundly atop the white cushion, her in his lap and their legs tangled together. His handsome profile is scruffy, his nose buried in her long, pinkish blond hair. The strands twitch, alive with magic. Her gauzy wings are folded behind her like a butterfly's at rest.

They look so lovely together, the White knight and his fairy bride, in one another's arms at last. In spite of all they went through to reach this place, their love never faltered. They deserve this more than anyone I know.

My heart swells with happiness and I prepare for the tearing pain that's sure to follow. Instead, a small ripple echoes the emotion. It's like a dragonfly butting against my sternum—delicate and exhilarated. I take a deep breath, stronger and more at peace than I've been since I began this journey, maybe in my whole life.

Something stirs in the back of my skull. Red is still there, curled up in mourning, but she's losing power by the second. It's just a matter of time until she seeps out of me and withers away to nothing. I'm the only thing holding her inside, though I can let her go when I'm ready. Her spell on my heart has been mended.

How?

I look down at the vintage nightgown covering me. It's stitched of sheer white fabric and lace—as transparent as the glass surrounding this room—with slits in the back for wings. A lacy silver corset bodysuit offers a modicum of modesty underneath.

Fuzzy purple light twinkles behind the corset's bodice. The glow radiates from *inside* me . . . under my skin and behind my sternum.

My stomach flips. The last time I saw magic like this, it came from inside Jeb—a combination of Red's and Morpheus's strains.

Clacking footsteps bring my attention to the crystal doorway. A bald head shimmers in the shadows. Pink, dewy eyes glitter from inside the albino skin that hangs in rolls of wrinkles like a shar-pei puppy's.

"Late, I say. Queen Alyssa. Late I be."

I smooth my gown and smile. "Rabid. I was worried you were frozen."

"Invited to the castle of ice, were we. Before the winter summoned by Ivory-fair."

So that's what I saw in my first dream of Mom. Ivory brought her, Grenadine, and my royal advisor Rabid White to stay here, where they'd be protected from the doldrums.

Rabid's bunny-size silhouette waits in the hallway, unmoving.

"Please, come in." I wave him forward. He hops across the threshold. His frothy lips pout in concentration as he balances the ruby crown on a pillow atop his gloved hands.

His skeletal body knocks against itself inside his red tailcoat with each ambling movement. I put a finger to my mouth to hush him.

He glances at my sleeping parents and slows his hops to awkward steps, intuitive in spite of his grim and wide-eyed appearance. That's what makes him such a formidable royal advisor. Like most netherlings, he's ambiguous. Introspective and unreadable when necessary. That's how he tricked me last year into thinking he was out to kill me, when all along he only wanted to set me upon my throne.

He's dressed like he was that first time I met him, except today his coat is flocked and has black velvet buttons and a matching fur collar.

Sympathy rushes through me for the hideous form hidden under the lavish clothes. I will never forget how Red stripped him of his pride and his skin. A part of me wants to tell him the truth. That she caused his deformity; that when she saved his face from the acid, it was all a ploy to secure his loyalty. But what good would it do to tell him he was a pawn? Red isn't a threat anymore, to anyone. It's actually sad, how worthless and helpless she is now.

A twinge of deep remorse nudges inside my skull where she hides. It grows as Rabid gets closer to the bed, enough that Red whispers inside me, *"Please . . . relieve me of my misery. Let me tell him of my regret for my actions, then release me so I may cease to exist."*

Too little too late, I whisper back internally, fighting any inclinations toward mercy. *I've yet to decide your fate.*

Rabid arrives beside my bed and holds up the pillow. His fuzzy white antlers almost topple him as he kneels. I place a hand on his head to balance him. We went through some crazy stuff together when he snuck into the human realm before the prom-pocalypse. He's earned my everlasting trust and affection.

He sighs—a contented sound—then continues, "Time it is, Queen Grenadine says." Foam slathers around his mouth as he speaks. "Crown Queen Alyssa, she commands."

Puzzled, I take the pillow, setting it on my lap over the covers. Coiled in the crown's center is a new ruby-tipped key and filigreed chain. I place it around my neck. I've missed wearing the key to the kingdom against my chest. My fingertips trace the crown's intricate golden frame, and I hold it up so the rubies shimmer in the faint light.

"Alyssa, no!" Mom's startled voice causes poor Rabid to lurch headfirst to the floor. I set the crown aside, throw off the covers, and swing my bare feet down to help him stand. Mom and Dad are next to me in an instant, blinking their bleary eyes.

"Hi?" I say, more of a question. They hug me, sandwiching me between her floral perfume and his mossy clean scent. Mom kisses my forehead, and Dad nuzzles my curled and primped hair.

"We were so worried," Mom whispers.

"I'm okay," I answer. I glance up at Dad. "But I don't understand how . . . ?"

He opens his mouth, but clams up as Rabid scales the bed and digs through the blankets for the crown, holding it out once more. "Ready to serve Queen Alyssa, be I. Long time await. Have much and many debts to pay. Loyal, always and forever-evermore."

"It's not time yet." Mom wipes tears from her face and takes the crown from Rabid's hands.

Rabid hisses, his sharp teeth bared, eyes glinting hot. "Otherwise, Queen Grenadine says."

I place my hand on his head and he bows again, obediently relaxing.

"The plan has changed," Dad says, moving with caution as he helps the netherling climb down. He walks him to the door. "We sent word to Grenadine, but she must've forgotten. She doesn't have her ribbons to help her remember right now. Why don't you get Ivory for us? She'll explain everything."

Rabid's pink eyes lose their shimmer, hazy like cotton candy. Before the door closes he mutters, "Zombies in Toyland?"

Dad pauses shutting him out and exchanges a worried glance with Mom.

I giggle. "It's a game on my phone. Rabid beat my high score a few weeks ago." I smirk at my little advisor. "We'll play it again soon. I have to get my title back."

His eyes brighten. "Generous are you! Cookies, too? Rabid White hungry be. Always."

I laugh. "Yeah, always. I'll have Mom make you some cookies."

He grins, then hops away down the hall, looking more like a rabbit than a demented otherworldly being.

Dad shuts the door and both my parents stare at me as if I'm a mirage that could disappear any second.

"Okay." I'm done being in the dark. "What's going on?"

Mom's gaze falls to the purple glimmer radiating from my chest. I'd forgotten about it with Rabid's unexpected arrival. I hold my hand over the gown, pressing my key against the place that glows. A warm flash of happy memories surges: Morpheus and me as children, then Jeb always there during my middle school years. Their voices follow, blended together and filled with love and encouragement: *You are the best of both worlds . . . You got this, skater-girl-fairy-queen.*

I look up at my parents, seeking the answers I see in their faces.

"Where are Jeb and Morpheus?" I ask, my throat dry. "I can't believe they're not here. I almost died."

"They would've been here, but . . . Ivory will explain their absence." Mom turns her eyes to Dad. Behind her black lashes and blue irises flecked with turquoise, there's anxiety.

Absence? A knowing stirs in my gut. This change within my heart *is* a combination of them and their magic. I still have no idea how Jeb kept Red's power after we stepped into Wonderland from AnyElsewhere, but the biggest question gnawing at me is why aren't they here?

I waver as my mind rocks with horrible scenarios.

"Butterfly, sit down." Dad supports my elbow and slides me back onto the bed. He offers his Elvis smirk, but I'm not buying it because of the eyelid twitch that follows.

"The guys," I squeak.

"They're fine," he answers. "They'll be by to see you soon. They're busy right now."

I let out a breath, my relief so palpable I can almost taste it. "Busy with what?"

"Re-creating Wonderland," Mom answers.

I stand back up. "*I* was supposed to help Ivory with that. It takes two queens working together, from both kingdoms. This is one half my world, and wholly my responsibility."

Dad's face flushes. He drapes a quilt around me. "It takes two queens' crown-magic. Ivory will explain. And you need to get some clothes on if you plan to leave this room—"

"She can't leave," Mom interrupts. "Allie, there are instructions for the magical sutures."

I tie the quilt around my neck, forming a robe. "Sutures?" I back up to the bed and prop my hips against the mattress's edge. "But Red said there was no magic she knew of that could help me."

"That is true." Upon the sound of Ivory's voice, I look over at the door. Both her milky skin and her layered floor-length dress glisten like the crystallized ice on the walls of this room. "This brand of magic has never been experienced by Red, or by most netherlings." She steps inside. Chessie sits atop her left shoulder and Nikki on her right, confirming I didn't imagine the little sprite earlier. There's only one explanation: Jeb repainted her.

"Jeb wasn't drained of Red's magic," I venture.

Ivory's wings sweep behind her, resembling a feather cape. "His muse has been forever altered. The tie was so strong between his creative drive and Red's closed-minded obstinance, they fused together and became an entity. So although Morpheus's magic returned to its original vessel, Red's stayed within your mortal knight. His talent for painting is a living thing now, retained within him. And it is more powerful here than it was in the looking-glass world, for there is no iron to taint or weaken his creations. They cannot be washed away with water. They become as real as you or I."

As outrageous and unsettling as the concept is, it makes sense. "So, because his power comes from Red, it retains her royal bloodline and her crown-magic. *He* helped re-create the landscapes with you."

"Yes," Ivory says, smiling. "And Morpheus guided us, as he knows every nook and cranny of Wonderland, even the wilds occupied only by the solitary fae. It was his place to make the sketches for Jebediah to follow. We are finished now."

A strange wave of sadness washes over me and I sit again. "I was supposed to be a part of it. It was my duty."

"No, Alyssa," Ivory scolds. "Your duty was to rest and heal, for your kingdom needs a queen, not a corpse. Correct?"

I nod in agreement, but it's halfhearted.

Mom sits next to me, her arm around my waist. "Allie, there's still something very important for you to do. Only you can decide what will become of Red. Are you going to cast her out and destroy her? Or give her back to Sister Two as a restless spirit?"

Restless spirit. Red's the furthest thing from that. I've never seen anyone so dejected and weary. Her unforgotten memories are immovable chains around her.

She whimpers inside me, curling up tighter.

It's not so easy to crush her now that she's remembered. Now that she has regrets. She even knows what became of her king, how he's forever imprisoned in the jabberlock box, because of events she set into motion. Her vendetta has lost all meaning.

I tell myself I'm keeping her alive to punish her, but there's more to it than that.

"I came to kill her," I say, seeking counsel for my conflicting feelings.

"Maybe it's enough that you reminded her there's more to living than death and destruction," Dad says, stroking the top of my head.

"You must decide soon," Ivory adds. "In just a few hours, after the landscapes have stabilized, I will be waking all the denizens who sleep in my spell. We shall have a banquet, and together assure them our world is safe and strong. However you choose to dispose of Red will set the precedent for how your subjects view you as a queen."

As if things are too serious for his liking, Chessie dive-bombs me, his eyes relaying his relief that I'm well. Nikki follows yet watches me shyly, with a stranger's eyes. She's not exactly the same little sprite. She's an updated version, but Chessie is still delighted to have her back.

I smile and open my hands so he can nestle there. Nikki perches on my thumb, cautious and inquisitive.

I glance at Ivory. "What about the magic that healed me?"

Ivory looks at my parents. "Might I have a moment alone with your daughter?"

Dad nods and squeezes my shoulder. Mom kisses my cheek reassuringly. Holding hands like teens, they leave the room and shut the door behind them.

"This magic"—Ivory points to my chest—"is made of the most innocent love, Alyssa. The love of children. Pure and unconditional."

Chessie launches from my hands and flutters about the room with Nikki in tow. I look down at the faint glow behind my sternum. "I don't understand."

"Come." Ivory leads me to the fireplace. The silver flames blink, brushing Ivory's pale irises, eyebrows, and eyelashes with glitter, like snow in moonlight. We sit together on the crystal lounge and she winds her waist-length silvery hair to one side on the white cushion. Nikki settles atop the coiled spiral and spins herself up in the strands.

The graceful turn of Ivory's long neck reminds me of the swan form she sometimes takes. Just like Morpheus takes the form of a moth. It fully hits me that my alternate appearance is my human one . . . that my magic will never have a telltale color, because I'm a half-blood. This sets me apart, just like my dreams and imagination. It makes me special to both worlds. Which is what Morpheus has been saying all along. Which is exactly what Red hoped to accomplish by spawning a race of half-bloods, before she lost sight of her original noble intentions.

Red stirs at the back of my head, shrinking in agony.

Ivory holds out her palm and a softball-size bubble appears, luminous and clear.

"Another vision?" I ask, remembering all too clearly the last one she showed me and the life-magic vow that ensued. I don't plan to make any more vows for a while.

"This is not a vision. Rather, it is a glimpse into your recent past."

Chessie drops down and, with a poof, dissipates to orange sparkles and gray smoke. His haze drifts across the bubble like a cloud, bringing clarity to the blurry image that takes shape inside.

All of my senses tune in: I see, hear, smell, feel, and taste the moment:

Morpheus carries my unconscious form into this room and places me on the bed atop the snowy quilts. He pauses, staring down at my face, the jewels under his eyes the stormy gray of a tempest. Mom moves around him, her wings fluttering nervously. He steps back as she blots blood from my lips and collapses over me, crying.

Chessie hovers anxiously.

Morpheus turns to him, jaw clenched. "Go through the mirror passage . . . bring Thomas and Jebediah. Hurry!"

Chessie flurries away.

There's movement at the doorway and Ivory steps inside. "There is only one means of saving her now."

My mom looks up, the whites of her eyes rimmed with red. Even in her sadness, she's beautiful, her skin luminous and smooth as if she were twenty years younger. "No. Not yet. She still has another life to live."

Ivory winds her snowy white hands together. "If you want her to live at all, this is the only way. I've already summoned Grenadine to send the crown via Rabid. They're in the north tower, so he shall be here soon."

"We can't do this." Mom stiffens her shoulders. All vulnerability has faded from her expression. Her wings rise tall behind her. She's determined, ready to fight.

Ivory steps closer and places a hand on her arm. "By putting the crown on her head, we will renew her netherling heart. She will return to the age she was when she came last year, the age of her coronation. And she will be stronger than ever before."

Mom arranges the dreadlocks around my head. "But her human half is too weak to endure the surge. It will die. And she'll always be haunted by its absence."

"We can give her a forgetting potion," Ivory suggests. "Banish the memories. She'll be the Red Queen, with nothing human to impede her reign."

"And in the process," Morpheus says from beside the fireplace, "you'll destroy some of her best qualities."

Mom and Ivory glance at him, as if taken aback to hear those words coming from his lips.

He sits hard on the chaise lounge, wings draped over the back, then slouches with elbows on knees. The silvery flames flicker across his bejeweled face. "What of her whimsy and curiosity, her compassion and loyalty? Her imagination, her dreams. These are all part of her humanness."

My mom stares at him in disbelief. "This is thanks to your schemes. You pressured her to choose you . . . to choose Wonderland over her other side. What did you think would happen?"

Morpheus hunches lower, miserable.

"Alison." Ivory sits beside Mom on the mattress. "You are being too harsh. This rift was not caused merely by her efforts to choose between her worlds or between her love for Morpheus and her mortal knight. Red put a spell upon her netherling side, in hopes it would dominate and destroy the other one. You cannot blame him for that."

"I can, because it all started when Allie came here last summer." Mom glares at Morpheus again. "Now you're finally going to get what you wanted. To have her here in Wonderland with you. To have her break all ties with mortals forever. You should be celebrating. You won."

"Won what?" Dad asks from the door.

Before anyone can answer, Jeb comes up behind him. He curses and rushes to the bed with Dad.

Ivory moves aside while explaining everything, including the plan on the table.

Dad starts toward Morpheus. "Are you happy? You made it all about Wonderland. Now she'll be a queen without a family who loves her."

Jeb grabs Dad's arm before he can get across the room. "Thomas, it wasn't just him. We were pulling her apart, too. Trying to convince her to stay in our world. We have to be unified now, to think of Al and how to keep her alive." There's torment behind his green eyes, because he knows he's about to give me up forever. But there's no doubt, only pained resignation.

"Jebediah is right." Morpheus meets Jeb's gaze. An unspoken understanding passes between them. "But this isn't the path to Alyssa's salvation. Were she able to speak for herself in this moment, she would insist there must be another way."

"I can think of none, and we're out of time," Ivory answers sadly. Her wings hang low at her back, appearing heavy.

"Put her on ice then," Morpheus suggests. "Freeze her heart and give us a chance to come up with options."

Ivory agrees.

An arctic surge rushes through me and my blood slows in my veins, like icy slush. The pain in my chest vanishes.

Mom pets my frozen hair and Dad slumps to his knees next to Jeb, burying his face against my frosted gown.

"If only we still had the diary," Jeb says absently, rubbing my fingers inside his, as if trying to keep me warm. "The magic inside. Maybe we could've used it somehow."

Morpheus tilts his chin. "The diary. Of course." He stands and stares pointedly at Ivory. "We're looking at this all wrong. We need to think of her heart as an object . . . like a toy. What makes abandoned toys such powerful casings for Sister Two's souls? 'Tis not so much what they are, but what is used to seal them."

"A child's love magic." Ivory purses her pale pink mouth. "It could work, since you've both shared her childhood at different times."

"It's worth a try, at the very least," Morpheus adds.

Ivory nods, then casts a wise and knowing glance from him to Jeb. "The seal would only be a temporary fix, to hold her together until she can heal. You both must be willing to compromise . . . see past your needs, and accept that she is meant for more than fulfilling your expectations for her. You will have to support one another as constants in her life if you're to bridge her human and netherling heart. She must live in both worlds for equal amounts of time. This will allow her heart to grow and mend, piece by piece. Once it has healed and is unified, she'll no longer need the sutures, and she can endure being crowned without losing either part of who she is. Are you willing to let her have this dual future? The decision falls to you. She's too weak to make it for herself. Red's greed and vengefulness saw to that when she made Alyssa's heart the battlefield."

"I'll do whatever it takes," Morpheus and Jeb answer simultaneously without hesitation.

The bubble in Ivory's hand bursts, Chessie rematerializes, and the moment is gone.

I frown, overwhelmed by Jeb's and Morpheus's devotion, but still confused.

Ivory lays my palm over my heart. "What do you see inside?"

I curl my fingers into a fist. "Some of my happiest memories with each of them, when we were younger. But it's from their points of view, not mine."

"Therein is the magic. They have both loved you with a child's love, and now a man's. It is the child's love that holds you together . . . cemented by the moments you shared with them that they treasure most. They had to bare their minds, hearts, and souls to one another and send the sentiments directly into you, riding on their magic to seal the two halves of your heart. Those are the sutures. And their love for you as men has given them the strength to look past their pride and compromise. Throughout the day, you will spend your human life in the mortal realm, but at night, as you sleep, Morpheus will bring you here in your dreams. You will continue to learn the politics of our world and acquaint yourself with your subjects and your dominion; you'll learn to trust, understand, and work with him, so one day—should you choose to wed one another and reign together—your bond will be unbreakable. And Wonderland will be unassailable."

I'm astonished that both guys would agree to the arrangement. Especially Morpheus . . . because he has to go back to dream duty and wait to be with me in reality. He said he was done waiting. Would he really postpone our life together and the birth of our son? *Our son . . .*

I grasp Ivory's hand. "Wait. Sister Two. We have to appease the need for borogroves in the cemetery. There must be dreams for the restless souls. Or else she'll keep taking human children. She won't have a choice."

Ivory studies my face. "At last you realize the rules are there for a reason, even if they seem barbaric. But in truth, I should like to see this particular practice altered, every bit as much as you. Our kind has never been in the business of seeking the most humane way to do things. We're of an ends-justify-the-means mentality. But with two queens who care enough to find another way, this can change. And our realm will be stronger once we need not rely on outside commodities." The black dragonfly-wing markings that flank her temples crinkle in thought. "For now, we have a compromise that will last as long as your mortal knight lives. He has volunteered to be Sister Two's dream-boy."

My stomach falls.

Dream-boy. I'm slammed with the image of my Dad's brain being siphoned of dreams and nightmares as a child. My hallucination in the hospital a month ago comes full circle: Jeb sheathed inside a thick sheet of spider silk, me slicing it open, then him staring dead-eyed back at me. Was it a vision all along?

Ivory didn't mention him in her earlier explanation of my future, only that I would live out my life in the mortal realm.

Jeb is planning to sacrifice his existence so no more humans will suffer, because that's what he does. He protects the vulnerable. No matter what it costs him.

My skin flashes hot and cold. *Not this time.* Not when he's finally found his way.

Without another word to Ivory, I scramble up and sprint out the door, insisting Chessie show me where Jeb is. He takes to the air in front of me with Nikki skirting behind. Ivory calls out, but time is too precious. I don't stop.

I turn a corner that opens to a long, sleek corridor.

There's no traction on the white marble floors. My bare feet slip. Righting myself, I untie my makeshift robe and leave it behind as I release my wings and take flight down the wide expanse. I pass a dozen or so elfin knights who watch with detached curiosity, but make no move to stand in my way.

I don't even feel embarrassed that I'm wearing a transparent gown. There's no need to be proper or modest. I'm the Red Queen: untamed, wild, and maniacal. I *dare* anyone to question my choice of clothes.

I'm on a mission. Sister Two isn't going to use Jeb up until his heart stops and he's a dreamless corpse.

That is not the ending my mortal knight deserves.

DREAMSCAPES

Chessie and Nikki lead me to the highest tower that overlooks Ivory's kingdom, then flutter off before I can thank them.

Panting to catch my breath, I wait outside the open door and absorb my wings. The large room is windowless. Windows are unnecessary in a palace with transparent walls. Unlike the chamber I was in earlier, no frost or ice impedes the view. Daylight reflects off the snow outside and illuminates the surroundings with sunny brilliance.

Finley is taking canvases off their easels, his back turned to me. There's no sign of Jeb.

I step quietly inside. Stacks upon stacks of canvases lie on the floor, all of them slathered with beautifully bizarre landscapes. I'd recognize the handiwork anywhere.

I look to the world outside the glass tower, where patches of color on the horizon bleed Jeb's paintings into being. The fluid metamorphosis reminds me of when I was small, when I would sandwich crayon chips between sheets of waxed paper, and with a hot iron, Dad melted them into gleaming "stained-glass masterpieces." I never thought I'd see such vibrant, visionary bursts of color in anything but a kaleidoscope, certainly not to scale across an entire world.

I'm awestruck.

Movement in the sky catches my attention. The graceful arc and lift of giant black wings swoops through the clouds, making holes that close again before I can blink. Even though he's cloaked in the white fluffy haze, I know it's Morpheus, supervising the rebirth of his beloved home. A part of me aches to be with him. To climb to the top of this tower and dive off so we can soar together, hold hands, feel the wind whipping through us. I want to watch the jewels on his face flash through that thrilling rainbow of emotions.

But something else is calling to me right now, an equally strong pull . . .

Jeb has outdone himself. He brought our world back to its full freakish splendor, and Wonderland will be forever in his debt. I won't allow him to sacrifice anything else.

Finley stops working, preoccupied with a standing mirror in the far corner. His body blocks the reflection he watches.

Just like in my vision, he's wearing an elfin knight uniform: black pants that fit like well-worn jeans, a silver chain linked in and out of two belt loops, and a cross of glistening white diamonds on the left upper leg. The shirt is long-sleeved, made of stretchy fabric that clings to his muscles—silver with vertical black stripes.

"Where did the artist go?" My question comes out sharper than I intend.

Finley turns. Upon seeing me, he looks down and rakes a hand through his dark blond hair in an awkward gesture, reminding me how sheer my gown must be with the sun filtering through.

My face flushes, but I don't turn away.

"He took the mirror passage." Finley sets aside the canvas he's holding, revealing the looking glass's surface.

I step closer. A vast hollow blinks in the reflection, filled with ice-slicked weeping willow trees. An endless array of teddy bears and stuffed animals, plastic clowns and porcelain dolls, hangs from webs on the drooping branches.

The restless souls.

My breath catches as the image disappears.

So Jeb is in the cemetery, beyond the dead and barren willows, in the shelter of ivy where a thick sheath of web thrashes with light and breath. The glowing roots may already be attached to his head and chest, siphoning away his dreams and imagination.

I swallow a moan. Every nerve in my body fizzes with rage.

"Envision where you wish to go," I whisper, and picture Sister Two's lair—the deepest part, where she stores her dreamer, the one who provides entertainment for those wretched, restless souls to keep them at peace.

The glass crackles and Jeb appears in the reflection. He's not wrapped in web or hooked up to the tree roots yet, but the spidery grave keeper is standing over him, her eight legs pinning him in place. The striped fabric of her skirt bubbles wide like a hoop around her spinnerets. Her upper torso, deceptively human, tenses beneath a matching bodice. Her left hand, a pair of gardening shears in place of fingers, prepares to strike, moments from rendering him a vegetable.

Riding an adrenaline rush, I lift my key to unlock the mirror's glass.

Finley stops my hand. "I can't let you do that, miss. Ivory asked they not be disturbed."

I snatch my hand free. With one glance across the room, I conjure a pile of drop cloths in the corner to rise and hover over him like angry ghosts. Two of them stretch out with clawed fingers and clamp his arms. The others cast blue shadows across his face, awaiting my command. I'm surprised how effortlessly my feral side took over. Surprised and pleased.

"Ivory would make an exception for the Red Queen," I snarl.

Even with my phantoms holding him, Finley doesn't flinch. Realization crosses his face. He obviously had no idea. I can't blame him. I don't exactly look the part of royalty right now. "Forgive me, Majesty. I'll be here to open the mirror from this side, when you're done."

I allow the cloths to fall to the floor while inserting the key into the hole formed by the cracked glass. The reflection ripples like liquid and I step in. A haze of sepia swirls around me, and a prickly sensation sweeps through my skin.

I shake off the disorientation and the scene opens to reality. A stale-smelling chill hangs on the air and snow blankets the ground. The cries and wails of restless toys pierce my eardrums.

Above it all, Jeb's agonized scream slices through my soul.

Racing toward the sound, I stop a few steps behind Sister Two.

She holds up her scissored hand, slicked with blood. Her translucent skin and graphite-colored hair are both splattered with red.

Jeb clutches his right wrist. Shimmery red lines streak from his tattoo into the grooves between his fingers, then drizzle into the snow and along his paint-stained tunic, leaving fresh bright dots.

He collapses to his knees, wailing.

"Jeb!"

He winces up at me through his pain.

Before Sister Two can react, I summon the webbed casing she's prepared for him. The sticky strands wind around her, trapping her within her own net.

She struggles, but everything, from her multiple legs to her arms, is wrapped in a cocoon. Her blades can't even open to snip at the binds. "How dare ye set foot on this hallowed ground!"

The voice that once tapped on my spine like branches on a windowpane has no power over me now. Instead of evoking terror, she stokes my anger—reminding me of everything she's done to my loved ones: planning to bleed my dad dry and leave him for dead, trapping my mother here, stinging Morpheus, and chasing Jeb with the intent to hold him here forever.

"I'm a half-blood, *witch*," I seethe. "My powers aren't affected by this place. So you're going to have to roll out the welcome mat. Your days of answering to no one are over. And Jeb is *not* going to be your dream-boy." I animate another strip of web so it slaps across her lavender-colored lips, effectively silencing any response. Her blue eyes harden.

Jeb still crouches, holding his wrist. "There's no reversing what's already been done." His voice is husky and tight.

What I thought were droplets of red blood on the snow merge

together to form a pulse of light. It tunnels underneath the web surrounding the grave keeper. It doesn't stop there. Snaky, glowing strands separate and spread into the roots beneath the ground that lead to every tree. The light seeps into the writhing toys, feeding them. One by one, they settle to a disturbingly serene hush.

Jeb stands. His tattoo that once glowed with power and magic—that was bleeding moments ago—is the color of his skin, healed and raised like a scar. Not even a blink of light shimmers behind it.

His eyes are different, too—a darker green, like moss in shadows. Some integral part of him has changed.

"Jeb." I fist my hands at my sides. "I made a promise to you. For a life together."

He shakes his head. "I release you of your vow, Al."

At his words, I feel the difference . . . the bind I made breaking free. "No!" I lurch forward and clutch Sister Two's neck. "What did you do to him?"

Jeb gently peels my hands off the spidery woman. "What I asked her to do. Didn't Ivory tell you?"

"That you volunteered to be the dream-boy? Like my dad was? That's why you're letting me out of my promise. So I won't be tied to a corpse." My voice is high-pitched and desperate. Nothing like a queen's should sound.

Jeb frowns. "You didn't give Ivory the chance to explain, did you? You went flying all over the castle half-naked to find me without letting her finish."

I clench my jaw.

He turns me to face him. His face flushes with color and he looks strong and healthy again. His frown turns into a smile, those dimples a vision too lovely for words. "Classic Al."

"This isn't funny. What you did . . . we have to undo it. There's another way to give Wonderland dreams."

He squints. "By you having a child with Morpheus? Are you ready for that today?"

My throat constricts. I finally know who I am without a doubt, but I'm still learning who Morpheus and I are together. I don't want to bring our son into the picture before we've had time to grow, to work side by side and accept one another.

I want to do everything right this time, so I'll never hurt Wonderland again.

Jeb takes both my hands in his. "You've made enough sacrifices. Your heart was ripping in half, trying to appease everyone and everything you love. You didn't get to make the choice of where to live. It was made *for* you. So from this point on, anything that happens between me and you, or you and owl-bait, will be your choice. Not because of some magical promise you made me when you were desperate to save my ass from no-man's-land. Not because of a dream-child you're prophesied to bring into this world someday. Neither of those things should play any part right now. They've been taken care of. So you get to choose what role we'll have in your lives, your terms. No time limit. No pressure."

I squeeze his fingers. "*I* get to choose? How, when you're staying here in the cemetery?"

"It's not like that. Sister Two has the power to pull netherling spirits out of a possessed body. She used the same process to isolate my muse and coax it out of me, because it's an entity now . . . made up of my dreams, nightmares, and imagination, brought to life by Red's magic. That's what will take the place of human children." He's trying to reassure me, but his words are far from comforting.

"It will keep Wonderland's cemetery balanced, keep it supplied for as long as I live."

I take a shaky breath. I'm relieved he's not giving up his life. But just imagining him without his ability to paint makes my chin quiver. "Why should you have to fix my world? You already painted it alive again. That's enough."

"It's my world, too, because it's part of the girl I love. That's why I did it, Al. Okay?"

"But we could've found another way."

"There's no other way for me to be human again. I'm ready to go back . . . to take care of my family. Be who I was born to be."

My throat swells. "Twice, I've watched you give up your life for me. I can't let you give up your gift." My voice is stern, hiding the helplessness I feel.

"Giving up the magic is the only way for me to move forward." He releases my hands and helps free Sister Two from her sticky cage. "It's my decision. And it's done."

Sister Two glowers at me as she scrambles free in the snow, kicking up powder with her eight legs. "Ye are unwelcome in the garden of souls, halfling, lessen ye be bringing me a soul to keep. Queen or no queen, power or no power, there be rules and customs ye must abide if ye wish to live in our world."

Fury flashes through me, scalding hot. My skin sparkles, casting tiny dots of light along the webs and trees. "Fair enough. But there's a new rule for you, grave keeper. I understand you're tired of searching out dreamers. Well, problem solved. Now that you have an ample supply, you have no business returning to the human realm. Your place is here, tending your charges. The portals out of Wonderland will be heavily guarded. If I ever find you sniffing around them, I'll strap you up in your web and let you hang for the rest of eternity."

We stare each other down. She hisses but keeps her distance, wary of my magic. Jeb takes my hand and drags me toward the image of Finley waiting on the other side of the mirror to let us into the castle.

The moment we step through, the glass crackles and becomes solid again. All that's left is a reflection of me in my see-through gown. Jeb grabs one of the drop cloths at Finley's feet and covers me with it.

"Thanks for keeping watch," he says, shaking Finley's hand.

Finley offers a key to Jeb for the mirror, then bows to me. There's serenity in his amber gaze as he says, "Hope to see you both at the banquet this evening."

For a young man once so tortured and suicidal in the human world, he seems at peace and in control. All along I thought he was a hostage, but by loving him and appointing him a position in her army, Ivory has given him a purpose . . . a reason to live.

Red once had a constructive purpose, too. If she hadn't lost sight of it, maybe she could've found peace. The knot at the base of my skull doesn't budge this time. Her regret has consumed and incapacitated her.

What if the same thing happens to Jeb? For so long his identity was wrapped up in his art. What's his purpose now?

Once Finley leaves the room, Jeb pulls me close in a wordless hug. I nestle against him, savoring the scent of paint. A scent that will be fading soon, forever. The only sounds between us are our pounding pulses and our clipped breaths. I'm so devastated, I can't speak.

He holds me tighter, until his chest crushes to mine. My heart draws toward his, almost magnetized. It's a breathless, intense innervation—warm and wonderful—as if starbursts of energy pulse within the organ. The sensation must be caused by the magical bridge he and Morpheus constructed within me, and I wonder if it will always feel like this when one of them holds me now.

Jeb backs me to a transparent wall and whispers, "Look at your world, fairy queen."

I turn my head to view the dizzying heights below, the genesis of Wonderland blooming everywhere. My wing buds tingle, craving flight.

Jeb gently holds the drop cloth around my collarbone. "It's fitting. That my wanting to know who you were inspired my first paintings. And that my knowing through and through inspired my last." He has the strangest look on his face—alert and renewed—as if he's just woken from a nurturing sleep. He doesn't look like someone who's quitting. He looks like someone who's just beginning.

"Is it so easy to say good-bye to that part of you? Are you walking away from me, too?"

The world outside explodes in a riotous transformation of color and light, reflecting in patterns across his olive skin.

He tilts his head, studying me thoughtfully. "Saying good-bye to my art is . . . it's terrifying, Al. Ivory offered to give me a forgetting potion, so I wouldn't have to live with the ache. But I refused. I don't want to forget anything, because it's those experiences, those losses, that helped me see there's a lot more to me than a brush and watercolors. Other parts that haven't been tapped yet." Behind his dark, long lashes, his eyes glimmer with a potency that has nothing to do with magic. He pulls me to him, warm breath dancing along the fringe of my lips. "We can figure them out together."

His thumb touches the dimple in my chin, then drags along my mouth, sending prickly sensations from my lips to my chest to my belly.

"And just so we're clear, I will *never* walk away from you unless you ask me to. I almost did once, but only because I thought I'd hurt you." He works a necklace from inside his shirt.

I hadn't even noticed the chain glistening at the curve of his neck. I help him drag it out, revealing the engagement ring that he melted in the ocean, the one that Morpheus melded into a clump of metal. It's been painted anew. Indestructible.

"Oh, Jeb . . ."

"I can't give you all the things I once hoped to," he says. "But I can give you a family and a home. I love you, Al. I just hope you can love a simple mechanic."

I wind my fingers through the wavy hair at his neck. I admire this side of him most of all . . . his fragility, his flaws. His strength in spite of them. And now, he sees that strength with as much clarity and confidence as I always have.

"There will never be anything simple about you," I whisper. "And I already love you."

He lifts me until I match his height, my feet dangling, and presses me into the glass wall with his body. My heart reacts again—humming with life. His mouth and labret cross my forehead, soft yet persistent on their way down my face.

My mind blurs to a ripple of pleasure when his soft, full lips at last make contact with mine. He starts to deepen the kiss, but pauses, intent on the glass behind me. "You gotta be kidding."

I glance over my shoulder. Outside, Morpheus hangs on the glass in moth form, level with my head, glaring at us with his bulbous gaze. Even without a face, his smugness is apparent. His favorite pastime is interrupting Jeb's romantic moments. I try not to laugh, but can't help myself.

"Cocky son of a bug." Jeb sets me on the floor and draws the dropcloth tighter around me.

A barn owl swoops from the sky and skims the glass. Morpheus launches off in a tizzy, trying to outrun the bird. Now Jeb's the one laughing.

I slap his shoulder. "Hey, that's not funny."

"Ah, he'll be okay." Jeb raises an eyebrow, watching the aerial pursuit taking place outside the glass. "It's a new genus of vegetarian owls. They're only in it for the chase. Besides, Morphie-boy can change to his other form anytime he wants."

I smirk. "That owl is one of your creations?"

Jeb's grin widens. "It was for bug-breath's own good. Dude's ancient . . . he needs to stay in shape."

I bark another laugh. It's so wonderful to see his playful side again.

Jeb's smile gentles, then his expression fades to serious. "Can you finally admit it, your feelings for him?"

My elated buzz evaporates to a nauseated coil in my stomach. "There will always be two different sides to me. And each one loves you and Morpheus in different ways." I look him in the eye, unashamed of the confession because of the honesty behind it. "I know it's not fair to ask either of you to be okay with that."

Jeb tips up my chin with a fingertip. "You didn't ask. And I don't want fair. I don't want easy, either. I want one lifetime with you, and every crazy complication that comes with it. We've gone to hell and back to be together. I've proven I'm more qualified than any other human to handle what's thrown at us. Magical or otherwise. Besides, how is you having two lives any different from any other woman who remarries after her husband is gone?"

"Because Morpheus will visit me in my dreams every night. Do you trust him?"

"I trust you. You're as strong—no, *stronger*—than he is. He knows it, too. That's why he gets off on testing you. You just need to prove it to yourself, like I had to prove things to myself. And you're about to have twenty-four hours alone with him to do that."

My shoulders slump. The drop cloth wrinkles between the wall and my back. I'd forgotten about my vow to Morpheus. "As soon as I'm free of Red."

Jeb tucks the ring necklace under his tunic again. "I'm going to keep this until you tell me you're ready. It's a huge sacrifice, to build a human family and walk away from it someday. If it's too much, or if after your time together, you decide you want to be with him now, I'll move somewhere so we'll never have to see each other. You need your time in the mortal realm to heal, and I won't risk ripping you in half again." His eyes are sincere and intense, his jaw tightened in an effort to be strong, even though I can tell it's the most difficult thing he's ever said.

His strength amazes me. I pull him into a hug. Just the thought of living my human life without him triggers pain in my newly repaired heart. Not a rip, but a heaviness, as if it's filled with rocks. I snuggle under his chin, pulling his chest close so I can feel that magical current between us once more . . . so it can lighten the weight.

He strokes my hair. "About Red. You can't let her sit dormant inside you forever. What's your plan?"

I shake my head, grateful for the subject change. "I was going to release her spirit. Let her wither away. But I want to do something else. Something . . . meaningful."

He pushes us apart and narrows his eyes. "Something she deserves, I hope."

I trace the smudges of dried paint and blood on his tunic. "She loved Wonderland once. Before she lost sight of her good intentions, she wanted to change it for the better. Like you said, Sister Two zones in on spirits and drags them out. Since your muse has the residue of Red, maybe Red's spirit can be joined with it. Then Red could help supply the dreams. She'll be imprisoned, never able to escape, but at least she'll be contributing something. It will extend the life of your muse. And it will send a message to my subjects, that if they step out of line, I'll find a way to make them serve Wonderland forever. Most importantly, it will give Red peace."

Jeb's eyes brighten with something akin to pride. "You're going to make one hell of a queen, you know that?"

A rush of satisfaction warms my cheeks. "I'm going to give it my best shot."

He kisses my forehead. "Okay. I'll stand guard here . . . let you back through when you're done."

I start for the mirror, but Jeb stops me. I look up at his concerned face, convinced he's changed his mind and wants to come along since Sister Two and I aren't on the best of terms. I'm prepared to argue with him, but all he does is lift one of my hands and curl my fingers into a fist.

"You got this," he says, and bumps my knuckles with his. "She's wanted Red back in her keep for over a year. You hold all the cards."

"Exactly my thinking." I smile at him.

He smiles back. "And one more thing . . ."

"Yeah?"

"It's time for you to find peace, too. The bad is behind us now."

I caress his face, then turn to the mirror. Sliding the drop cloth off my shoulders into a pile at my bare feet, I release my jeweled wings and envision the cemetery in the glass. My reflection looks back as I wait for the destination to appear: netherling eye patches, glittery skin, hair that's wild and alive.

I see what Jeb saw, the reason he'll never try to be my protector again. It's a great feeling, knowing I'm strong and capable.

Maybe he's right. Maybe the bad is behind us.

I can't be sure until I know where things stand with my mentor-tormentor; the wisdom keeper who saved my life more than once, who holds the other half of my heart in his manipulative hands, and who made my metamorphosis to Wonderland's Red Queen a possibility in the first place.

Fair Faryn

Gossamer hovers next to my ear as I stand in one corner of Ivory's enormous crystallized banquet hall. The sprite has visited me throughout the day, providing pleasant company in spite of her unrequited affection for Morpheus. Working together to lead the mome wraiths from my school gymnasium a month ago seems to have bonded us.

As for Morpheus, I haven't seen him since the owl chased him from the tower. He's even stayed out of my head. Although he sent a message via Gossamer, concerning how pleased he is with my decision for Red.

Silver flaming candles, floating upside down from the ceiling, softly light the room. A string quartet plays without players; the frosty, glacial instruments glow and pulsate with the colors of the rainbow. The music is as crisp and breezy as morning air, yet muted, like melodious whispers echoed in a cave of ice.

Gossamer and I are playing the role of wallflowers beside an open doorway, watching Mom and Dad waltz alongside Ivory and Finley. The four of them—graceful and beautiful—stand out like pristine toppers for a wedding cake among the bizarre netherlings dancing spastically around them.

I danced earlier with some of the guests. Chessie, Nikki, and Rabid. Zombie flowers, shrunken back to their original size. Sprites. Hobgoblins. Even Herman Hattington joined in, his face switching like a TV screen between me and our other dance partners, the Doormouse and March Hairless.

Jeb stole me away once for a slow, romantic song. He's gone now, shut up in his room in the castle. He was exhausted. Having wrangled Red's and Morpheus's magic for a month, survived facing his demons in a barbaric otherworld, breathed life into a dying landscape, and given up his muse forever, I'm not surprised. Yet I can't help but wonder if the main reason he left was because he doesn't want to be here when Morpheus comes to whisk me away.

I stare at the door Jeb took when he left, unable to shake him from my thoughts.

"Your mortal knight is most unique," Gossamer says in her chiming voice as she follows my line of sight. Her coppery bulbous eyes, glowing green skin, and glittery scales seem almost phosphorescent in the dimness.

I bite my lip, considering her words. My tongue stings pleasantly from the cinnamon-red lipstick the other sprites applied earlier with my evening makeup.

Hovering in front of my nose, Gossamer tilts her teensy head. "Which bids the question . . . Before all this. Before the compromise for your heart. Had you reached a decision? Which man? Which future?"

I return her steady gaze, still not sure if Morpheus is willing to compromise anything. "I was going to choose Wonderland, and rule alone. I could never live an eternity knowing I'd broken one of their hearts for the other. Especially now that I know how excruciating a broken heart can be." I let out a shaky sigh. "Maybe I still should choose that. It seems wrong, for them to endure so much to bridge my two sides. It feels like I'm being selfish."

The sprite makes a tiny sound, something between a snort and a sneeze. Her astute dragonfly eyes reflect the rainbow-colored lights from the instruments.

"What?" I lean against the door's icy frame, amazed by how the ice isn't cold to the touch, yet it can freeze a damaged heartbeat or suspend a rotting landscape.

The sprite perches on my shoulder, her wings tickling my ear. "You're thinking like a human again. Seeing things in black-and-white."

It's my turn to snort. "Right. I forgot. It's all about the gray in Wonderland."

"It is. I once told you that no one knows what he or she is capable of until things are at their darkest. When you were dying, both your men came face-to-face with that moment. They combined forces, looked within one another instead of themselves, and found the gray—the common ground."

I frown. "Are you saying that it changed them?"

She sits down and, propped against the curve of my neck, lifts one leg at a time to adjust the pointed green shoes on her feet. "You've always brought out the softer side in my master. But he hasn't changed. He's as changeless as he is ageless. He'll always be selfish, manipulative, untamable. He knows no other way to be, for he is all things Wonderland. The event simply gave him a new means to determine the direction of his actions when dealing with you."

"What do you mean?"

"A mortal moral compass. Just as your Jebediah now understands Wonderland's magic and feral desires, Morpheus understands the human world's emotional needs and insecurities. He and your mortal knight have always been your perfect mate, split in twain. But now each of them has gained enough insight to provide what you need in either realm. It is not the men bridging your heart. It is your heart bridging *them*. They are wiser because of their love for you. I daresay even happier. Yes, they could subsist without you, but they are better men *with* you. They are the ones who need *you* to be complete, to be all they were meant to be. That does not make you selfish. It makes you indispensable."

I smile. The idea is empowering, and as fascinating, twisted, and beautiful as Wonderland itself.

My attention wanders back to the dance floor and the guests representing the Red kingdom, the White, and even the solitary of our kind. I recognize a few more of the attendees: Mustela fae—ferret-like creatures with long, venomous fangs and vulnerable craniums, a hedgehog being with the face of a sparrow, a pink woman with a neck as long as a flamingo.

There are also some that are new to me, with batlike wings and fishy faces, or sensuous females as dark as mud, with amphibious plants sprouting out of their supple skin.

I may not know every netherling, but I know their gifts and powers. Morpheus taught me in my childhood.

The bridge troll's dreadlocks are enchanted with a telepathy that brainwashes his victims into being so fearful of staying in place, they cross his bridge even when they know he's waiting on the other side to turn them to stone. And the nameless muddy vixen uses an alluring song to draw lesser-minded beings into the water where she sucks the life from them.

Not all of them are deadly, but each one is deranged and strange enough to tease my darker side with the possibility of chaos. I'm eager to start visiting in my dreams so I can learn their weaknesses and how to manipulate them, because reasoning is never the law of the land in the Red Court. It's all about who's the trickiest, who's the wiliest with words. And who's the most determined to get their way.

Which is why Morpheus will be the perfect Red King one day.

Jeb mentioned earlier that he and Morpheus talked while I was recuperating from being frozen. He told Morpheus he was letting me out of my vow, in hopes Morpheus would play the gentleman, too. But I don't expect him to fight fair. Just as I know he doesn't expect me to be an easy mark.

I fidget in the dress he sent over this afternoon: white corset bodice with miniature crimson rosebuds sewn upon the neckline and satiny black laces that crisscross, then dangle in a bow at my waist. A fitted red and white pin-striped, ankle-length skirt hugs my lower half, and a matching choker collar is secured over my key necklace. Per his request, my hair is loose and long, and writhes around the roses pinned in place. Every part of my ensemble feels like a seduction. Even my long sleeves—sheer poufs of black netting with twirling swirls of red ribbon woven throughout the length—cling like soft kisses to my arms.

"Did you tell him my last message?" I ask Gossamer as one song ends and another begins. Earlier, I thought upon the wording of my life-magic vow: that I was to give him one day and one night. I never stated consecutive hours, or that they would be spent in Wonderland. Since I've pointed out that we accumulated at least twelve daylight hours together in AnyElsewhere, he'll have no choice but to agree that only the night half of my vow is unfulfilled.

"I did tell him," Gossamer's bell-like voice chimes. It's obvious by her crossed arms that she's not about to share his reaction.

"So, he's pouting, right? That's why he missed the ceremony," I say over the instruments.

"He's been away from his home for some time. He had things to do. To prepare for your night together." Gossamer's furred wings buzz into action, lifting her off my shoulder.

"Sure." I smother a smile. "We both know he didn't come because he would've been bored to tears. There's too much orderliness for his liking."

She giggles in agreement—a tinkling sound that blends with the music.

Earlier, Ivory gave a speech, introducing me as the reigning Red Queen, assuring everyone that my blood is tied to the crown that Rabid White is keeping under lock and key until I can place it on my head again.

Two of my subjects from the Red Court stepped forward to thank Jeb for his contribution to our world: Charlie, a dodo bird with the head of a man and hands protruding from the tips of his stubby wings, and his wife Lorina, a parakeet-like netherling with a humanoid face slapped onto crimson feathers as if it were a mask. They presented Jeb with a key to the cemetery gates delivered by five of Sister Two's smelly, silvery pixies. The fact that a human boy earned the Twid Sisters' respect gained him quite a fandom among the guests.

After that, the music began and food was laid out.

Honey-scented tea steams invitingly from the pots, and the food sparkles with ice and magic. Plates are piled with moonbeam cookies and other unusual confections, such as starlit marzipan tarts and lightning-bug meringues, each of them waiting to pour delectable light into every guest's mouth with one bite.

Ivory's idea of entertaining is different from the banquets I've attended with Morpheus in reality, dreams, and visions. Everyone is on their best behavior due to the hundreds of elfin knights posted at every entrance and exit. Several of my card guards have joined them for extra security.

The gathering is proper and refined.

I suspect that one day, if Morpheus and I rule together, I'll have to attend such things by myself, given the flighty-wicked side of him that both annoys and entices me.

Something tinkles above my head. I glance up at some cherry-flavored chimes made of sugared icicles, suspended in midair by fairy enchantments. All it would take is a stretch of the arm to capture one. But that's not nearly as challenging or fun as chasing a roasted duck with a death wish around a table, mallet in hand.

"I'm getting hungry," I say to my spriteling companion.

"I already told you. The master wishes to share a picnic. It will be worth the wait." Her glimmering eyes zero in on me, scolding.

"You're misreading her implication, pet." Morpheus's deep voice warms the top of my head from behind. I turn to find him peering around the doorway, wearing that smug smirk. He hands me a long-stemmed rose that matches the ones in my hair. "Alyssa was referring to her hunger for a walloping good adventure. Isn't that right, luv?" He offers a palm, his jeweled eye patches flickering between violet and pink.

Instead of admitting how well he reads me, I silently take his hand. As we start out the door, I glance over my shoulder in search of my parents, who are now lost in the crowd.

"Gossamer," I begin. "Would you mind—?"

"I will tell everyone you have gone for the night." She flashes Morpheus and me a mischievous smile. *"Fennine es staryn, es fair faryn."* Then she flitters away.

Morpheus leads me past the elfin knights and out of the glass castle into the evening air. I make a marked effort not to notice how debonair he looks in his white tailcoat suit and the black and red pin-striped vest underneath, or how high and proud his wings rise behind him.

Instead, I take in our surroundings. The sun and moon twist together in the purple sky. Their combined light coats everything with an ultraviolet hue. In the distance, past Ivory's icy domain, plants of all kinds flourish in psychedelic colors—pink bushes, yellow flowers, orange trees, and rainbow ground cover.

I bask in the beauty of it all. Threading my fingers through Morpheus's, I ask, "So, what did Gossamer say?"

He leans in to hear me over the scuffle of some fashionably late dust bunnies who sneeze as they pass us on their way to the entrance. "An ancient blessing from our realm. *May the fairy goddess light your footsteps with stars, and may your travels be fair, however far you roam.*"

"And how far are we planning to roam?" I ask, my netherling side almost salivating upon the sight of our carriage. It's a reasonable facsimile of the moth "hot air balloon" he'd intended us to use in AnyElsewhere. Although this giant mushroom basket is enclosed to keep us warm, and is drawn by thousands of moths harnessed to glowing blue strands of magic. The same magic forms luminescent wheels. They remind me of the glass tubing on neon signs, molded in circles and spokes.

"Every part and parcel of your kingdom will be laid at your feet tonight," Morpheus answers. "With so many of your subjects here at the castle, it is the perfect opportunity to take the tour. From the checkerboard deserts to the chaotic cliffs to the overgrown wilds. We shall make a few special stops along the way. I had Jebediah paint some scenes from the past as I remember them. The cave Alice was held in . . . birdcage and all. The cocoon from whence I was born anew. They're part of the history we share. And now they're preserved forever."

I'm touched by the sentiment and move close enough to get a good look at his top hat in the moonlight. "You're wearing your Seduction Hat. Why am I not surprised?"

He offers a pirate's smile. "Did you notice . . . I've a new embellishment?" He makes a show of adjusting an owl's tail feather in the band.

I bite back a giggle. "Vegetarian barn owl, I presume?"

"Won't be bothering me again for some time."

"I can guarantee it's not the only one out there."

He loops my arm through his. "Good. I'm always up for a worthy chase."

I shake my head. "Which brings us back to the Seduction Hat."

He smirks. "I'm wearing it because it matches your dress."

"Sure," I say, even though his top hat—one-half crimson and one-half white, with black moth garland and rosebuds at the brim— actually does match me, perfectly.

"It appears Gossamer found your parents." Morpheus motions to one of the towers, where Mom and Dad are watching us leave. "Hope she told them not to wait up," he quips.

My parents have made peace with Morpheus after he proved how much he cares for both my human and netherling sides, but they weren't thrilled to learn of my vow. Then they saw Jeb's example, how he's trusting me to make my own choices. After that, they only wished me strength of mind and heart. I assured them I had both in spades because of their examples.

Morpheus helps me climb into the carriage. The compartment is big enough to accommodate his wings, and the seats are made of red velvet. Striking purple curtains hang across the window, and animated fluorescent swirls move along the walls. The interior is like Morpheus in every way . . . elegant and polished, yet at the same time jarring and mesmerizing. I settle into the seat opposite him, clutching my lace-clad hands around the rose he gave me. Hookah smoke hugs every breath. Two hurricane-style candelabras are mounted on either side of the window, filled with fireflies that cast an ultraviolet glow, bluing the paler shades of our clothes and Morpheus's porcelain skin and lovely lips.

"So, where to first?" I ask. "Bear in mind, we only have twelve hours."

He pulls the door shut and leans forward, elbows on knees. "About that. When I went back to my manor to prepare, I had some time to think about your vow. You deliberately left out the 'after we defeated Red' clause in your *recollection*. Which, technically, doesn't quite encompass our hours in the looking-glass world, now does it?"

My arrogant bubble bursts. "Um . . ."

"Precisely," Morpheus says, pulling white gloves into place on his hands. "However, to prove I can be every bit as conciliatory as your mortal prince, and to reward you for the effort of manipulating me, I'm going to let it slide. You shan't be held accountable but for one night."

"How gracious," I grumble.

His jeweled markings sparkle, the color of orchids in spring. "It is, in fact. Considering that originally, before our tour of Wonderland, I was to take you dancing in the clouds and serenade you with the wind. Then dining on candied spiders and sipping dandelion wine, so we could appease your sadistic tendencies regarding flowers and bugs."

I fake a pout. "Are you ever going to let me live that down?"

"Not in this lifetime. Perhaps in the next." He pushes back the purple curtains, revealing a window big enough for us both to look through. "We'll have to forgo the dancing. I packed a picnic and we'll eat as we explore."

We lift to the sky and I watch Wonderland's majesty pass below.

I give in to my stomach's rumblings and try a candied spider. It's not too bad, other than that it wiggles going down and leaves a faint soapy aftertaste. Morpheus rewards my daring effort with moonbeam cookies and dandelion wine. The wine tickles my throat with effervescent bubbles, giving me the hiccups. Each time my mouth pops open, the carriage's interior blinks from the moonbeams coating my tongue.

Morpheus laughs deliriously and I can't help but join in.

Within four hours we've seen so much of Wonderland, my mind is spinning in resplendent ultra-violet hues and bizarre terrains.

I can't wait to capture them in my artwork. Sadness chases that thought, thinking of Jeb and his orphaned muse.

Our last stop before Morpheus's manor is the flower garden outside the rabbit hole's door. Most of the flowers are away at Ivory's castle. Those that aren't cower when they see me, having heard of my victory over Red and the slaughter of hundreds of prisoners in AnyElsewhere at my hand.

With Morpheus's patient coaching, I embrace the chaos within and command the wraiths that live in the soil to reverse their damage to the rabbit hole. In a maelstrom of ear-shattering wails and black inky cyclones that whip through our clothes, they obey, putting everything back as it was in the beginning, little-boy sundial statue and all.

"What will the human realm think when they wake up to the change tomorrow?" I ask Morpheus as we board our carriage once more, my awareness heightened and my nerves still skittering. I'm half manic after joining forces with the wraiths. My skin feels hot and my face flushed.

"Perchance that some Good Samaritan came in the night and replaced the sundial," Morpheus answers. "You were once like them . . . easily lulled to complacency."

"That's because believing you're alone in the universe is less terrifying than admitting you might have an otherworldly audience."

Morpheus studies me appraisingly. "And *that* is a human weakness. Use it, when it's time to clean up all the messes your absence from the human realm has made over the past few days. When it's time to explain where your mum and Jebediah have been for a month. Your duality gives you an advantage in this world, Alyssa. But also in the other. Never forget that."

We arrive at his manor and he deposits me in his windowless chamber, promising to be back shortly with tea.

I turn on my heel to view the wild and stunning decor. Soft amber light falls from the giant crystal chandelier spread across the domed ceiling. Velvet hangings drape the walls in shades of gold and purple, intertwined with strands of ivy, seashells, and peacock feathers.

The multi-tiered crystal shelves catch my eye. I touch one of the many hats embellished with dead moths. When I was a girl, I was fascinated watching him string the garlands.

I turn to the tiny glass-dollhouse terrariums. Cocoons coat the panels—caterpillars transforming. In other places, moths flit and perch on leaves and twigs.

Their graceful antics remind me of how Morpheus affects me now as a woman and a netherling. Being here works like a tonic . . . taking me back to that monumental moment over a year ago when he transformed me—awoke my darker side with afternoon tea and a living chess game.

The waterfall that serves as his bed's canopy trickles behind me. I step toward it and reach out a hand. The liquid curtain reacts to me as it did then, lifting back like a living thing so I can see the mattress. Velvety golden quilts and pillows cover the expanse, and hundreds of red rose petals are scattered across, filling my nose with their delicate scent.

I back up, letting the curtain fall, and bump into the glass table that doubles as a black and silver chessboard. The jade chess pieces must be put away in their box, all but Alice and the caterpillar, newly carved, because I have the original at home.

A sentence hovers atop three of the silver squares as if by magic, in tiny glowing script: *Sleep with Alyssa.*

"Let me clear the dust away, luv." Morpheus's hand appears from behind and sweeps across the glass, smudging the words.

Tense, I turn to face him. He's taken off his jacket, vest, and gloves. His toned, pale chest peers out from the half-buttoned frilly white shirt. He's breathtaking, and far too alluring for my comfort.

My jaw clenches. "I won't do this."

"What, have tea and crumpets?" He balances a tray with cups and a kettle on his other hand and places it on the empty end of the table. "Why ever not?"

I stand my ground. "Jeb wants to grow old with me. The human in me wants that, too. To experience what Alice never did in the mortal realm. He was willing to risk his one life and face Red so I could have a future with you. My happiness was more important to him than his own. Yet you're asking me to walk away from him after all he's given up for Wonderland?"

"What makes you think I am?" Morpheus hangs his hat on the arm of his chair as he pours cranberry-colored liquid into one cup. Wisps of steam fill the room, carrying notes of mint and lavender.

"The sentence you wrote."

"Ah. That . . ." He motions for me to sit. When I don't budge, he seats himself, crossing his legs at the ankle. His wings hang wide on either side of his chair. "Alyssa, think. Have I ever taken advantage of your innocence?"

"No."

"Have I had means or opportunity?"

"Many, on both counts."

"All right. You've learned so much on your journey. Surely you haven't already forgotten the most important lesson: how words can say one thing, but mean another." He lifts his cup and regards me over the rim while sipping, then sets it on his saucer with a clink. "It's crucial, as queen of the Red Court, for you to keep that upmost in your mind in all situations. You must always consider every angle of every statement before you react emotionally."

So, this night is both a lesson and a test. He's teaching me the politics of Wonderland, but at the same time, testing me to see if I can practice what I preach: trust him the way I expect him to trust me.

"Now," he continues. "I brought the tea to relax you. But you are by no means obligated to drink it. Although, at the very least, after all we've been through, one would think you could sit and speak your heart to me. If it would make it easier, use the chess pieces, like when we were little."

I take a deep breath, gather my skirt around my legs, and sit in the chair across from him.

Concentrating on the Alice figurine, I imagine her alive. She retains her teensy size, but begins to move, stretching out her arms and legs as if she's been asleep for years. She prances over to the caterpillar and curtsies.

"How do you fare this evening, Mr. Caterpillar?" she says in a milky voice of innocence. "I should like to thank you for not crowning me earlier, for finding another way. It was quite noble."

Morpheus grins. The blue light at his fingertips snaps out and wraps around the caterpillar chess piece, wriggling it in front of the Alice caricature as if it were moving. He's the master puppeteer, exactly as he was in our games as children. Exactly as he was in the human realm. Exactly as he always will be.

"Far from noble, My Queen." His voice is comical and high-pitched. "Self-serving, in fact. Without any memory of your humanness, you would not be the girl I shared a childhood with.

And, I'm loath to admit it, living out your life with the humans you love will make you a better ruler here. You know I always do what's best for Wonderland."

Those words have never sounded more beautiful or poignant. I coax my tiny Alice to drag a foot along the board. "You said you were done waiting," she mumbles under my command. "And you're right. I cannot ask you to wait any longer. You should find someone else." As much as it hurts to hear the words leave her lips, Morpheus deserves to be happy.

He dips his chess piece, as if it were slouching, and answers in that nasally lilt. "Bless it, little majesty, have you forgotten what I am? As a solitary fae, I do not require company. In fact, I find the constant give-and-take of companionship tedious on the best day. Although I expect to discover the charm in it, some sixty years or so down the line."

Tears sting my eyes, but I won't let them fall. Instead, minuscule streams trickle down Alice's cheeks. "Then I should like to add that I'm sorry. I'm sorry you have to wait so long for so many things."

Morpheus's gaze flashes to mine, then back to the chess piece wrapped in his magic. "Stop crying," his quirky voice scolds. "Queens don't cry. I taught you better than that."

I bite my quivering lip, and tiny Alice strokes the caterpillar's face. "But you're crying . . ."

Morpheus lowers a wing and shades his cheek along with the transparent glimmer of his jeweled markings. "Well"—his shrill voice cracks slightly—"contrary to my preferences for lace and velvet, I'm not the queen. So I can cry all I like."

My answering snort is clipped with a sob. I cover my mouth with my fingertips, guiding Alice to dry her face with her pinafore.

"I love you. I don't want to hurt you," I murmur behind my hand.

Morpheus's jaw spasms, his magic tightening around the caterpillar until it twirls in place on the board like a top set to spin. "Your pity is misguided." His childish voice lowers an octave. "As I've often told you, time has no constraints in Wonderland. Jebediah may have your days for now. But an eternity awaits me and you. He's the one getting the short end of the stick." The corners of Morpheus's mouth twitch wickedly. "Which is fitting, considering he's short in so many other aspects."

"Shut up!" I say, laughing hysterically. Alice transforms back to an inanimate jade piece as I toss her. My aim is off and she plops into Morpheus's tea, splattering him and the chessboard.

With a graceful sweep of his hand, he retracts his magic. Tea drizzles down his face as his inky eyes turn up to mine, alight with something both dangerous and daring, shifting moods faster than I can blink.

"Careful, plum." It's his deep cockney accent now. He wipes his face with a napkin. "Don't start something you have no intention of finishing."

"Oh, I'll finish it," I say—spurred by the dark confidence fluttering at the edge of my psyche. The side of me that knows I'm his match in every way. "And you know I'll win." I rise from my chair to scope out the room for weapons, vaguely aware of the prisms of glittery light reflected off my skin onto the surroundings.

"I know I'll *let* you win," Morpheus says, standing up. "I won't even put up a fight." His white-toothed smile spans to something forebodingly provocative, as though mimicking the spread of his wings. "Well, perhaps a small one, just for sport."

I inch toward the middle of the room, wrestling the smile trying to blossom on my own face. My heart flutters in an effort to get closer to him, that same magnetic invigoration in my chest that I felt when Jeb hugged me. Yet Morpheus isn't even touching me.

He studies me knowingly, as if he can *see* my heart's reaction to him.

"On second thought, playtime can wait." He snatches my wrist with his blue electrified strands before I can unleash my magic. "You're too easily distracted, luv. That's something we'll work on." He drags me over, picks me up, and carries me to the bed.

"Morpheus," I warn, squirming in his arms. I know, with just a thought, I can bring the chandelier crashing down on him like a cage.

"Tut. Don't do anything rash," he scolds as if reading my mind. Swiping the waterfall aside, he lays me atop the fragrant, silky rose petals. "I'm only asking one thing of you tonight. And it will not compromise your human future. We'll keep on our clothes. No hanky-panky." He presses his palm over his heart in pledge fashion. "I vow on my life-magic never to come between you and Jebediah Holt again."

I gasp. The profoundness of such a gesture, from a self-seeking fae, touches my soul. The only thing predictable about my future king is his unpredictability. "You once told me you wouldn't be a gentleman. You lied."

He leans over and caresses my cheek with his knuckles, so tender it hurts. "Oh, I stand by that statement, little blossom. For you see, there's the chance *you* will break down and come between the two of you. Every night we're together, I will tempt you to the edge of madness. I will tease you to torments. You will have to earn Jebediah's happy life by being strong and unbending, as all good queens should be. Though *this* night, I'm giving you a lull."

His words come back to me from our afternoon inside the

mountain: *Yes, we will quarrel incessantly and fight for dominance. And yes, there will be ravishes of passion, but there will also be gentle lulls. That is who we are together.*

"When next I see you in your dreamscapes," Morpheus continues, bringing me back to the present, "our trial by fire will begin. You wanted it, you shall have it. I intend to push you to your best, infuriate you to your worst. It is the only way for you to rule over a world of creatures both mad and cunning."

I let the smile I was suppressing have free rein, because I'm up for any challenge he can throw in my path. The chance to prove it thrills me beyond all reason. "I understand now. What the sentence on the chessboard means. That you want to sleep with me . . ."

He crawls across my body and lies on the other side of the bed, leaving the liquidized curtain open behind me. "Do tell."

Covering up with one of his wings, I surround myself with the scent of licorice and honey. "You want to hold me while I sleep. You want to watch my face as I dream like you never have—from the outside."

He traces my eye markings with an elegant fingertip. "That will be my memory to cling to, until you're mine forever at last, both in waking hours and sleep. The question is, do you trust me enough to give me that? To rest in my arms tonight?"

I hold his soft palm against my cheek. "Will you sing me my lullaby?"

He weaves his fingers through my hair and presses my forehead to his. "Forever and always," he whispers.

As he hums the tune that has been inside my mind and heart all my life, I close the waterfall canopy, cocooning us within our own frozen pocket of time.

EPILOGUE

Jeb and I lived out our life in Pleasance, with Mom and Dad visiting often when they weren't in London with the Skeffingtons.

I'll list no other details: how many children and grandchildren, the nieces and nephews given to us by Corbin and Jenara, how old Jeb was when he died. All I'll say is that our mortal life together was everything and more than I'd hoped. Even when death claimed my family members—one by one—there was happiness in its wake, a wash of treasured memories and laughter hanging like priceless art on the walls of my heart.

I made a name for myself with my mosaics, while Jeb was renowned for marble maze toys so intricate and ingeniously crafted they were compared to Rube Goldberg designs. Although the true legacy he left for our children and grandchildren wasn't the wealth or awards he obtained with his mechanical prowess. It was his gentleness, sense of humor, and unconditional love.

Mom and I wanted our descendants to have the normal life we never did, and I was able to silence the bugs and flowers in their ears simply by commanding it—a perk of my crown-magic. Still, I left them an opportunity to stumble upon their Wonderland heritage: hundreds of mosaics filled with bizarre and mystical landscapes, and a box full of heirlooms along with a map and a key. I hid everything in the attic for them to find should they go looking for answers.

Maybe they'll think it's the ramblings of a senile mind. Or maybe they'll believe and take that same leap of faith that once led me, and a curious little girl named Alice, to venture into the rabbit hole.

I'll be there to welcome them, if they do . . .

Leaving my human family behind is the hardest thing I've ever done. After faking my death, my final sojourn to the rabbit hole is less of a leap than a fall. Morpheus is there to catch me. He takes my wrinkled and age-freckled hand, helps me inside, and kisses away the tears from the old, frail, white-haired woman I've become.

He doesn't recoil or flinch. He sees past my age, to what I am inside. To the ruler he's helped shape in my dreams since my childhood: adept at pandemonium and manipulation, tempered by wisdom.

He places the crown on my head and my hair thickens and warms with the pale blond of youth, alive with magic. My bones, skin, and muscles smooth and straighten to toned suppleness. My wings sprout anew.

I am sixteen once more.

"I shall give you time to grieve," he whispers, but the desire burning in his eyes belies any patience.

Though my heart is heavy, it is also strong and unbreakable, thanks to two men who put my needs above their own.

Morpheus and Wonderland have waited long enough for their queen, for their dream-child. I touch the bejeweled face I've come to love so dearly, not in spite of his infuriating tactics, his word wizardry, his tender malice . . . but *because* of them. "The Red Court needs a king," is my answer.

We marry, surrounded by a mishmash of creatures: some clothed, others naked, all more bestial than humanoid. They are our subjects, and my heart brims with affection—for their weirdness, for their madness, for their loyalty.

Morpheus and I both wear red: me, a gown of real roses, netting, and lace; and him, a beautiful crimson suit.

When the moment comes, I proudly state, "I do."

He lifts my hand and presses soft lips to the scars that mar my palm. "I always knew you would," he teases. Then he smiles, his jewels glistening gold and bright.

Donning our ruby crowns, we fly together into the sky.

"Shall we dance in the clouds, luv?" my King asks.

I remember a vision from a lifetime ago—our souls and bodies bared to a brilliant inferno—and answer, "I want to waltz on the sun."

And there, in the midst of blinding orange, yellow, and white flames, our forever begins.

ACKNOWLEDGMENTS

First and foremost, gratitude to my family for turning a blind eye to dusty furniture, mountains of laundry, and TV dinners when deadlines loom.

Hugs and a hat tip to my Agent Goddess, Jenny Bent, whose business savvy, diplomacy, and faith in her clients know no bounds.

Thank you to the prestigious Abrams family: Maggie Lehrman, Tamar Brazis, Nicole Sclama, and countless copyeditors and proofreaders for helping me polish each diamond in the rough until they sparkle and shine. Also, gratitude to Laura Mihalick and Morgan Dubin, my in-house publicists; printing press specialists who oversee the pages and special effects; marketing advisors; and everyone who plays a part behind the scenes in the making of the books.

A deep bow to Maria Middleton, designer extraordinaire, who always finds the perfect symbolism for each cover, and to Nathália Suellen, one of the most talented artists I've ever encountered. You made me believe in magic by breathing life into my characters via your enchanted artistry.

A standing ovation to my local crit group, the Divas: Linda Castillo, Jennifer Archer, Marcy McKay, and April Redmon. You read everything I pen, yet still consider me talented.

High fives and hugs to my online critters and beta readers: Rookie (aka Bethany Crandell), the White Chocolate to my Godiva; POM (aka Jessica Nelson), who loves coffee and brownie mix almost as much as I do; Stacee (aka @book_junkee), for cheering me on (if anyone could convince me to trade my parasol for an orange jumpsuit, it would be you); Owly (aka Ashlee Supringer), for knowing my characters almost better than I do; Marlene Ruggles, whose keen eye is always on the lookout for unseen typos; and Chris Lapel, my number one fan.

Head butts to my #Goatposse, who are wiser and funnier than the average domesticated ruminant animal. Also, a hollah to the WrAHM girls and to all the Splintered series fans online via Goodreads, Facebook, Tumblr, Pinterest, and Twitter.

A hearty shout-out to the Twitter Splintered RP players who made the wait for Ensnared bearable and fun for the fans: @SplinteredCrew, @LongLiveTheMuse, @AlyssaPaints, @PunkPrincessJen, @seductive_fae, @MorphTheMoth, @NetherlingQueen, @splinteredivory, @tyedribbions, @RabbitNotBeMe, @taelor_tremont, @ChevyLovingJock, and @ChessieBlud.

Thank you to Nikki Wang at Fiction Freak, my very first mothling, who lent me her name for a sprite both sweet and fierce, much like her namesake. Also, thanks to Sarah Kate for bringing my characters to life via adorable plushie counterparts.

My respect and awe to all of the talented fans who send artwork for my Pinterest board and write incredible fan fiction, thus allowing my characters to breathe outside of the books' pages.

Thanks to Jaime and Rachel at RockStar Book Tours for mastering the blog tour ropes and being so supportive and generous with their time.

A debt of gratitude to Lewis Carroll and Tim Burton for inspiring me to dive headfirst into this weird and twisted Wonderland world.

And last but not least, gratefulness to the One who gives me the ability to write and continues to fill my creative well with characters and stories, each waiting for their turn to be told.

ABOUT THE AUTHOR

A. G. Howard wrote *Splintered* while working at a school library. She always wondered what would've happened if Alice had grown up and the subtle creepiness of *Alice's Adventures in Wonderland* had taken center stage in her story, and she hopes her darker and funkier tribute to Carroll will inspire readers to seek out the stories that won her heart as a child. She lives in Amarillo, Texas.

This book was designed by Maria T. Middleton. The text is set in 10.5-point Adobe Caslon, a revival of the mid-eighteenth-century classic created by the legendary engraver and type designer William Caslon. Designed in 1990 by Carol Twombly, Adobe Caslon is based on William Caslon's original type specimen drawings. The display font is Yana Swash Caps I, designed by Laura Worthington for Umbrella Type.

This book was printed and bound by Courier in Westford, Massachusetts. Its production was overseen by Elizabeth Peskin.